The Horror of F

M . R . C . Kasasian was raised in Lancashire. He has had careers as varied as factory hand, wine waiter, veterinary assistant, fair-ground worker and dentist. He lives with his wife in Suffolk in the summer and in a village in Malta in the winter. He is the author of two previous historical mystery series, published by Head of Zeus, including the bestselling Gower Street Detective series.

M.R.C. KASASIAN

THE HORROR OF HAGLIN HOUSE

San Diego, California

Canelo US

An imprint of Printers Row Publishing Group
9717 Pacific Heights Blvd, San Diego, CA 92121
www.canelobooksus.com

Printers Row Publishing Group is a division of Readerlink Distribution
Services, LLC. Canelo US is a registered trademark of Readerlink
Distribution Services, LLC.

This edition originally published in the United Kingdom in 2023 by
Canelo.

Published in partnership with Canelo.

Correspondence regarding the content of this book should be sent to Canelo
US, Editorial Department, at the above address. Author inquiries should be
sent to Canelo, Unit 9, 5th Floor, Cargo Works, 1–2 Hatfields, London SE1
9PG, United Kingdom, www.canelo.co.

Publisher: Peter Norton • Associate Publisher: Ana Parker
Art Director: Charles McStravick
Editorial Director: April Graham
Editor: Angela Garcia
Production Team: Beno Chan, Julie Greene

Library of Congress Control Number: 2023949702

ISBN: 978-1-6672-0729-2

Printed in India

28 27 26 25 24   1 2 3 4 5

For Tiggy with love

1: THE FLIGHT OF THE RAVEN

5th July 1894

HETTIE GRANGER TIDIED my veil though it was tidy enough already. She was trying to distract us both, I suspected.

'You look lovely, Violet,' she told me, her opal eyes iridescent in the sunlight through the great window of Thetbury Hall.

'The image of...' my mother began and finished, unable to think of anyone that I resembled. 'Yourself,' she ended weakly.

My father was tall, sturdy, Roman-nosed and square-mandibled, the opposite of me, his older daughter, in almost every aspect. He had, however, given me a thick head of black hair and a blue right eye. My mother – tall, sturdy and aquiline-nosed with a pointed jaw – had donated my green left eye and my pale complexion.

Don't do it, Ruby urged for the third time that morning, but I shushed her. Just because she would never marry did not mean that I must follow suit. *It is legalised slavery.*

Romulus, my second cousin, trotted down the stairs, splendid in his Suffolk Regiment captain's uniform with its gold-braided, yellow-cuffed red coat.

'What a stunner,' he remarked.

'Why thank you, Rommy,' my mother simpered, though I rather thought that he had been looking at me, and Romulus winked. He was the closest contemporary male relative I had, all my brothers having been lost to disease, violence, the cruel sea or just lost.

Rose, my last surviving sister, peeked out, uncomfortable in her coral dress. She would much rather have been in jodhpurs persecuting vermin.

'Your carriage is here,' she announced, and I glimpsed the coach on the driveway, the Thorn crest with its ram rampant azure on a maroon shield.

It would have been quicker to have walked the hundred yards to the family chapel, given the time that it took to arrange and rearrange my satin dress as I clambered in and out, but my father would not hear of it.

'You might as well arrive by bicycle,' he had told me, and I rather cared for that idea.

It would have made Jack laugh.

The Reverend Methews stood cassocked in the porch, but there was something more than usual wrong with him. He was slumped and hesitant and one might have thought that he was conducting me to the gallows from the expression on his normally irritatingly cheerful face.

It is because he wants you for himself, Ruby asserted, *but at a hundred and forty a year he will have to settle for a thick-waisted parlour maid.*

Methews ran his fingers through his ginger curls, scuffed the soles of his brown boots on the gravel and cleared his throat.

'You look more nervous than I feel,' I teased, but he did not even attempt a smile as he held out the envelope with *Lady Violet Thorn* written in block capitals. Before I could take it, however, my father had whipped the letter away and was ripping it open.

'Is Mr Raven unwell?' I enquired. Surely, if Jack had died, they would not have let me come this far before delivering the news?

It is Jack's handwriting, Ruby told me impatiently for she had heard my thoughts when none of my family could. *And dead men do not write.*

They do in séances, Inspector Havelock Hefty asserted and I left them to argue the point. There had never been any love to lose between those two characters.

'It has just arrived,' Methews mumbled, unable to look me in the eye, so it was obvious that he had some idea of its contents.

My father's fist closed around the letter and his face screwed up so tight that I feared his monocle would either cut into him or shatter.

'I shall flay him alive,' he swore, and Hettie touched my arm. 'The filthy coypu,' my father raged.

2

In retrospect this seemed an odd choice of animal since none of us had ever seen one outside of a coloured plate in *Fortescue's Natural History of South America*, but I had other things to worry about at the time.

Romulus prised the ball of paper from my father's grasp and opened it out, standing at my side so that we could read it together.

'He shall suffer for this,' Rommy vowed grimly as I looked over the short note again in disbelief.

All that stuff about sticks and stones is nonsense, I discovered. I had not known, until that moment, that words can hurt one physically and that what should have been the kindest of them could be the most cruel.

With all my heart, your ever-loving Jack, it was signed with an X for the kiss that he would never give me.

Letting my bouquet fall, fatally wounded, onto the gravel and, no bicycle being available, I ran back to the family home.

Agnust, the maid, was the first to find me, for she knew all but two of my hiding places.

'He said he is unworthy,' I whispered in disbelief.

'Unworthy is as unworthy do,' she affirmed, grasping my shoulder in one massive six-fingered hand and turning my chin with the other to make me look her in the face. Hers bore a new expression which I thought at the time was biliousness, but I realised later was hatred. 'You do want me to kill him?'

'Do not worry,' I said calmly. 'I shall do it myself.'

2: FILTHY FIENDS AND THE MAGIC PENCIL

RUBY GIBSON HESITATED, but the muzzle of the Mauser C78 was pressed beneath her breast and she could not hope to overcome her nemesis with her hands tied and her feet shackled.

'Lie down,' the count commanded and Ruby, defiant to the end, obeyed reluctantly. 'You have fortunate,' he told her, in his thick Bragislanian accent, 'for I have give you a casket which is more than you have give my brother.'

'He was a foul fiend,' Ruby told him, 'and I am only sorry that the piranhas devoured him so quickly.'

The count fingered the old scar on his cheek, a souvenir of their pistol duel on the north face of the Matterhorn.

'At less I have his head to bury in the vault of my noble family's,' he snarled, 'but you, Miss Gibson, shall go scattered to the winds.'

'You will not get away with this, Count Vorolski Zugravescu,' Ruby warned staunchly.

'I fear the proverbial boot, as you English says, fit on the alternate foot,' he sneered, his yellow eyes glinting like those of a serpent in the flickering flame of the torch that Igorovich was holding over her. 'You do not get away from me this time,' the count gloated, blood trickling from the rapier wound that she had inflicted upon his simian brow. 'This casket he is made of inch-thick solid steel. I shall bolt and padlock him. There is no airholes and, believe me Miss Gibson, you will pray to lose conscious before Igorovich light that pit of fire below and beneath you.'

'You filthy fiend and ungrammatical brute!' she cried and Count Zugravescu laughed maniacally.

'Farewell, Miss Ruby Gibson. You have foil me for the last and final time,' he cackled as Igor slammed the lid, plunging her into a darkness deeper than pitch.

4

No sooner had the bolts slid into place than Ruby Gibson felt the steel coffin growing hot, but she was an Englishwoman and would not despair.

'You are not as clever as you think, Count Vorolski Zugravescu,' she muttered defiantly for, only seconds from an agonising death, Ruby Gibson, Extraordinary Investigator, still had one more trick up her sleeve.

–

I put down my Aikin, Lambert and Co magic pencil, the green barrel inlaid with mother of pearl flowers. I dislike writing with pens. As my fingers have testified many times, ink splots, splatters or smudges too easily and heaven help you if you get the pages wet.

Blimey! I thought. *How the blazes do we get out of this one?*

From the way this coffin is heating up 'blazes' is the apposite word, Ruby told me. *Do something, Thorn, and do it soon.*

I shall, I promised and I would, just as soon as I had worked out what.

3: THIN ICE AND CUTTHROATS

5th July 1895

THERE WAS A nearly full moon and, once we had left the gaslit streets of Upper Montford, we were glad of it. Monastery Park had no lighting since the lampposts had all been vandalised – by cutthroats, it was rumoured, but there had not been anything so exotic in our Suffolk market town since the Montford Maniac was on the loose.

Here we slowed down. The path, running straight through the park, was just about wide enough but the earth, rutted in the wet spring, had baked hard in the summer heat so that Gerrund and I had to hold hard to the straps to stop ourselves sliding into each other or bouncing onto the floor. In my youth I would have had a full bustle to cushion my back and many layers of material to sit upon. Now my russet cotton dress and single petticoat gave little padding between me and a lumpy leather bench.

'This is the coolest I have been all day,' I commented, retying the ribbon of my bonnet, for there was a welcome breeze in the open spaces.

'Wouldn't object if it turned into a gale.' Gerrund ran a finger under his carefully arranged emerald cravat.

'Do not tempt the fates,' I warned, remembering the time that he had complained about the tedium of a journey only for our train to be derailed at the next bend.

I had told my man that he need not wear his green waistcoat under his navy woollen jacket, but he was adamant that he was not going to let the summer heat lower his standards. A poorly turned-out manservant reflects on his mistress, he had insisted, but a heavily perspiring manservant made his mistress even more uncomfortable.

Where are we going? Ruby asked.

Wait and see, I said, which was annoying, I knew, but she had been pestering me repeatedly since Zugravescu had entrapped her.

I will make you a deal, I had told her over breakfast. *I will let you out during the day if you allow me to sleep at night.*

You cannot blame me for your restless nights, she had protested, but we both knew who had yelled *Get me out of here!* at twelve minutes past three that morning.

Very well, she had agreed reluctantly for she did not like making concessions, but I knew that she would keep her side of the bargain. *I cannot speak for all the others though*, she had warned.

There was a rustling to our right and Gerrund, alert as always, twisted towards the sound.

'Clear off,' Friendless, who had a better view from his high and more comfily sprung perch, shouted. The figures of a few children emerged from the shrubbery, hands outstretched in supplication. 'Or I do give you a taste of my whip.'

I banged on the roof with my parasol.

'Wint be sunny,' Friendless had warned when he had seen me carrying it and listened incredulously to my explanation that the material matched my dress. Even his trouser legs were of different patterns.

'Do not hurt them,' I called.

'They're street slugs,' he protested, an unkind local word for urchins. 'They int got feelin's.'

'Stop a moment.'

'Can't stop moments,' he philosophised, for Friendless was nothing if not literal. 'They just goo on fr'ever.'

'Stop,' I simplified the command.

'Not likely,' he defied me but Old Queeny halted anyway. Neither she nor her master were so heartless as to run over the little girl who had stepped out in front of her.

Friendless raised his whip threateningly but I had never seen him use it, especially not on his horse.

I unclipped my handbag, dipped into my small-change purse and tossed out a handful of coins, the children scrambling after them through the sparse dry grass.

'Goo on.' Friendless flicked the reins and we set off again. 'Things like that 'courage them,' he informed me.

'To do what?' I asked. 'Eat food? You can tell at a glance they get too much of that.'

'Actu'lly,' our driver mused, 'they look half-starved to me or half-fed. Not sure which. Anyhap,' he decided, 'they should be in the workhouse.'

I did not like to remind him that he could not ply his trade forever and, having no family, might well end up there himself but Gerrund had no such qualms.

'Visiting you,' he muttered, but we were distracted by the bark of a fox.

'That was a fox,' Friendless explained, 'barkin'.'

I nearly said, *Oh really? I thought it was a nightingale*, but could not face the prospect of him explaining how wrong I had been.

We reached the humpbacked wooden bridge over the River Mont that bisected our town, Old Queeny struggling a little with the climb while I looked wistfully down. As a child I would swim in that water and I would give a gold sovereign to be able to do so now. Over the other side we went, Friendless hauling the reins as Old Queeny skated down the smooth slats. I had seen a cart overturn there once when a horse lost its footing. The driver had been thrown into the river, which a group of visitors thought hilarious until he was fished out dead and quite spoiled their picnic.

We were near the far side of the park now and Lower Montford lay dark and uninviting in front of us. Despite the sharing of a name, this was a different world. Upper Montford was relatively prosperous. Lower was populated by what Charles Booth, the reformer, would have classified as the lower classes, vicious and semi-criminal. Only I was not sure about the semi-part.

'Not too late to turn around,' Gerrund suggested.

'Turn round you say?' Friendless misheard, deliberately, I suspected.

Cowards, Ruby jeered for she had hardly hesitated to enter *The Village of the Dead*.

'No,' I insisted. 'Go on.'

Forebodingly, a cloud passed over the moon, but I was never very good at heeding warnings. *I told you the ice was thin*, Shillidge the pigman had said the moment that I regained consciousness.

4: COCKLES AND THE WEARING OF FACES

CHARLES JOHN HUFFAM Dickens stayed at the Splendid Hotel and it was a source of resentment to the locals that, while he had immortalised the Angel Hotel in Bury St Edmunds, Montford had not even merited a mention in *The Pickwick Papers*. Allegedly, though, he had compared our town to a smile on the face of Suffolk. If that were true, Romulus had declared, Lower Montford was its rotting molar.

Upper Montford boasted tree-lined squares and well-kept gardens. Lower crammed its mean rows of terraced houses into narrow winding streets, many of them not even cobbled. The lunar illumination had been dimmed to half-moon-power, so Friendless stopped to light the lamp on the front edge of the roof. I hoped that it helped him and, more importantly, Old Queeny to see the way because it did little for me other than improve my view of her hind quarters.

We left Monastery Park and crossed Salvation Road to where Lower Montford stood, grim medieval hovels leaning across the roads, some so badly tilted that you could have stepped across from one third storey to another if you were not encumbered by skirts.

'She dint like it here,' Friendless told us, though I suspect it was more the driver than his mare who was nervous for Old Queeny plodded placidly down the first street without a moment's hesitation.

I could not say that I blamed him, for I had not heard all sorts of reports about the place, only bad ones. Inspector Stanbury of the Central Suffolk Police Force had told me that he never sent a solitary constable in there and, if there was the slightest hint of trouble, they went in fours. Sergeant Whyte, who had ventured in alone five years ago, had never been seen since despite a hovel-to-hovel search.

'Duck your head,' Friendless advised himself as he passed under a cockeyed balcony, but still almost forgot to do so.

We came to a sharp left turn quickly followed by a sharper right and a long, winding way traversed by alleys, some of them hardly wide enough to walk along. A few doorways were open, but little or no light came from the dwellings and the inhabitants stood or sat on their front steps watching us sullenly.

Under Gerrund's instructions we headed zigzagging towards the centre, or so I trusted, for I had soon become disorientated by the frequent changes of direction. The town was not so much a warren as a maze within a labyrinth, and had I been dropped off there I would have been hopelessly lost. To make matters worse our route had been made more complicated by our having to go back on ourselves when the way was blocked where the flint and mud wall of a cottage had collapsed across it.

'One day they will light these streets,' I forecast with more hope than confidence, it being unlikely that any company would go to the expense of laying pipes for the impecunious inhabitants.

'They'd do better to tear them down,' Gerrund grumped and banged on the roof with his cane. 'Next cockle, driver,' he called.

Friendless was a good cabby but his mother, not content with giving him such an unappealing first name, had let him pick up a hot coal to teach him a lesson when he was a toddler and it had *cockled*, or withered, his left hand. This, however, proved to have one advantage, for Friendless was greatly handicapped in his profession by his inability to distinguish left from right.

'Are you sure?' I checked because I had an impression that we were going back on ourselves.

'I think so,' my man said less positively than I had hoped. 'I don't normally come this way.'

He is lost, Ruby asserted. *Hopelessly lost.*

'Who goo there, Jam?' a man asked from the shadows.

'Uppers,' another, presumably Jam, replied and I made out two silhouettes in a first-floor window.

Anyone not from Lower was presumed to be an Upper or, worse still, a foreigner, which was anybody from outside Suffolk.

'Heave a brick at 'em.'

'If you hit Mr Gervey you'll be wearing your faces inside out,' I warned, unsure what that meant but hoping that it sounded menacing.

'Wha'?' Friendless asked.

'I will,' Gerrund confirmed in a high, presumably Gervey-like pitch. Unlike me, he had actually met the man.

'Crick me!' the one not Jam exclaimed.

'Gervey int…' Friendless began.

'We do joke,' not Jam explained unconvincingly.

'Tha's right,' Jam confirmed and the figures disappeared, their boots clumping on bare boards.

I used that trick in The Haunted Oak, Ruby complained.

Yes but I have the copyright – for all the good it has done me.

'Gervey int here,' Friendless declared in confusion, but by then their footfalls were fading.

'He was make-believe,' I explained as we continued.

'No he int,' Friendless argued, 'I see him twice more than twice.'

'Uncockled,' Gerrund called and we swung to the right.

'I thought we came up this street five minutes ago,' I speculated; that dead mongrel looked familiar.

'You mean you think it five minute ago or we do it five minute ago?' Friendless sought to clarify.

'Yes,' I replied and left him to puzzle it out.

'I'm sure this is the right street,' Gerrund declared in a way that made me think he was not sure at all. He craned forward and screwed up his eyes in an effort to see better, but I never found that worked and it did not seem to help him either. 'Nearly,' he modified his claim.

I listened for a moment.

'It sounds promising,' I conceded.

Though not especially enticing, Ruby opined.

There was a burst of light twenty yards ahead and a swell of noise so raucous that it was difficult to judge if the occupants were having a celebration or a riot.

'It's probably just a fight,' Gerrund failed to reassure me as we edged to a halt. 'They get a good few of those.'

A sea of light gushed from the doorway flushing a dishevelled woman out onto the street. She floundered in the current, wading unsteadily to the shore and stumbled into the shadows. The door slammed and we were in near darkness again. The sky was even more overcast by now, so I was glad to see the yellow flame of a lamp high on the wall ahead.

We came to a halt.

'That's it,' Friendless announced through the hatch.

'But we still have ten yards to go,' I objected.

'On your foots,' he told me. 'I dint see it but old Queeny do.'

Gerrund leaned over the flap and sideways.

'There's a trench,' he announced, 'going straight across.'

'Oh good,' I breathed.

'Int good at all,' Friendless corrected me. 'It's blimmid bad. I'll have to back out backward and the horse as an animal int constructed to do tha'.' He spat into the night. 'Her face forward it do.'

'Is there not another way round?' I enquired.

'No,' our driver stated flatly. 'Faces alway face forward.'

'There is,' Gerrund replied. 'But we would have to go back and around the town and come in on the other side. It would take the worst part of an hour.'

He adjusted his hat a fraction. It was dyed emerald too – one of at least six different coloured bowlers that I could recall seeing him wear.

'Bother,' I muttered.

'You think so?' Friendless quizzed me. 'It's more than a bother. It's a blimmid bother.'

Gerrund drew a safety lantern out of his satchel, raised the glass chimney and struck a Swan White Pine Vesta, the flare briefly dazzling us. He lit the wick and lowered the chimney again, blowing out the match and snapping it to be extra sure before tossing it away. Neither of us would forget our visit to Kelham St James, where he had ignited the methane from a cesspit, blowing up a derelict dairy and almost us in the process. My eyebrows had taken months to recover from that experience and I was not sure that my lashes would ever uncrinkle again.

Friendless pulled the cord to let us out and Gerrund, being on my cockle side, went first.

'Mind your step, Lady Violet,' he warned, and I saw that there was no pavement and that the gutter was overflowing with excrement.

I wrinkled my nose, unconvinced that the slurry was all of animal origin and took the hand he proffered, my own hand enveloped by it. Down onto the board I clambered and raised my skirt a few inches to skip over the channel, only saved from slithering onto my back on the slimy cobbles by my man's steadying grab of my sleeve.

'Begging your pardon.' Gerrund released me.

'I would have been more affronted if you had let me fall,' I assured him.

'If he had you do come a cropper,' Friendless explained.

'The only way over is that plank,' Gerrund informed me.

It was probably the first time that the rough-hewn length of lumber he pointed to had been dignified with such a title. It looked like a clumsily split telegraph pole.

'Oh marvellous,' I sighed.

'Marv'lous?' Friendless interjected. 'You int seen many a piece of timber to think tha' one a marvel.'

'One day I shall explain sarcasm to you,' I promised and he cocked his head.

'Sarsasm? Who's tha' then? Somethin' to eat?'

'Quite so,' I agreed because it was easier to do so.

'Sounds French.' Friendless spat again. He was good at doing that. I had seen him hit a costermonger in the eye from at least fifteen feet when the man was blocking our way with his cart.

A bottle smashed on the wall alongside us and Old Queeny shied.

I knew I should have brought a squad of burly constables, Hefty huffed, but I was not sure that I had room for any more in my head.

'You cannot wait here,' I told our driver.

'I can,' he argued, 'bu' I'm toasted on toast if I do.'

'If you wait by the park gates I shall send for you,' I said.

'How?' he demanded, but I did not know the answer to that one.

'Let milady worry about that,' Gerrund told him with unwarranted confidence, and I certainly would.

'Will you be able to find your way?' I worried.

'No,' Friendless replied cheerfully, 'but Old Queeny do. Like a homing pigeon she is... only she int got no wings.' He glanced over his shoulder. 'Or feathers.' Friendless triple-clicked his tongue and she began to edge backwards.

'Safe journey,' I wished him.

'Int safe at all,' he contradicted me, edging away.

There must be other drivers who will come out at all hours without notice I pondered, but there were probably not many and Friendless was one of the few who would venture into the Lowers, let alone at night.

'And she dint lay eggs,' his voice reached us as he disappeared around the corner.

Gerrund eyed our route warily.

'I can still fetch him back,' he offered.

'Are you frightened?' I asked.

'Of course not,' he bridled, which was a shame because I was absolutely terrified.

Watch out for the man with no ears, Ruby warned, which was good advice for he was a cold-blooded sadist but he was in one of her adventures and not one of mine – I hoped.

5: THE MUNKY AND THE MATTRESS

I TOOK A deep breath and wished that I had not. It was the fetid air and not my fear, I told myself, that made me feel queasy.

'I shall go first,' I decided, pushing as many misgivings as I could collect into the attic of my mind.

Being fifteen inches taller than me at six foot one and robustly constructed, Gerrund was a great deal heavier than I and, if he broke our makeshift bridge, he might make it across but I would be left behind.

He handed me his lamp and I peered over. It was more of a crater than an earthwork.

'Why the devil would they need to make it so large?' I wondered.

'They probably had an extra big hole going spare,' he joked as I stepped out tentatively. 'Have a care, milady,' he fretted, though I had not been intending to be reckless.

The alleged plank felt solid enough despite it bowing down worryingly in the middle. The trench was about eight feet wide and I was probably halfway across when the beam wobbled.

'Oh dear,' I said mildly.

'Damnit!' Gerrund contributed less mildly.

Broggit! Ruby contributed with no attempt at mildness at all.

Parasol grasped in my left hand and lantern in my right, I stretched out my arms either side to improve my balance. I had seen a tightrope walker do that when I was a child and it was probably not his fault that the tower had tipped, sending him plunging to his death.

Do not think about that, I told myself sternly, but myself rarely listens to my advice.

I slid another foot forward. Walking boots would have given me a better grip, but I had been expecting to step straight indoors, not to perform acrobatics en route. The plank wobbled again even more violently and I windmilled my arms to regain my balance.

Do you know what this is? Ruby enquired.

No, I replied warily.

Dangerous, she said.

Be quiet, I snapped and, for once, she did as she was told.

'How deep do you think it is?' I was too unsure of my stability to lower the lamp for a closer inspection.

'Only about six feet,' my man estimated.

Perfect depth for a grave, Ruby observed, rarely silent for long.

'I'll stand on my end to steady it,' Gerrund proposed.

'Please do,' I urged, wondering why he hadn't done so already, but it still felt unsteady when I moved again. 'I hope there is an extra-large mattress at the bottom.'

'Bound to be,' he assured me, 'with linen sheets and plumped-up pillows.'

I took another tentative step and the plank rocked alarmingly.

'I thought you were supposed to be steadying it.'

'I am,' he said, 'or you'd have spilled for certain that time.'

To hell with this. I took a deep breath and ran three frightened steps to the other side.

'Well done, milady,' he called.

I hooked the lamp on the end of my parasol and held it out towards him. Gerrund hesitated. Surely the man who had scaled the outside of the clocktower at Newmarket was not going to baulk at such an obstacle?

'Just thinking,' he said. 'If I shift it over a bit…' He crouched and dragged the end of the plank a foot or so to his right. 'The ground looks more level here.' He set one boot on the plank and then another. 'That's better,' he declared with some satisfaction and ambled over as casually as he might have taken a country walk, his cane jauntily over his shoulder.

'Thank goodness you did not think of that before I went,' I commented coolly.

'I couldn't see the problem until you tried it,' he defended himself.

My feet were wet and I lowered the lamp to find that the whole street ran with effluent, a steady stream trickling into the ditch.

'Oh for goodness sake.'

Hems were up to ankle height by this time, but mine had still got saturated.

'I did advise you to wear something old,' my man reminded me.

'I do not have anything old,' I told him, 'other than you.'

Gerrund bristled; at an estimated age of forty-two he was hardly decrepit.

'Not gone rusty yet,' he muttered.

We sloshed on, my Wilber-Lowe bespoke shoes squelching with every step until we reached a hanging sign with a peeling picture of something resembling a misshapen sweep's boy proclaimed to be The Green Munky. The confused sounds of what I hoped was revelry came from within.

'Why are all the windows boarded over?'

'Glass doesn't last long round here,' Gerrund explained.

'It sounds like they are doing good trade.'

'Not much good about it,' he grunted.

The moment he pushed open the door the light and the noise hit us, but not as hard as the stench. I had thought that the street air was foul, but it was rosewater compared to this.

I could have stayed at home, I pondered, but the newspapers, I tried to tell myself, were full of blood-curdling accounts of people who had thought that they were safe behind locked doors.

Ruby fingered her silver revolver. Mine lay usefully in my desk.

Here goes, she said gamely and we stepped inside.

6: THE DONKEY AND THE OWNERSHIP OF FEET

THE SALOON OF the Green Munky was crammed, mainly with men who clearly expended more cash and time on alcohol than their toilet and wardrobes. Perhaps two hundred of them were crammed into a space that would have been uncomfortable for half that number and the tobacco smoke would have had the most experienced of firemen on the retreat. Two alleged pianists were hammering at battered instruments a few yards either side, but hardly a note reached me above the shouts and raucous laughter.

The room was lit by paraffin lamps hanging in protective wire cages from a ceiling painted brown by the fumes.

'This way, milady.' Gerrund used his bulk to force a way through and I followed close behind, wishing that I had worn one of my smaller hats. The brim of my bonnet was being reshaped already.

'Here!' An irate man in a drooping tam-o'-shanter snarled at me, his breath less fresh than a diseased dog's. 'Whose foot you think you tread on?'

I glanced down at the patchwork boot sewn together with frayed twine.

'In the absence of any evidence to the contrary,' I said, 'I shall assume that it is yours.'

I pressed on, feeling quite pleased with myself for that response until a jaundiced woman, clay pipe clenched between her jaws, barged into me, slopping most of her beer in my hair and down my dress. It was only a little thing that Pierre Auberge of Bond Street – in Norwich, not London – had run up for me, but I preferred the right shoulder puff not to sag soggily.

'Scrot-eyed blixen!'

I could not recall having been called that before and made a mental note of it though it would not pass the censuring pen of Ted Wilton, my agent. He had refused to submit a manuscript in which a villain said a word represented by twelve asterisks, though I had challenged him to tell me what obscenity he thought that represented.

The woman waved her mug, spraying me with the rest of its contents.

'How the frock I s'pose to see you down there?'

To be fair she was all of three inches taller than me even in her gnarled bare feet.

'Possibly,' I suggested, 'by looking.'

The woman chewed her pipe furiously. It had worn a semi-circle in what remained of her upper teeth and a white scab on her lower lip but, before she had the opportunity to formulate a Wildean riposte, she stepped backwards and into another woman who was either in full mourning or exceedingly dirty.

'Scrot-eyed blixen!' my new acquaintance cursed and, disappointed that the epithet was not exclusively mine, I left them to debate why people did not take more care.

Gerrund twisted round to check on my progress, but whatever he said was drowned out by a voice that could have been used to warn shipping, screeching 'Old Danny's Donkey' into my left ear.

Old Danny's donkey's back leg was wonky, I was informed.

'Don't listen, milady,' Gerrund advised as if I had a choice. 'It's the bawdy version.'

I must say that surprised me, for I had not known that there was a respectable one.

After a great deal more battering from the mob and a brief dispute with an Irishman as to whether or not I was an unintelligent female dog, we reached a green door guarded by a burly man in a long black leather coat. It was not only the donkey's limbs that were crooked, according to the human klaxon but, it being unlikely that I should ever meet the unfortunate creature, the information was of little interest to me.

The doorman was enormous, making even Gerrund look almost frail. His head was the size of a football but the shape of a roughly chopped beet and of a similar colour.

'No kids,' he boomed.

'I should hope there are not,' I concurred, and he bent to take a closer look at me. I had seen that face before.

'What are you? Some kind of dwarf?'

'I am petite,' I told him haughtily.

'Dint ask your name,' he sniffed.

'No,' I agreed, shouting to be heard, 'but I know yours. It is Sledgehammer Smith.'

'Tha's right,' he agreed, holding up the right hand that had earned him his nickname. It had been twisted into a tangled lump by numerous fractures caused by causing numerous fractures over the course of his career.

'I had a guinea on you when you knocked down Pat Simpson,' I told him and he frowned.

'One pig?' he rumbled. 'I'm worth more than tha'.'

'I was told that you had three cracked ribs.'

'Put tha' 'bou' to raise the odds,' he grinned and I was surprised at how many teeth he still had, though they had been rearranged in rather an eccentric manner. Smith turned to my man. 'You int takin' a lady down there, Gerry?'

I had not known that Gerrund was on such intimate terms with any pugilists, but there were probably a great many things that I was better not knowing about his private life or past.

'Don't you fret about her,' my man assured him. 'She isn't nearly so giddy as she looks.' He caught my eye. 'That's a compliment,' he protested, and I wondered what he might say to insult me.

I slipped Sledgehammer a coin. 'Have a drink on me,' I said. 'Only next time tip me the wink.' But we both knew that there would be no next time. He was getting old and slow by then and a damaged eye had left him vulnerable to a left hook.

'Any trouble let me know,' he said and Gerrund bristled.

'Milady will let me know first,' he growled, and the old prize fighter nodded slowly, opened the door and stood aside.

I could have stayed at home, I pondered again, for the newspapers, I knew all too well, were full of blood-curdling accounts of people who had ventured out from the safety of their locked doors.

Live a little more, Ruby urged and I was not sure that she meant to add *but die a little less* out loud nor even that her advice made sense.

7: BLOOD IN THE BASEMENT

GERRUND WENT FIRST, leading me straight down a long steep flight of wooden stairs. The steps creaked and swayed worry-ingly, but this was small onions compared to our recent travels and, to judge by the buzz of voices coming up to us, a great many men had been down them already and survived.

'Are you sure about this?' Gerrund checked and I nodded, though this was not how I had envisaged spending what should have been the first anniversary of Jack's and my wedding.

Are you sure you're sure? Hefty, ever the cautious one, double-checked and I nodded again, though I was not very for I disliked venturing underground at the best of times and this did not promise to be one of those occasions.

We reached the bottom and turned right into a cellar, concrete-floored and whitish-washed-walled with a low rough-plastered ceiling and dozens of lamps set around. Here the class of customer had risen. While not quite up to the Royal Enclosure at Ascot's standards, there were a good many well-brushed toppers to be seen bobbing about. This was the night of champions, after all, and only those capable of laying large wagers had been admitted.

Above the buzz of animated conversation came the yaps, snarls and howls of a pack of unseen dogs.

'Looks like we are just in time for the big one,' Gerrund observed as a man in red-and-white striped trousers tucked into his tasselled Hessian-style boots, topped by a long white-and-red striped jacket, strode across the room followed by two lads carrying a large cloth-covered box, about the size of a tea chest between them. To judge from the way that they strained, whatever was in it was heavy.

'That's Bill Bradley, the landlord,' Gerrund told me and went into action. 'Make way for the lady,' he cried, muscling through.

'What sort of lady would enter here?' a walrus-moustachioed gentleman enquired stuffily.

'The sort for whom a true gentleman would make way,' I retorted and he stepped aside reluctantly.

A younger man with beautifully waxed moustaches looked shiftily away.

'Good evening, Crump,' I greeted him and the Right Honourable Percival Crumpinton-Chove took his arm from around the waist of a girl who looked uncannily unlike Lady Crumpinton-Chove. He forced an uneasy smile. 'She slipped and I was helping her to her feet,' he explained utterly convincingly.

'Feet?' she cackled, giving his sideburns a playful tug. 'Dint usually worked on those.'

The Rt. Hon. winced, more in embarrassment than pain, I suspected.

'You are kindness personified, Crump,' I commented, 'and I do not doubt, bearing this evening in mind, that you will be kind to me too if ever I need a favour.'

The man was a wimp but he had two useful assets – wealth and powerful relatives.

'Oh most definitely,' he hastened to assure me and I moved on.

The ring, like most sporting rings, was a square. Surrounded by a solid wooden fence about four feet tall, it was already splattered with fresh blood, though some attempt had been made to smear it around the floor with a mop.

'My lords, ladies and gentlemen,' Mr Bradley was announcing, 'the moment for what we all do wait for. The unbeat, undispooted champion of the world two year runnin' in a row. I give you the one the only...' He flung his arms in the air. 'Li'lllle TICH!'

Little Tich, the comedic star of the musical halls, might have disputed that claim, but he would have been gratified by the enthusiastic cheers that greeted the announcement. From the other side of the ring a door opened and six men pushed through in a column, each of them looking like he could survive a good few rounds with Sledgehammer.

Gerrund bent to put his mouth close to my cheek and for a bizarre moment I thought that he meant to kiss me.

'The so-called Master,' he hissed in my ear, and I saw the men part to reveal the infamous Mr Anton Gervey.

Physically, the man who had terrorised a great deal of East Anglia for two decades was unimpressive. He was not much taller than I and even less sturdily assembled. His hairless face was pinched and sallow. His nose was prominent, but his chin receded.

From his incongruous clerical hat to his patent leather shoes Gervey was dressed in black, the only contrast being a glimpse of white shirt behind a tidy cravat.

'Is he in mourning?' I asked, only to be told that he always dressed like that.

Inspector Hefty stepped forward boldly.

Anton Aloysius Gervey, he declared, *I am arresting you on charges of extortion, blackmail and…* Hefty paused to give his last word more emphasis. *Murder.* But the dapper detective had yet to find a way to make himself heard from inside my skull.

Gervey clicked his fingers. He had the hands of a child and it was difficult to imagine them wielding his notorious razor, though those who survived could testify to his effectiveness with it. The Master's proudest achievement was to create the Suffolk Smile, a grotesque grin achieved by slicing off his victim's upper lip.

A stocky middle-aged man stepped forward in a velvet-collared frock coat, carrying a black-and-tan terrier that could have been called Miniscule Tich without fear of contradiction. I had never seen such a short, slender example of the breed.

'Won't be pretty,' my man warned.

'Oh,' I feigned disappointment. 'I felt certain that it would be.'

Little Tich had been lowered into the ring and was trotting about, sniffing the barrier excitedly.

'Let's give him a taste,' Bradley suggested and whipped off the cloth to reveal that the two lads were holding a cage.

About three-foot square it was crammed with a mass of live rodents, and I tried hard not to squirm as much as they were doing when the landlord raised a flap in the lid and plunged his hand straight inside.

'I am amazed that he does not get bitten,' I commented as he brought out a fat, wriggling rat.

'Oh he gets nipped all right,' Gerrund assured me and I saw that the tip of Bradley's thumb was missing and the web of it cratered.

'It looks nearly as big as Tich,' I observed.

'Don't let that fool you,' Gerrund said. 'Greased lightning he is and jaws like a trap.'

'And I thought you spent your spare time reading improving books.'

'I do,' he assured me. 'Improving books on sporting form.'

Little Tich watched eagerly as his prey was held high over his head, struggling in the landlord's fist, tail thrashing and long yellow teeth bared. The landlord let go and the rat fell, the dog leaping up to meet it and snapping while it was still in the air. A quick shake and he dropped the rat, neck broken, to the floor.

This was greeted with wild enthusiasm by the crowd. Sledge-hammer had had to fight thirty-four rounds against Yankee Joe to get such an ovation. Little Tich's handler leaned over and, taking him by the collar, lifted him out to hold him aloft again.

Gervey watched impassively, his arms crossed with his right hand under his coat.

'And now,' Bradley shouted over the hubbub, 'the moment you all do wait for.' At a signal from him, the lads lifted the cage over the barrier. The landlord fiddled with a catch and the bottom of the cage dropped, a squirming mass of rats falling onto the concrete. 'Fifty on 'em,' he declared and I shuddered as they scurried around the ring looking for escape routes. 'Who wants more?'

It transpired that almost everybody did – though I did not express a preference – and a second cage was fetched.

'One hundred rats,' the landlord bellowed as they too were tipped in. 'Anyone want get in and count 'em?'

Not surprisingly, there were no volunteers.

I stood on tiptoe, straining to reach over and prod a particularly large specimen with the tip of my parasol.

'Have a care he doesn't run up it,' Gerrund warned.

'Why are they so sleek?' I asked, more used to seeing the bedraggled specimens that scurried from derelict buildings and drains.

'He gets them from a breeder in Essex.'

'They farm them?'

'By the million,' he probably exaggerated. 'The sewer rats carry too much disease. They've had dogs die from a simple nip so owners stopped entering any quality animals.'

That took me aback. I was all in favour of killing vermin, though I wondered about the type of person who would find the process entertaining, but to raise creatures for the sole purpose of slaughtering them was sheer cruelty. Little wonder that there were calls to have the alleged sport banned.

Bradley clicked his fingers and the lads brought a blackboard. It was in two columns.

'The left hand is how many he kills in five minutes and the right is the odds,' Gerrund told me, 'but I don't need to explain those to you, milady.'

I took a look at the figures.

'He's offering eighty to one against Little Tich killing them all in that time,' I noted and Gerrund tipped his bowler back.

'He can offer a thousand to one for all I care.' He flipped his hand dismissively. 'It can't be done.'

'Two crowns says he cops for sixty,' a skinny man in a round fur hat said, handing five shillings over.

'A sovereign says the same,' a whiskery gentleman called.

'I'll have a bit of that,' Gerrund joined in.

'Where did you get ten shillings from?' I asked after he had laid his bet. 'I must be overpaying you.'

'No danger of that,' he replied without rancour, for we both knew that I had taken him on when nobody else would and gave him more than the going rate. 'My winnings from brag.'

'Why is Gervey not backing his own dog?'

'He'll have backed him all right,' Gerrund assured me. 'But Bradley couldn't stand for the kind of wager he would lay. Besides, Gervey will be taking his slice of the profit.'

'What is the least time in which that Tich could dispatch them all?' I enquired.

'The record for a hundred is five minutes and twenty-eight seconds by a dog called Jacko,' my gambler's encyclopaedia replied, 'but that's held for thirty years now and some say the clock was fixed to run slow.'

I called my fiancé Jacko once, I recalled, though he had turned out to be more of a rat than a dog.

I took another look at Little Tich. He was straining in his handler's arms desperate to return to battle.

'Then it is about time that the record was broken.' I pushed my way over. 'Five pounds says he kills the lot.'

'Don't, milady,' Gerrund urged.

Bradley snorted. 'Save your money, gal.'

'I am not a gal,' I said, bringing out my notecase, 'and I am entitled to place a wager.'

The landlord turned away.

'Here.' Gerrund grabbed his sleeve. 'Don't you show your back to milady.'

'Take the stoopid mare's lolly,' somebody urged from across the ring and a few others joined in. No bookie was supposed to turn down a bet. I followed his gaze across the ring and saw Gervey incline his head a fraction. Bradley stuck out his hand angrily for my notes.

'He's never so reluctant to take my rhino,' a young toff complained.

'I reckon she knows something,' his companion declared. 'Here Landlord I'll venture a pound on that.'

'Me too,' another voice added.

'Stick 'im in, Cecil,' Bradley yelled holding up a stopwatch. Gervey gave a nod and the handler virtually threw his dog into the ring. 'All bets closed,' Bradley announced to widespread disgust, but there was no time to argue as everyone's eyes fixed on Little Tich.

The terrier set to work the instant he landed, tossing the nearest rat aside and clamping his teeth on the next without pause. The rats scattered but Little Tich was on them, breaking their necks with an efficiency that any hangman would have envied. I had not thought it possible for such a small dog, but twice he took two rats at once. At the same time as he was killing them, Little Tich seemed to be herding his prey to the sides. Some tried to scramble up the barriers, but there were overhanging ledges on the corners and no shortage of volunteers to knock those who made it up the sides back again with their canes. Others scrabbled frantically at the floor in hopeless attempts to burrow to safety. One rat he had grasped by its hindquarters managed to twist and bite Little Tich on the ear, but I doubt the dog even felt it. He was in a frenzy of slaughter, launching himself with undiminished vigour into the last group, huddled in a corner.

'Stop the watch,' somebody yelled.

Bradley affected not to hear but Gerrund strode over and snatched it from him, pressing the button at the same time.

'Blimey!' he marvelled, staring at the face. 'Four minutes,' he yelled, 'and fifty-two seconds. A new world record!'

The crowd erupted. They had all lost, but they had been witnesses to a moment in history.

'They int all dead,' Bradley protested.

'Show us a live one and I'll give it a cuddle,' Crump's companion called back to great hilarity.

The poor girl must have been feeling dizzy, for he was holding her tightly again.

'Give milady her winnings,' Gerrund demanded and the landlord's eyes flicked side to side.

'I int got tha' much,' he whined.

'Now,' I said and lowered my voice, 'before I tell them what you have been up to.'

'Dint know wha' you mean,' Bradley protested, but he was busily sorting through his satchel as he spoke.

'There's somethin' fishy goo on here,' a fresh-faced youth speculated and the crowd began to mill around.

Bradley held out a wad of notes.

'Do you really imagine I do not know what four hundred pounds looks like?' I asked indignantly. 'Or shall I make an announcement?'

'My mistake,' he muttered hurriedly, counted out the rest of his notes and added a fistful of coins.

It was still short, I suspected, but it was all he had. I thrust a handful of the money into my handbag and clipped it shut, passing the rest to Gerrund who put it into his satchel. I hoped that his lantern was out properly.

Gervey, I noticed, was already leaving through the back way.

'Time to go,' I told my man and we set off. The greater part of a hundred people had witnessed me collecting my winnings and a fair proportion of them would hope to take my prize from me.

A hand grasped my shoulder from behind so I did what any other well-brought up young lady would have done. I turned my head and bit it.

Next time bring a stiletto, Ruby advised but, fond as I had grown of the place, I was not planning on making a return visit. I raised my skirt and, Gerrund in my wake, cantered up the stairs.

8: BEEMAN'S AND THE GREEN FAIRY

IN RESPONSE TO Gerrund's urgent knocking, Sledgehammer opened the door. There were already footsteps clattering close behind us.

'Do you think that you could keep it closed for a minute?' I asked and passed him a crumpled note.

'Give you two for tha',' he promised, slammed the door shut, bolted it and leaned back on it for good measure. Somebody was pounding already on the other side. 'Wish I could hear 'em over this racket.' Sledgehammer shook his head sadly.

I wiped my mouth, resisting the urge to spit. The hand that I had nibbled had been neither fresh nor delicious.

If anything, the saloon was more crowded than before and I had a torn sleeve and a hanging hem by the time we had battled back onto the street. I put a hand to my bonnet. It felt more like a mob cap now.

At least the moon was out again and we did not have to wait for Gerrund to relight his lantern.

A gentleman passed by with his hat down and a muffler pulled up over his lower face despite the heat.

'Somebody doesn't want to be recognised,' I commented.

'And I think we can both guess why,' Gerrund replied and puffed out his cheeks.

'Come here, girl,' the stranger called to somebody unseen and I recoiled to think that he actually meant girl rather than young woman.

'Got a long walk back to the park,' Gerrund remarked. 'Friendless will never hear us from here.' He glanced uneasily over his shoulder. 'Wish I'd brought my revolver now. This sword stick isn't much use against a mob.'

'There is a hansom on Salvation Road by the park gate,' I shouted to his puzzlement. 'Sixpence to whoever fetches it to the end of this alley.'

About ten figures emerged from the dark doorways across the road, all children, scattering back up the street, an old man struggling after them on crutches.

'Go back to sleep,' I told him and slipped a florin into his clawed hand, enough to feed him for a week if he did not drink it away.

Gerrund relit his lamp and we hurried, sloshing through the stinking sludge, back up the road until we reached a deep stream. Abandoning any pretence of decency, I hitched up my dress and waded across.

'Yick,' I breathed as it seeped over the top of my shoe.

What a silly word, Ruby said, annoyingly, for I had been thinking of giving it to her. *I would rather roast*, she asserted which was a distinct possibility.

Gerrund peered back.

'They're coming,' he warned, and I made out perhaps a dozen people running after us.

'There they goo,' somebody yelled. It was the old man who had managed to hobble after them and he was pointing down a side alley.

'Thank you,' I breathed as they went towards it.

'No they dint,' a woman lord–bless–her cried. 'They goo there.'

Cancelling my relief I broke into a messily sploshing gallop.

Crossing the hole was not something to which I had been looking forward, but the act presented much less of a challenge since Gerrund had straightened the plank. Once we were both across I peered back.

'They are catching up.'

'Soon stop that.' Gerrund crouched in the sludge, grasped the plank and heaved, tipping it crashing with a splash into the crater.

'But how will the children get home?'

He dipped gingerly into his pocket to bring out a handkerchief.

'Home?' He wiped his hands. 'They haven't got homes.' He tossed his handkerchief into the hole. 'But don't you fret, milady.

Like alley cats they are. They'll go over the rooftops if they want to, in fact some of them sleep up there.'

The urchins were gathered around our cab when we got to the junction, all clamouring to take credit for having summoned it.

'First one touch my horse take a lick of my whip as'll put his eye out,' Friendless threatened and the children left him to swarm around us.

'Have a care, milady,' my man warned. 'They'll have the laces off your shoes and the gold out of your teeth given half a chance.'

I did not have any stoppings, but this was not the time to compare our experiences of modern dentistry.

'Stand away,' I warned, holding my bag close. 'Or not one of you will get a farthing.' I stepped backwards, feeling my way carefully and, while Gerrund held up the lantern, sorted through my winnings. 'Form a queue,' I instructed, 'and I shall give you all something.'

'Wha's a coo?' a tiny girl demanded.

'A soup-line with no soup,' my man explained, and they jostled each other into some kind of order.

I handed the biggest and, therefore, first child a half crown and he eyed it suspiciously. He had probably never seen so much money at one time.

The next followed and then another. As the last, a bow-legged child, held out his or her hand, Gerrund slapped it on its shaved head.

'I let you go twice already,' he said. 'Don't be greedy.'

After I had finished paying them, we climbed aboard.

'Home driver,' Gerrund called, pulling the flaps shut.

'Tint home,' Friendless corrected him. 'If it is you dint need me.'

Not for the first time I wondered if his mother had known how richly her baby would merit his name.

'So what was Bradley up to, milady?' my man asked as we emerged onto the open road and I took a deep breath of the air that would have been fresh had it not stunk of me and Gerrund.

'He thought that nobody would bet on the dog killing them all in that time,' I explained. 'But I had more faith in Little Tich than that, besides which, the rats were drugged.'

'Drugged?' Gerrund repeated incredulously. 'I've known of it with horses and greyhounds and even a prize fighter but rats!'

'They were all too sluggish.' The cab rose over an unseen obstruction and I braced myself for the fall. 'The one I prodded with my parasol hardly reacted.'

'Blimey,' Gerrund said for the second time that night.

'Blimey indeed,' I agreed, finding the little box I kept in a side pocket of my bag.

I had been dying for a Beeman's. My father's cousin Gertrude had sent him a case of the chewing gum from her home in Boston – not the proper one but the place in America. It contained pepsin, which she thought might help his heartburn. He had hated it, but I had tried some and loved it. There was something wonderfully horrible about the *delicious natural and artificial flavors* with no *u* and I soon became a hopeless addict, consuming two packets a day, sometimes even having a stick before I got out of bed in the morning. Before my supply ran out, I had arranged regular shipments from the city posing as Cleveland, always keeping a crate aside in case of delays or loss at sea.

Gerrund sniffed disapprovingly as I unwrapped a stick. He would rather that I adopted a more ladylike habit such as cigarettes, or his personal favourite. He brought out his coffin-shaped snuff box and took a couple of pinches of something white that perked him up more than pulverised tobacco ever could. I for one had been quite invigorated enough for one night.

'Why did Gervey need so many men around him?' I wondered.

'A show of power,' Gerrund explained, 'and protection. There's a war brewing with the Braise Shotten gang for control of the Hams.'

These were the surrounding villages, the largest being Great Bardham, which was almost a town, and the smallest Kelham, little more than a hamlet. Together these settlements made up a sizeable population, enough from which to make a dishonest living at any rate.

I knew Cane Braise by sight. He was a huge jolly man, always smiling and laughing, tipping his tilted slouch hat to the ladies and dispensing coins to street children. On cattle market days he would be seen rubbing shoulders with the farmers, discussing their livestock and buying drinks – a gentle giant one might have thought if one did not know of his fondness for roasting people on a spit. *Braise is as Braise do*, he was alleged to chuckle through their screams.

'The girl I love is sweet and fair. Her heart is kind and trooo-oo-oo,' Friendless sang mournfully, the tune lost somewhere in the mists of his mind.

Where were you while all that was going on? I asked Ruby.

Cooking, she reminded me and, of course, she meant being rather than doing for, like Dracula in reverse, she had to be back in her coffin by midnight.

'But come the day I lose my hair she lose her heart to you-ooo-ooo-ooo-ooo,' Friendless wailed. 'Her name wa—'

Be quiet, Ruby commanded quite nastily, I thought, and he stopped abruptly so perhaps it had not been Ruby after all.

–

Gerrund fetched a jug of iced water from the cellar, half-filled my absinthe fountain and bade me a good night, though I rarely had one. The fountain looked like a miniature brass lamppost with two taps off the chamber at the top. I only ever needed one. The ritual comforted me, placing a cube of sugar on the slotted silver spoon and watching the water drip slowly through, clouding the clear green liquor, but never diluting it enough to take away the bite nor sweeten it enough to mask the bitterness.

'You swore that you loved me,' I said aloud.

You are better off without him, Ruby asserted, and I knew that she was right but it did not feel that way.

And to think I turned down Timothy Curtin, I fumed. Tim was a sweet man with forty thousand a year and a castle in Buckinghamshire near the pretty village of Milton Keynes.

Men, you cannot live with them. You can live without them, Ruby asserted.

It is said you cannot drown your sorrows and that may well be true, but you can certainly anaesthetise them, as I was proving almost every night.

Never trust a man, Ruby had advised and so I found some comfort in the company of Hettie who lived three streets away. She was a portrait painter and a very good one I thought.

Except me, Havelock Hefty chipped in, rather late to join the conversation and conveniently forgetting how he had investigated me for the murder of my great aunt the Dowager Herbena Lady Strainge.

It had not been my fault that she had drowned in a vat of pickles, I mused as the first sip ran onto my tongue. Some people thought her demise suspicious since she had bequeathed everything to me, but her fortune was not so much dwindling as dwindled. Strainge Comestibles was already in debt following the failure of its jellied bovine colons and her late husband, the baron, had lost heavily on a scheme to breed Manx cats with tails.

I rolled my drink around my mouth, wondering if I would become a sour spinster and waiting for Ruby to tell me that I had already done so, but she lifted a loose tress of my hair, placed it gently behind my ear and said nothing.

The one object of value that I had inherited from my aunt was Break House, tucked oddly into the corner of Seraphim Square in Montford, eighteen miles from our family seat in Thetbury. I say *oddly* because it was a wedge-shaped building, two rooms off the hallway at the front, fanning out to four at the back.

I swallowed, feeling the liquid trickle down into my waiting stomach.

Jack had vowed that he would die for me. If my father, second cousin or maid ever caught up with him he would find that promise fulfilled. Gerrund had made no threats, but I had seen the way he had gripped his meat cleaver when he had found out. Out of those three, my money would have been on Agnust. Few things escaped her though she had yet to discover that my *green fairy*, as some referred to the spirit, was not a herb-flavoured peppermint cordial.

'I loved him,' I told the absinthe.

It did not reply of course, but Ruby had plenty to say on the subject.

What is love? she philosophised. *A flutter of the heart or a surge of blood in the brain? Doctors will find a cure for it one day.*

From my readings of poetry I had hoped that there might be more to it than that, but I was forced to admit that she could be right.

Poets, Ruby snorted. *What do they know? They think that clouds are lonely.*

There had been little to inspire me in sleepy Thetbury and so I moved into the town to discover that the major differences were the readier supply of coffee and that the bumkins lived closer together.

From there Jack Wastrel would die horribly in my next book *The Revenge of Rose Rachet*. It was otherwise an uneventful existence, but I was quite content to have my excitement on paper. Life, however, had other plans and you cannot argue with life because it can always threaten to leave you and, if it does, you can never woo it back.

9: KIPPERS AND CHOLERA

AGNUST FLUMPED A plate in front of me.

'I hear you do get yourself in a scrape last night,' she began.

Who had snitched? Surely not Gerrund?

Apart from being loyal to me he would have got the edge of her tongue too.

Well don't look at me, Ruby protested. *I was tucked up in my coffin until a moment ago.*

Breakfast was two oak-smoked Yarmouth kippers. They were from a batch sent by my mother who, having sampled a disappointing sandwich at Montford railway station eight years ago, was convinced that there was no proper food to be had in neighbouring Suffolk.

'Just a little one,' I admitted warily and Agnust plunked her sizeable fists on her even more sizeable hips.

'Now you listen to me young lady,' she began and I promised that I would, though not that I would heed her words. 'When I come down from civ'lisisation...' By which she meant Thetbury Hall, just over the border in Norfolk. 'I promise your dear mamma I look after you.'

'And you do,' I assured her, helping myself from the rack of toast.

Agnust thrust out her chest, not that it needed projecting any further. She was a large woman in every dimension.

'And how do I do tha' when you're off fightin' rats?'

'I did not fight them. A dog did.'

'And galivantin' with crinimals,' she continued.

'Gerrund was there to protect me and I did not do any galivanting,' I objected. 'I ran away.'

'Runnin' away from crinimals at all hours?' She jutted her jaw. 'Wha' kind of behavin' way is tha' for a young lady of old breedin'?'

'I was doing some research for my book.'

'And tha's another thing.' Agnust folded her powerful arms under that bosom. She could have done a few rounds with Sledgehammer, I pondered, and not come off much the worse for it. 'Young ladies of old breedin' do not goo writin' shockers.'

'They are what makes the money,' I informed her though *The Mangrove Street Massacre* had yet to recover its meagre advance.

I did not ask how she thought I paid her wages because my father did that. Taking Agnust with me was one of the conditions that I had had to agree to before they consented to my moving from home. 'What has Montford got that we have not?' my father had demanded. 'Apart from smog and cholera?' And it was useless to argue that we were no smokier than any other market town or to point out that the last outbreak of cholera had been ten years before I was born.

'You should write romances,' my maid and self-appointed literary adviser advised, 'like Miss Primrose Delight.'

'I hate romances,' I told her, 'all those swooning heiresses falling in love with handsome brutes.'

Agnust shook her head at my nonsense, for she had read *Withering Hills* at least twice and told me about it ten times more than that.

'And do you see the state of your dress?' she demanded. 'It look like you goo paddlin' in a cess pit.'

That was actually not far from the truth but, when all was said and done, it was my dress and it was not her job to launder nor repair it.

'Might I have my coffee now?' I asked more timidly than I had confronted members of the underworld, and Agnust begrudgingly poured me half a cup.

'Int good for you,' she muttered, though I should have thought that my beverage would have been the last of her worries after my night spent mingling with crinimals and brawlin' with vermin.

'How did you know about last night?' I enquired.

She was there in disguise, Hefty theorised unconvincingly. *It didn't make a fool of me though.*

What did then? Ruby asked, filing a fingernail and I wished she would not do that. The debris made my thalamus itch.

'You write it in your diary,' Agnust explained and I sat up indignantly.

'My journal is private.'

'Well,' Agnust refolded her arms and the cuff of her dress rose to reveal some of her scars, 'if you do leave it lyin' 'round in a locked drawer you have to 'spect people to read it.'

But how, I wondered. The lock had not been forced and I could not imagine my maid having the dexterity to pick it.

She has seen you leaving the key in that ginger jar, Ruby explained, and it occurred to me that most employers would have their maids packing their bags after that explanation but, not being most employers, I only said, 'I see,' in a tone that I hoped would give Agnust pause for thought, but if she paused at all it was only to glance at her reflection in the mantle mirror and stroke the furry mole on her upper lip affectionately on her way to the door.

'And dint you goo chokin' on any bone,' she admonished me, though I had never done so yet.

Alone at last I opened my post. A relative I had never heard of was being held in a Turkish prison and would be beheaded if he could not pay his fifty-guinea fine for insulting the sultan. I might have given it a little more attention if the postmark had not been Preston and, heartlessly, I left him to his fate.

I browsed the day's *Times*, hardly giving the front page of advertisements a glance. I had no need yet of liver salts nor electrical devices to stimulate my sluggish circulation, though I did wonder if I might benefit from Professor Frobisher's Brain Tonic, guaranteed to help any lady think more sensibly – like a man presumably. I turned the page, getting hardly any butter on the lower edge.

Sidney Grice, the famous Personal Detective and his goddaughter March Middleton had managed to track the mysterious Honest Publisher to his hiding place in Wimbledon. Many had thought that he must be a mythical figure.

There was something sharp in my throat and I coughed as gruffly as a bilious colonel, but the sharp something was still there. Hastily I chewed and swallowed a piece of toast, which not only failed to shift it but got stuck too. Choking now, I hurried to the sideboard, sploshed out a cup of, mercifully cold, coffee and managed to wash the bolus down, hurrying back to my chair as heavy footsteps approached.

Agnust eyed me suspiciously. She must have heard the commotion and I was probably flushed, but she made no comment except to wonder if I believed that she did not have enough to do without my slopping beverages. I assured her that I did not. If she had not returned I would have mopped it up myself, but she had caught me brushing crumbs off the tablecloth once and enquired if I were after her job.

'I shall have a quiet day today,' I sought to reassure her as she cleared.

'And tonight?' she asked distrustfully. 'Gooin' bear baitin' or cock fightin' with the nasty-men are we?'

Nasty-men were garrotters and, twenty years after the scare in London, the panic had struck in East Anglia. A man had been strangled from behind in Gorham and three women in Ipswich, not to mention assorted parlour maids, milkmen and vicars similarly dispatched around the county. One of the many troubles with these accounts was that they had always happened to somebody that a friend of an acquaintance knew, but the teller could never recall their names. The stories were in all the papers they would assure you, but they must have been in different editions to the ones that were delivered to my house.

'Are we?' she pressed.

'You are not,' I replied and was about to add that I was not either when the doorbell rang.

'Now who do tha' be?' Agnust cocked an ear.

'There is only one way to find out,' I replied but, on reflection, there were at least three, though answering the door was the easiest and most conventional way.

I sat and waited. It was not Gerrund's job to respond unless Agnust was not available, and I was fairly confident that it was not mine either. She unwound her arms and huffed.

'S'pose I best goo,' she decided. 'But, if tha's one of your friends, you int not gooin' out to play.'

It was seventeen years since an eight-year-old Lady Violet Thorn had run with her hoop in front of a hay waggon and I had been right as rain within the year, but neither Agnust nor the dent in my skull would ever let me forget it. Few things sound more horrible than the cracking of bones, especially if they are one's own.

10: *BLUE ROSES AND THE HABSBURG JAW*

FROM THE SOUNDS of the door opening and closing and the low conversation afterwards it was obvious that the caller was not a tradesman, postman or telegram boy, for none of those would have got over the threshold without at least a scuffle and Agnust had returned unscathed bearing a silver tray with a white calling card upon it.

'There's a lady do wish to speak with you, she do,' she announced, rubbing her chin, which had been sprouting a few black hairs recently.

Automatically I touched my jaw. Was that a bristle? I was relieved to find that it was a fine kipper bone, though it said little good about my table manners.

'Did she say what it was about?'

'She say it do be pers'nal.'

She wants money, Ruby asserted.

'And she int lookin' for money,' Agnust continued.

Definitely money then, Ruby insisted, and I was just about to tell my maid to send the woman away when she added, 'Oh and one straculiar thing...'

Straculiar meant strange and peculiar, at least it did in Thetbury.

'And what was that?'

'She do say she like your books.' Agnust raised a hand to show that her list of wonders was not complete. 'All on 'em,' she marvelled.

'Then I had better see her,' I decided for admirers were scarcer than pelicans in Piccadilly Circus.

Perhaps you should display this one in a glass case, Ruby advised.

She was a little crabbity that morning, having had a bad night in her casket.

'Put her in the front sitting room and I shall be through presently,' I said, ignoring Agnust's muttering.

She had a strong aversion to doing as she was told which, I suspected, was one reason my parents had so generously donated her to me.

Alone I checked myself in the mirror, wondering as always why the good Lord had seen fit to give me such a tiny nose. Was that a dot of butter on my chin? Strange how Agnust, who rarely missed an opportunity to scold me, had not drawn my attention to it. I wiped it off, noticing some ink stains on my fingers, though I had not used a pen for two days, but decided that, otherwise, I was presentable.

My visitor was a small woman but, at a couple of inches over five foot, she still had the advantage on me. Aged about thirty-five, I estimated, she had golden-brown hair under a straw boater. They were all the rage that summer, though Gerrund asserted that they made people look like thatched cottages. She wore a simple powder-blue skirt with a short matching coat, over a white shirt and rather a nice rope of cream pearls around her slender neck.

'Good morning.' I held out my hand and she shook it firmly.

'It is good of you to see me out of visiting hours,' she said.

I rather liked her perfume, but it was probably premature to ask her what it was.

I know what it is, Ruby told me. *Expensive.*

'You are Mrs Ryan?'

'I am,' she agreed, 'but I prefer to be called Martha, if that is agreeable to you.'

'In which case I am Violet.'

She looked about uncertainly.

'Take a seat, Martha.'

I indicated to the left hand of the two chairs placed at forty-five degrees to each other and before the long sash window. They were box-shaped with high railed wooden arms and upholstered to match my rose-and-trellis wallpaper. The material of my seat had been stretched and sagged noticeably from when Agnust had stood on it in her boots, trying to swat a fly which had been annoying her all morning, only for her to realise that it was something floating inside her eyeball – a *dooleybug* in local parlance.

'How lovely and modern.'

The chairs were separated by a small low table, more in fashion since dresses became less voluminous and not as likely to swish off ornaments.

'William Morris,' I told her. 'Not everybody approves. They think his furniture too plain.'

'Oh no,' she disagreed. 'I am half sick of all the fussy over-ornamented stuff with which we cram our homes. After all, we are heading towards the twentieth century.'

'They are more comfortable than they look,' I assured her as she sat in one. 'Those pegs can be repositioned to make them recline,' I explained, not unlike the shop assistant who had sold them to me.

'How clever.'

Martha sat, straight-backed, clipping and unclipping her handbag on her lap. It was rather a nice bag, blue of course – for this lady's outfit was nothing if not coordinated – and embroidered with intertwined tulips.

Before us lay Seraphim Square, the broken remains of the old flint monastery walls running along the left-hand side punctuated by the great cube of the gatehouse with its high arch through which people passed into the gardens. The Splendid Hotel – not such a vainglorious name as it sounded, having been founded by a Mr Walter Splendid – faced it to our right. Straight ahead at the far end was the Pythagorean, a two-storey building, white plastered with faux Greek friezes and a statue of the great man over the portico. It was a club for men of philosophy, science and literature and so I was excluded on every count.

'Will you take tea or coffee?' I enquired.

'Coffee would be lovely,' she said.

This was a woman after my own heart; an infusion of stewed leaves was always something I drank more from politeness than for pleasure. I went to the bell pull and was about to tug it when Agnust appeared.

She often stood at the door when we had new callers. It was not just nosiness – extravagantly endowed with that as she was – but she had not forgotten the lovely old lady who had stabbed me with a tuning fork in my protectively raised wrist for *stimulating* her husband. My sin was to use the words heaving and breast in the same sentence, even though they were unconnected and I had been writing about a man.

'Dint blame me if you dint goo sleep after lunch,' Agnust muttered and I promised that I would not, though I thought that I was four years old the last time I had been sent for an afternoon nap.

'Neither shall I,' Martha Ryan assured my maid with such a twinkle in her hazel eyes that I warmed to her even more.

'You have a good view of the square,' she commented when Agnust had gone.

The main market, unsurprisingly, was based in Market Square but some stalls were set up in Seraphim Square – mainly luxury goods and souvenirs or refreshments for visitors. Garish and inaccurate china models of the monastery gates were surprisingly – to me at any rate – popular gifts, but it was difficult to imagine that they would be received and displayed with unalloyed pleasure.

'And it has a good view of me,' I said for I did not favour net curtains, 'but I like to watch the world go by.'

'Looking for characters?'

'I try to.'

The eel woman was there. She was not a circus act but the seller of foul-smelling stew from a hubbling-bubbling cauldron that she stirred with a rusty steel ladle. She always set up with her wooden spoons and bowls near the statue of Edmund the warrior king, who was armed only with a cross. In the winter people would gather to warm themselves around her charcoal brazier, but how she withstood the heat in the blazing summer of '95 was beyond me.

'I have read one of your novels,' Martha declared, and my heart dipped like a float when the trout takes a tentative nibble.

One? Agnust had said that it was all of them.

'Oh yes? Which one?'

'*Death Visits Mars Mansions.*'

'Utter tosh of course,' I muttered to Ruby's indignation.

She had tracked a rabid baboon through Hampton Court maze in that adventure.

'On the contrary,' Martha Ryan disagreed, 'I enjoyed it enormously. It kept me up half the night. Ruby Gibson is so clever.'

I most assuredly am, Ruby preened while my visitor continued, 'I am still not sure how she knew where to find that dagger.'

Neither am I, I thought, heart bobbing back to the surface, but said, 'I try to keep my readers guessing.'

'You unquestionably succeed,' she enthused. 'I only finished it on Monday and this morning I went straight to Elkin and Lovat's Bookshop to order the rest of the series.'

'Thank you,' I said. 'I hope that you enjoy them.'

'I am sure I shall.'

Much as I relished the unusual experience of being flattered I decided not to further the conversation for I had the impression that my visitor was procrastinating.

'I believe there was something personal that you wished to discuss,' I said and she ran a hand under the arm, surely not checking for dust?

She had long fingers with a wedding ring on her left hand and a good-sized diamond on the other.

'I feel foolish now that I have come to say it aloud,' she admitted.

'There is no need to,' I assured her, though she might have an excellent reason to be embarrassed for all I knew.

'Obviously I do not know you,' she began.

Obviously, Ruby concurred impatiently, starting to pace back and forth in my mind.

'But I fell into conversation in the Café Cordoba with a lady who is, I believe, a friend of yours – a Miss Hettie Granger.'

'We have known each other for many years,' I agreed, omitting to mention that Hettie was to have been one of my bridesmaids.

'And she spoke very highly of you.'

'I have a good opinion of her too,' I said, trying to sweep the memories of Hettie's escapades under my mental carpet while Ruby was trampling over it.

'So I am correct – am I not? – to believe that I can rely on your discretion?'

Keep still, I told Ruby and she huffed but froze mid-step like a child playing statues.

My visitor was so obviously agitated that I leaned back a fraction. If you lean forward you may look attentive, but equally you might give the impression you are ready to pounce.

I taught you that, Hefty reminded me, primping his already-primped moustaches.

'I do not gossip,' I confirmed, 'well not about anything told to me in confidence at any rate, unless,' I added to make it quite clear, 'an innocent person is in danger.'

If she wanted to make use of my limited literary skills to plot a murder I would need a compelling reason to oblige her. Come to think of it, Martha Ryan might make an excellent murderess in my next book. She was so patently innocent that nobody would suspect her.

I would, Ruby said, almost toppling over. *Her eyes are too lustrous.*

Shush.

My visitor clipped, unclipped and reclipped the bag, and I nodded in what I hoped was an encouraging way.

'What did you want to talk about, Martha?'

'I am not sure,' she replied unhelpfully. 'It may be that you can do nothing.'

'But?' I coaxed, brushing aside my character's mutterings about telling her to stop wasting our time and go away.

But find out what perfume she uses first.

'I have come about a friend of mine,' Martha began tentatively, and I sighed though not, I hoped, audibly. One of Ruby Gibson's clients had claimed that he was just enquiring for a pal in *The Mystery of Waterworks Road*. It had not fooled my heroine for long and it would not do so for one tick of the golden fob watch that hung on a chain around my neck now.

'Is he or she in trouble?' I enquired coolly.

'That is why I am here.' Martha unfastened, fastened and unfastened the clip again. 'I do not know.' She dipped into her bag and brought out one of those silly lace handkerchiefs that women are expected to carry, and which are useless for anything other than waving loved ones off to massacre foreigners.

Agnust entered with tray.

'Leave it here,' I told her.

'Oh and there I was 'tendin' to take it away again,' she retorted not quite under her breath and I resolved to have a word with her later, for all the good that would do. I liked sarcasm, but I much preferred to be the sarcasmer doing the sarcasming than the sarcasmee, to coin three words that were probably best left unminted.

'Shall I pour, milady?' she asked as if she were offering me her last drop of blood.

'No I shall.'

'Lady Violet Independence now,' she breathed, and Martha watched her leave in surprise.

'You have an unusual maid.'

'She is my Habsburg jaw,' I told her. 'Not my most attractive asset but I inherited her.' I poured our coffees. 'Help yourself to milk and sugar.'

'Thank you.'

She took both as did I.

'I am sorry,' she said, folding her handkerchief to drop it back unused. 'But I feel stupid. I am sure my concerns will sound quite ridiculous.'

Only 'quite'? Ruby mocked and I resolved to give her a good shaking afterwards. *Just try it*, she challenged and I abandoned the idea. There are few things more undignified than being trounced by one's own imaginary characters.

Imaginary? she fumed.

'Please continue.'

'Well, Violet,' Martha began hesitantly, 'you will not laugh?'

'Certainly not,' I assured her, hoping that I could keep my word. It is often the way I find that, when people tell me something will make me giggle, I know that it will not and that I will feel obliged to force a smile but, if they tell me not to, I am stifling a guffaw before I have even heard about some awful mishap.

Martha took a breath.

'My best friend will not speak to me,' she said softly.

11: MUNGO PEERS AND BLOOD ON THE SALT

THERE WAS A spider on the ceiling. It was quite a big one, but I only spotted it when I raised my eyes heavenward. If I had not already braced myself I might have found Martha Ryan's statement mildly amusing. More likely I would have wondered from which nursery she had absconded. My first thought was that she could not be serious. Had somebody sent her to play a practical joke upon me? But I did not have that sort of friend – certainly not Hettie – and if I had any enemies surely they would not be so gentle in their revenge. Looking at my visitor, though, it was clear that she was troubled and I had no difficulty at all in keeping a straight face. She swallowed and clutched the handle of her handbag.

'I see.' I picked up my cup. 'But how can I help you?'

'It may be that you cannot,' she said, 'but I should like you to find out why.'

'Do you want me to ask her?' I enquired in mild surprise. It seemed an odd request to make of a stranger.

'Good heavens no,' she replied hastily. 'I would like you to investigate.' Martha must have observed my sceptical expression and misinterpreted it, because she added, 'Unless you are too busy.'

You are much too busy, Ruby insisted.

You most certainly are, Inspector Hefty agreed for he was still languishing in one of my many unfinished manuscripts.

'It is not that,' I said, dragging my thoughts back to the matter in hand. 'I can find the time but...' I hesitated. 'You do know that I am not a detective?'

Martha flushed slightly.

'Well of course.'

'It is just,' I put in hastily before she took too much offence, 'that I have had some highly intelligent readers confuse me with my heroine.'

They were actually people with half a brain in search of a companion and I was surprised that they could read, but I was trying something that Miss Kidd, my governess, had despaired of teaching me – being tactful.

Martha smiled wryly.

'I have not escaped from the Dewbury Hall asylum.'

'I know that you have not.'

I stirred my coffee.

If this were one of my Hefty stories, I would have made some clever observation but, anxious that my visitor was not under any delusions about my deductive powers, I explained, 'The director is a relative of mine and he would have told me if anyone had absconded.'

Martha nodded.

'I did consider employing a private detective,' she told me, that being the first resort of anyone who has ever fallen out with a friend. 'But one hears such dreadful stories of how unscrupulous they can be.'

'One certainly does,' I concurred, Hettie having had distressing experiences at the hands of the Barfolemew Pentigin Agency.

'And how would I explain their bills to Arthur, my husband?'

'Arthur and Martha,' I mused though, as Miss Kidd had instructed me when I was a child and Agnust had reiterated only last week, one should never comment upon people's names. They might think that you are mocking them and the chances are that they would be right.

'Quite so,' Martha agreed with no sign of resentment. 'The similarity of our names struck me as humorous before I was married. There has been precious little to amuse me since.'

Do not ask for details, Ruby advised, *or she will never leave.*

The postcard boy was strolling to his patch in front of the great flint and mortar arch that had guarded the monastery gates. Once there he would sit on the low ruins of the wall, contorting his legs in grotesque imitation of a crippled child.

'So your husband does not know about your friend?'

'It would only confirm his belief that the most intelligent of women are scatter-brained.'

'He is not alone in that opinion,' I commented and Martha lowered her head.

'Alone describes how I feel quite perfectly.'

'Do you have any children?'

Martha exhaled heavily.

'Four boys,' she said, 'all stillborn.' She pinched the bridge of her nose. 'Dolores was the only person I could turn to after the last one. Arthur had lost interest in my grief by then.'

Martha blew her lips out.

So now she has latched onto you, Ruby said nastily but possibly accurately, and I was about to disengage myself from my visitor as gently as possible when Ruby added, *Get rid of her.*

If there was one thing Ruby, Agnust and I had in common it was a dislike of being told what to do and, to borrow a phrase from Friendless, I was *dripped on dripping* if I was going to be bossed about by my own creation.

'I will do whatever I can,' I promised though I had not the slightest idea what that might be.

Do not worry about me, Ruby said lemon tartly. *I can smell burning.*

Martha Ryan squeezed my hand.

'Thank you,' she said. 'You and Hettie are the first people I have met in a long time who I feel I can trust.' She unclipped her bag yet again – a tribute to British craftsmanship that the catch had not broken. 'Do you mind if I smoke?'

'Not at all,' I said, though I disliked the acridness of cigarettes and the way it seeped into my clothes and furnishings, but at least she had the courtesy to ask. Most people assume that nothing would give one greater pleasure than to bathe in their fumes.

I got back to my feet, went to my desk to open a lower drawer and brought out a Limoges ashtray. It was a present from a friend for her to use on visits. The picture was of a lady and a shepherd. Only a town dweller could imagine that the brutes who guard sheep are romantic figures.

'Let us start with some details,' I suggested, if only to settle her down. 'Where do you live, Martha?'

'Cranberry House,' she told me, reaching into her bag. 'Orchard Square.'

'That is a nice area.'

And expensive, Ruby remarked. *You should charge her a fee for our time.*

Martha produced a silver box of vestas but, instead of a matching cigarette case, followed it with a red rectangular box, hinging open a lid inscribed *LITTLE QUEEN* and *Perfumed cigarettes*. The cigarette itself was encircled in a gold band on one end and the name was printed, also in gold, along the side. It was so elegant that I was almost tempted to cadge one just so that I could hold it.

'What is your friend's name?' I asked as she slotted her cigarette into a silver holder, cast in the shape of a snake with a gaping mouth.

'Mrs Dolores Poynder,' she told me. 'Her husband is a doctor.'

'Dr Edward Poynder?' I knew of him, though I had never required his services.

Yet, Ruby chipped in.

'Yes.' Martha gripped the holder between her straight white teeth.

Actually teeth are never white, Ruby corrected me, *they are light yellow at best because their dentine shows through the enamel.*

Yes but…

Also, she spoke over me, *they cannot be straight. They follow the arcs of the jaws.*

I knew that she was correct, but my visitor had good teeth and *curved light yellow* did not do them justice.

Martha struck a vesta, dipped her head towards the flame, and shook the match out. 'He has a consulting room in their house and gives two days a week at the nursing home and another in the infirmary.' She snapped the match deftly. 'Oh and, just to ensure his place in the heaven he repudiates, he does good works amongst the slum poor.'

Dr Poynder had an even greater claim to sainthood than that, I recalled.

'That poor little boy,' I said automatically.

'Yes,' Martha said. 'Edward was quite the man of the hour.'

I watched as she sucked the smoke deep inside her. Had there been a tinge of irony in her tone? I could not imagine why there would be.

The papers had been full of the events for weeks. The vultures had even swooped on Montford from the heights of Fleet Street, for the story had everything of which they could wish to pick the bones – the murder of a child, a handsome hero, an innocent man in custody and the same handsome hero to the rescue.

–

Dr Edward Poynder had just finished seeing a patient in his house when he heard Sheba, his English Setter, barking wildly and then squeal as if in pain. Hurrying out into the back garden, Poynder was horrified to see his pet dead on the terrace, blood pouring from a slashed throat.

In the corner of his eye he glimpsed the figure of a man in a long black cloak and fedora making his way from the shrubbery through the side gate. Poynder gave chase and was just in time to see the man fleeing around the corner down Gainsborough Gardens. He would have followed, but found himself presented with an even more ghastly sight, a small boy staggering in the road, bleeding heavily from chest and neck wounds. As the doctor ran to help, the boy collapsed and, try as Poynder might, he could do little to staunch the haemorrhages.

At that moment Jacob Kaufman, a salt-block seller, arrived on his cart. He was clearly distraught and despite the doctor's attempts to restrain him, cradled the child in his arms as the boy expired.

Kaufman identified the victim as Mungo Peers, the ten-year-old son of a local grocer who was prosperous enough not to put him to work. Mungo was a popular child. Good natured and something of a chatterbox, he would often sit outside his father's shop striking up conversations with whoever passed by. Kaufman had the reputation of being a solitary, sometimes surly, man but even he was taken with the boy. The two struck up a friendship and Mungo began to take rides on the cart, running to the tradesmen's entrances of private houses with orders wrapped in brown paper parcels.

Mungo made friends with kitchen maids who often gave him slices of bread and butter or cake. While the boy dallied, Kaufman would continue on his round, stopping at every house to deliver regular orders or check if any were required so it was easy for Mungo to rejoin him. On this occasion, the child not having caught up, Kaufman had circled around in search of his young friend only to find him on the brink of death.

Poynder summoned Montford police station on the telephone. Sergeant Gorbals was the first to arrive with two constables. Having a clinic booked at the Newbury Nursing Home, Poynder gave a brief statement, then returned home to wash himself and change his clothes. After instructing his man Wormwood to bury Sheba in the garden he set off for work.

It was PC Canning who, seeing how Kaufman was covered in blood, searched his cart. There were bloodstains on the block of salt and a machete-like knife hidden under a sheet of tarpaulin. The handle of that knife was also covered in blood. Had Kaufman not panicked, he could have explained that he used the knife to cut the salt and was in the habit of covering it over to prevent its theft when his back was turned, and that he must have got blood on it when he put it away after comforting Mungo. But the salt seller had been in trouble with the police before. A maid had accused him of lewd behaviour and he had been treated roughly until the other servants had vouched for him. He panicked and claimed, foolishly, that he had gashed himself but, on being unable to show any cuts, was arrested and charged with murder.

When Dr Poynder arrived at Montford police station to make a statement he was told that Jacob Kaufman had confessed to murdering Mungo Peers and killing Sheba and was asked to take a look at the guilty man who had tripped down the flight of stone steps to the cells. Kaufman, it was explained, had fallen out with Dr Poynder's cook and had killed the dog in retaliation for her cancelling their regular order and, his bloodlust up, had turned on the child who, being fond of Sheba, had tried to intervene.

To be fair to the *Montford Chronical* it tried to give a balanced view of events, but few other newspapers made any attempt to do anything other than sensationalise an already sensational story. As for Kaufman, *The Englishman's Weekly* reminded readers, it was well known that Jews ritually sacrificed gentile children.

Poynder was unconvinced by these stories and by the sergeant's account of how Kaufman received his injuries and so, when the salt-block seller retracted his confession, the doctor appeared at the inquest with his version of events. The man he had seen fleeing, he insisted, bore no resemblance to Kaufman; the weapon used was a carving knife Poynder had seen the murderer cast away; and the failure of the police to follow up on his evidence had allowed the guilty man to make his escape.

The accused man was released without trial, to a thunderous article in the *Englishman's Weekly* accusing the police of allowing their antisemitism to cloud their judgement, but Kaufman found himself a pariah. People were sceptical about the nature of his friendship with Mungo and maids became nervous of dealing with him.

Mud sticks, Ruby commented, *but blood stains and it can never be washed away.*

12: *CHAOS AND THE MENDICANT*

MARTHA INHALED DEEPLY, the expression of Saint Theresa in her ecstasy being decidedly languid compared to my visitor's rapture as the nicotine flooded into her brain.

I know precisely how she feels, Hefty observed, never having forgiven me for breaking his favourite cherry-wood when it deflected a bullet. He might have recovered from being shot, he had complained at the time, but his pipe had been unrepairable.

'Where do the Poynders live?' I asked, trying to blow the smoke away without making it obvious that I was doing so.

'Haglin House, Gainsborough Gardens.'

'Another nice area,' I commented, scanning a map of the area in my mind. It was a bit messy after Ruby had circled all the public houses in red ink. 'And adjacent to Orchard Square.'

'The backs of our gardens adjoin,' she told me, 'which is how we met.'

I got up and pulled the lower sash window up a few inches.

'You do get a good larrupin' if you dint behave,' a grim-faced nanny threatened the howling girl who she was dragging past, and I wondered if mothers realised how much some servants loathed the children that the parents adored but could not be troubled to tend.

'I prefer to be cool,' I excused my actions, wondering why I felt obliged to.

My attention was taken briefly by a ragged woman in a patched dress and battered bonnet standing on the cobbles in the square. The perimeter road had been coated with tar in an attempt to stop the macadam stones flying at pedestrians from speeding carriages, and it had been a great success until the summer heat had started to melt the surface. Now cabbies complained that an oily black treacle stuck to their wheels, sprayed onto the woodwork and clogged their horses' hooves.

'Tell me about that first meeting,' I invited for, if I were to form an opinion upon what the relationship foundered, it might help to know upon what it was founded.

A cloud billowed from Martha's nostrils, as I returned to my chair, reminding me of the terrible Thetbury Dragon who, I was told, would incinerate any children foolish enough to play in my father's wine cellar.

'Dolly – I mean Dolores – has a cat called Chaos and rightly so,' Martha – not very draconic after all – began. 'He managed, Lord knows how, to climb a tall monkey puzzle tree on our side of the wall and she asked if she could come into my garden to rescue him.' Martha tapped her ash off. 'It took a while but eventually we managed to coax him down. For some reason we were instantly comfortable together. I invited her in for coffee and she returned the invitation the very next day. Our friendship blossomed from there and we became inseparable, the sisters that neither of us had ever had.'

I leaned over to pour more easily.

'How long ago was that?'

'Just over eight years. Monday March the fourteenth.'

'How can you be so precise?'

'I keep a diary.' Martha stiffened a fraction. 'But it is personal.'

'Then I shall not ask to read it,' I assured her.

It might have been useful. A woman will confide things to her journal that she would not dream of sharing with her best friend, and many a wife has been ruined by her spouse's discovery of its contents.

'Did you ever argue?' I asked, for I had yet to come across two women, *sisters* though they may have been, who did not.

'Once,' Martha admitted. 'Dolores was singing Edward's praises as usual, telling me how wonderful he was to devote so much time to helping Adelaide Cotton, who was suffering from loss of weight. I was bored and told her it was wonderful how wealthy Adelaide's father was.'

'Is he…' I began.

'The manufacturer.' She confirmed my supposition before I had even voiced it.

When I was a child I imagined that Cotton Traction Engines must be made by seamstresses, but as I grew older I realised that they were made by breaking men's bodies in foundries and factories.

'I suppose I should not have told you her name,' Martha realised, though I would have thought that her friend was more at fault for breaking medical confidences.

'You can rely on my discretion,' I said. 'What happened then?'

'Oh it was stupid,' Martha admitted. 'She told me that he charged her no more than any other patient, but I was too stubborn to retract.' Martha dotted the air with her cigarette. 'But I sent her a dozen white roses the next morning with a note apologising.' She took an interest in her upturned left hand. 'Dolores called upon me immediately. We hugged and made up and the matter was never mentioned again. That was almost two years ago.'

'So what went wrong?' I asked, and she brushed an invisible speck of ash from her sleeve.

'Dolores accompanied her husband on a five-month tour of Europe. He wished to instruct his colleagues in some new technique he had developed,' she said. 'We bid each other an affectionate farewell, saying how much we would miss each other and promising to keep in touch. We hugged and Dolores cried. She was always more emotional than I but this time I joined in her tears.'

I watched my visitor carefully. She looked as if she were about to repeat the act.

'And then?' I asked quietly.

Martha looked out across the square, but I had the impression that she was not seeing anything, not even Jolly Jimmy Jones who frightened small children and irritated older ones with his raucous tomfoolery. *Lawks but I have lost my head*, he shrieked, pulling his coat over it and trotting around an exasperated seller of linnets.

If only that were true, Ruby said with feeling; she disliked any jokes save her own.

'That was the last time we spoke to each other,' Martha said simply and, sure enough, her eyes brimmed with tears.

Tell her to pull herself together, Ruby urged for she hated what she saw as *drippy* women, but I had a better idea.

'Would you like a sherry?' I suggested, and Martha dabbed her eyes with one corner of her flimsy lace frippery.

'I don't usually drink at this time,' she said.

Of course she does, Ruby jibed. *Look at her bloodshot eyes.*

That is from crying.

'Neither do I,' I told my visitor. 'Would you prefer sweet or dry?'

'Dry please.'

Well she didn't take much persuasion, Ruby, the woman who had drunk a druid under his sacrificial altar, said primly as I went to the cabinet – the rosewood panels painted with vividly coloured parrots perching on floating branches.

'Did you receive any communications after you said goodbye?' I enquired.

The bottle looked less full than I remembered. Surely not Agnust? She had refused plum pudding on Christmas day because it had brandy in it. And Gerrund regarded sherry as a drink for ladies and vicars, of which he was neither.

Don't look at me, Ruby protested as I extracted the cork. *I'm a whisky woman.*

She started to run through her preferred brands, none of which I stocked, but I was trying to listen to Martha's reply to my question.

'One postcard saying that they had landed in Calais,' she was saying, 'but nothing since and I was not familiar enough with her itinerary to be able to reply.'

Martha pulled the stub of her cigarette out of her holder and ground it out in the ashtray.

'And when Mrs Poynder returned?'

I poured two small measures, then, deciding that they looked what they were – mean – topped them up.

'I left her a week to recover from her travels before I called only to be told that she was not at home.' Martha reloaded her holder. 'I tried three times more with the same result. I rang on the telephone four times and was informed that she was unavailable. I wrote to her but received no response. My last letter was six weeks ago.'

I put the glasses on a round papier-mâché tray – there were robins in flight under the lacquered surface – and placed it on a little low table between us.

A blind man was wending his way across the square, a ragged buff-coloured canvas coat hanging loosely about him. He had on a floppy wide-brimmed hat with a shallow crown and his head was down. He moved cautiously sliding his feet as if he were testing for thin ice, tapping the cobbles not with a white stick but a neatly furled gentleman's black umbrella, and I wondered whether he had found or stolen it.

'Perhaps your friend is unwell,' I suggested, hoping that I was not adding to her anxieties.

Martha struck another vesta and lit her cigarette.

'I wondered that,' she admitted. 'In fact I asked Wormwood, who is the only servant allowed to answer the telephone, but he refused to respond to any of my concerns about Dolores's well-being.'

Wormwood, Ruby chewed the name suspiciously. *He has to be evil. No hero could have a name like that.*

It is what flavours our absinthe, I reminded her, for she had introduced me to the liquor.

Martha drew on her cigarette. 'But surely, if Dolores were ill, she would welcome my company.'

'Perhaps she has contracted something contagious,' I postulated and Martha shrugged.

'It is possible.' She balanced her cigarette and holder on the ashtray. 'But I cannot understand why she would not let me know. If she had to be isolated why could we not speak through a closed door or at least correspond with each other?'

The blind man moved slowly towards us around a pile of cabbages. They had been dumped rotting three days ago, presumably having been unsold in Market Square. The stink of them drifted into my sitting room, though they did not appear to trouble the dog-collar seller who stood beside the mound, chains draped over his shoulders and leather straps dangling from his belt.

Martha picked up her drink and, as I followed suit, it occurred to me that there was a simple explanation for all this.

'Do you think it possible,' I began, as delicately as I could, 'that Mrs Poynder has just decided that she wants, if not to break your friendship, at least to make it less… intense?' The hurdy-gurdy man was passing by, and I hoped that he was not going to set up with his instrument of torture too close to the window. I had had a whole afternoon of his constant drone and scratchings last week. 'That may not be the best choice of adjectives,' I conceded while Martha held up the glass.

'It is an apposite word,' she assured me and, before I could question her further on the subject, added, 'I tried to tell myself that I might have been too intrusive, but Dolores drove our relationship onwards as much as I.'

'Sometimes, when people are away from something, they see it from a different perspective,' I hypothesised. 'I have an uncle who lived for his garden. Then he had an accident and was bedridden for two months. He fretted dreadfully but, after he recovered, he never picked up his secateurs again. He realised that what he had thought gave him joy was an obsession and oppressed him.' I sipped sherry, so taken by my story that I almost wished it were true. 'Having gone away and had the opportunity to be more objective about your friendship,' I continued, 'Dolores may have decided that it was not what she wanted and, rather than suffer a confrontation, taken the coward's exit by simply avoiding seeing or speaking to you.'

'I was coming to that conclusion myself,' Martha admitted, 'until...' She tapped her cigarette. 'I received this.' She opened her handbag, dipped her hand in and pulled out a creased white envelope. 'A letter,' she explained, fiddling with the clasp.

Well blow me down, Ruby exclaimed in mock surprise. *I thought it was an emperor penguin.*

'May I see?' I asked and Martha handed it over.

'Steeplejack's cat not missing after all,' the newspaper vendor bawled. 'Read all about it.'

13: THE CANDLESTICK CALL AND THE LOCKET

I COULD NOT bring myself to hate Miss March Middleton – in fact I admired her enormously – but her accounts of her investigations with the Personal Detective, Sidney Grice, made my Ruby Gibson adventures seem what they were – very trivial indeed.

They may be trivial to you, Ruby objected, *but they are life and death to me.*

If Mr Grice were present he would have sniffed the envelope and detected a rare blend of pipe tobacco or a perfume produced exclusively for a Hungarian countess. He would have discovered the wing of an extinct beetle or a curry stain that could have only come from one particular village in the Punjab. The list was endless of what he could have deduced from the ink.

I surveyed the envelope. It was creased, once white and pre-gummed as were most modern examples. The address was handwritten, though not very neatly, in purple-black ink, presumably iron gall. PERSONAL was scrawled in block capitals in the top left-hand corner.

The flap was open, of course, and I lifted it back to pull out the letter. It was written with the same ink and handwriting but on torn-out blank paper, probably the fly leaf of a book.

'Does Mrs Poynder not have her own headed notepaper?' I asked in surprise, for even Agnust had a box of that, given to her by a would-be gentleman admirer in the vain hope that she would enter into a correspondence with him.

'She always has had,' Martha told me, 'but, even if she had run out, Edward would not have done so and,' she added, 'the envelope was crumpled like that when it was delivered.'

A sense of unease came over me. This had all the hallmarks of being secretly written and possibly smuggled. But why? The woman was not in prison.

T, I read to myself, *I have made a terrible mistake. If you can find it in your heart to forgive me, PLEASE meet me today at one in the Café Cordoba. I really need to see you. D +.*

There were so many things wrong that it was difficult to know where to begin.

'Is this her handwriting?' I asked incredulously.

A skivvy might not be ashamed of it, but we were discussing a doctor's wife.

'No,' Martha admitted, 'but I am convinced it came from her.'

'Why?'

'Well the T for a start,' she began. 'It was a joke between us and the kiss at the end. She always put them horizontally.' Martha drew it in the air with her index finger. 'Like a plus sign... and the accent over Café.'

'Grave instead of acute,' I observed.

'She said it was because she was left-handed and had been forced to use her right.' Martha drew on her cigarette, leaned her head back and blew smoke into the air.

I glanced at the back of the letter, which was blank, refolded the note and was about to put it back when I discovered what to Mr G would have been the clue that solved the entire case instantly. I, however, was not at all sure even that there was a case. I peered into the envelope.

'Is Mrs Poynder's cat white?' I asked and Martha nodded.

'Black and white. Why?'

I licked my finger and dabbed it to pick up and show her my find – a long hair.

'Chaos moults a lot.'

'So I see.' I gave myself a mental pat on the back. 'And he has kindly provided us with more evidence that it came from your friend.'

'I suppose so,' she conceded, not nearly so impressed by me as I was.

Well I thought you did quite well, Ruby defended me for, while she might disparage my efforts, she usually rallied to support me against outsiders.

'When did you receive this?' I asked coolly, remembering that this woman had imposed herself upon me and could have at least tried to look astonished.

'Four weeks ago today.'

I realised at once that I could have deduced that for myself from the postmark and hoped that my visitor did not come to the same conclusion. Sidney Grice could rest on his laurels a while yet, I reflected ruefully.

'And did you go?'

'Of course,' Martha said but, before my hackles had had a chance to stir she hastened, 'I am sorry. There is no of course about it. You are not to know if I could find it in my heart to forgive her slights.'

It was also possible that Martha had had a previous appointment that she could not or did not wish to cancel or she might have not read the letter in time, but I restricted my response to, 'What happened?'

I handed the letter back and she tucked the flap back into the envelope before returning it to her bag.

'I waited an hour and a half but she did not come.'

'And there was no message or any subsequent communication?'

'No, nothing,' Martha said, crestfallen. 'I went every day for the week in case Dolly had been delayed somehow but there was no sign of her.'

I sampled my coffee. It was tepid at best.

'So what did you do?'

Martha twisted her cigarette around in its holder for no reason that I could discern other than to distract herself.

'I made another telephone call.'

'When?'

'In the afternoon after my second and third visits to the Cordoba, then the next morning and one early evening, a Thursday when I knew Edward would be doing a private session at the nursing home. Dolores and I used to meet up in each other's homes for a drink those evenings or even have dinner together if Arthur was at his club.'

Martha balanced her cigarette holder on the edge of the ashtray.

'What happened?' I asked. 'When you rang?'

'Wormwood always told me that his mistress was not at home.' Martha shifted uncomfortably. 'The penultimate time he said that she had instructed him to say that I was not to call again. On the last occasion he replaced the receiver the moment he heard my voice.'

I do not trust her, Ruby hissed in my ear. *She dyes her hair.*

Well I do.

Dye your hair? At least she had the grace to sound surprised. *Trust her.*

All right then, she challenged. *Prove it.*

I brought out my little red notebook with my magic pencil.

'Could you write her full name, address and telephone number for me?'

I handed them over, having first pulled the ring to extrude the lead, and Martha took them questioningly.

'I thought I could call Haglin House,' I explained and, seeing her alarm, added, 'There is no need to worry. I will not break any confidences.'

'But why can I not simply tell you the number?'

'People more often misremember numbers when they say them out loud,' I said. 'Most commonly they reverse the order of the last two digits but they will be absolutely convinced they have been correct. Or I might mishear you,' I ended as a sop.

Her writing, I was pleased to note, looked nothing like that on the note that she had shown me. Apart from having an educated hand, Martha's H, for example, was done in straightish lines, but the one Dolores had supposedly written was crumpled as if somebody heavy had sat upon it even after I had smoothed the paper out.

Happy now? I demanded.

I shall be happier when…

I am dealing with it, I snapped.

'Are you all right?' Martha asked, in a tone I might use to check on a dipsomaniac in the gutter.

'Yes,' I assured her. 'I was just thinking.'

I got up and crossed the room to where my telephone stood on a table. It was the latest candlestick design and a great improvement on the old box with the handle that I used to have to crank like a miniature butter churn.

'I am not sure...' she worried, but I was already asking the operator for the number and, after a few clicks and crackles found myself being put through. 'What will you say?'

She hurried over to listen and I put a finger to my lips.

'Dr Edward Poynder's residence,' a man's deep voice declared.

'Summon your mistress, Wormwood,' I commanded, lowering my own voice half an octave in the hope that he would not identify it if we spoke again.

'I regret to inform you that Mrs Poynder is not at home,' Wormwood told me in that tone all servants adopt when they do not regret a thing at all.

'When will she be home?'

'I fear I cannot say, madam. Whom may I enquire is calling?'

No matter how superior they pretend to be, butlers always get who and whom mixed up. It is almost one of their duties along with saying madam so respectfully as to border on insolence.

Tell him he may not, Ruby urged.

He already has, I countered before remembering that my conversation was supposed to be with Wormwood.

'Dr Poynder will be most unhappy,' I forecast, 'when I inform him that you did not recognise me.'

I replaced the earpiece and the hook dropped, cutting the line.

'I am not sure what that achieved,' Martha fretted.

'Wormwood told me that his mistress was not at home before even asking for my name,' I told her. 'Which means that she is unavailable to everybody. It appears that she is either unwilling or unable to speak and you, Martha, are not the only one who would like to know why.'

'I know why.' Martha returned to her chair brushing against her handbag so that it fell onto my Kashan rug, spilling its contents on the floor. 'Oh for goodness sake!'

The box of vestas had come open, scattering them over a surprisingly wide area. She crouched to pick them up and I knelt to help.

'It is all right. I can manage,' she said, staring at the debris but making no effort to do anything with it.

A gold locket with no chain had gone under the desk and I fished it out. The lid was cast into a stem and leaves crowned by a ruby and turquoise flower.

'This is lovely,' I said and the lid sprang open.

'That is why I do not wear it,' Martha told me. 'The catch is faulty. I keep meaning to get it repaired, but I do not like to be parted from it.'

'A gift?' It did not look old enough to be an heirloom.

'From Dolores.'

'A generous lady.'

'She is,' Martha confirmed. 'Very.'

There was a lock of corn-gold hair woven into a spiral behind glass in the left-hand compartment and a photographic portrait in the right.

'Is this...'

'Dolly,' she told me. 'She had it taken before she went away so that I did not forget her.' Cracks ran across the surface of Martha's voice. 'As if I could.'

I handed the locket back to her but not before I had seen the subject of my enquiries – a young, light-haired woman with the profile of an innocent child.

'I gave Dolores a locket with my portrait in return,' Martha recalled. 'It was nothing like as expensive as this though.'

A metallic clattering rose above the general hubbub of street-sellers and carriages and we both looked up.

'Captain Heavers,' I diagnosed. 'He often drives his motor car through the square.'

A Daimler motorised carriage came into view, the captain steering expertly with the handlebars around a Capricorn Brewers' waggon turning down the side of the Splendid Hotel. The giant Suffolk Punch hauling the beer barrels edged away nervously.

'I'm surprised nobody throws one of those cabbages at him,' Martha commented disapprovingly.

'Not with Hector on board.' I referred to the mastiff sprawled over the back seat. 'The last man who tried something like that almost lost an arm.'

There had been attempts to ban motorised vehicles from the town centre. Apart from their disturbing the horses, Squire Crow had crippled a child in Bardham when he had lost control of his vehicle and run off the road. Poor Crow had been most discomforted by the incident and was forced to dismiss his housekeeper, the child's mother, for moping.

I gathered Martha's address book and card case.

'You said that you knew why your friend is incommunicado,' I reminded her.

'Yes.' She finished collecting her things, clipped her long-suffering bag shut and we both rose to our feet.

There was a faint grubby mark on my dress, I noticed. Any other mistress would reprimand her maid for allowing the rug to get dirty, but I had a shrewd suspicion that I knew who would be scolding whom.

'I did not want to say, when I first came, in case you thought I was hysterical,' Martha hesitated. 'But I feel certain that I can trust you, Violet.'

'You can,' I avowed.

I wish I could, Ruby piffed.

In my experience beautiful women do not commit crimes, Hefty contributed. *They have no need to.*

I did not mention Francesca da Grimini, who had almost killed him in the whispering gallery of St Paul's, breaking three of his fingers and his heart in the attempt.

What about sweet little Francesca? Ruby taunted and he reeled away.

Cane Braise was going past, the children flocking around his bright yellow gig while he tossed toffees to their outstretched hands.

Martha lowered her head and, for a while, I thought that she was not going to say any more but then she raised it, quickly as if she had been jolted awake.

'Because Edward Poynder is keeping Dolores prisoner,' she whispered, seemingly incredulous at her own words.

14: BLOOD IN THE GUTTER

I DIGESTED MARTHA Ryan's statement sceptically though distractedly. Was that a hot air balloon in the distance? Ruby had escaped a Bavarian Castle in one of those and I would have loved to have been floating over the town in it. Apart from the view, it might be cooler up there. The balloon sank rapidly as my fears for the occupants rose, until I saw that it was a child's vulcanised latex toy bobbing on a string in the breeze.

I told you that you need eyeglasses, Ruby reminded me.

You also told me to jump over that puddle, I reminded her.

How was I to know that it was an open manhole?

Martha coughed politely and I shook my brain to scatter the daydreams.

'You think he locks her...' I began, my concentration broken again but this time by a double bang.

The second bang was what scientists call an echo, Ruby explained.

'What on earth?' Martha cried and we both jumped up.

Cane Braise looked up in surprise, lowered his head and whipped his horse into a gallop, scattering the children in his path as he disappeared down Angel Street.

A passing piebald horse shied in panic, crashing the hansom that it was pulling into a pump.

'Just the engine detonating,' I reassured her, though she must have heard the sound before, but she was not the only one to have her nerves stretched for an unseen woman screamed in alarm.

Captain Heavers chugged in Braise's wake, seemingly oblivious to the chaos that he had caused. The pump was wedged between the wheel and the cab, but a couple of amused clodhoppers helped the driver reverse his hansom free and, cursing volubly, he manoeuvred it back onto the tarred road before clambering down to inspect the damage.

Two well-dressed men in derbies were bent over someone, and it was only when one of them stepped aside that I saw it was the ragged woman. She was on all fours and appeared to be searching for something. Her bonnet had come off and lay brim-down in the gutter, but she ignored that and grabbed hold of a lamppost to haul herself up. Her face was covered with dark sludge. Had she slipped in shock at the noise and fallen into a pile of horse droppings? The cobbles were supposed to be swept clear, but vendors used horses to carry their stalls and wares and rarely worried about any mess that was not on their patch.

As I watched, the woman sagged and slid down the post, letting go to stagger a few steps sideways into the road. One of the men tried to take her arm but she pushed him away, took two paces forward and fell face down. The other man went on his haunches and took hold of her shoulder.

I heaved the lower sash up higher and put out my head.

'You there,' I called and they looked over. 'Do not move her. I am coming out.'

I rushed past a puzzled Martha to the door.

'Has she fainted?'

'I am not sure. Wait there.'

I flung the door open yelling, 'Gerrund! Agnust! Emergency!'

Almost immediately Gerrund emerged from the kitchen at the end of the hall and, a few seconds later, my maid from her sitting room.

'What is it, milady?' she asked.

'There has been an accident in the street,' I told her as Gerrund rushed past. 'Bring the medical chest, Agnust,' I ordered and followed close at his heels out into Seraphim Square.

Freda, the bearded lady, was lounging in the doorway.

'Spare a bottle o' gin for a poor widda woman,' she beseeched us, but Gerrund brushed her aside.

The woman lay supine, probably having been turned onto her back by some well-meaning person, and she did not appear to be conscious.

Gerrund was arguing with a cabby.

'If my mistress says she isn't to be moved, she isn't to be blooming moved.'

'But I've got a fare and she's blockin' my passage,' the cabby objected as I hurried over.

Gerrund jabbed a finger at the man's face. 'I'll block your passage good and proper, chum,' he threatened, then, catching sight of me, added, 'begging your pardon, milady.'

As the cabby hesitated a gentleman in an Inverness coat joined us. Why on earth did he need that on in this weather?

'Get her out of the way,' he commanded. 'I have an appointment.'

'My man will make you an appointment with your dentist, if you touch her,' I told him, wondering fleetingly if Anton Gervey might have a vacancy for me in his *insurance* business.

'I will,' Gerrund agreed and the stranger, realising what a couple of ruffians he was dealing with, backed away.

I crouched to take a closer look at the woman and tried to recall some of the little knowledge that Romulus had taught me. I had learned the most when he was a student and I was helping him to prepare for his examinations. As a result of his studies I knew enough about the structure and functions of the kidneys to put me off eating them, but that was of no use at the moment or in any foreseeable event.

The woman's face was smeared with straw-spiked horse droppings. I automatically wiped some away with my thumb, lifting her excrement-caked black hair aside and saw that her nose was badly broken, presumably by her fall, and bleeding so heavily that I could not see her left eye.

She was, as I had suspected, unconscious, but at least she was breathing through her gaping mouth, albeit noisily.

A crowd was gathering, an assortment of the curious, caring and cantankerous. Agnust pushed her way through with my bulky medical kit resting easily on her left hip under her muscular arm.

'Stand you back and give the woman some air,' she bossed the bystanders, "stead of your befouled breaths.' She elbowed a coachman aside. 'Your box, milady.'

She did not like to call it a chest, believing the word not decent in or out of company.

Agnust bobbed. She often treated me with exaggerated courtesy in public for, if I were a grand lady, she must be a grand lady's maid. She had a folded copy of *The Times* under her arm. Surely she did not think that I wanted something to peruse? But, sensibly, she laid it on the ground putting the box on top.

Romulus had made it up for me. Having seen a mother try to stop a nosebleed with a tourniquet around her little boy's neck, he was very keen that everybody should learn some basic medical assistance measures, but few attended the free courses that he had organised because he had omitted to promise refreshments.

The chest had three drawers and I could not remember what was in them, having only used it once before when Gerrund had stabbed his hand opening an oyster that wanted to stay closed. I pulled out the top one. Ointment for bee stings, another for wasp, smelling salts, scissors and tweezers. Amongst other things the middle had a sling, a finger-splint and an eyepatch. The bottom and largest held a bottle of gentian violet; Romulus had read a paper in a German journal claiming that the dye killed germs. Packed around it were rolls of bandages, cloths and gauze. I took a wad of the last and wiped the manure from the woman's cheek, tossing it aside and making a fresh pack for her eye. It was only then I realised that she did not have one. Where the left eye should have been was a crater, too big to be an empty socket. It went into the side of her nose.

Oh dear God!

The unfortunate woman must had fallen on a spike of some sort. Knowing better than to poke around, I took another and bigger pad and laid it over the wound. It was saturated with blood immediately, but there was nothing I could do about that. For all the good it would do I poured the gentian violet over it, unrolled a bandage and wrapped it around, lifting her head as little and as gently as possible. Romulus had warned me about the neck injuries that could result from falls.

'Scissors,' I said. Agnust handed me a pair and I cut off the excess roll. 'And a safety pin.'

She already had one to hand, having attended one of the courses with me but leaving when my cousin started demonstrating how to strap a sprained ankle on, to her disgust, a young lady. It made no difference to my maid's mind that the lady in question was Jane, Rommy's wife.

I pinned the bandage.

What next? I ran through his instructions in my head. Loosen clothing? That was for people who had fainted or were having a fit. Reassure the patient? She was beyond that.

Call for medical assistance, Ruby prompted.

'Good idea,' I said aloud.

A ragged girl stood close by, her face and hands polka-dotted with fleabites. She cannot have been more than ten or twelve years old, but it was difficult to judge. Undernourished children develop slowly, if they live long enough to develop at all.

'Do you know her?' I asked, praying, *Please God do not let this be her mother.*

'I know I int sayin' no to those boots,' she replied. 'Only when she's dead,' she added hastily, lest I accuse her of insensitivity, ''cause they wint be no use to her then.'

I glanced down. The girl's feet were wrapped in filthy torn cloth knotted around her ankles.

'A shilling if you fetch an ambulance,' I offered and she turned up her nose.

'Tha's a long ways,' she objected. 'Three shillin's and the boots throwed in.'

'It is a five-minute walk,' I told her, 'and the boots are not mine to give.'

'Forge' tit.' She tossed her head contemptuously, her yellow matted hair glued rigidly to her head.

'Give you a good clip round the ear if you don't,' Gerrund threatened.

'I goo,' a lad in a telegram messenger's uniform volunteered. 'Be more quicker on my bike.' He pushed his peaked cap back a fraction. 'Only, like the tyke say, it's three bob.'

'Here tha's my job,' the girl objected.

'You dint wan' tit,' he reasoned, threw his leg over the crossbar and pedalled off.

'Frebbin' gimp,' she yelled after him. 'I was negoshiatin'.' She turned back to me and, despite the awfulness of the situation I found myself stifling a brief smile.

I was surprised she even knew that last word let alone what it meant.

'Here.' I handed her half a crown. 'Get yourself some boots.'

'And a pint of strum,' she grinned and skipped off.

Strum was a local rum-like drink made from beets. It was not delicious but it was certainly strong. Romulus used to use it to preserve anatomical specimens, the pride of his collection being a cyclops baby he had delivered stillborn in a field in Lower Downhill Up. The mother had absconded while he was trying to revive it.

The beggar woman's right eye opened and she struggled to raise herself, whimpering in pain. I put a hand to her shoulder.

'Lie still,' I urged. 'Help is on its way.'

She flopped back.

'Came to warn you,' she gasped, her eye flicking from side to side.

'Try not to speak,' I advised and she coughed, spraying blood over my dress.

'He do kill you if you dint stop interferin',' she gasped.

'Who?' Gerrund demanded.

'The...' she managed.

'Who?' he pressed her.

'Let her be,' I ordered.

'The Master.'

'Gervey?' he checked in surprise.

The woman grasped my hand and tried to pull it away.

'Lie still,' I implored as she twisted side to side. 'The doctor will be here any moment now.'

She put her free hand to her head, clawing at the bandage.

'Scrise!' she hissed. 'It hurt.' She coughed again. 'It do.'

And, before I could tell her to leave it, she fell back, her head smacking the kerbstone, took one last useless gasp of air, exhaled and was still.

I knew there was little hope but I bent low to put my ear to her chest.

'Quiet everybody,' Gerrund barked and the chatter that I had hardly been aware of paused.

Her ribs jutted into my cheek but there was no beat beneath them. I wiped my face on a small white towel and my hands on another, dropped the waste into a steel kidney dish and closed the drawers.

'A woman doctor,' a rather grand figure with a tall beaver-skin hat deduced in error and disgust. 'It is not natural.'

'If you are an example of what is natural,' I muttered, 'I am thankful that I am not.'

The beggar woman's right eye was open so I closed it for her. The warmth would soon leave her body.

'May the Lord receive your soul,' I heard and was aware of Martha, white-faced at my shoulder.

'Soul?' the cabby said scornfully. 'She's a street slug. She int got no soul.'

For a few seconds I was sorely tempted to strike the man but I did not, of course. I stood up, flicking my head hard back to administer what the locals called a *dobbin*.

'Clumsy crust-eyed fritch!' he cursed, staggering back and feeling his nose gingerly. 'Nearly jolt my brain out of its box.'

'Brain?' I said scornfully, gratified to note a trickle of blood peek out from his right nostril and wend its way through his tatterdemalion moustaches. 'You int got no brain.'

What on earth do you think you are up to, brawling on the street? Ruby tutted. *You are no better than I.*

15: THE MADONNA AND DRIFTWOOD

MARTHA RYAN HUGGED herself as if she were caught in a blizzard.

'Are you all right?' I asked inanely, for it was obvious that she was not.

She was trembling, her face was drained and she swayed worryingly.

'I do feel a little light-headed.'

Agnust lumbered up saying, 'Come you with Agnust, madam. I soon do set you aright,' and took her by the arm along with the medical chest back towards Break House.

'Her immortal soul has risen to join our heavenly father,' a man in a butcher's striped apron observed reverently. 'Well,' he sighed in wonder. 'At least we can shift her now.'

'Not yet,' I insisted.

'Give me a hand,' he told the coachman.

'Lay one finger on her and I'll snap it off,' Gerrund threatened and they hesitated, neither of them willing to put him to the test.

'We should call a priest,' somebody suggested.

'Bound to be one about,' a matronly woman in a patchwork shawl asserted. 'This hot weather brings them out – like flies,' she explained inexplicably.

'Did anybody see what happened?' I asked and a flower girl appeared. Her basket was empty so she had probably been to the Splendid Hotel. Many of the guests and staff liked to sport a buttonhole.

'I do, lady,' she volunteered. 'You wrap up her head and she do die.'

'I meant before that.'

'What?' she demanded. 'Yisdee?'

I think she means yesterday, Ruby told Hefty who was making notes.

He had already put a pigeon feather into his cigar case in the hope that it might yield a vital clue, never having forgotten how a crushed berry in the British Museum had put him on the trail of the *Mistletoe Murderer*.

'What caused her to collapse?'

'You do be the quack,' she declared, and I wondered if that were now so widely accepted that I would find people queuing at my door and, if so, I speculated how much I could charge for a consultation. 'Got a fag?'

I carried cigarettes to offer as incentives or rewards sometimes, but she had not earned one yet.

'I do not smoke,' I answered truthfully.

'Precious small wonder you do be such a runt.'

Talk about the pot, Ruby fumed, indignant on my behalf.

'Did anyone hear a bang?' I asked the assembly and they looked at each other.

'Depends,' a clodhopper, the bottoms of his trousers rolled halfway up his shins, told me. 'If you want me to, I do. If you dint, I dint.'

'Did anybody see what happened?' I called.

'What's it wurf?' a shaven-headed young woman asked.

'Nothing,' I said, unwilling to pay for people to invent stories and she spat on the pavement.

'Nothin'?' she checked incredulously for her time was immensely valuable. 'Then tha's 'xactly what I see.'

A constable arrived, truncheon in hand, though I had no idea what he thought he was going to need that for. He had a lean weather-beaten look about him and his helmet was too big, the rim resting on his shaggy eyebrows.

'Move along now,' he told me, ignoring everybody else.

'This woman is dead,' I declared.

'Right then.' He hung his truncheon back on his belt. 'We best get her shifted.'

'Is that it?' I asked, taken aback by the speed of his investigation.

'Course not,' he reassured me. 'We do get a cart to waggon her off.'

I was not sure he had got that the right way round, but I was fairly sure that I did not care.

I took a breath. 'Is that the end of your enquiries?'

'Well,' he ruminated, 'what else is there to enquiry 'bout?'

'How did she die?' I asked and he shrugged.

'There's somethin' wrong with her. Anyone can see that.'

'Yes but…'

'Why else do she goo see a sawnbones?' he reasoned.

Was I missing something? There was no doctor's card clutched in her hand.

'How do you know that she did?'

The constable snorted, doubtless wearied by a career wasted in explaining simple things to simpler women.

'I use my policely trainin' and notice wha' goo on.' He tapped the side of his forehead as if checking for woodworm and neither Ruby nor I would have been astonished if he had found any. 'She do get bandaged she do.'

'But I did that,' I protested.

'She do,' a scrawny man wearing a fat man's collar confirmed. 'She wrap up her head and splosh ink all over it and she do die.'

The flower girl's statement had become an established truth, along with the Madonna of Woolpit, who appeared to the daughter of a cheesemonger telling people to eat more Suffolk Crumble.

'She do,' rippled through the crowd like driftwood in the sea.

Was I being blamed and would I find myself being lynched like the beekeeper of Gorham village, accused of trying to set fire to the parish church when he was smoking a nest out of the bell tower? It was unlikely, I decided, since none of them seemed to be perturbed.

The constable looked at the mess I had created.

'Ink?' he checked incredulously.

'Antiseptic,' I told him.

'Aunty who? Is she a witness?'

'No,' I said, not troubling to answer his first question about which he appeared to have forgotten anyway.

'Then why mention her?' he challenged.

'She's all confoosed, the buffle-headed mare,' the clodhopper explained gallantly thereby resolving the matter to the constable's satisfaction.

The postcard boy, his twisted legs temporarily cured, was inspecting an umbrella, the one the blind man had been carrying, I assumed, until I saw that it was broken and the cloth shredded.

'What a shameful shame,' a young woman in a tartan shawl sighed, so at least somebody cared. 'That's a good pair on two boots goo waste.'

Thank heavens for the education acts, Ruby sarcasmed.

'And what about her?' I cried.

'Dint you fret and get the vapours,' the constable advised me. 'She do get a proper pauper grave.'

'And it's the like of us what pay for it,' an ancient nut seller in a black beret complained at the beggar's selfishness, though I doubt the old man had paid a farthing tax in his life and he would probably be disposed of in the same way.

'Have you no human feelings?' I asked the assembly. 'What is wrong with you all?'

The crowd, which had been starting to disperse began to drift back, sheepishly I thought.

'Well I goh a chesty cough,' the butcher told me, bits of offal squashed and smeared over his striped apron.

'And I'm a touch liverish,' the gentleman added, tapping where his offal nested under his waistcoat.

'I do get a broked nose,' the man I had *dobbined* exaggerated.

'Is that all you care about?' a young lady with rather a nice blue bonnet scolded them. 'I have an ingrowing toenail but you won't hear me complaining about it.'

'Oh you poor little goose,' the constable commiserated.

'I try to be brave but sometimes...' She burst into tears. 'It hurts.'

'Sympathy,' Miss Kidd had said when I had fallen off a summer-house roof and broken my wrist, 'comes from the Latin *sympathia*, which in turn comes from the Greek *sumpatheia*. Nobody is sure where it came from before that but, rest assured, Lady Violet Elizabeth Antoinette Cordelia Thorn, that it did not come from me.'

So many people shared Miss Kidd's philosophy, I was to discover, that I was surprised they did not take over the world. Perhaps, I mused as I returned to Break House, they had already.

16: WOOL-GATHERING AND THE FRAGILITY OF LIFE

IN THETBURY HALL the only running water came through the roof when it rained. In Break House it came through the modern installation of lead pipes, though admittedly it usually ran either steam-and-cold or cold-and-cold, the gas geyser being something of a prima donna.

I washed my face and hands and quickly changed my dress before joining Martha in the sitting room. Agnust had installed her with a generous measure of Martell cognac in an armchair, thoughtfully selecting one facing away from the window.

'You must think me awfully feeble,' Martha said, stubbing out her Little Queen.

As weak as an Australian, Ruby affirmed, being inordinately proud of having beaten Wombat Walter, the Tasmanian champion, in an arm-wrestling competition.

'Not in the least,' I assured Martha. 'It was a shocking death.'

'But you were calmness personified.'

'I did not feel it.'

My visitor put her drink on the low table before her and I was tempted to pour myself something equally inebriating.

'I was rude about your maid,' she admitted, though I did not think that she had been especially, 'but she is a treasure in a crisis.'

And a tribulation the rest of the time, I thought uncharitably.

'She is a good woman at heart,' I told her, though I had heard the same said about Janit Parstay, who had buried two husbands and her sister-in-law alive because she had accidentally purchased a job lot of coffins in an auction and did not want to let them go to waste.

Martha fiddled with her necklace.

'I feel ashamed,' she confessed. 'Compared to what happened today my problem seems trivial indeed.'

'On the contrary,' I said, 'it reminds one of the fragility of life and the importance of safeguarding what we value. You appear to have lost a cherished friend and I believe, at the very least, that you are entitled to know why. Can you come back tomorrow?'

Martha lay her cigarette holder in a hinged, black-lacquered papier-mâché box and put it away.

'Are you sure?' she checked. 'You must have far more important matters to worry about.'

'Nothing urgent.'

What? Ruby Gibson demanded. *I am seconds away from death. How much more urgent can it get?*

'Shush,' I said unintentionally aloud and hurried to shut the window and cover my mistake. 'The man who invented hurdy-gurdies has a lot to answer for.'

'I did not hear him,' Martha said.

'He is just untuning up.'

How do I get myself into these muddles?

By wool-gathering, Miss Kidd replied, rule raised to rap my knuckles. How I would have loved to have the chance to tell her that I was paid to daydream now. Much as I disliked her, she had not deserved her ghastly fate. Come to think of it, being a real and – as far as I knew – living person, she had no rightful business invading my head.

'Would the same time be agreeable?' Martha asked, and I tumbled out of the clouds back into the real world.

I could have pretended to consult my diary, but that was the sort of thing that head waiters did in overpriced and under-frequented restaurants.

'Perfectly,' I agreed as she picked up her handbag. 'But by all means finish your Martell.'

'It was very kind of your maid to give it to me but I have not touched it.' Martha stood. 'I'm afraid I do not care for brandy.'

'Neither do I.'

It had been a present from Ted Wilton, my agent, who had been given it by a grateful client and did not like it either. I was reminded of a vase that I had sent to my godmother. It had been passed along a chain of recipient-donors for nine years before she received it from a neighbour for her birthday and gave it back to me for Christmas.

'Why did that poor woman say that somebody would kill you?' Martha remembered, through her shock.

'I think she was confused,' I replied. 'I had never seen her before.'

I accompanied Martha to the door.

'It was not an accident when you collided with that cabby, was it?' she asked more lightly.

'I am only glad that I had not put a bonnet on,' I told her. 'It would have been ruined.' I touched my scalp. 'My head is slightly bruised but I console myself with the belief that his snout feels a great deal worse.'

Martha laughed and took the hand that I offered her, but also leaned forward to kiss my cheek.

'God bless you, Lady Violet Thorn,' she said, and there was a time when I believed that he had.

–

I could have a phial of an extra-powerful acid that eats away the steel in seconds, Ruby suggested so suddenly and loudly that I almost choked on my Beeman's.

But that is what you used to dissolve the bars in that Tasmanian prison, I reminded her crossly, coughing the gum up into its wrapper.

This is not going to be another 'Bones of Borneo' fiasco, is it?

She had never let me forget how I left her being boiled in a pot by head-hunters.

I never did finish that story, but was mortified when Grantham Hogarth's highly successful Hydrangea Devine was placed in the same peril and escaped in exactly the way that I had discussed with Ted Wilton.

'You cannot copyright what you have not written,' Ted told me shamelessly when I complained.

Coincidentally he also represented Mr Hogarth's more lucrative interests. 'Besides which, I gave you the idea of the carnivorous zebras disposing of a corpse.'

'And if I ever use that device I shall be grateful,' I promised.

'Well actually you can't now,' he informed me. 'I mentioned it to Grantham and his book comes out next month.'

Agents, Ruby scorned. *They may only take ten per cent of your royalties, but along with publishers they take one hundred per cent of your soul.*

You should be grateful to them that you have one, I told her. Had her adventures not been printed, she would have gone the way of Baroness Bournemouth, Barnaby Brighton and all the other heroes languishing in the limbo of my manuscript chest.

Let us out, they clamoured, little realising what a ruthless proof-reader might do to them.

17: TORTOISESHELL AND TUMBRILS, THE ATHEIST AND THE STAIN

BREAKFAST WAS DEVILLED kidneys – Gerrund having no truck with my squeamishness about the organs' functions – scrambled eggs and toast.

'Goodness what a lot of food,' I commented as Agnust poured my coffee.

Even at such an early hour and in the shade of my dining room the heat was uncomfortable, and I would have been quite happy with a couple of rounds of toast.

'Gerrund do try to build you higher,' she told me.

'A little late for that.' I had not grown an inch in ten years.

'Tint nine on the clock yet,' she observed, dripping some coffee on the tablecloth and tutting at my clumsiness.

Agnust was very proud of being able to tell the time, the first member of her family, she claimed, to have acquired that skill. Being the only survivor of fourteen children, she was also likely to be the last one available to make such a boast.

'Quite so,' I conceded and dug in.

When did servants start dictating the size of their employers? Was this the start of the revolution and would I end my days with my head in a basket in Trafalgar Square?

I foiled the anarchist plot to massacre parliament, Ruby reminded me, as if I could forget. The title alone of *Rivers of Blood* had caused such outrage that it was far and away my best-selling book so far. I had not been allowed to call the next one *Gore in the Gutter*, however, and its sales under the title *Demise on a Damp Wednesday* had been very nearly good enough to be disappointing.

I browsed *The Chronic*, as the *Montford Chronicle* was known. A carpenter who had gone missing nine years ago had been found dead in the cellar of an empty house in Bridge Street. It was thought that the stairs he had been constructing had collapsed on top of him and that, trapped but otherwise uninjured, he had starved, a process made slower by there being a water tap within his reach. With unintended irony the widow was accusing the police of not having taken enough *steps* to find him. I cut out the article to file with my other clippings of unusual deaths, including the steeplejack impaled on a lightning conductor and the laundress who had been boiled to death in her own copper of scalding water. A tasteless joke about missionaries and cannibals had circulated about that incident.

Having finished my breakfast, and while enjoying my first stick of Beeman's, I flicked through my mail. A man of considerable wealth wished to marry me and would let me have a photograph of himself in his bathing costume if I sent him a postal order for ten shillings. I would do so, I resolved, the very moment that I lost my sanity.

I was not aware that you had found it, Ruby quipped, but I was torn from my reveries by the sound of the doorbell. It was unnecessarily harsh and I intended to have it replaced. When it came to domestic improvements, however, I was always one for not putting off until tomorrow what I could put off indefinitely.

Builders must have crept in and extended the corridor considerably since I last went along it, to judge by the time and effort that it took Agnust to respond.

'As if there int 'nough to do without me doin' my job,' I heard her grumble as she went past.

Voices murmured, the front door shut and she reappeared.

'It's tha' Mrs Ryan again,' she announced. 'What she do back here at this time?'

'Mrs Ryan has an appointment.'

'You never tell me.'

'I do not have to.'

'Well.' The fists were plonked on the hips. 'We'll see 'bout that.'

'We shall,' I agreed. 'Put her in the sitting room.'

'You never do speak to me like that four and twenty year ago,' she complained.

'Twenty-four years ago I was struggling to say mama and papa.'

'Pity it dint stop there,' she muttered, whisking my unfinished cup away.

'And we shall have a tray of coffee,' I called after her.

'She'll have coffee coming out of her neck next,' she forecast as she left. Had she, too, imagined me being guillotined?

I got up to check myself in the mirror. My hair was fastened up in a knot at the back with a tortoiseshell comb. Like most of the Thorns, I was overly proud of my thick black hair but was that a grey one? I plucked it out and saw that it was almost white. What next? Would I start going bald?

You made me wear a hairpiece once, Ruby reminded me, but that was so she could smuggle a bomb into the lair of Otto Strattinger, the Strasburg Strangler, and I was not planning to hide any explosives in my coiffure that morning.

Stop maundering about wigs, I scolded, remembering how she had complained about it for days afterwards.

I straightened my alizarin crimson dress. Agnust did not approve of my addiction to red clothes, but I had two excuses prepared for her. Its brightness gave tall people fewer excuses for not seeing me, and it was a warning to would-be child-strippers that I might be dangerous. One of them, misjudging my age had threatened me on a visit to Ipswich and I had been obliged to insert the ferule of my umbrella into her tonsils before she desisted. 'You could carry a samwidge board to tell folk that,' she had reasoned, and I would have loved to have seen her face if I had taken her literally.

Martha stood in the middle of the room. She was in a light green that day, her dress, jacket, parasol and handbag embroidered in ferns, her summer bonnet decorated with a little foliage too. I followed London fashions avidly and reasonably successfully, I had thought, but my new acquaintance only had to step into the room to make me feel like an unemployed clodhopper's wife.

'Good morning, Violet,' she greeted me, taking both my hands in hers and kissing me in an unaffected natural way. 'What a lovely dress,' she remarked as if she truly meant it.

'Are you feeling a little better this morning?' I enquired, trying but probably failing, not to simper.

'I was until I came into the square,' she said. 'Then it all came flooding back. I do not understand what happened to her.'

I let go of her hands, envious of those long, slender fingers. Mine, like the rest of me, were short.

'I thought that she must have fallen on the spiked railings around that statue of King Edmund,' I told her, suddenly realising that I still had the gum in my mouth, 'but, when I went around the square at first light...'

I must have been chomping on it all the time but what could I do now? I could hardly spit it and Agnust had warned me that it would block my chitterlin's, which included almost every internal organ by her reckoning, if I ingested it. But I knew better and swallowed it only to discover that she had been right. The gum went halfway down and wedged in my gullet. I coughed and it came up a bit only to go down again but the wrong way this time.

'Are you all right?' Martha scrutinised me in consternation and I managed to nod, but I could not have been convincing because she put a hand on my shoulder and asked, 'Is there a medicine you should take?'

I waved a hand dismissively. When I was a child I had a breath-holding contest against the man who came to unblock our drains. He had won, but I had managed just over one and a half minutes before I was forced to give in. I must have almost reached that limit now but with no such opportunity to quit. I coughed again as hard as I could, which was not very because I could not take a breath to give me something with which to do it.

'Goodness,' Martha said in dismay. 'You have gone a very odd colour.'

That is never something that a woman wants to be told, especially when it might be the last thing she hears. I coughed a third time, doubling over with the effort.

'Let me help.'

There was a blow to my back that Sledgehammer Smith would have been proud to deliver. I huffed in shock and the gum shot out of my throat and mouth. I did well to catch it and hastily closed my hand but a fraction too late.

'Is that chewing gum?' Martha enquired.

'Possibly.' I waited to be told how disgusting a habit I had, from a woman who thought it perfectly acceptable to inhale the combustion products of leaves.

'Oh,' she said with interest. 'I have never tried that.'

'Would you like to?' I offered. 'I mean a fresh one, of course,' I assured her hastily and wrapped my piece in a sheet of paper before tossing it into the wastepaper bin – a new painted metal one since Uncle Hawley had set fire to my basket with an unextinguished cigar.

'Yes please.'

Agnust came bearing a tray.

'Got you at it, has she?' she asked. 'Filthy habit.' And that from a woman who put spiced tobacco powder up her nostrils because she had heard that the Prince of Wales took snuff, his practices being a splendid example to his future subjects.

She put the tray down and stomped off.

'Is she ever happy?' Martha asked in amusement.

'All the time,' I assured her. 'She would be miserable if she had nothing to grumble about and I keep her well supplied.'

Martha smiled and we sat at the desk.

'What do you make of the gum?' I asked and she chewed it thoughtfully.

'Deliciously horrible,' she decided.

'That is exactly what I think,' I told her. 'It is claimed to aid the digestion.'

'It didn't do much for yours,' she reminded me and I laughed. 'Do you mind if I…'

'Use the wrapper,' I said, holding my bin out when she had done so.

I settled next to her, both looking out.

Mad Harry, as he called himself – and who was I to argue? – went by, waving his placard THE END OF THE WORLD COME YISDEE. My mother had often told me that, if I did not organise myself better, I would miss the event and it appeared that she had been right.

'I suppose it was true for that poor woman,' Martha mused. 'You were telling that you went out.'

'Yes,' I recalled, for there are few things more distracting than nearly choking to death. 'To look at the railings. The spikes are even sharper than I thought but the fence is higher. She was probably taller than I, but she would have to have been well over six foot to have fallen onto it.'

'What do you think happened, then?'

'I may have a clearer idea this evening,' I told her. 'My cousin is a doctor and he has agreed to take a look at her body.'

Romulus had not taken much persuasion.

'Just let me at her,' he had said when I called him on the telephone, and I could almost hear him polish his surgical saw with glee.

Martha fiddled with the clasp of her handbag.

'Feel free to smoke,' I told her since it was obvious that she wanted to do so.

'You are sure?'

'If you do not mind me opening the window.'

I pulled up the lower sash.

'Read allll about it,' the newspaper vendor bellowed. 'Montford man come third in standin' still contest.'

'Crikey!' I said. 'That makes me feel proud.'

'There were probably only three entrants,' she chuckled and I sat next to her again.

'You were saying yesterday that you thought your friend's husband is keeping her prisoner.' Martha stiffened as if what I said had come as a great shock to her.

'That was the first time I have spoken my fears.'

There was a small stain on my dress and I hoped that it did not smell of kidneys.

'But how?' I wondered. 'Does he lock her in?'

Martha could not have clutched the handle of her handbag any more tightly if it had been the only hold she had to stop herself falling down a cliff.

'Not exactly,' she said carefully. 'At least not all the time.' She raised her warm hazel eyes to look into mine. 'Oh,' she noticed. 'You have one blue eye...'

'And one green.'

'I am sorry I...'

'It does not worry me,' I said. 'My mother used to tell me that God, unable to decide which colour would suit me best, chose to compromise and gave one of each.'

'I am sorry,' Martha said again. 'I am avoiding your question. It all sounds so silly when I say it aloud.'

'Most of our fears do,' I told her. 'It does not mean that they have no basis in reality.'

She sighed.

'I would give anything to find that mine are imaginary.'

'Then help me to help you,' I urged and she inclined her head briefly.

I released her hand and got up. Daisy Dixon the Diamond Queen went by, hundreds of glass beads sewn into her parti-coloured dress and glittering in the sunshine. Usually she was accompanied by her common-law husband Danny who, being no relation of the wonky donkey, strummed a ukulele while she danced with surprising grace for such a monumental woman. Today she was alone, her sparkling tambourine hanging from a hook on her belt.

'Does Mrs Poynder leave the house at all?'

'Call her Dolores, please. It sounds so impersonal.'

I did not remind her that, for me, it was impersonal. After all, the closest I had come to her friend was glimpsing a portrait and lock of hair.

Martha picked up her cup. The coffee would be cold by now and she had not touched it yet but she took a sip and then a longer drink.

'She goes to church,' Martha said finally. 'St Etheldreda's.'

'The patron saint of sore throats.'

'How did you know that?'

'She is an East Anglian saint,' I replied, 'and a doctor advised my mother to pray to her when my little brother Marcus had diphtheria.'

'Did she help?'

Like hell she did, I thought but only said, 'I am afraid not.'

'Oh my goodness.' Martha rubbed her brow. 'How old was he?'

'Six,' I said. 'He would have been twenty-four next month.' So would his twin, Magnus, I reflected. 'Have you seen her there?' I asked.

'Yes I saw her,' Martha replied. 'But I could not speak to her. He was there – Edward who, Dolly told me, is an atheist. He would not even let her go to mass alone. Doesn't he trust her with the vicar?'

'Priest,' I murmured automatically. 'Did he stop you talking to his wife?'

Martha put the holder between her teeth, realised there was nothing in it, and took it out again.

'He did not get the chance,' she replied bitterly. 'I slunk off home.'

There was a disturbance in the square. Daisy the Diamond Queen was gesticulating at the eel woman. At first I could hear nothing of their argument, but the cries of the hawkers petered out and the crowd became muted as everybody turned to enjoy the spectacle.

'I int touched your old boy,' the eel woman was asserting indignantly. 'I dint want the ganty-gutted snaggled-toothed git.'

Ganty-gutted meant skinny and was an apt description of Danny, who was a sapling beside his oak tree wife.

'Ganty!' Daisy repeated in outrage as if he performed a strongman act. 'We do see 'bout tha' you ranny mawkin.'

I was not convinced that anybody could be a shrew and a scarecrow simultaneously, but I smiled at the description.

'We'll see 'bout tha',' Daisy roared and grasped the cauldron in both hands.

No doubt she intended to toss the contents at the alleged Jezebel, but the speed with which she let go revealed that it had not been the most intelligent of schemes. Daisy threw up her hands with a shriek. I would have gone out to help her but she ran off, knocking a display of painted flowerpots over in her hurry, and through the monastery gates yelping like an injured mongrel.

'This is a peaceful area as a rule,' I declared and Martha shrugged.

'I am sure it is,' she said without conviction as we settled back.

'Does Dr Poynder know you?' I asked and she tip-tapped her fingers on the arm of the chair.

'We have met on a number of occasions,' she told me coolly. 'But Edward does not approve of me.'

'Do you know why?'

'I encouraged Dolly to engage in frivolous pursuits – tennis, picnics, playing cards...' Martha's voice tailed away.

A grey pigeon landed on the window ledge and she watched it, though it was not an unusual sight. Montford was infested with creatures who served no purpose other than to deface the statues of men who were probably not as important as was believed at the time, since many of them are barely remembered in, let alone outside, Suffolk.

I waited assuming that, if she wanted to tell me more, she would.

'Edward likes his wife to be unthinkingly obedient to all kinds of authority, especially her husband's.'

I had an itch and put a little finger in my ear but stopped myself from puggling about just in time to pretend that I was lifting my hair over it.

'He is by no means unique,' I commented as she loaded her holder. 'Many men have two kinds of servant, those they employ and those they marry. The former are more fortunate for they can quit.'

Hefty cleared his throat but maintained a tactful silence. He knew that I had not espoused that opinion when I had set off for the Thorn family chapel little more than a year ago.

'Oh dear.' Martha's mouth twitched. 'Edward would regard that assertion as little short of treason.' She grimaced. 'He believes that the Married Women's Property Act is an abomination.'

A larger, presumably male, black pigeon with white streaks joined the first who exercised her feminine wiles by pretending not to notice – much as I did when Clitterton the Curate at Thetbury tried to impress me by exercising with Indian clubs at the vicarage tea party. He was doing quite well until one club went flying and knocked out Miss Partridge's front tooth.

'I am quite sure that he and I would get along splendidly,' I quipped as she snorted.

The pigeons were bobbing their heads side to side with locked beaks now, her neck feathers glittering green in the sunlight and his glowing purple.

'Well he was born in the year of the coronation,' she informed me, 'and I am not sure that his ideas have evolved since then.'

A simple sum, Havelock Hefty chuckled, but his brow furrowed as he pencilled the figures into his notebook. *Seventy-nine*, he announced and frowned in disapproval.

'Fifty-eight,' I calculated as the birds broke away to preen their feathers.

Jack and I had watched the jubilee parades along with a large proportion of the population. We had stood before Buckingham Palace trying to convince each other that we had glimpsed a royal blob on the balcony.

'They should put him in the Natural History Museum,' Martha piffed. 'The world's youngest fossil.'

I laughed.

'How old is your friend?'

'Thirty-six.'

'That is quite a gap,' I commented, 'but not especially unusual. How long have they been married?'

'Eighteen years.'

She drummed her fingers on the desk.

'Is she happy in her marriage?'

'Is any woman?' Martha asked.

I liked to think that I would have been. I had never felt so close to anyone as I did to Jack, but now I had never felt so far from him.

'Do you think it is possible that he is just being protective of her?' I asked. 'I mean he is easily old enough to be her father.'

'There is paternal and there is tyrannical,' she said. 'And Edward is the latter.'

'Does she love him?'

'She says so.'

'But you have your doubts?'

Martha flicked the catch on her handbag open and I rubbed my ear. It still itched.

'I think she loves him in the same way that she loves God. I do not mean she thinks he is God, but there is something dutiful in the way that she regards him.'

The pigeons had gone back to locking beaks, breaking off to preen each other and would probably have proceeded to perform deeds that would have had Agnust shooing them away in disgust with her little-used duster, but a third and even bigger bird alighted on the ledge and they scarpered.

'Does he love her?' I asked.

'In the same way a man loves his dog.'

'Sounds like his dislike of you is reciprocated,' I said, and Martha shook her head.

'No,' she said, 'it runs much deeper than that. I absolutely hate the man.'

She ground her cigarette out vengefully.

'I will have a think about your problem,' I promised.

'Thank you.' She packed her things away and stood. 'I only hope that I am not wasting your time.'

Your hopes, like the Hesperus, *are dashed upon the rocks*, Ruby told Martha and I showed my visitor to the door.

18: ROMULUS, BAZALGETTE AND THE HANDS OF TIME

AGNUST FLUNG OPEN the door with a flourish.

'Romulus, Viscount Thorn of Thetbury,' she announced as if this were a grand ball and he a complete stranger, though she had larruped him more than once when he was a child.

'Rommy,' I greeted him with a kiss.

'Good evening, Vi.'

My cousin gave me a hug. He was the only one allowed to *Vi* me. My parents, taking the opposite approach, called me Violetta even though they had had me christened Violet.

'I swear you look younger every time I see you, Agnust,' Romulus told her as he released me, and my maid blushed.

'There do be no swearin' in this house,' she told him but skipped from the room, the bottles in my cabinet rattling with every impact of her boots.

'Whisky and soda?'

'Just a drop.'

'Of whisky?'

'Of soda.'

I poured us a large one each, diluting mine much more than his.

'You look well,' he said and we clinked glasses, 'though I may have to bill you for that opinion.'

'You still owe me for breaking my dolls' house.'

Romulus was a Thorn through and through with the hooked nose, sapphire eyes and thick head of straight black hair. He was even taller than my father and more willowy. I, as Agnust liked to tell me, had been the *grunt* of the litter. 'You look worn out. How is Jane?'

His face fell.

'She is in such pain.' He gulped his drink. 'I feel so useless. She cannot spend her life in laudanum slumbers.' He drained the glass. 'What little is left to her.'

'Is the new treatment not helping?' I had tried to ask him when I telephoned, but he had given me to understand that his wife was within earshot.

Romulus put his tumbler to his lips, oblivious to the fact that it was already depleted.

'Mine is a dishonourable profession,' he asserted, dabbing the lower borders of his waxed moustaches with his handkerchief. 'The extraction of money from the sick is often little short of fraudulent.'

'There are some good doctors,' I protested. 'You for instance.'

He snorted.

'I try,' he said, 'but even so I find myself giving people false hopes rather than admit how little I can do for them.'

'But surely people are living much longer now.'

He looked at his tumbler, surprised to find it empty and, surprised to find how quickly he had emptied it, I took it to refill.

'We have the likes of Bazalgette and their sewage systems plus some improvements in housing and diet to thank for that,' he said, peering at the bust of Tchaikovsky on my mantlepiece. For all my cousin's advanced views, he did not enjoy modern music.

We stood by the window. An empty hearse was going by, a black boy riding at the back sticking his tongue out at a little girl in a brougham. She would go home to her feather bed, he to sleep under the counter in the undertaker's shop.

'I am sorry,' I said and took his hand. 'She does not deserve...'

'I took a look at your woman,' Romulus broke in. 'At and inside her.'

'And?'

'You were right about the injury being unusual.' My cousin put his drink down untouched on the mantlepiece. 'I have never seen the like since Burma.' Officially the country had been in rebellion but my cousin, regarding it as a bid for independence from the British who had no rightful business to be there, had resigned his commission and returned to Norfolk, some said as a coward, though no one who knew him or had seen his medals shared that opinion.

'So what do you think caused it?'

Romulus delved into his tweed jacket for a small cylindrical corked bottle. 'This.'

He handed it over. There was a silvery-grey lump inside, shaped like a miniature rock-cake.

'Looks like a bit of lead.' I held it up to the gas mantle.

'That is exactly what it is,' my cousin confirmed.

'Where did you find it?'

The surface was pitted.

'Lodged on the inside of the skull behind the cerebellum.'

'The little brain,' I recalled from his studies. 'But that is...' I racked Ruby's brains for she had done additional training in Zurich. 'In the base at the back is it not?'

I have just told you as much, she grumped, miffed at my lack of confidence in her superior knowledge.

'At the top of the spinal cord,' he confirmed. 'I thought it looked like a bullet wound the moment I saw it, but I was surprised not to find any sign of an exit hole.'

'I heard a bang but I thought it was a motor car,' I admitted, turning the bottle to and fro. 'It does not look much like a bullet to me.'

'It was so soft that it would have flattened the instant it hit bone, in this case the eye-socket,' Romulus said. 'I have seen men survive being shot through the head. A high-speed bullet can make a very neat tunnel through the brain and, if you are lucky, not hit anything vital, but this was designed to make as much mess as possible.' He grimaced. 'And, believe me, it did. For lack of a better word, a great deal of her cerebrum was a mush.' Romulus fiddled with his watchchain. 'Whoever fired at that unfortunate woman was determined to kill her.'

'But she was just a beggar,' I protested, and he puffed out.

'Remember what you said to Jerkins, our old estate manager, when he threatened to horsewhip that girl? Nobody, you told him, is just a beggar.'

'I meant that she was unlikely to have been so important or such a threat...' I struggled to explain.

She was not actually begging, Ruby ganged up on me with relish as she had feelings for Rommy that she made little attempt to camouflage.

'I take your point,' he said.

'So who was she and why was she murdered?'

Romulus took up the tumbler again and swirled it around. The glass, big as a bucket in my hand, was small as an eggcup in his.

I have told you before about exaggerating, Miss Kidd scolded, and Ruby railed because my governess had no business mingling with my characters.

'You said that she died in the square?' Rommy checked.

'Just out there,' I pointed.

'Let's take a look.'

We went into the hall where he took his cane from the copper-and-iron stand.

'You will require that for our long journey,' I mocked gently as I selected a bonnet from the table.

'Just as you will need your parasol,' he riposted, donning his grey bowler and opened the door.

Seraphim Square was almost deserted in the gathering twilight. A well-dressed courting couple went by, surreptitiously holding hands, their chaperone, a rather grand lady I had seen in her own box at church, affecting not to notice.

'Show me,' my cousin said and we went outside.

I jumped.

'Oh for goodness sake!' I exclaimed and rubbed my ear. Did that hurdy-gurdy man never sleep? 'I hope his heart breaks.'

'It's not like you to be so vindictive,' Romulus commented and we crossed the road.

'It is the name of the song,' I explained, though he probably knew that. He had frequented Morley's Music Hall many a time before his professional status obliged him to avoid being seen in such disreputable venues.

There were traces of stains on the kerb and some between the cobbles as we had not had any rain since the incident and nobody had troubled to wash the blood away.

'Will this heat never end?' I lamented.

'I shall remind you of that when you are complaining about the snow in winter,' he promised, bobbing to take a closer look and then peering at the sky. 'Where was she standing?'

He stood again.

'Just near that lamppost.' We walked towards it. 'She tried to keep herself up on it before she staggered and fell in the road.'

'And which way was she facing?'

'Towards Break House.'

'All the time?'

He flicked an apple core to one side oblivious to Ruby's objections that it could be a vital clue. She was fond of reminiscing about how she had tracked Count Craven by the traces of his specially formulated tooth powder on a discarded cucumber sandwich.

'She seemed to be staring at my window,' I recalled, 'but I was not really watching her.'

Shame on you, Hefty scolded.

'Inspector Hefty would not be impressed,' Romulus rebuked me.

'He is not,' I assured him and I hoped that he was better at hiding his feelings when coming across patients whom he believed to be mad.

'The problem we have,' he told me, 'is trying to work out from where the shot came.' He clicked his tongue. 'She was a midget not much taller than you.'

'If you listen carefully,' I told him, 'you will hear the bonds of second cousinly tolerance starting to snap.'

'So,' he continued unabashed, 'if the bullet entered through her eye at about this height...' He held his cane by the side of my head. 'And travelled in a straight line to the back of her skull around here.' He angled his cane, pointing down at about forty-five degrees. 'Then it must have come from the top of a building at about fifty feet.' He scanned the square. 'Which means that the shooter had either climbed on top of your observatory...'

'He cannot have weighed very much,' I remarked. 'As you know, it is thinly framed glass.'

'Or...' my cousin swung his cane up and around to the far corner, 'she was facing the other way and it came from the roof of the Splendid.'

The hotel occupied a good third of the side of the square to the right of my house from the far corner – five storeys of red brick with a grand colonnaded entrance manned by a heavily bearded Sikh commissionaire so resplendent in his blue-and-gold turban and matching robes that it was difficult to believe that he was John Smith, a laundress's son from Lower Montford.

'Was there anybody important around?' Romulus asked. 'A cabinet minister or a member of the royal family for example?'

'I do not think anyone like that has been here since King Edmund,' I said, 'and he was only passing through. Why?'

'Whoever fired that shot was either shooting randomly or a very fine marksman indeed,' he speculated, 'but in Montford and in public?'

My cousin shook his head in disbelief.

Pity the hurdy-blinking-gurdy man wasn't in the line of fire, Ruby said grumpily as he ground out another dirge.

'Before she died...' I began, and was about to tell Rommy about the victim's warning to me when Pottager cleared his throat discreetly.

If I might be so bold, milady, Ruby's manservant said softly, and I stopped in my tracks for he rarely spoke unless he had something important to say. *Do you not think that Dr Thorn has too many worries already with his wife's illness and the pressures of his profession?*

You are right, of course, I conceded, *I am being selfish.*

I would not say that, Pottager murmured in a way that made me suspect he thought it though.

'Before she died...' I began again and Rommy glanced at the clock tower, presumably watching the hands of time move on. 'Cane Braise rode past my window. He scarpered when he heard the shot.'

'Braise?' Rommy checked in alarm. 'You did not tell me that.'

'I did not think much of it.'

He frowned.

'Remember how Ruby Gibson castigated her manservant for omitting to tell her that the arsonist had freckles?' Romulus reminded me. 'How can your character be cleverer than you?'

'Because she does not have to live in the real world.'

And I am going to die in the world you created if you do not get me out soon.

'Do you think...?' I suggested.

'Anton Gervey,' Rommy confirmed. 'Though Braise was not his target.' I opened my mouth to question that statement, but my cousin was already explaining. 'He must have been thirty or forty yards from the woman and even you would not be that bad a shot.'

I huffed indignantly.

'When we had that competition,' I reminded him, 'I hit the bullseye first.'

'On my target,' he countered as if such petty details mattered. 'If Braise had been killed there would have been open warfare, but what better way to fire a warning shot than to show your willingness to kill and in as public a way as possible?'

There was a wonderful silence and I was pleased to note that my persecutor was packing his instrument of torture away.

'Keep a sharp eye out and your curtains closed, Vi,' Rommy advised grimly. 'I doubt that either man cares much about who he kills.'

You may be a professional assassin, Van Dyke, Ruby said, blowing smoke into his monocled eye, *but you are no match for the British amateur.*

'Be quiet,' I commanded her.

'Why? Did you hear something?' my cousin whispered after a few seconds.

'Only Ruby Gibson,' I replied as if it were the most normal thing in the world but, if anyone would understand, it was Romulus and, if Ruby did not behave, I would never let her out.

19: THE MIDNIGHT MANGLER

MONTFORD POLICE STATION stood on the corner of Cannon Street and Water Lane, the blue lantern almost always lit to reassure the populace that, while our navy kept our shores safe, the Central Suffolk force tried to do the same for our streets. But, while the navy succeeded, the police had an impossible task. One only had to venture into the Lowers to realise that.

I had waited until the afternoon, when the station was more likely to be quiet. The majority of crimes are committed at night because the greatest proportion of them are stimulated by alcohol. Turn up in the morning and you will find young swells, who have been out celebrating, rubbing shoulders with vagrants who were seeking shelter.

At two o'clock there was only the desk sergeant, who was busily occupied in pushing a wooden splinter between his upper molars.

'Good afternoon, Sergeant Webb,' I greeted the officer as he raised his massive head. It was said that his application to join the force had been rejected because there was no helmet large enough for that colossal cranium, but an uncle who ran a public house in Lower Montford had organised a whip-round to have one specially made, his customers contributing in the mistaken belief that one of their own would turn a blind eye to their activities. One of his first actions on donning his outsized uniform was to have the pub closed down.

'Afternoon.' Webb put his makeshift toothpick into the nib box. 'Found the Midnight Mangler?'

Neither of us believed that the killer existed. The *East Anglian Gazette* had linked a couple of unconnected murders, a missing glazier, a suicide and an accident with a ladder, as the work of one man. It sold a great many newspapers and created a great deal of paperwork with numerous witnesses coming forward to regale the police with vital misinformation.

'Surely that is your job?' I replied.

'Thought you liked doin' it for us,' he goaded.

I would never be allowed to forget the time Agnust and I had tackled a stranger who was behaving suspiciously only to find out that he was a constable in plain clothes.

'Is Inspector Stanbury here?'

'He most assuredly is,' a voice called and, a moment later, a figure appeared from the open doorway of the second room along the corridor. 'Good afternoon, Lady Violet.'

Alfred Stanbury was about average height for a policeman, i.e. tall. He paid good money, he had told me, for his suits. If so, his tailor was either incompetent or bore him a grudge because they never quite fitted. The charcoal jackets were always a little baggy and the almost-matching trousers even more so.

It is his fault for being the wrong shape, Ruby told me. *He is too...* She stopped, unable to decide in what dimension the man exceeded in or fell short of requirements. He seemed fairly well proportioned to me. *Well proportioned*, she concluded.

The inspector shook my hand warmly, his black hair – mistreated by a similarly inept barber – fell loosely over his ears and in a strand over his forehead. I had presented him with a bottle of macassar oil one Christmas in the pretence that it was a joke, but in the hope that he would use it. He had recognised the joke but not my aspiration.

'Come into my office.'

Stanbury left the door wide open. He did not have to tell me the kind of stories that would circulate if we were closeted together. They would not especially worry me, for a single woman pursuing such a disreputable career as mine must expect to be the subject of all sorts of rumours. Any scandal, real or imagined, however, could do untold harm to a police officer's career and, at thirty-three, the inspector still harboured hopes of rising to the rank of superintendent.

I settled on a wooden chair while he stood at the side of the desk. His moustaches were a little disarrayed, for he may have trimmed and combed them but he never applied any wax.

'To what do I owe this pleasure?' Some men's eyes sparkle. Stanbury's did not. They were toffee-coloured with such a soft glow that I always felt warmed by them.

'I would like to report a crime,' I said, and he tilted a little to his left, surveying me.

'Your maid has attacked another of my men, has she?' he mocked gently.

'She was defending her mistress,' I told him, though he knew full well already what had happened. 'Sergeant Little should have identified himself before trying to detain me.'

Stanbury snorted in amusement.

'Love to have seen it,' he said and, to the relief of my cricked neck, went to sit on his chair on the other side of the desk.

It was a large room with a splendid view of Mark's Alley and the fire-gutted block of apartments on the other side of it.

Unlike Stanbury's attire, the office was tidy with files neatly stacked in trays or put away in one of his two steel filing cabinets. Even the painted tin ashtray – a souvenir of a holiday in the seaside resort of Sackwater – was clean. Although he was fond of cigars, he always cleared it out when he had finished one.

'I am talking about a woman who was killed in Seraphim Square,' I said, and he picked his cylindrical ebony rule out of the wooden tray.

'I heard about that,' he said. 'A beggar slipped down and hit her head, didn't she?'

'She did fall,' I conceded, 'but she did not slip.'

'Tripped up then?' He paused and scratched his clean-shaven chin. 'Or are you saying somebody pushed her over?'

He pointed the rule towards me.

'Take a look at this.' I put the specimen bottle on his desk and he put the rule down to examine Romulus's find.

'Bit of lead.' He rattled it in the bottle.

'A bullet,' I told him and he arched a shaggy eyebrow.

'Not like one I've ever seen.'

'Nor I,' I admitted. 'Romulus found it lodged inside the woman's head.'

'Blimey!' the inspector breathed. 'Stupid question but how did it get there? You're not suggesting somebody walked up and shot her in the middle of Seraphim Square?'

'Not quite,' I agreed. 'We think there was a marksman on the roof of the Splendid Hotel.'

'Rommy thinks that too?' Stanbury checked. He was on familiar terms with my cousin since they had fished together as boys on the River Angle. 'So it isn't just a plot for Ruddy Gibson?'

I forgave the deliberate misnaming of my heroine because I had unwittingly brought ridicule upon him by having a Sergeant Cranberry in *Death at Mars Mansions*.

I wonder how blasé you would be if he called you Lady Violent, Ruby sniffed.

He used to, I told her, *when we were growing up.*

'It was Rommy's idea,' I said, forcing myself to ignore Ruby's barb about my not having grown up yet.

Stanbury put the bottle down on his virginal blotting pad. 'So why isn't he here?'

'He had to attend an inquest,' I told him. 'Dazlina Dazzles.'

'Patience Dove,' the inspector affirmed because Dove was written on her death certificate, though she had many other names. 'Is he still sticking to his theory?'

'I think it is a more than a theory,' I protested, though I had to admit to being sceptical myself. Not many keepers of disorderly houses are strangled to death with a dead grass snake while attempting to rescue a fire eater who was being eaten by fire in Kelham Green. 'But he is quite happy to talk to you another day.'

'Were there any witnesses?'

'None that a sane person might think reliable,' I replied. 'I heard a shot from my front sitting room but I thought it was a motor car.'

'Did you see the vehicle?'

'Captain Heavers in his Daimler.'

'That man is a menace,' Stanbury muttered. 'Wouldn't be surprised if he started the uprising.'

I laughed. Heavers was a hero of the Zulu wars and it was rumoured that he would have been recommended for a Victoria Cross had he not been seduced by his colonel's wife.

The inspector went to his filing cabinet. 'Constable Cooper attended the scene,' he announced, sitting back at his desk with a thin brown folder. 'He's a steady sort.'

Steady, I knew, meant *plodding*, but Stanbury was not going to denigrate one of his own men in front of a private citizen.

'I have no wish to criticise him,' I said to prepare him for my doing so, 'but I cannot help but feel that he was a little too ready to dismiss the incident as an accident.'

The inspector rolled the rule to and fro under his right hand, the back still scarred from when it had been impaled on a weather-vane.

'He had little reason to suspect a shooting.'

'That is true.' I had not deduced it either. 'And there was something else. The victim warned me that I would be killed if I did not stop interfering.'

'Fat chance of you doing that,' Stanbury jibed without malice, but then asked seriously, 'interfering with what?'

'I have no idea,' I assured him. 'She talked about the Master and I wondered if she meant Gervey.'

He picked up the rule again, grasping it like a truncheon.

'And how have you interfered with his business?'

His grip tightened.

'I did come across him at a rat-baiting in the Lowers,' I said, and he raised a shaggy eyebrow. 'But we did not meet.'

'You have an unusual social life,' the inspector commented and scratched under his left sleeve with the stick.

'And I won four hundred pounds.'

I won one hundred thousand roubles playing Russian Roulette with Kropotkin the nihilist, Ruby boasted, but we both knew that she had cheated.

'Blimey!' Stanbury raised the other, slightly less shaggy brow. 'He would not have been happy about that.'

'I did not wait to find out.'

'Very wise,' the inspector snorted. 'I can't see him ordering a public execution because of it though.' He slid his chair back. 'I'll have a think about it,' he promised, 'but there doesn't seem much point in interviewing him. He will not admit to anything and it would only alert him.'

I took the chair-sliding cue and stood up.

'I'll let you know if I find anything,' he promised.

'I am sure that you will find something if only that there is nothing to find,' I assured him and he huffed as he got to his feet.

'I'll see you out.'

Well I thought it was a good aphorism, Ruby protested, while I wondered if I could find somebody to proof-listen to her remarks before I broadcast them.

20: THE LONG GESTATION AND THE SHORT SERMON

IT WOULD HAVE been quicker to have walked I reflected, as we finally managed to pull into Broad Road, but – rather like my father on my jilting day – neither Gerrund nor Agnust would hear of such a thing. They could not have their lady reduced to the level of those who inhabit the streets.

'Never guess who I have in my cab yisdee,' the driver called down.

'Not on the basis of that information,' I agreed.

The pope, Ruby speculated.

'Old Dizzy,' he told me with great satisfaction. 'Lord Beaky-field.'

Beaconsfield, Ruby corrected him, annoyed at her guess being wrong.

'But Disraeli is dead,' I protested, and the cabby laughed knowingly in an unpleasantly high pitch.

'Tha's what they do want us believe,' he said. 'Gedoudovit!' he yelled at an elderly man in a towering topper who had put a foot on the road. 'Can't stand shufflers.' A shuffler being a pedestrian. 'If God want people to walk he wint give them me and my magnificent carriage.'

I gave up cricking my neck. He was no more worth looking at than he merited listening to.

'Course he deny it,' my driver confided, 'but shavin' off his beard dint make no fool of me.'

'I wonder what did then,' I muttered, relieved to see that we had arrived.

St Etheldreda's was an odd concoction. The bulk of the building a brick cube, flat roofed with no tower or spire, but then the architect must have taken a Cook's Tour to Athens and found a Greek temple going cheap for there it was, stuck on the front, white marble pillars with a simple iron cross screwed on top as an afterthought.

Having left in plenty of time, I had not calculated for a tortuous diversion caused by scaffolding collapsing across Eternal Road. It would be impossible to go in so late without drawing attention to myself so I decided to wait outside.

A heavily pregnant woman in a patchwork cotton dress leaned on the gatepost of a low front wall, but she waddled forward in unmatched carpet slippers as I approached.

'Spare a farthin' for a starvin' mowther,' she pleaded, though I had yet to meet a beggar who would be satisfied with so little.

I gave her thruppence.

'Lord love you, miss,' she trembled.

'I do hope your baby is not born as lopsided as your bump,' I said and she glanced down.

'Broggit,' she cursed. 'Blimmid stuffin' do shift.'

She shuffled her bulge about.

'How long have you been with child?' I enquired and she wiggled her nose.

''Bout five year now,' she reckoned. 'I'm blind afore tha', but I get fizzed with people droppin' stones in my can thinkin' I dint see.' She scratched her bosom. 'Fine kettle of frogs when the public goo as tricksome as me.'

A muffled hymn and discordancy had started.

'Wint be much longer,' she forecast. 'Tha' Father Green dint give a long sermon. Too much of a rush for his breakerfast.' The doors opened and she perked up. 'How do I look?' she enquired.

'Awful.'

'Thanks,' she grinned as the first of the congregation began to emerge, and uncleared her throat to issue a piteously croaking, 'Spare a farvin' for a starvin' mowther, madam.'

An elderly woman hurried by, miraculously cured of her need to shuffle.

'Spare a farvin' for a starvin' mowther.'

A young couple in all their Sunday finery paused.

'Do not despair,' the wife said compassionately. 'The Lord will provide.'

'How 'bout you helpin' him?' my new acquaintance suggested unheeded.

A family of giants emerged and positioned themselves in front of me as their fellow worshippers spilled out. I scuttled sideways. Was that lady in black Dolores Poynder? I hoped not because she had an impenetrable veil on. She was too heavily built, I decided, and glimpsed a woman in brown who was more the right size but was probably about three decades too old.

The beggar woman was working hard but fruitlessly, and I understood then why the singing had been so bad. Every single one of them must have been stone deaf.

A rotund gentleman in a short grey cloak came by, rotund wife in a long grey cloak at his side.

'Bother,' I breathed and stepped back hastily, opening my parasol to shade my face. The veil was too flimsy for me to feel secure and the last thing I wanted was for him to bawl out, *Good Morning, Lady Violet Thorn*. It was clear that he recognised me too but even clearer that the last thing he wanted was for me to bawl out, *Good Morning, Mr Asterisks-for-legal-reasons. Are you still a client of Phillis Fishnet's on Straight Street?* For I had bumped into him exiting the building a few weeks ago.

Pay attention, Thorn. Ruby was the only one allowed to *Thorn* me. *That is her now.*

As almost always Miss Gibson was right. A lady was exchanging a few words with the priest – telling him to get that boil on the side of his nose lanced, I hoped – and she was unmistakeably the object of my visit.

Mr Asterisks froze, spun on his heel and strode off so abruptly that he almost knocked over a flower girl who was rearranging the display in her basket.

'Crust-eyed screep,' she called after him, not very affectionately.

Dolores Poynder paused to dip her first two fingers in the holy water stoop, made the sign of the cross and stepped out. I was maybe a dozen feet to her right, but Mr and Mrs Gargantua and their monstrous brood were milling about between us and Dolores was bent over, looking down. I wished then that I had had the foresight to ask Martha for a description of Dr Poynder, but I could check with her later. He was a slender man, with a profile that reminded me of Michelangelo's David – a straight nose under a heavy brow and above full lips, the upper adorned by short neat moustaches and his face framed by tidy dark brown mutton-chops a little greyed. He was much more appropriately dressed than Goliath's nemesis, though, in a Prussian blue coat with a matching silk hat.

Dr Poynder had hold of Dolores's arm, but there was something wrong about the way that he was doing it. He took her through the small, paved forecourt to the pavement and seemed to be heading for the line of hansoms that was gathering to whisk the churchgoers away, but the couple swung around towards me, his expression so grim that, for a second, I thought he was going to confront me – until I told myself that he would have had no reason to do so. The doctor was looking straight past me and his wife could not have stared at the ground more intently if she had dropped her ticket to heaven.

I stood back but his shoulder nearly brushed against my parasol as they passed. It was only then that I got a good look at Dolores. It was definitely her, but she had changed dramatically in the months since that photograph had been taken. The woman who drifted by now was grim-faced and haggard, as if she had hardly slept in all that time.

A spoke of my parasol scraped against the wall and Edward glanced towards me, but without interest, and they both walked by. Dolores looked awful. Her skin was bleached and her eyes dark-rimmed. She must have been doing a lot of crying to make them so bloodshot. What on earth had that man been doing to her?

I had planned to speak to Dolores on some pretext, but two things stopped me as they walked slowly away. The first was her expression. I had seen that look before and hoped not to see it again. It was undisguised fear. And the way that her husband was holding her was not an affectionate gesture but more as if he were making an arrest. I had thought that Martha sounded like something from Wilkie Collins when she had claimed her friend was being kept prisoner, but was it possible that there was something in what she said?

Have a care, Thorn, Ruby said so clearly that I spun around. *That man is dangerous.*

Stop being so histrionic, I rebuked her, but I had a feeling that Miss Gibson – handsome, brave and resourceful according to a review by Mrs Rachel Chick, excellent reviewer of the *Suffolk Whisperer* – could be right.

21: *THE MOAT, THE MAID AND THE JEMMY*

GAINSBOROUGH GARDENS WAS almost a miniature park in itself, large and railed, lawned and well-stocked with flowers, shrubs and trees to our right. To our left, the road was bordered by some rather splendid houses, all individually and magnificently constructed. I doubted that you would have much change from a thousand guineas for any of those properties in such a location.

We trotted gently around the perimeter.

'There it is,' Friendless announced pulling on his reins. 'Whoa girl.' We came to a halt. 'Haglin House.'

He pulled up the catch for me to clamber out.

A romp in a haystack – and I had a few of those in my youth – does little more to disarray one's clothing than a short ride in a hansom. The vertical magenta stripes of my cinnabar dress, straight when I set off, were wavy now and the shoe fairy had undone one of my laces.

'Int a bad gaff,' Friendless commented.

All cabbies are keen critics of other people's residences, often annoying me by contemptuously dismissing properties that they could never dream of possessing. This time, however, I found myself in agreement. It was not a bad gaff at all.

Haglin House was a good-sized red brick building, three storeys over a semi-sunken basement, substantial without being imposing. It was double-fronted, the two bays with iron balconies on the first floor and rising to peaked red-tiled roofs. There were none of the showy towers and spires beloved of the previous generation. This, I decided, was modern architecture at its tasteful best.

There were spiked railings separating the property from the pavement, but they were little more than three feet tall and the gate was unlocked when I tried it. A red-tiled bridge led over the basement moat to matching steps straight ahead, nine of them I counted for I was trying to train myself to be observant.

You need a better teacher, Ruby scoffed, though I did not need to remind her that I had seen the giant bird-eating spider two pages before she had.

A wide path ran alongside the house in either direction.

Unusually the front door was to the left of the open porch rather than straight ahead, which struck me as eminently sensible. The usual design allows a wind to sweep whatever weather is available straight into most hallways.

The doorbell was a brass disc cast in a paisley pattern, with a white porcelain button printed with the word 'Press' for anyone tempted to try to extract it. I followed the instruction and heard a pleasant chime.

If a man with a cutlass appears, run, Ruby advised, though she had stayed to fight when one had confronted her.

Through the stained glass a figure appeared and a maid answered my summons.

'Good morning, miss.' She was a pretty girl aged about eighteen, I estimated, her auburn hair tucked neatly under a starched white hat. Agnust used to wear one of those, against my wishes, until Gerrund told her that she looked like a white-crested duck and she abandoned it that very day. This maid looked very smart in hers.

'Milady,' I corrected her because a title is often more effective than a jemmy for gaining access to a building.

'Milady.' She eyed me dubiously, for I had left my tiara on the mantelpiece. 'Can I help you?'

'I am calling on Mrs Poynder,' I announced.

'I'm afraid my mistress is not at home, miss-milady.'

'Oh but she assured me that she would be,' I lied, resisting a childish urge to cross my fingers behind my back. 'And I have come such a long way.'

'I'm afraid my mistress is not at home,' she repeated slowly enough for the words to percolate through my sluggish mind.

'If you could tell her who I am...'

'To anyone,' she told me firmly.

'When do you expect her?' I enquired, aware that I was breaking one of the cardinal rules of etiquette and she raised her chin, also aware that I was breaking one of the cardinal rules of etiquette.

'I'm sure I don't know,' she replied quite correctly, for she could not know whether her mistress would ever be *at home* to me.

I tried to peer past, but she had only opened the door a little and filled most of the gap and, seeing what I was doing, she pushed it to a little more. It was then I did something unpardonable.

Call her.

I cannot do that.

Call her, Ruby insisted.

'Dolores,' I called. 'Dolly.'

I did not really expect a response from Mrs Poynder and I was not sure even that it was worth a try, but I did anyway and found that it was not.

'Well really, miss!' the maid exclaimed, my splendid title cast contemptuously away with what little respect in which she had held me. 'Anyone would think you are an American.'

And with that damning assessment she shut the door.

I went down the steps and back onto the pavement.

Thank you so much for embarrassing me, I fumed.

At least I never made you pretend to faint in the Sistine Chapel.

You had to do something.

So did you.

'You do be right 'bout not being long,' Friendless conceded. 'Old Queeny int hardly got her breaths.'

His mare was contentedly munching on a bag of oats he had attached to her harness.

'I am happy to wait,' I assured him. 'In fact there is a water pump on that corner and it is shadier. Why do you not go there and I shall take a walk in the gardens?'

He gave my suggestion some thought.

'Why do you say I dint goo there?' he enquired. 'When that is where I goo presently?'

Without waiting for an answer – which was just as well because I did not have one – Friendless clicked his tongue and flicked his reins and, nose still in canvas, Old Queeny plodded on.

My father often told me never to give up, but I did not subscribe to that dictum. As Sledgehammer Smith could testify but probably would not, there are times when the best thing to do is to throw in the towel. I was not quite beaten yet, however, for I had noticed that the maid, smartly attired as she was, was wearing her outdoor boots.

'You are not as clever as you think,' I muttered defiantly for, many decades from a peaceful death – she hoped – Violet Thorn, Lady Novelist, still had one more trick up her sleeve.

22: THE MAN IN THE SHRUBBERY

IT WAS THE hottest part of the day as I strolled across the road, and I was coming to think that my rose-pink bonnet might not have been worth the three guineas I would have to pay for it when Mrs Grayside's monthly account arrived. It may have been all the vogue, but the silk was too flimsy to protect my head from the beating sun and I was loath to put up my parasol. It was a new one from Batterby's of Bond Street. Mr B had folded it immaculately and I doubted that I could ever achieve the same result.

The way to the gardens was open so I ambled in, positioning myself behind a rhododendron – mercifully in the shade of a sycamore – where I could just see the gate of Haglin House. There I waited. It was possible, of course, that the maid had those boots on because she had just come in and had not had time to change them before she was summoned, but I had nothing to lose other than a little of my not-especially precious time.

How many chestnut, bay or dappled horses would come along, I wondered but quickly tired of that game. Hardly anything passed by and it is no fun betting against yourself for you win and lose simultaneously.

After five minutes that felt like fifty, the peace was broken by a clattering not unlike the sound of a small train approaching at speed. Craning my neck, I saw a Benz Patent-Motorwagen appear, go by and rattle off at a breakneck walking pace. The driver was a portly gentleman who appeared to be having trouble steering it with the lever on a horizontal wheel. 'Sorry! First time,' he called over the racket to two young ladies forced to leap backwards as he weaved towards the pavement. Romulus had almost bought one of those machines until I told him that it looked like an oversized invalid carriage.

The noise died down and a donkey cart clipped by. Having nothing better to do, I stifled a yawn then, having nothing better to do, I yawned.

'Looking for something?' a masculine voice at my shoulder enquired and I jumped.

It was a young man, in an ecru linen suit, loose-fitting with the sleeves short enough to show half an inch of white shirt cuff as was becoming the fashion. He tipped his straw boater.

'Sorry,' he said though he did not look it. 'Didn't mean to startle you.'

'Not at all,' I dismissed his apology. 'I was looking for a butterfly that flew into here.'

The young man had a nice smile and was clean-shaven. I for one was glad that profuse facial topiary was going out of style. My friend Kitty had complained once that, if she wanted to be affectionate, she had to rummage through the undergrowth to find her husband's mouth. By which time he has usually fallen asleep, she had sighed into her third glass of cider.

'Plenty to choose from.' He swung his silver-handled, lemon-painted cane to indicate at least a score of them quivering amongst the branches. 'Was it a special one?'

'I thought I saw a...' I racked my brains. Romulus was a keen lepidopterist and kept a display case in the study. He had tried to teach me about them but I told him it was a cruel hobby. If he killed everything for its beauty, he would have Lillie Langtry and Kitty Loftus pinned out on boards. *And you*, his friend Robin had added in one of the strangest compliments I had ever received. '*Asellus compernis*,' I bluffed wildly.

'Knock-kneed haddock,' the young man translated effortlessly. 'I must see this.'

He moved forward until we were standing barely six inches apart and peered into the bush.

'You are spying on that house, aren't you?' he said softly.

'Of course not,' I blustered and waited for an apology.

'You are too well-dressed – not sure about the bonnet, by the way – pretty but inadequate – to be a burglar,' he continued, my wait clearly in vain. 'At first I thought you might be suspicious of your husband,' he said, 'but then I realised you are not wearing a ring, besides which, having seen you at close range, no man would cuckold a wife like you.'

I felt my face go even hotter than it was already, but one of the blessings I am fortunate to have been granted is that I never blush.

'I am sorry,' he said. 'I have made you blush.'

He has, Ruby confirmed and I could not gainsay her or him for they had a better view of me than I did.

'You are very forward,' I told him severely.

I knew that we were approaching a new century and that things were a little less formal than they had been, but such familiarity from a stranger was almost casual enough to be improper.

'I know,' he agreed. 'My wife used to tell me that.'

'Has she changed her mind?' I could not see why she would have.

Was that a shadow of the front door opening? I screwed up my eyes to peer more closely and decided that it was not.

'No,' he replied, his expression entirely serious. 'She passed away on Christmas Day three years ago.'

'Oh how awful,' I said. 'So did one of my brothers.'

It was not like me to confide in a stranger, especially after so short an acquaintance but, for some absurd reason, I felt that I knew this man already.

Absurd is the word, Ruby warned. *You do not even know whether or not he likes jam in his rice pudding.*

Would you like me to investigate? Hefty, anxious to prove himself useful, volunteered but I told him that I would not.

'How awful for you too,' the man-who-I-did-not-know-already commiserated. 'My wife died in childbirth.'

'My brother did not,' I said and stopped aghast at the crassness of my words.

You cannot blame me for that one, Ruby said, taken aback by the crassness of my words.

The young man coughed and stepped back, and I was about to apologise and explain that I had not meant to mock his bereavement when he burst out laughing and, to my astonishment, I found myself joining him.

'Oh my goodness,' I said. 'What monsters we are.'

'Not in the least,' he assured me. 'Marigold's departure broke my heart and, from the way you spoke, the loss of your brother...'

'Magnus,' I inserted in the pause.

'Broke yours too,' he continued. 'We were not laughing at their loss but at the absurdity of what you said.'

I could have taken umbrage at that but, on reflection, I could not.

'That is the first time I have found any humour in the subject,' I said.

'And I,' he said. 'She is coming out.'

I looked across. This was most unprofessional, allowing myself to be so easily distracted.

But you are not the professional anyway, my Extraordinary Investigator reminded me.

The maid was making her way down the steps.

'I say,' the man said. 'If he were your husband you would be right to be mistrustful of him with her. She's a corker.'

He did not exaggerate. Apart from having a waist that you could put a necktie around and still have plenty left with which to make a flamboyant bow, the maid had that slight sway in her walk that men find highly attractive. I had assumed that she would proceed along the pavement, but she was crossing the road towards us.

I edged into the bush a little.

'Excuse my familiarity,' the young man said and stepped close to and in front of me. 'But what I would like to know is what he intends to do about it,' he said loudly.

He was a pipe smoker, I discovered. My father would approve of that if nothing else.

Steady on, Thorn!

It was a perfectly innocent thought.

Since when have you been either perfect or innocent?

'What are you doing?' I whispered.

'Shielding you and pretending we are engrossed in a conversation,' he explained.

'You sound like you are addressing a public meeting.'

He grinned.

'I suppose I do,' he said quietly. 'You have unusual eyes.'

God had matched his to his dark brown hair.

'I did not know that,' I replied, hoping I had not sounded as tart to him as I had to myself.

'And you are sarcastic,' he remarked. 'I like that.'

'Brandy Flake,' I said without thinking.

'You know your pipe tobaccos,' he said approvingly.

'I knew Magnus's.'

'How many siblings have you got?'

'Just one sister now.'

'I have five sisters, all married off, thank Jupiter. I could not possibly support any of them, in fact I am hoping that they will support me one day.' He twisted his neck. 'She has gone now.'

He stepped back and I tried to tell myself that I was glad.

The maid was disappearing behind a shrubbery.

'What now?' he asked.

'I wait,' I said.

'For whom or what?'

I did not need Ruby to tell me that this was absolutely none of his business, but she did anyway.

'To leave a few minutes gap.'

The young man produced a leather pouch out of an inner jacket pocket. 'Now let me think.' He lifted the flap of his pouch and brought out a polished briar. 'You have arranged to meet somebody in that house and did not want the maid to catch you out.' He pulled an unconvincing expression of horror. 'An assignation,' he hissed.

'Certainly not,' I protested. 'And I would strongly advise that you do not attempt to make a career on the stage.'

'I shall bear that in mind.' He dipped the bowl of his pipe into the pouch to plug it. 'That maid turned you away,' he surmised, 'and you are hoping her substitute will admit you.'

'You have been reading too many cheap novels.'

'At least I am not trying to re-enact one.'

'I do not know what you mean.'

He closed the pouch and slipped it back inside his jacket, creating a slight bulge that I had not noticed before. I tried to take a pride in my powers of observation, but was coming to the conclusion there was little about which I could be conceited.

'Skulking in the undergrowth.' He patted his outer pockets. 'Trying to trick your way into a house. All that you lack is a false beard.'

'I left it at home,' I huffed.

Was I really that transparent?

Like lead crystal in candlelight, Ruby told me.

'I could lend you one of mine,' he offered.

'How many do you have?'

'Only eight... No really.'

'What are you? Some sort of criminal?' I joked.

'Well, just between ourselves,' he said, 'I'm a murderer.'

I started to laugh but got no further than parting my lips, for one glance at the stranger's expression was enough to convince me that he was entirely – not to say deadly – serious.

23: THE DEVIL AND LADY DERRINGER

I COULD HAVE screamed in the hope that a big strong man would rush over to protect me; I could have run but the murderer would probably have been faster; but, for some reason, I did not feel afraid. That, however, could be how he worked, I meditated, by lulling his victims into a false sense of security. Had he been sent by Anton Gervey to assassinate me? Gerrund often nagged me to carry my gun. He favoured an Enfield .476 revolver for himself, but it was much too bulky for me so, with his guidance, I had purchased a Lady Derringer. It only held two bullets, but I had never needed either of them yet. I had not thought to put it in my handbag today.

How many times have I cautioned you? Ruby sighed. *But do you ever listen?*

Who are you to talk? I demanded. *I warned you repeatedly not to enter that cave.*

No you did not! You sent me in there.

'On the stage,' the young man explained.

'The thing I advised you not to go on?' I recalled ruefully.

'The very same.'

'I can only apologise.'

He folded his arms in the way that parents do when contending with fractious children.

'Please do.'

'I am sorry,' I mumbled. 'It was meant to be a joke.'

Leave the jokes to me, said Ruby, who had once entertained an audience in Lusby's Summer and Winter Palace for forty-seven minutes while her man Pottager ripped the lining out of all the hats in the cloakroom in a fruitless search for a copy of the French plans to sink the Isle of Wight.

The young man frowned and rubbed his chin, a reaction that could have been seen from the highest of the gods.

'I shall overlook it,' he decided, patting his pockets again. 'Bother. Forgot my vestas.' He slipped his briar into his outer breast pocket.

A rather beautiful red-and-blue butterfly alighted on the brim of his boater though not, I suspected, an *Asellus compernis*.

'What are you in?'

'Not the sort of thing you would enjoy,' he began.

'You do not know me.'

'I know you are a lady.'

'Oh dear,' I said. 'Would it make me swoon?'

'Not you, who intrepidly tracks down unfortunate fish through the undergrowth,' he mocked gently. 'To give you an idea, it is called *The Devil Stalks the Strand*. Utter tosh of course.'

'And you are playing Peter Stimpson?' I checked, swishing my parasol so casually that, had the man not jerked his head back, I might have caught him in the eye.

'Well Gerald Spender is,' he admitted, rubbing his neck either from bashfulness or from having cricked it in avoiding my flail, 'but I am his understudy and...' He stopped mid-sentence. 'It has not come out yet. How did you know his name?'

'Because I wrote that utter tosh.'

It was then he did something that I thought I never did but did apparently, and I had rarely seen a man do though I found it strangely attractive. He blushed.

'Oh.' He cleared his throat and pushed the boater back on his head. 'You must be Lady Violet Thorn.'

'I simply must,' I agreed icily and, while I folded my arms, the butterfly folded its wings. It looked like a flake of old bark now and I hoped that my action had not had a similar effect upon my appearance.

'I can only apologise.'

'Please do.'

'I'm sorry,' he mumbled. 'It was meant to be self-deprecating. I would actually be thrilled to get the role.'

I did not trouble to frown or rub my chin.

'Perhaps Mr Spender will accidentally drink a sleeping draught before the curtain goes up,' I suggested.

If advanced ticket sales were anything to go by – *Which they are*, Ruby insisted – the opening night would be the closing night for the devil would be stalking a house packed with empty seats.

'You are a devious woman, Lady Thorn,' my acquaintance said admiringly.

That was my idea, Ruby complained. *I did it in* The Reckoning of Roger Raiment.

'And now you have the advantage of me.'

'Anthony Appleton at your service, milady.'

'Well it was a pleasure to meet you, Mr Appleton,' I said, ignoring the outstretched hand. I liked to think that I was a modern woman, but I had not abandoned quite all proprieties. 'However…'

'I have not seen you at rehearsals.'

'You have not,' I agreed, unwilling to admit that the director had banned me for groaning repeatedly at his actors' skill in making humour humourless and pathos humorous. 'However,' I tried again, 'I have work to do.'

He clicked his fingers.

'Researching another book?'

'Quite so,' I agreed, thinking he might make a rather good Inspector Hefty.

He is far too good looking for the part, Ruby asserted.

Perhaps he could play you then, Hefty retorted and I stamped my foot as I set off out of the gardens.

If you two are to continue to occupy the same brain, I chided, *you had better start being civil to each other.*

I am always civil, they chorused simultaneously and untruthfully.

Friendless was still waiting on his high perch on the corner and had turned his cab around, presumably to be able to see me coming, but his head was bowed so that I could only see the top of his pith helmet. He had found it discarded that morning at the back of the infirmary and believed, erroneously, that it suited him. I hoped that he had not fallen asleep, for it was not unknown for Queeny to get bored and wander home.

Over the road, across the pavement and up the steps I went, turning to make sure that the maid was not returning. She was nowhere in sight but Anthony Appleton was and he waved cheerily.

Go away, I telepathed – and if that was not a verb it should have been – but he only waved again and even more ostentatiously. I shooed him and rang the bell. It was a longer wait this time.

'Butterfly lady,' came yelled from behind me and I turned again to see the young man still waving but more urgently this time. He cupped his hands to his mouth in a homemade megaphone. '*Cave servus,*' he called, which did not require a great deal of Latin to translate as *beware the servant* and I saw that the maid was returning but, because she had come down the side rather than straight across the garden, she had been out of my line of vision until then.

The door was opening as I started back down.

'Dear me, wrong house,' I called over my shoulder in high pitch so that she would not recognise my voice if I spoke to her again.

I thought you did a low pitch for that, Ruby reminded me of my telephone call to Wormwood.

I am versatile, I told her unconvincingly.

I had just reached the pavement and gone a few yards along it when I saw that the maid was crossing the road diagonally towards me rather than the house, doubtless intending to challenge my loitering.

'At last!' I declared.

Nobody says things to themselves that loudly, Ruby informed me.

'I was starting to think that I should never manage to find a cab,' I boomed before deciding that she was right, and rushed off.

'Thank you for waiting,' I called as I clambered a little breath-lessly aboard.

I pulled the flaps shut and slumped into my seat. 'Young ladies of old breedin' dint slump,' Agnust had told me repeatedly, but she was wrong about that. This young lady of old breedin' sagged like a half-empty sack of potatoes.

'Dint need thank Old Queeny,' Friendless told me, though I had been peering up at him. 'I give her no choices.'

He clicked his tongue and we set off so gently that it was a moment before I realised that we were moving.

Desperate for a stick of Beeman's, I delved into my handbag.

'Stop here,' I called.

'Whoa!' he yelled, hauling on the reins as if we had been careering down an icy mountainside towards the edge of a cliff. 'You int gettin' out again?'

'I am not.'

'Why do we stop?'

'Because you pulled on the reins and called *whoa*,' I replied, proving that we can all take things literally if we choose.

There was no sign of Anthony Appleton at the entrance to the gardens and the only reason I was disappointed, I told myself, was that I had wanted to thank him. I twisted to my right to look at Haglin House. The maid was standing on the steps watching me. A policeman at the scene of a crime could not have been more suspicious of my activities had I been wielding a bloodstained axe, and I was about to tell Friendless to drive on when a movement caught my eye.

There was the figure of a woman in the top left-hand window. I screwed up my eyes, made her blurrier and unscrewed them. Her straw-coloured hair hung loosely over her face so it was impossible to be certain, but I was half convinced that she was looking back at me. She raised her hand as if in acknowledgement but pulled it down quickly.

I did not have the best of views and she was already turning away, but it was when I saw her side on that I knew at whom I was looking. I had seen that profile in Martha Ryan's locket and again outside St Etheldreda's. But why would she be in what must have been the servants' quarters?

Juniper! Ruby exclaimed. *She looks worse than you do every morning.*

Thank you, I said tartly.

Why? she challenged me. *Do you think she looks better?*

I waved her aside and tried to look harder, but I had yet to discover a means of doing that.

As far as I could judge from what could not even be described as her coiffure, Dolores Poynder looked what Dobsy, the chirpy cockney in *The Murder of Mrs Mulliver*, would have described as a real Aunt Bess, which, in my fictional London dialect, translated as a mess.

24: BLOOD AND EARTH AND THE
DEVIL'S CLAWS

I WENT FOR a walk in the morning. This was partly to cogitate over Ruby's plight away from the confines of my study, which was failing to inspire me.

A bad writer blames her desk, Ruby cobbled a proverb that I doubted would merit an entry in *Brewer's Dictionary of Phrase and Fable*.

I was good enough to invent an excellent heroine, I defended myself and she conceded gracefully.

My main reason for going out though was to escape my maid. Agnust belonged to the tiny Sect of Pre-Markians who believed that the gospels of Mark the Evangelist were forged by Satan in 666 AD. Amongst other practices the believers crossed out a word of his writings upon rising every day, knowing that when they reached the final *it*, the world would burst into flames. This did not seem an especially worthy ambition to me, but it had all been revealed to Ethel of Ickworth in a dream and was, therefore, unalterable. I only wished that Ethel could have had another dream that maids should act respectfully to their mistresses.

It was Pre-Markian Christmas Day and Agnust had been warbling such stirring hymns as 'Oh Little Town of Ethel-lyhem' and 'Once in Royal Ickworth Village' at the top of her voice since dawn. To make matters worse my larynx had decided to act independently and hum along.

There was a concrete cube near the ruins of the monks' refectory in Monastery Gardens. Approximately ten-foot high along each side it was not a thing of beauty, but it attracted more sightseers to the park than the shrine of Saint Aegbald had done for centuries. This was where Marvellous Farthingale – not his real name, I suspected – had partly performed his greatest trick. The astonishing Mr F had allowed himself to be manacled, shackled, blindfolded and encased in a block of concrete from which he was going to spring unscathed after it had set. Eight years later we were still waiting.

There were moves to have the block broken open or even interred in its entirety, but there was such vigorous opposition to these suggestions from hawkers of postcards, paperweight models of the block and refreshments that the council let it be.

Some still believed that Marvellous was going to escape and swore that, if one pressed one's ear to the side, one could hear him chipping away industriously as he burrowed towards the surface. At Agnust's insistence I had tried, expecting to hear only the ocean though that could not possibly be in there because it was in every shell and empty teacup already. To my consternation, though, I had definitely heard a regular faint clinking. It was the fob watch around my neck, Ruby had explained patiently that night. Her condescension might have been understandable had it not been her who had excitedly drawn my attention to the sound.

I headed for the block, intending to view not it but the profuse deep pink flowers of the oleander bushes, and in the forlorn hope of finding a cool breeze in the shade of the horse chestnut trees. It was then that I spotted him – not Mr Farthingale, of course, but a man standing on the grass.

A slightly built man in a tattered buff-coloured canvas coat and with a shallow-crowned floppy wide-brimmed hat, I recognised him immediately.

Immediately after I reminded you, Ruby said, though I rather thought that it was I who had refreshed her memory.

It was the blind man I had seen in the square before that poor woman had been shot and this time he was wielding a walking stick. He appeared to be beating at something in the undergrowth. An adder? We had had a few of those that year and a cow had died near Stolham St Ernest from being bitten, probably after accidentally treading on one. If it was a snake though, how had he detected it? Perhaps he was not completely blind.

Or a fraud, Ruby suggested. She was sceptical about all beggars after a pauper had attacked her on St Patrick's Day with a shillelagh swaddled like a baby.

Leanbh, Ruby translated, for she had learned a little Old Gaelic while searching for the only Tyrone man claiming not to be descended from the last king of Ireland.

This was a remarkably resilient snake though; the beggar was raining a good many blows upon it as I approached. It was then that I heard a squeak. Was he thrashing a dog? If so, even one of those blows would have been inexcusably brutal.

I quickened my pace and it was then that I heard a small cry of *No!*

'You there!' I called and broke into a trot.

Ladies never trot, Agnust had told me and, when I asked how they played tennis, had insisted that they did not, for jumping about muddled their insides so that their children would be born with tangled chitterlings.

The man stiffened, stick raised high over his head. Then, when I was still twenty feet away, he lowered his stick and shot off.

A fraud, Ruby reasserted, though I had already come to that conclusion myself, for no blind man could have skirted the memorial stone to Biffo the brave cat who had saved a man's life by running for help, but I suspected that the animal, bored of watching his master lying unconscious, had wandered home for its supper.

I would have chased him and could possibly have caught him as he was not especially fleet of foot, but my primary concern was the object of his attack.

A young woman lay supine in the bushes. Her hands were raised, crossed over her face, but I could see a large weal traversing her mouth up to a swollen left eye.

'Please,' she whimpered and I knelt beside her.

'You are safe now,' I assured her. 'He has gone.'

I glanced up to check but the man had disappeared, probably towards one of the smaller side gates in the tumbled monastery walls.

The woman uncrossed her arms and touched her cheek gingerly.

'He's mad,' she whispered.

A signpost had fallen across her legs. I lifted it aside and the board reading *Floral Clock* fell off.

'Do you know him?'

'No. He come at me from behind.' She was neatly, though not expensively, dressed in a light blue skirt and a white shirt discoloured with dust and splattered, as was her flaxen hair, with blood. 'I never see him proper.'

Properly, Hefty corrected her.

Was that really the best that London's premier police detective could contribute?

'We need to get you to a doctor,' I said and she winced.

She was little more than a girl, I judged.

'Crumbs! It hurt.' She felt her nose tentatively. It was bleeding heavily. 'Excuse my language, miss.'

Crumbs hardly merited an entry in a lexicon of expletives, but I have often noticed that the speech of those lower in the social orders is milder than that of their alleged *betters*, for it is the servants who are castigated for their language while their masters curse like Cornishmen.

I looked about. I did not want to leave the girl unattended while it was possible that her assailant might return but there was nobody else in sight.

'Can I help you?' a man said suddenly at my side.

Now you know why I never take you on my escapades, Ruby said. *Looking about involves more than glancing over one shoulder.*

I know that, I said testily, *now*.

'This woman has been attacked,' I said.

From his green coat and trousers and matching peaked cap I could tell he was one of the park keepers, whose main purpose seemed to be threatening unaccompanied children in danger of enjoying their visits.

'By you?' he guessed. Being the only person about, I must be the suspect.

'No of course not.'

'Only,' he said edgily, 'from the way you grasp that cudgel…'

I had not realised that I was still holding the post and let it fall, narrowly missing Inspector Hefty, who was slipping a suspicious-looking daisy chain into a manilla envelope.

'It wint her.' The girl insisted, patting herself as if checking that all her limbs were still present. 'Least I dint think so,' she added less insistently.

It's the devil's claws for you my girl, Ruby forecast with relish, the claws being the arrows on a convict's uniform and, if her forecast proved correct, I resolved to take her with me.

'Of course it wasn't me.' I tossed my head haughtily, not easy to carry off when you are kneeling with your neck cricked to look backwards and up. 'I am Lady Violet Thorn.'

A title, as everyone knows, guarantees that the holder's word is unimpeachable.

What about… Ruby began.

I was not talking about him, I broke in.

Or…

Nor her, I snapped before she trotted out the whole of *Burke's Peerage*. We both knew full well that there were as many aristocratic criminals as poor ones with no lineage behind which to shelter. *I was commenting on the public's perception of the nobility.*

'A lady,' he marvelled thereby proving my assertion. 'I int never caught a real lady afore,' he added with great satisfaction, thereby disproving my assertion. 'Prob'ly get a medal.'

The girl struggled to a sitting position despite my attempts to restrain her gently.

'It wint her,' she declared again but this time, to my relief, she did not recant.

I was not seriously concerned about spending the rest of my days on a penal treadwheel, but I could imagine with what relish *The Chronic* would report my being taken in for questioning.

'Are you sure?' the park keeper asked in disappointment.

'It do be a man,' she remembered. 'A stranger.'

'A stranger what?' he puzzled.

'What did he look like?' I asked as she inspected her shirt in dismay.

'Evil,' she stated.

Hettie Granger occasionally helped the police by drawing wanted posters and a description like that would give her plenty of scope, I mused – glaring yellow eyes and a slavering mouth of fangs.

'Did you see his face?' I pressed gently as she rearranged her skirt.

'Yes.' The girl grabbed my wrist in both hands. 'It look evil.' She hauled herself onto her feet and, very nearly, me off mine. 'And he was blackened,' she added, 'like a sweep.'

Clearly she had seen her attacker a great deal more *proper* than she had led me to believe.

'I know it,' the keeper asserted, though he had known no such thing.

He made another spitting action but was disappointed to find that he had run short of saliva.

Something glinted on the dry, cracked earth and I picked it up – a florin.

'Is that yours?' I asked the girl and she snatched it from me.

''Tis now,' she declared.

'Bribin' a witness.' The park keeper wiggled his moustaches as if trying to shake them off and I could not have blamed him. They were meagre and unkempt. 'Tha's a criminal 'ffence.' She had already exonerated me so I ignored him.

'Did your attacker say anything?' I enquired and he spat spitlessly again.

'Of course,' she told me crossly. Everybody knows that attackers engage their victims in conversation. 'He say *You shouldn't have worn that hat.*'

I glanced around and saw it lying a few feet away, a battered but otherwise inoffensive straw bonnet with a blue ribbon tied in a twisted bow at the back.

'Anything else?' I pressed her and she struggled onto all fours. 'What time is it?'

'He dint need beat you to find tha' out,' the keeper commiserated. 'Unless you wint tell him.'

That would make his actions perfectly acceptable, Ruby fumed.

'I need to know,' the girl clarified. 'I'm back waitin' table at noon.'

I checked my watch.

'It is twenty minutes to twelve.'

'Lorr!' she cried getting to her feet in a disjointed way that was painful to watch and must have been agonising to perform.

'Mrs Frow-Fulford goo crackle-headed.'

I had come across Marjory Frow-Fulford. She ran the Empire Café in Market Square and I could not imagine her going insane, but then I had not expected Petra Volent to decide that she was a cormorant and launch herself off the cliffs at Sackwater.

'You cannot go to work like that,' I told her. 'I will explain the situation to your employer.'

The girl shook her head and my hand off her arm.

'And do you explain why I'm late yisdee and day 'fore yisdee?' she demanded. 'Int my fault I do be unreliable.'

''Tis,' the keeper assured her and it probably was, but the girl was brushing aside my offers to take her to a doctor or accompany her to the café, hobbling and half-tumbling towards the main entrance as if the ground were the deck of a ship in a storm.

'She leave her hat,' the keeper noted. It was little more than broken straw now, though the ribbon might be salvageable. 'You better take it otherways it's litter.'

I glanced back at the block.

Marvellous is getting out! Ruby exclaimed, poking me in the ribs excitedly and, sure enough, I saw it – a grey fist emerging triumphantly from the top of the concrete block. *Oh,* she said disappointedly as it moved closer towards the edge. *A squirrel.*

25: THE MAN WHO DIED BACKWARDS

OLD QUEENY PLODDED even more wearily that afternoon, but I did not like to comment because a worn-out horse was a hobble away from the knacker's yard. It was a cruel fact that no cabby could afford to feed a useless animal.

'She have a bad dream last night,' Friendless explained, though I had not asked. 'I tell her daint eat cheese afore bed but will she listen? Will she?' he demanded. 'She wint,' he answered his own question rancorously.

'From where does she get it?' I asked.

'Me,' he said simply. 'We alway share our supper.'

'But you do not eat hay.'

'Not much,' he agreed. 'She do get steamed if I do, she do.'

We turned onto Frog Lane and came to a standstill. Another cab drew level and a middle-aged gentleman in a grey frock coat and a well-brushed beaver-skin hat leaned over to get a better look.

'Ahoy little girl.' He prodded his ebony cane towards me. 'I'll wager you like chocolates.'

'Not nearly as much as I like being left alone,' I replied and he giggled, sounding more like that little girl than I did.

'I like a lass with spirit,' he sniggered, tugging playfully at one of his curled moustaches.

I could have tugged on them both for him though not quite as playfully.

'And I like a man who leaves women alone,' I retorted.

'Oh but I do,' he assured me. 'I never touch a girl over fourteen.'

I took a good look at him. He was probably a respectable family man and I was just about to express my disgust when a young man jumped in front of us with a bucket.

'Clean your cab for a tanner,' he offered, slopping water – brown with horse from previous jobs – over the window with a grubby rag.

'Clear off.' Friendless waved his whip menacingly.

'Give me a chance, pal,' the boy entreated.

'Where are you from?' I enquired because that was certainly not an East Anglian accent.

'Guildford.'

'Ruddy foreigners,' Friendless spat, 'comin' here stealin' our...'

'How fast can you run?' I asked the boy.

'Faster than any copper,' he boasted.

'Jobs and...' Friendless attempted to continue but even he realised that nobody was interested.

'Well you had better scarper,' I told him, and he looked over his shoulder edgily. 'After you have given that gentleman a bath.'

I tried to toss him a florin, but the coin had plans of its own and flew high over his head and plopped into his bucket.

'You mean...?' The boy delved to retrieve it, undismayed by the state of his sleeve when it emerged, and I nodded.

'That is exactly what I mean.'

He grinned and crossed over to the adjacent cab.

'Clean your cab for a tanner,' he called.

'Tan your hide for free,' the other cabby threatened.

'Wish I think on that,' Friendless sighed and the boy stepped forward.

'Give me a ch...' he began and tripped over his own feet.

Dan Leno, the music-hall comedian, would have been envious of that boy's sense of timing. The diluted manure shot out of his bucket so forcefully that it knocked the passenger's no-longer-well-brushed hat sideways, soaking his face, his primped-up moustaches collapsing into curdled droops.

'You...' the man gasped, but the boy had not boasted in vain for he was off like a greyhound, dodging through the traffic to disappear behind a soap-seller's cart. The man mopped his face with an already sodden handkerchief. 'You told him to do that,' he accused me.

'Did I?' I wafted the stink of him away with my hand.

'Look at me,' he raged. 'I'm absolutely filthy.'

'If it is any consolation,' I told him. 'You were absolutely filthy before you got wet.'

Good for you, Ruby cheered admiringly, *though aqua fortis would have been more dramatic.*

I forgot to pack any nitric acid, I told her.

Silly you, she tutted, her admiration brief as ever.

Oblivious to our conversation, the man was half-rising in his seat.

'You ruggy sow!' he cursed.

'Show some respect for my passenger,' Friendless warned, 'or I do learn you some manner.'

But not any grammar, I thought.

'You threat'nin' to whip my passenger?' the other cabby demanded.

'I'm surprised you have to ask that,' Friendless reflected in all seriousness, 'but yes I am,' he admitted unwisely, I judged, because his colleague was a big man with a face that showed he'd had a few scraps in his time, whereas Friendless could have shadow-boxed and lost before leaving his own corner.

'Be my guest,' his colleague grinned and pulled open the catch for the flaps. 'Out,' he called through his hatch.

'What?' the bedraggled gentleman gasped.

'Can't have you in my cab stinkin' like tha',' the driver told him. 'Hop it.'

I would have loved to have stayed and seen the outcome of that confrontation, but we were on the move again and the rest of our journey was disappointingly uneventful.

'I may be some time,' I told Friendless when we had halted.

'A second do be some time,' he informed me. 'So do be a year or more.'

'Somewhere in between those,' I replied.

'So long as I know.' He folded his arms, completely satisfied.

Gainsborough Gardens bustled with children playing, half-watched by resentful nannies gossiping in the shade of a sycamore. A few adults strolled about, some arm-in-arm, one couple clearly at odds with each other.

'It is all your fault,' I heard him insist as they passed.

Well it would be, Ruby snapped.

'Well it would be,' the lady snapped, and not for the first time I wondered if other people could hear our dialogue.

Of course we can, I thought the man told me before I realised that it was Inspector Hefty trying to be funny. He never did have much of a sense of humour. *That's because you never gave me one*, he retorted with justification.

There was a bench at the side of the path a few yards in and, by sitting on that and twisting to my right, I was enabled to get a reasonable line of vision to the front of Haglin House. I took out my opera glasses. They were an improvement on the naked eye but not as powerful as I had remembered from my last visit to Morley's Music Hall.

There was no sign of any activity inside or out of Haglin House as I scanned it.

'What is it today?' Before I had even turned I knew the voice of Anthony Appleton. 'A sabre-toothed wasp?'

He was in a fuchsia blazer with mustard waistcoat and trousers and his boater had a bright pink ribbon, but I refrained from enquiring if his tailor worked in the dark.

'Do you live in these gardens?' I asked instead.

'Yes,' he said simply. 'Well not under a bush, but in the top floor of Petunia Villa.'

He waved his yellow cane – from where on earth had he got that? – to the opposite side.

'Well, Mr Appleton, I am looking for an Egyptian nightjar.'

'Sounds like a cosmetic cream,' he commented and I peered through my glasses again, but Haglin House was still quiet. 'Please call me Anthony.'

'Not Tony?'

'Certainly not,' he bridled. 'I am not a digit and a joint.'

Toe-knee, Ruby explained to a puzzled Hefty.

'Matilda, the maid is out,' Anthony told me, 'and will not be back until this evening.'

'How do you know that?'

He tipped his hat with the handle of his cane rakishly to the side.

'I come here most mornings for my constitutional,' he told me. 'Rather generously the Poynders give their servants a half-day off every week, and this is hers.'

'Where does she go?'

'Pretty as she is…' Anthony, realising that he had gone too far, corrected the angle of his hat to slightly less rakishly sideways. 'I do not follow her.' He allowed himself the hint of a smile. 'Well not far at any rate. Wormwood, the manservant is also out, by the way and, from the carriage-clock-shaped parcel under his arm, I would say he is going to Huskin's to have it repaired and…' He pulled out his half-hunter and glanced at it. 'Since they do not reopen for another forty-three minutes, he will not return for at least an hour.'

If he is after my job, Ruby said sourly, *he is welcome to it and we shall see how readily he wriggles out of his coffin.*

'Have any other visitors called while you were doing my job more efficiently than I have been?' I asked, returning to my surveillance.

'Not one,' he said simply. 'Unless you count the coalman whose horse bit the ear of a child in a sailor suit, but that was half an hour before you arrived.'

'You have a great deal of time for leisure,' I remarked, and he sniffed loudly.

'I am working,' he protested. 'Peter Stimpson is a leisured gentleman and I am accustoming myself to the role.'

'I trust you are not accustoming yourself to his homicidal deeds.'

A gigantic bird of prey swooped towards me and I almost ducked into the shrubbery before I remembered that I was looking through glasses and realised that it was a mistle thrush.

'The chemist was out of strychnine,' he told me sadly.

The man is hopeless, Ruby scoffed. *I extracted my own from Saint-Ignatius' bean.*

Purchased from the local greengrocer? Hefty proved that he could also scoff and that my talking-to had done no good whatsoever.

'Well I must not detain you,' I told the man who could not even extract the simplest though deadliest of poisons.

'Oh but you must,' he assured me, unabashed by his failure.

'Good day, Mr Appleton.'

I slipped the glasses back into their brown leather case and dropped them into my bag.

'Anthony,' he reminded me as I set off.

My mother, my maid and almost every respectable lady I had come across would have been appalled by my forwardness with a stranger and, when I lived at Thetbury Hall, I would have disapproved of such behaviour myself, but there was a general feeling that we were heading towards a new and less formal age. Perhaps I was jumping the gun, but nobody – except Agnust, of course – had scolded me for apprehending a burglar at Thetbury Hall and detaining him with conversation before we had been properly introduced.

26: HETEROCHROMIA AND THE SCARLET WOMAN

I RANG THE bell, hoping that Anthony was right and that Matilda had not returned without him noticing. It was a different girl who answered my summons – a kitchen maid to judge by the stains on her dress beneath the clean apron she was still trying to tie at the back.

'I have an appointment to see Mrs Poynder,' I stated.

'She int home,' the girl said.

Tell her again.

I am going to.

Then do so.

'I have an appointment,' I repeated firmly, and the maid dropped an apron string.

You are learning, Ruby conceded, *albeit at a pace that would make a garden snail resemble a cheetah.*

Not a simile that bears analysis, I criticised and, before she could make a pun about bruins that we would both regret, the maid scratched her neck and said, 'Um.'

'I had better come in,' I decided for her and took a step forward.

'You do best come in,' the maid translated my statement into Suffolkese and stepped back.

Haglin House was an even more impressive *gaff* inside than out. The hallway was a broad rectangle stretching the length of the house to a glass-panelled door, through which I glimpsed a rose arch and, beyond that, a birch tree with bark that simply implored the younger Violet to peel it off for making into pretend paper.

Did you notice the lock? Ruby whispered. *It's a night latch – much easier for you to force than a deadlock.*

I am not going to break in, I assured her over Hefty's spluttered remonstrations about criminal offences.

I would, she asserted and he reached for his notebook.

The maid set off and, not having been instructed to the contrary, I followed but then she remembered.

'You best wait here,' she told me and so I did.

The walls were plastered in a marble effect and separated from the stucco panelled ceiling by a wide cornice decorated in blocks of fern leaves. The floor was tiled in polished limestone, nice and slippery when washed, I imagined. To the right was a wide, gradually rising staircase with a light green runner, the bannisters and rails painted white. The whole effect was light, spacious and uncluttered with not a painting nor an aspidistra to be seen. The hall table was slender and the umbrella stand made of light wood slats rather than the all-too-popular amputated elephant's foot.

There was one door to my right before the stairs and there were three to the left before the hall branched to either side. The maid disappeared through the second door, leaving it open as she announced, 'There's a lady to see the mistress, sir.'

'I have told you that Mrs Poynder is not at home,' a man said, and I hoped that I had not got her into trouble.

'But she do have a n'appointment,' the maid explained and the man huffed.

'What is her name?'

'Dint know, sir. I forget to ask.'

He huffed again.

'Go back to your work, Susie.'

'I'm sorry, sir.'

'It is all right,' he said to my, and doubtless her, relief and Susie came out, scurrying down the corridor to disappear behind the stairs without even a reproachful glance in my direction.

A moment later Edward Poynder appeared, rather formally dressed in a mid-grey morning coat buttoned up with dark grey trousers and a light grey waistcoat, all matching slightly greying neat black hair, brushed back and oiled into a parting. His soft grey eyes peered over gold wire-framed half-lensed spectacles. He had not been wearing those outside the church.

I suspect you will find they are called 'reading glasses', Ruby said.

'Can I help you?' he enquired amiably enough, considering that I had tricked my way into his home.

Presumably he realised from my attire that I was not going to try to sell him anything.

'Good afternoon.' I held out my card. 'I am calling upon Mrs Poynder.'

He glanced at the wording and his brows rose. If it is true that the English love a lord, they extend almost as much affection to a lady. If Sir Glynn had not swapped sides at the last minute in the battle of Brandon Ford he would not have been given the Thetbury Estate and I would be plain Miss Thorn, forced to earn an honest living or to entrap a man of means in unholy matri-money.

'I am afraid my wife is not at home, Lady Violet,' he told me, 'but my maid said that you had an appointment.'

'I fear I must have confused her,' I lied. 'I told her that, if your wife could not see me, I wished to make an appointment.'

He eyed me quizzically.

'Might I ask why?'

'I met Mrs Poynder some time ago,' I said, keeping it as vague as possible, 'and she expressed an interest in joining a committee to help orphaned babies.'

'Is that not the job of the foundling hospital?'

'It is indeed,' I agreed, 'and they do an excellent job, but we believe that children are best placed in families rather than an institution and so our aim is to encourage people to give them homes.'

'A worthy cause,' he concurred. 'Well I must not keep you, Lady Violet.'

'Perhaps I could call tomorrow,' I suggested.

'I shall see that my wife gets your card,' he told me firmly, as polite a way of saying *clear off and don't come back* as I had heard in a while.

'I am sorry to have disturbed you.'

I smiled to show him that I was not really and was about to turn when he declared, 'Heterochromia iridium,' and put up a hand. He had long, unusually thick fingers, smooth and well-manicured. 'Forgive me,' he said. 'I was thinking aloud – a bad habit. I was referring to your...'

'Eyes,' I broke in.

'That's right,' he agreed, mildly impressed by my not-exactly encyclopaedic medical knowledge. 'Differently pigmented irises are common enough in some mammals such as cats but quite uncommon in humans.' He waved his hand, stained blue-black.

Iodine, Hefty diagnosed rather obviously.

'I'm sorry. I should explain.'

'Mrs Poynder told me that you are a doctor.'

'I am,' he concurred and fished out his hunter by its silver chain. 'I have a clinic for which I must leave in twenty minutes and, by the time Susie could manage to organise tea, I would be seeing my first patient. It takes her half an hour to come up from her bed in the mornings. Would you care for a sherry?'

I would not especially for it makes me sleepy during the day, but I told him that that would lovely and he ushered me through into a large, sunlit study overlooking the gardens across the road. Having settled me into a high-backed leather armchair, Dr Poynder unstoppered a decanter, the silver tag swinging on its chain as he poured.

'Do you have any particular medical interests?' I chatted, as everybody likes to talk about themselves.

'In a country town like Montford a doctor has to fulfil many roles.' He restoppered the decanter. 'I am primarily a physician, but I perform minor surgical procedures here and slightly less simple ones in the infirmary.' He turned towards me. 'For any major operations I call in a specialist.'

'Dr Cronshaw?'

'You know him?'

'I know of him. My second cousin, Dr Romulus Thorn, has worked with him.'

'Dr Thorn.' Poynder nodded approvingly. 'We have met twice I believe. He attended my lecture on new techniques in anaesthesia and I his on diphtheria.'

We Thorns had good reason to take an interest in that illness.

A furniture van trundled by with the reassuring slogan painted fairly neatly along the side. We Will Not Break Your Furniture, Smash Your Ordaments or Steal Your Valubuls.

'I do not recall my wife speaking of you.' Dr Poynder was not as easily distracted as I had hoped.

'She may not even recollect me,' I admitted as he placed the two drinks on the table between us. 'We only met once when I attended a mass at St Etheldreda's. I handed out leaflets about our society and she expressed an interest. I promised to call and tell her more.'

It occurred to me that Edward Poynder might ask for further details, which would force me to improvise – rarely a good idea – but he settled in a chair facing mine and said, 'Dolores will be sorry that she has missed you, but I am not.' He half-smiled. 'She is involved in far too many charitable causes already and I subscribe to the unoriginal belief that charity begins at home.'

I generally find that, for people who quote that biblical misquotation, charity does not begin at all but I only said, 'That is as may be but surely it does not end there?'

'In my wife's case it certainly does not.'

There was a lightness in his manner that rather threw me off balance. The man I had seen coming out of church was grim-faced and I had expected him to be forbidding, if not downright sinister, but Edward Poynder did not strike me at all as a modern Mr Rochester, keeping his mad wife in the attic. Far from avoiding the subject, he spoke of Dolores easily and, it seemed to me, affectionately.

We sipped our drinks. I do not know much about sherry but it was dark and left a rich warmth on my tongue.

'I was interested in your eyes,' he told me, 'because I read a paper a few months ago by a Dr Hirschsprung, linking Hetero-chromia to other conditions, the nature of which I shall not be so indelicate as to describe.'

I knew that he was referring to bowel problems because Romulus had told me but, fortunately, I was not afflicted by them.

'Unless you are referring to arrested growth,' I said, 'my general health is good.'

'I am glad to hear it.' He took another sip. 'It is thought that Heterochromia may be inherited. Might I ask if any other members of your family have the same condition?'

'They do not,' I told him. 'Nor are any of the others of such a short stature.'

I smiled nicely.

Grinned like a Cheshire cat, Ruby corrected me.

'Does that mean that I have been adopted?' I enquired and Poynder smiled.

Now that was a nice smile, Ruby declared, *and not remotely feline.*

'It does not.'

'I thought it might explain my interest in orphans,' I said, though I had thought no such thing at all, and he chuckled.

'If our interests were hereditary I would be out now chasing foxes,' he told me. 'From November to April you will hardly find my parents out of the saddle during the hours of daylight, but I detest the practice. It is glorified rat-baiting for the gentry.'

I laughed. This was probably not a good time to boast about my experiences with that pursuit.

'They would find a kindred spirit in my father,' I said, 'but my mother and I are more in accord with your way of thinking.'

Neither of my parents went with the hounds. My mother could not ride since she had an accident and my father preferred to shoot God's creatures. Countless birds, rabbits and hares and a good many deer filled the pages of his game diaries before some of them reached our plates.

'Your wife told me you do good work for the poor,' I recalled from Martha's dismissive remarks.

'If I do not nobody else will,' he said modestly.

'Are you not afraid to go into Lower Montford?' I had been, even with Gerrund to protect me.

Dr Poynder puffed his cheeks.

'I was the first time,' he admitted. 'If truth be told I was terrified, but a man had been stabbed and could not be moved. It transpired that he was an associate of a Mr Gervey. I do not know if you have heard of the gentleman in question.'

'I have,' I confirmed, 'though I am not sure that the term *gentleman* applies to him.'

Poynder sniffed in mild amusement.

'I was able to help the man and, as a token of his gratitude, Mr Gervey gave me his guarantee of safe passage.' He rubbed the back of his neck ruefully. 'But, having treated a few of those who find themselves on the wrong side of him, I use it as infrequently as possible.'

'Few would use it at all,' I observed for dear Anton's word was not known for being his bond.

Poynder took out his watch again. It was a full hunter and bulkier than most modern examples and so possibly a twenty-first birthday present from his vermin-stalking father.

'I am sorry,' he said, rising to tug the bell pull, 'but I really must go.'

I drained my sherry and rose.

'It is I who should apologise for delaying you,' I assured him and he followed me to the hall.

'I would offer you a lift,' he said, 'but I take it you came by carriage.'

'By hansom, thank you.'

This was missing an opportunity to converse with him more, but I could hardly claim to have walked from Break House.

'I did not see one through my study window,' he said. 'I hope your driver has not deserted you.'

'He has just taken his horse to the water trough,' I said and held up my charm bracelet to reveal the silver whistle.

'Does it work?' he asked in surprise.

'Oh yes,' I assured him. 'I just put it to my lips and blow.'

I demonstrated softly, for it had a piecing sound at full breath, and his eyes crinkled in amusement, if not something else. A man does not have to be a physician to know when a woman is flirting. Agnust would have tried, but failed, to send me to bed with no supper for such outrageously lewd behaviour, but a woman does not have to be scarlet to know the power that she can wield over a man with a look, a word or a whistle.

27: *DIABOLO AND THE GROWLER*

ONCE OUTSIDE, EDWARD Poynder shook my hand. His grip was firm and his gaze direct.

'It was a pleasure to meet you, Lady Violet,' he said and I felt fairly confident that he meant it.

'And you,' I told him.

'Shall I stay with you until your cab comes?'

'There is no need thank you,' I assured him. 'I shall take the air in the gardens first.'

'And he will keep waiting for you?' Poynder asked in surprise.

'He knows that I shall reward him,' I said and he raised an impressed eyebrow.

Why was only one of his eyebrows impressed? Ruby wondered. *Was the other one more jaded?*

'Well I shall bid you a good day.' The doctor swung easily into the waiting hansom, settled back and was gone, giving a slight tip to his black silk hat with the silver head of his ebony cane.

I crossed the road and had not even gone through the gate when I saw her.

'Is that who you are looking for?' Anthony Appleton asked, after I had ignored his proffered hand.

He jerked his head in the direction of Haglin House and I followed his gaze.

There was definitely somebody in that top left-hand window again. I opened my handbag for my opera glasses.

'Take these.' He unclipped his case and produced a pair of binoculars. 'I'll wager you could hardly see the soprano's face with your toy, but you could inspect her tonsils and the wiggly thing in between with these.' He held them out. 'You turn the wheel to focus and…'

'I do know how to use them.'

'I was only going to explain which end to look through,' he protested, 'and that you have to point them at your object of interest.'

'Thank you.' I took them from him. 'I did not know any of that. Do I need to keep my eyelids separated?'

'It might be best to.'

Hurriedly I adjusted the focus and the blurry blob that had attracted Anthony's attention sprang out at me.

'That is her,' I breathed.

'Mrs Poynder?' he asked.

She was standing, looking out, her hair still hanging loose over half her face.

'How did you know that?'

'You do not have to be an Extraordinary Investigator to find out who lives on your road,' he told me.

'I suppose not,' I conceded and, as I watched, Dolores Poynder stiffened.

At first I thought that she had spotted me, but her head was turned to her right and I lowered the glasses to see a sailor-suited boy trotting along the opposite pavement followed by a young nanny carrying a picnic basket. He held two sticks with a string between them and was tossing an hour-glass-shaped bobbin high in the air to catch it again on the string.

'It's called a diabolo,' Anthony explained.

'Do you like being annoying?' I asked, going back to Dolores.

'I do rather. It was my main motive for taking up the trumpet.'

'Your neighbours must love you.'

'I fear they believe themselves to be under no such obligation.'

She was rapping on the windowpane and the nanny glanced up. Dolores waved and at that moment the boy, who had been doing quite well, missed his bobbin. It bounced off the kerb and rolled into the road and I heard him howl from thirty yards away, even above the racket of a growler rumbling by. The nanny waited for it to pass and dashed out to retrieve the toy, just managing to skip away from a lady riding side-saddle who showed no inclination to rein in her chestnut stallion or change direction. The nanny stuffed the bobbin into her basket, and I hastily lowered the binoculars as they crossed the road towards the entrance and us.

'I'm sure it was a fan-tailed red finch,' Anthony said loudly. 'You can tell by the green plumage.'

But the nanny was too busy telling the boy to stop snivelling and that no, he could not have his toy back until they were away from the road.

I trained the binoculars back at the window just in time to see Dolores moving away. It seemed a sudden movement. Was she stepping back hurriedly or had she been pulled?

'Why would a red finch have green plumage?' I challenged Anthony.

There was no sign of anyone at any of the windows now.

'That's what makes it so rare,' he said. 'The first to be spotted in these parts for one hundred and thirty-two years.'

'I feel privileged,' I said and returned his glasses.

'Do you want me to keep an eye on the place?'

Do not trust him, Ruby warned. *He is too cheerful and... hand-some.*

He is hardly a Greek god, Hefty mumbled.

While you are more like a Greek dog, Ruby told him.

'No thank you.' I spoke over them.

I would have liked it very much, but this was supposed to be a discreet enquiry.

'I shall anyway,' Anthony promised. 'I have a good view from my sitting room.'

And I have seen prettier sea slugs than you, Hefty retorted and Ruby laughed contemptuously.

I had no idea your tastes were so exotic.

Stop this minute! I scolded, glad that Friendless was not there to explain that you cannot stop minutes. *Or I shall maroon you together on a desert island.*

That should silence them for the time being, I told myself, but Ruby only said, *Buck up, Thorn*, and I realised that a hand was waving like a metronome in front of my face.

'Excuse me but is Lady Violet at home?' Appleton was enquiring and I jerked my head towards him.

'I am sorry.' I shut the door on Ruby and Hefty before anybody else could hear their bickering.

'You've been a long way away.'

'Yes.'

'Thank you for coming back to me.'

A strange thing to say, I thought, after such a brief encounter.

'You are interested in ornithology?' I raised the binoculars questioningly.

'My interest in birds begins and ends with what they taste like and when they are in season.'

'Then why...'

'I am nosey,' he responded. 'I could help it but I don't want to.'

I laughed.

'Thank you for letting me use them.'

I handed his glasses back.

'Did you see what you hoped to?'

'No,' I replied, 'but I might have seen what I feared.'

Never fear, Ruby advised me, *unless there is something of which to be afraid*.

As usual, though, her counsel was no better than my own.

28: STEAMERS, CHIMERAS AND THE SNIPER

MARTHA CAME THAT evening. She was dressed simply in a plain white cotton skirt, with a black bow tie and belt, grey shirt and short black jacket with mutton-chop sleeves. Her hair was tied up under a black-ribboned boater. Despite the heat, her admittedly short cab ride and her ascent of four flights of stairs she looked fresher than I felt.

I had had a shower when I got home and changed, though it had not been as refreshing as I had hoped. The supposed-to-be-cold water was not.

'I am sorry to make you climb all those stairs,' I said after we had kissed in greeting, 'but I thought that we would be more comfortable. The house is stifling and there is at least a breeze up here.'

'This is lovely.' Martha looked around my octagonal observatory. All four French doors were propped open wide as were the four windows, and the shades were down and under the domed roof. 'What a wonderful view you have.'

The previous tenant of Break House had been Framling Deakon, the astronomer who had built the observatory. His great claim to fame was his discovery of another planet in our solar system that he had modestly named Deakonus, and his descriptions of its movements might have brought him everlasting fame had it not disappeared the moment he had polished the mirror in his telescope.

'It is the glory of this house,' I said. 'There were more spacious properties with bigger gardens but none of them had this. At night I have the heavens.' I pointed to the telescope still set up on its tripod. 'And in the day I can spy on people in the square and gardens with little chance of being seen.'

I was trying to learn to interpret what people were saying but without much success. It disappointed me how little most of my subjects moved their lips when they spoke and how many men hid their mouths behind their facial foliage.

'I am having iced ginger beer,' I told her. 'Would you care for a glass?'

'I would pay a guinea for one,' she vowed.

Hold her to that, Ruby advised while I opened the insulated box.

'Where on earth do you find ice in this weather?' Martha enquired, unpinning her hat.

'My parents have an icehouse in our Norfolk home,' I explained. 'They sewed a block in canvas, wrapped it in several layers of wool, crated it and sent it in a shaded carriage to me. I think they lost about half of it on the journey but there is a deep well – dry at this time of year – under my cellar so I had it put in there. Gerrund descends by a rope ladder and chops a chunk off when we need it.'

I suspected that he spent a great deal longer down there than was necessary and helped himself to a few chippings, but I could not begrudge him those.

I poured Martha a tall glass and she pressed it to her brow, clearly not as cool as she looked.

'Oh this is heaven,' she breathed after her first drink. 'If your house is broken into do not be surprised to find me with a block and tackle.'

'If the well were big enough I would put my bed in it,' I said.

Except that you do not like cellars, Ruby reminded me. *Or winkles. Or oxtail soup*, Hefty contributed.

We sat in two steamers side by side, enjoying the flow of air.

'Have you any news?' Martha asked, fanning herself with her boater, and I wondered why she did not take off her jacket for I was not wearing one.

'I went to Haglin House today,' I announced, omitting to mention my first experience as illustrating my incompetent approach too clearly, 'and spoke to Dr Poynder.'

She sat up.

'Edward let you in?' she asked in surprise.

'Matilda was out, but Susie the kitchen maid did. She said that her mistress was not at home, but I misled her into admitting me.'

'I wager Edward was thrilled.'

'He was very civil,' I told her, 'and gave me a sherry.'

Martha gaped.

'Are you sure you went to the right house?'

'Quite sure. I pretended that I was hoping to recruit his wife for a charitable committee,' I said, 'but he said she did quite enough of that already.'

'She does do a lot of good work,' Martha confirmed. 'Or at least she did.'

'We chatted about my eyes and he left for work.'

Martha sipped her ginger beer.

'So you did not find out anything?'

Her disappointment in me was obvious.

'I went into the gardens afterwards,' I continued, though I could see she was hardly listening. 'And from there I saw Dolores – at a window on the second floor.'

'How could you be sure it was her at that distance?'

'I had a pair of binoculars.'

I note you have not told her that you had to borrow them, Ruby remarked.

At least I did not steal them, like you did that theodolite.

You cannot steal a stolen item.

Martha put her drink on the low table between us.

'But that is the servants' quarters. What would she be doing up there?'

'I do not know,' I said. 'But at least we know that she is still living...'

Martha jumped.

'You had reason to think she might not be?'

Something caught my eye – a movement where I would not have expected to see any.

A pigeon, Inspector Hefty suggested and, not for the first time, I considered giving him a pair of spectacles.

'Not at all,' I hastened to reassure her. 'I meant that she is still living there.'

Or a cat, he added, strengthening my resolve.

There was a man on the roof of the Splendid Hotel, though I could only see his head and shoulders. I did not know the height of the parapet but, assuming it was in the region of the usual three feet, he appeared to be crouching.

'Did she look well?'

'She looked tired,' I replied tactfully, leaned forward and shaded my eyes with my hand.

It was difficult to be sure at that distance, but it looked like the man was training a rifle on the people below and, as I watched, he swung it slowly around and up to point it directly at me.

I jumped to my feet.

'What is it?' Martha asked.

'Go to the cabinet,' I said and she eyed me in bemusement.

'I beg your...'

'Now,' I insisted, pulling down a roller blind and Martha's face tightened but she did as she was told.

She would be out of sight of the marksman there, if that was what he was. I rushed to the telescope and swung it round towards the doorway. The focus was set for Venus and I cranked the wheel furiously as far as it would go before peering through the eyepiece. The sun was to my left so it was not difficult to avoid. Romulus had warned me of a case where a man had blinded himself in one eye in a foolish attempt to view an eclipse.

'What is it?' Martha asked.

'I am not sure.'

The only thing I was certain of was that I hoped I was wrong because I was in full view of whoever was lurking on that rooftop.

The tower of Saint Aegbald's church got in the way and then a weathervane shaped like a Suffolk Punch carthorse. That must be the roof of the Capricorn Brewery in Canticle Square. I skimmed anticlockwise and down past its tall chimney to the side of the Splendid Hotel then more slowly up to the stone topping.

'What are you looking for?'

'A man,' I replied brusquely, trying to concentrate on the task.

I have yet to find one worth finding, Ruby quipped.

Where was he? I adjusted the fine focus. The object of my attention was standing with his back to me. There was something familiar about that slightly tousled hair, ruffling in the light wind for lack of macassar oil, and a glimpse of the strawberry birthmark peeking out above his collar confirmed my identification. The rifle, I saw clearly now, was a walking cane and Inspector Stanbury had it casually over his shoulder as he strolled towards the water tank and the brick room beneath it that must be the top of the stairs. He walked around it and disappeared.

I swung my telescope back towards the apex of my observatory.

'I am sorry,' I said. 'There was a man on the hotel roof.'

'Probably a workman,' she speculated, returning to her chair, the ice almost melted in her ginger beer. 'I know they had some trouble with leaks last winter.'

'Probably,' I agreed for there was no point in scaring her.

'But, why did it alarm you so?'

Tell her you have the plans for a secret submarine that the Germans are trying to steal, Ruby suggested.

That is a ridiculous idea.

You made me say it in Death in the Deep, she reminded me.

'I am sorry,' I waved a hand wearily. 'I have been working too hard on my next Ruby Gibson story.' I finished my drink. 'And it can be difficult coming back into the real world.'

Real world! Ruby echoed resentfully. *Excuse me, Lady Violetta Thorn, but my world is as real to me as yours is to you and, in case you have forgotten, I am in imminent danger of quitting it.*

'I wish I had your imagination,' Martha said, but I doubted that she would enjoy it at two o'clock in the morning when the chimeras who lurk in the recesses during the day come out, more sinister than I would ever be allowed to put in the pages of a book.

'Anyone could write that twaddle,' I murmured automatically, ignoring Ruby and Hefty's protestations. At least, if nothing else, they were united in their indignation.

Also at least, Martha had not spoiled the evening air with one of her elegant but foul stinking sticks, I reflected as a box of Little Queens appeared almost magically in her hand.

–

Alone with my characters and my absinthe that night, I thought over the tumultuous events of the last few days.

Most shocking to me was the murder that took place in front of my house. Who would want to kill that destitute woman? She could have nothing worth stealing and would Anton Gervey really be so openly contemptuous of the law as to perform such a public execution?

What is the point in having the privilege of knowing an Extraordinary Investigator if you do not call upon her for assistance? Ruby asked tetchily, all too aware that she would have to return to her fire-licked coffin soon.

Do you have any theories?

Not quite yet, she confessed, *but it would have been civil to have asked.*

Women, Havelock Hefty said dismissively, thereby offending both his creator and his greatest rival for my attention. *I have a theory. What if the beggar woman had stolen a Beryl Coronet, which had to be retrieved to avoid a national scandal?*

An interesting idea though not an original one, I told Scotland Yard's premier detective mildly, for I knew that he was trying to be of help.

What if, he tried again, *the beggar woman were sorting through a rubbish bin and came across a secret document and she was killed to retrieve it?*

I gave you that plot in The Dustheap of Death, I said a little impatiently.

Or to silence her, Ruby suggested, which was a possibility, though none of us could explain what she might have known or why she was executed so publicly.

What do you make of Dolores's letter to Martha? I asked, opening one tap a fraction to release my green fairy in a steady trickle.

A forgery, Hefty suggested, *though an extremely clumsy one.*

Let us assume that Mrs Poynder penned it, I proposed. *How did she get it delivered?*

Matilda, Ruby suggested.

Ladies' maids are accustomed to passing on secret messages, Hefty argued. *She would not allow her mistress's correspondence to fall into such a singularly poor condition.*

The kitchen maid? I suggested.

Would have no access to her mistress in the attic, he stated. *She sleeps below stairs.*

And how would you know that? Ruby challenged him.

Dr Poynder talked about her coming up from her bed in the mornings, he explained.

Which only leaves Wormwood, I summed up. *It would be simplicity itself for him to smuggle out the letter but there again, he would take better care of it.*

Perhaps Mrs Poynder screwed up the letter and threw it away, but one of the staff found it and thought it should reach its intended recipient, Hefty postulated.

He or she would risk incurring the wrath of both her master and mistress if she were caught, I countered.

What did you make of Dr Poynder? I asked Ruby as the last of the sugar cube dissolved and the last few drops fell.

A charming man, affable and not in the least part threatening, she replied, somewhat to my surprise for she was habitually harsh in her assessment of members of the male sex.

Why then, I puzzled, *did his wife look so frightened of him when I saw them coming out of the church together?*

In my experience it does not take much to frighten a woman, Hefty asserted and tried to look as if he had not flinched when Ruby said, *Boo.*

I poured my drink into a torsade lead crystal glass. It was one of a set of six, a present from Jack from our trip to Paris with his almost blind, very-nearly deaf Great Aunt Hecuba as our chaperone. We had dined by candlelight on the left bank of the Seine and sailed it by moonlight. He had fought off a gang of ruffians with his cane when we had ventured down the streets of Montmartre late one evening. He had made a policeman apologise for looking at me insultingly. And in the Temple of Love he had sworn his eternal devotion and asked me to be his wife, but I was not so easily won. I made him wait until he had finished speaking before I said, 'Yes. Yes please.'

For the thousandth time I took his letter out of my writing box and stared at the words.

'It was not for you to decide that you were unworthy,' I told him, though he could never hear my words.

With all my heart, your ever-loving Jack, I read yet again and, as always, in disbelief.

Burn it, Ruby urged.

I will, I promised, *the very moment that you throw Prince Rudolph's signet ring into the sea.*

Prince who? She puzzled and I remembered that I had not written that story yet.

'Forgive me,' I read aloud and, though the words never changed, I still could not believe them.

Strange, Hefty commented as he bowed his head to inspect the signature through his magnifying glass. *It smells of scallions.*

The whole thing stinks, Ruby seethed.

I took a large drink and let the sweet bitterness, cold in my mouth but hot in my throat, flow through my body before I refolded the letter and put it away.

29: DEATH IN ARGENTINA

CONSTABLE CANNING WAS installed behind the desk in an otherwise unoccupied lobby when I returned to Montford police station. He was a young man but did not look it, with his sallow complexion and his hair in its death throes.

'If you want the inspector he goo out on a case,' he told me in the same monotone children adopt to recite their tables.

'Where is he if I do not want him?' I quipped to his confusion.

'Out on a...'

'When will he be back?' I interrupted before our conversation could circumnavigate the world.

'Amara,' he said, which I translated as *tomorrow*.

'Well he will be furious when he does return,' I warned and the constable smirked.

'Why? Do you be a nowtery mawther?'

A naughty girl, Ruby interpreted for me, though I had taught her all the Suffolk dialect that she knew.

'I was more concerned with the man who is in Inspector Stanbury's office smoking his cigars,' I explained and set off down the corridor.

'You can't goo there,' Canning called after me.

'John Hanning Speke...' I began.

'I dint hear no one say nothin'.'

'John Hanning Speke,' I began again, careful not to pause for breath, 'was told he could not go there when he set off to discover the source,' I took the last part at a rush before he could ask me which condiment I meant, 'of-the-Nile.'

'Dint know where he goo...' Canning stood up, 'but he dint goo up tha' corriodor.' He lifted the flap to come out after me. 'Least not when I'm on dooty.'

'Good morning, Inspector Stanbury,' I called and, before the constable could collar me, his superior appeared in the doorway of his office.

'Good morning, Lady Violet,' he greeted me as his man caught up. 'It is all right, thank you, Constable. I think I can deal with her.'

''Bout time somebody do,' Canning muttered and strode back towards his desk.

'I overheard your deduction,' the inspector told me. 'We'll make a detective of you yet.'

'I am not convinced that East Anglia is ready for a woman police officer,' I said. 'They are still reeling from discovering that some doctors wear dresses and I am not talking about one of Phillis Fishnet's parties.'

'Come through,' Alfred Stanbury chuckled and I went into his office. His coat hung on a hook on the wall and his sleeves were rolled up almost to his elbows, though his collar was still buttoned up fully and his tie fairly neatly knotted. 'I told Canning I was not to be disturbed but it isn't you I'm hiding from.'

'Who then?' He did not strike me as a timid man.

'The general,' he told me, 'public. I have a fraud case to deal with and I need time to decipher the accountant's report undisturbed.'

He tapped an open ledger in front of him, the page crammed with dozens of columns of near-microscopic figures.

'I can come back another day,' I offered, but he waved me into a chair.

'I nearly came to see you last night, but I had promised my wife I'd be home in time to see if I could recognise any of our children.'

'And could you?'

He puffed on his cigar.

'Two out of four isn't bad,' he asserted – jokingly, I hoped.

'I saw you,' I told him, 'on the roof of the Splendid.'

'I thought I spotted you,' he said. 'At least I hoped it was you because it looked like there was a Gatling aimed straight at me.'

'That was my telescope and I thought you had a rifle,' I said. 'Did you discover anything up there?'

'Not much,' he admitted, 'except what I knew already – that there is an excellent view of Seraphim Square – but I didn't find any cartridges or footprints, not that I'd expect to in this weather. There's never any mud or snow when you need it.'

He blew a chain of smoke rings.

'Is it worth looking for the traces that fingers leave?' I had read something about a murderess in Argentina who had been caught after her thumbmark was discovered on a door.

The word you are looking for is fingerprints, Ruby told me loftily but too late for me to insert it into my question, and Alfred Stanbury snorted.

'There may be experts in such things down London way, but I've never heard of them catching anyone.'

I almost suggested that they contact Scotland Yard, but the wounds had hardly stopped bleeding from the *East Anglian Gazette*'s trumpeted *Clodhopper Constabulary Calls in Professional Police Force* eighteen months ago.

'I do not think we have had an assassination in the county since your ancestor was killed by a crossbow bolt.' Stanbury rolled his cigar between his fingers and thumb. 'And that was five hundred years ago.'

'And still unsolved.'

'Until a witness comes forward,' he agreed. 'Luckily it's not my case.'

'There was something else I wanted to discuss with you,' I began and he leaned forward.

'Oh yes?'

'I came to you because I know that I can rely on your discretion.'

'You can,' he agreed amiably and leaned back again, the legs of his chair creaking. 'Unless you wish me to hide a crime, in which case I would be obliged...' Stanbury's mouth twitched, 'to demand a very large bribe.'

I smiled. It was not for nothing that the inspector had been dubbed *Saint Stan*, though not always affectionately, by his colleagues.

'I can offer you a stick of Beeman's,' I said, and he put up his hands in refusal.

'I'm sure you've not forgotten it's an offence to threaten a police officer.' Like almost everybody else, he had not enjoyed the sample I had given him.

I made a resolution to stock up on even more supplies. It was unlikely that the fad for chewing gum would last – even amongst the undomesticated denizens of America – and I could not keep rechewing the same piece for ever after I had run through what I had.

There is always opium, Ruby suggested, never at a loss for a bad habit.

'A lady came to see me,' I began. 'She was worried about a close friend of hers who has suddenly stopped contacting her without an explanation. I know,' I said hastily as his lips parted, 'that it sounds childish and I tried to hint as much to her myself.'

The inspector rocked his chair dangerously far back.

'What made you decide there was something in it?' he enquired, plonking one boot and then the other on the desktop. Given the opportunity, Havelock Hefty could have made ingenious observations about the various specks on their soles, pinpointing Stanbury's travels for at least the last twenty-four hours, but Ruby was blocking his view and the dust was just dust to me.

'My client believes that her friend's husband is holding her prisoner.'

'Marriage is like a cage which the birds outside are desperate to get into and those inside are desperate to get out of,' Stanbury quoted, 'Michael de Montagnee.'

His pronunciation of Montaigne would have aroused the scorn of a scholar, but he would only ever have seen the name written down. Philosophy was not part of an officer's training.

'I'm impressed,' I admitted.

'That a flatfoot can read?' he asked defensively.

'That you can remember the epigraph so accurately,' I hastened. 'I could not have.'

It was a sensitive point with Alfred Stanbury that he had received so little schooling, but he had done his best to compensate for that by his weekly visits to the library and was better read than a great many allegedly educated men whom I had come across.

'The friend's husband is an atheist,' I said, and the inspector shrugged.

'Some say Darwin and geology killed God,' he mused.

'Others might say he rose again,' I riposted. 'But, when I tried to meet the friend at church, her husband was with her and I have seen you detain suspects less closely than he was guarding her.'

'Perhaps he is overly protective of her.'

'She looked frightened.'

'Maybe she had reason to and that was why he was accompanying her.'

'That possibility occurred to me,' I said, 'so I decided to pay her a visit. The maid told me that she was not at home, but I saw her looking through a window from the servants' quarters.'

'Which could confirm the theory that she feels threatened.'

Stanbury flicked his ash into the steel wastepaper bin on the floor beside him.

'It could,' I agreed, 'but, when I returned, I saw her again and she was banging on the window. Would you try to attract the attention of a stranger if you were in hiding?'

Stanbury rubbed his chin.

'Let's assume you're right for a minute, there's many a jealous husband keeps his missus on tight reins and, unless he manacles her in a dungeon, there's not much I can do about that. As you yourself said, he lets her out, even if he does accompany her.'

'There's something wrong about it,' I protested.

'Female intuition?' He raised an eyebrow.

'It is as good as a man's,' I asserted indignantly and he grinned.

'So it is and I often follow where my nose takes me, but I can't turn up at the man's house demanding to see his wife and I'd certainly never get a warrant on the strength of your instincts.' He lowered the front legs of his chair. 'Who is he?'

'Confidentially,' I began.

'That's an unusual name,' he commented and I winced.

'Dr Edward Poynder.'

The inspector pulled the corners of his lips down.

'Poynder? I know him. He's attended to an injured prisoner here more than once, and of course there was the Mungo Peers case.'

'Any progress on that?' I asked.

'Investigations are continuing,' he said, which meant *No*. 'But Poynder's a good man, I should say – certainly no Bluebeard.'

I exhaled, partly in despondency but also to blow his smoke out of my eyes.

'I do not suppose there is anything you can do, then.'

'You do not suppose correctly.'

Actually, Ruby chipped in, *that statement does not really make sense.*

I know what he means.

'Do you want my advice?' he asked.

'That is why I am here.'

'I would keep out of it.' The inspector balanced the still-smouldering cigar on the edge of his ashtray. 'Nobody will thank you for interfering between a man and his wife.'

I stood up.

'I am sorry to have wasted your time.'

He shrugged and turned back to the ledger.

'While you are here, how are you at double-entry book-keeping?'

'About as good as I am at Chinese,' I replied.

'Ha ching hoi cha,' Alfred Stanbury said, and I was not sure if he had studied Mandarin too or was making it up.

He was making it up, Ruby assured me as we stepped into the sunshine. *It should have been Hoy chi pin hoo.*

Now who is bluffing? I asked, though I could not help but wonder, as I reached for a Beeman's, was it possible for a character to have knowledge that his or her creator did not.

Of course it is, Ruby asserted. *I know the identity of Jack the Ripper.*

I have yet to meet someone who does not, I told her for I was bored to death of being bored to death by theories presented as facts. Sidney Grice, I had read, had solved the case, though I had also been reliably informed that Mr Grice was the murderer.

I hailed a cab but two young men had beaten me to it.

'Want to sit on my knee?' one called.

'I would rather sit on your…' I hesitated, unable to think of a part of his anatomy that would not sound disgusting. 'Inquest,' I came up with by the time they had gone.

Also, Ruby continued, *I know how I can escape.*

I would have a long wait, I suspected, for two things – an explanation and another hansom.

30: ROSALIND AND THE NUMBER OF THE BEAST

I WAS STUDYING a letter from a bank of which I had never heard. If I did not repay my forty-pound overdraft immediately they would be forced to take legal action against me and this was my final warning. To speed the transaction I should make out the cheque to the manager in person, a Mr Terrence Wise of Brighton. After much deliberation I filed it carefully in my wastepaper bin and turned to *The Chronic.*

No Dinosaur Fossils Found in Chalk Pit, it proclaimed and I leafed excitedly to page five for a fuller account.

The doorbell rang.

Agnust had a half-day off and Gerrund was out on business for me so I went to the door.

'Oh,' I said and, while Ruby was congratulating me on my quick thinking, my caller said, 'Good morning, Lady Violet.'

'Good morning, Mr Appleton,' I managed more articulately.

'I am sorry to disturb you at such an early hour,' he told me, though he did not look or sound it in the least.

'Are you?' I asked severely, but I doubted that I looked or sounded it in the least either.

'Might I have a word with you?'

Only if it is a repeatable one, Ruby quipped. She was a little irritable that morning, having banged her head on the lid of her coffin when she had woken up.

'You'd better come in.' I stepped back, brushing aside the knowledge of what my mother or maid would say at such forward behaviour.

'I shall not detain you long,' he promised, shutting the door behind him and peering about the hall. 'I have an audition at the

Duke of Cambridge Theatre in twenty minutes for *As You Like It*.'

Ohwah, Ruby yawned so theatrically that she could have gone with him, *Boring*.

'Then I shall not detain you either,' I promised.

He was soberly dressed that morning, if one has no objection to pink stripes and I did not, though I could think of a few people who would regard it as effeminate to the point for which Mr Wilde had been in the dock recently.

'It is just that I have been keeping an eye on Haglin House as you asked.'

'I most certainly did not.'

Anthony Appleton wrinkled his nose.

'I probably imagined that bit,' he conceded, 'but I know you wanted me to.'

'I think you imagined that too.' I smiled then, realising that he would not have turned up just to tell me that, added more seriously, 'I assume that you have come to report something.'

'When I was a naughty child or sometimes even when I was not,' he began.

'I thought you were in a hurry.'

Even if he were not, my coffee was evaporating.

'We did not have a cellar for my parents to lock me in.'

'I can find no words of consolation.'

Appleton cocked his head.

'I know I said I liked sarcasm in a woman,' he acknowledged. 'I didn't say I was addicted to it.'

'Do you not know I am a woman? When I think, I must speak.'

'Rosalind.' He recognised the quotation from the play in which he was hoping to perform. 'Perhaps you should come and audition with me.'

'Perhaps you should tell me what you came to tell me,' I suggested, reaching out unthinkingly to remove a white hair from his lapel, reminiscent of the one belonging to Chaos the cat that I had so very cleverly found.

'Yesterday evening, while I was spying – as I was not instructed to – on Haglin House— What a horrible name! It sounds like a small witch or a Scotch meat pudding.'

'It sounds more like you are straying from the point again.'

The hair was actually a thread and I tugged to snap it off.

'I saw her in the top left-hand window.'

'Is that it?'

'I am pausing for dramatic effect.'

'Save that for the casting...' I rooted through my brain, 'person,' I ended weakly and stopped pulling.

The material was puckering.

'What are you doing?'

He glanced down, but the damage was too high to be in his line of vision.

'You had some pollen on your jacket.'

'Thank you,' he said. 'It is so important to look my very best.'

Well done, Thorn.

You thought it was a hair too.

No I did...

'You will be late,' I warned and he gathered speed.

'She was holding a piece of paper. It was crumpled and obviously a long way away.'

'Obviously.'

He waited and so did I.

'But I could just make out the words with my binoculars.'

Appleton struck an unstatesmanlike statesmanlike pose.

Kick him on the shin, Ruby urged and, for once I was tempted to follow her advice.

Even the tick of the hall clock slowed. His tiepin was shaped like a rapier. Was that a diamond on the handle?

Hilt, Ruby corrected me, *and it is cut glass.*

'Aren't you going to ask me what it said?'

'No.'

'Why not?'

'Because you are going to tell me anyway.'

'Help me.'

'Help you to do what?'

He flapped his hands.

'No that is what it said. Just that and then she moved away.'

'Are you sure you did not imagine that too?'

He glanced at my clock.

'Cricks! I had better get going.' He inspected himself in the hall mirror. 'Should have had a haircut.'

'You look splendid.' I opened the door for him. 'Why was your parents' lack of a cellar relevant?'

'They used to put me in the attic,' he explained. 'Dash it! I've got a loose thread.'

'It does not show.'

'I tried the same thing.' He spoke quickly. 'Hoping that the police would come and arrest my mother, but a passer-by told them and my father dragged me away from the window.' He stepped out into the sunshine. 'She moved suddenly and sideways as if somebody had grabbed her arm and hauled her away,' he said. 'I must go.'

'Break a leg,' I called as he trotted off.

'Dint you goo threatnin' me,' the hurdy-gurdy man bristled, stopping to put his collecting tin on the pavement just outside my window.

The newspaper vendor trudged by.

'Missin' mouse found safe but tired,' he bawled repeatedly, his voice fading as he made his way towards the monastery gate.

What a relief, Ruby fanned herself with a copy of *Bicycling News*, though I had no idea from where she had got that.

'What a liberty!' I said, unintentionally aloud.

Why was Anthony Appleton looking for other roles? He was supposed to be in my play – well nearly.

31: PUNKAH WALLAHS AND NAG'S LUNG

I KNEW I had no right to complain for there were even more steps to my observatory, but the stairs to Hettie's *apartment*, as the landlord called her three attic rooms, were steep and narrow and smelled of all the things you do not want cats to do in a house. That and the invention of photography did little to promote Hettie's portrait business. Also I was hot. Crosby Street, where she lived, was too close by to be worth the hailing of a cab but too far for comfortable walking in those blazing *straw days*, as the drought was termed by local clodhoppers.

Hettie, having no servants to answer it for her, came to her own door and kissed me.

'Any news about that woman who was shot?' she asked as she took me through to her studio.

'None that I know of,' I told her, 'but I shall call in on the police this afternoon.'

The drapes were open and the sun, so reticent in most English summers, was pouring brassily though the big south-facing windows.

'I need the light,' she fended off my complaint before I mouthed it.

'I thought artists prefer light from the north.'

'Perhaps you would like to persuade my landlord to rotate the building,' she suggested. 'This was the best I could afford.'

Folding ladies' fans were much in vogue, especially those in the Japanese style decorated with cherry blossom, beautifully robed ladies with bamboo sticks in their hair or weirdly twisted willow trees. I always found the effort required to get what Mr Beaufort might have recognised as a fresh breeze heated rather than cooled me.

'You need a ceiling fan,' I told Hettie.

'Find me one that runs off oil,' she challenged, for she had neither a gas nor an electricity supply, 'or, better still, send me a punkah wallah.'

'You could at least let some air in.'

'Along with the grime and smuts of smoke,' she objected. 'And you have no idea what havoc an energetic fly can wreak on wet oils. The mayor's wife ended up looking like a case of smallpox after a bluebottle took a hiking holiday across her face.'

Hettie had four portraits underway, all hidden behind loose dustsheets. The bare floorboards were splattered with paint and scattered with squashed tubes around her easels. She had laid a sheet to make a path for her clients to walk to the low dais in the centre of the room. The chaise longue was draped with a claret cloth that morning.

The walls were lined with canvases, mostly half-done for, once completed, they would be framed and delivered to whomever had commissioned them.

'When is your next one due?' I asked.

Hettie glanced over at the mantle clock. It had been given to her by a client grateful that she had managed to give her repulsive son an appearance that she could look upon without shuddering while still being recognisable.

'One hour and nineteen minutes ago,' she told me. 'To be fair she has to make her way all across the square but I suspect she is losing her nerve.'

'Is this the lady who wants a nude study?'

'Certainly not,' Hettie corrected me in mock indignation. 'There is to be a strategically positioned samovar.'

'I wonder where people show these pictures.'

I picked a copy of *The Art Journal* from under a half-empty bottle of turpentine and a pile of rags on an old pine table against the wall.

'Well, the vicar of St Botolph's in Anglethorpe hung his wife, without even a fig leaf, in their entrance hall.' She wiped her mouth on the napkin. 'Or the ex-vicar of St Botolph's, as he is now. He sells buckets and spades on the beach. Hop on.' She nodded towards the platform.

'I do not have much time,' I stalled, fanning myself with the magazine.

'Then you had better not waste any,' she said, and I stepped up to sit on the sofa, my hands folded in my lap in a pose into which she had bullied me many a time over the years.

The portrait had been a work-in-progress for years now. Originally a present for Jack, if it were ever finished, I would give it to my parents in revenge for them giving me Agnust.

Hettie put on her cotton coat – more many-coloured than anything Joseph's father could have given him – and lifted the cover off a canvas to let it fall on the floor.

'There was a sad discovery in the yard yesterday,' she told me, selecting a brush from an old marmalade jar. The back of her studio overlooked the horsehair factory. 'A man was found dead in the drain.'

'How awful,' I said. 'Do you think he took shelter there?'

The conditions in which some people were forced to live never ceased to appal me.

'I'm not sure,' Hettie replied, gazing at me, her sapphire eyes sparkling. 'There were three policemen, which seems a lot if he was just another vagrant.' She picked up a caked palate, her thumb hooked through the hole. 'I don't mean *just* in that way.'

'I know what you meant,' I said. 'He would not have been important to the police.'

'And there was something else odd.' She squeezed a tube of orange paint onto her board. My dress was a light peach colour and I wondered what part of me was carrot coloured.

Your teeth, Ruby suggested spitefully.

'When they lifted him out he was in a blanket. Keep still,' she scolded.

I had watched Hettie work and she was patience personified with her clients, smiling indulgently at children who fidgeted when she was trying to do their hands, but that tolerance did not extend to me. *What are friends for if not to snap at?* she had enquired reasonably when I had pointed that out.

'Perhaps he was cold in there,' I suggested.

The dead usually are, Ruby observed.

I meant before he died.

'No I saw a constable bringing one,' she explained. 'I expect he fetched it from the infirmary and he was completely wrapped in it. I couldn't see anything of him.'

Then how... Hefty began but the same thought had occurred to me already.

'Then how do you know that it was a man?'

If this had been one of the inspector's cases, Hettie would have broken down and confessed at that point.

'Because I heard the plain-clothed policeman shouting, *Don't drop him again, Bunny*, which I assume was the policeman's name rather than a term of endearment.'

'Constable Bunleigh,' I laughed while Hefty stomped grumpily away. He did not like to give up on a suspect, having spent all summer successfully solving the strangling of Sister Cicely Sissons, the Sudbury Cistercian, only for her slayer to slip silently away.

'Oh for goodness sake, Violet!'

'Sorry,' I said, but my curiosity had got the better of me.

I got up and went to the back window.

'There is nothing to see now.' Hettie was waving her brush in exasperation and freckling her pale face in the process, and I knew that she was right but I had to take a look.

The wide square yard below was cobbled with bales of hair sorted into black, white and grey and stacked high against the far wall. An empty cart was leaving through the gate to my left, the mare pulling it placidly unaware that her mane and tail would probably be tied in separate bundles there one day and that the rest of her would be cat food.

You made me eat horse once, Ruby reminded me.

It was either that or starve, I defended myself, for there had been nothing else to be had in the middle of a Siberian winter.

The factory to my right was a two-storey brick building, the door and windows all closed when the workers must have been in desperate need of ventilation. Most of them were women who usually ended their days with *nag's lung*, gasping for air after years of inhaling the fine fibres through which they were employed to sort.

There was a manhole cover in the middle of the square.

'Was that it?' I pointed.

'Yes,' Hettie said, 'but why are you so concerned?'

'Because the police were interested,' I told her. 'Which implies foul play in which case he could be the second person to be murdered recently.'

32: TIGERS AND THE WHALE

I CALLED ON Alfred Stanbury again. I knew he had promised to tell me if there were any developments but I also knew what men were like, and if there had been any progress his first thought would not be to contact me. After all I had no official standing and he had always been more Romulus's friend than mine, for it is soppy to play with girls when one is young and then indecent when one is older.

The inspector was slipping his arms out of his sandy sackcloth jacket when I tapped on the door of his office. This was casual wear by official standards but, probably, he had hoped that the material would be cooler than his usual wool.

'Just got back,' he announced though I could have deduced that. 'And, before you ask, we are still making enquiries about that shooting.'

He hung his jacket on a nail in the wall.

'Somebody saw Mrs Poynder,' I began and he groaned but I persisted. 'Holding up a sign reading *Help me.*'

'Has it occurred to you…' He rubbed his brow irritably. 'That she is just another bored and excitable wife looking for attention?'

'If so she has an odd way of seeking it,' I commented. 'Locking herself away.'

'I'll think about it,' he promised in a tone that made me think he would not. 'But in the meantime I've got another murder case to deal with – a nasty one.'

He turned to his desk, obviously a cue for me to leave and so, obviously, I loitered.

'Do you mean *nasty* in the sense of horrible or garrotting?'

'Both.' He hung his coat on a wooden stand in the corner. 'A man found strangled in a drain near the horsehair factory. Normally he'd have been washed into the main sewer but, with the dry weather, he stayed put.' He grimaced. 'Must have been there a while by the state of him.'

'Decomposed?' I checked and he nodded.

'And the rats had been at him.'

I shuddered. Rats had featured more in my life than I cared for recently and it had been a wasted experience. The public did not want to read about Ruby baiting rodents in the slums, Ted Wilton had told me. They wanted her to have exotic adventures in glamorous locations, like hunting man-eating tigers in the Taj Mahal.

The last time I set out to do that you had me shipwrecked, Ruby sniffed. *As if a modern steamer could possibly get sunk by an iceberg.*

'Do you think that he was sheltering there?' I asked.

I had known the destitute to set up homes in the most unlikely of places, having come across a family living in a whale in Hadling Heath, though admittedly it was made of wood and canvas. It had been abandoned by a preacher who found it too cumbersome to drag around as he travelled the country refuting the claims of Mr Darwin and his Godless hordes.

'Probably not.' Stanbury flicked at a long eyebrow hair that was dangling into his lashes and clearly annoying him. 'I don't think he was a pauper.'

'But you could still tell how he died?' I asked.

'Cord wrapped tight around the neck.'

He blinked.

There would have been no shortage of that, Hefty observed, rather obviously.

'But not hanged?' I queried, and the inspector tilted his head sideways in the way people do when they have water in their ear.

'From the horizonal line I would say not.' He pursed his lips. 'Unlikely to be a woman.' He straightened up. 'Takes a great deal of strength to strangle a man even though he was slightly built.'

Daisy the Diamond Queen, Hefty asserted, but I was not going to accuse the woman on such flimsy grounds. Doubtless she would be suffering more than enough already with her errant husband and blistered hands.

'Muriel McManus had...' I began before remembering that she was fictional.

There'th many a man who withed I wath, Muriel lisped nastily.

She was punished harshly for her crimes, but my one regret was that I had not made the retribution harsher.

She doesn't frighten me, Hefty asserted, but I could not help noticing that he was standing well back.

'Who?' the inspector queried, plucking at the troublesome eyebrow with a thumb and first finger but unable to get a decent grip on it.

'I was just remembering that Muriel and I had an appointment to meet for coffee at the Café Cordoba on Thursday at eleven,' I blustered.

Why do you always do that? Ruby complained. *The more detail you squeeze into a lie the more likely it is to burst apart.*

'I see.' Stanbury sighed, more used than most to my digressions, and cleared his throat. 'There was something else.' He hesitated before revealing, 'The body was unclothed.'

'Completely?'

'As the moment he was born.'

I was born in a sailor suit, Hefty claimed primly for he was of the opinion that nobody should expose more than their hands, upper neck and head.

Stanbury licked a finger and managed to train the hair up and out of the way.

'A sexual fiend?' I suggested and he coloured a little at my indelicate use of language, though I could think of no more decorous way of expressing myself.

'Possibly,' he conceded. 'His body was in no condition to reveal much information about what else he had endured and there was no sign of his clothes.'

'Then how do you know that he was not destitute?' I asked, having had my theory on his sheltering there so cursorily dismissed.

'Hair cut short – not expensively like mine,' he explained with no apparent irony, 'but neatly rather than hacked.'

'Was he emaciated?'

'Not as far as we could tell.'

'Did he have rickets?'

'Not that I noticed,' he said cautiously, which probably meant that the leg bones were straight for he was not unobservant.

For a man, Ruby contributed to Hefty's irritation.

'What were his teeth like?' I asked.

'From what I could see the lower teeth were all right.' Stanbury suppressed a shudder. 'He'd had all the top teeth pulled out.'

'Was he wearing dentures?'

'No and there were none nearby.' Stanbury scratched the angle of his jaw. 'Why?'

'It seems a little odd if he were not poor,' I mused and, to give the inspector credit, he only bristled slightly for nobody enjoys having their professional judgement questioned by an amateur.

Sorry I must have nodded off, Ruby sarcasmed. *When, exactly, did you become an amateur detective?*

Four minutes and eight seconds ago, I bluffed.

'Do you think there could be a connection with the murder of the woman in Seraphim Square?' It seemed something of a coincidence that two people would be killed within such a short space of time in what was normally a peaceful town.

I delved through the clutter in my handbag.

'Unlikely,' he assured me. 'Murderers tend to stick to their methods either because they are tried and tested or because they get pleasure from that act.'

What are you looking for? Ruby asked in exasperation, for she could always lay a hand on anything in her specially compart-mented bag when she needed to.

Got you.

'So you are hunting two men now?' I checked and he nodded.

'Don't move,' I said and got to my feet.

Stanbury looked at me uneasily. Had I spotted that sharp-shooter on the charred roof of the apartment building across Mark's Alley?

'What's happening,' he asked as I leaned over.

'Hold still,' I ordered, nail scissors in hand.

I reached over to snip off the offending hair, and I was confident that I would not have nicked Inspector Stanbury's fore-head if he had been an untypical man and done as he was told. I would have helped to staunch the bleeding had he not expressed the opinion that I had done quite enough already and shooed me out of his office.

It only bled a little, I assured Little Myrtle who was terrified of blood, and with good reason, but she had swooned into the arms of a burly dragoon – for a different good reason, Ruby and I told each other knowingly.

Excuse me sir, Hefty called out to a stubby stubbled man stumbling by with an enormous mastiff on a lead. *Do you have a licence for that dog?* But the man did not even glance over except to leer at me.

At me, Ruby insisted and I did not argue.

The dog was an ugly brute but it was a canine Adonis compared to its master, though judging from the way it staggered, I was not sure that it was any more sober.

Drunk in charge of a human, Hefty observed, reaching for his notebook.

33: WORMWOOD, THE WEASEL AND THE IMAGE OF AN ANGEL

I HAD COLD beef for dinner. Gerrund had wanted to curry it and was in a sulk because I had told him not to trouble. Bread and pickles were all I needed, especially as he had been out working for me all day.

'Didn't realise we were poor,' he muttered, after Agnust had served, grumbled and gone. 'I could fetch you some jellied eels tomorrow.'

'Or a sheep's head,' I suggested.

'I know a good recipe for that,' he said and I hoped that he was joking.

I had eaten more than enough lamb and mutton in Norfolk and Suffolk without being served parts that should be reserved for stray dogs.

'Have you had any luck with your enquiries?' I asked, sprinkling salt over the meat.

Gerrund put a jar of English mustard reluctantly in front of me.

'Not much,' he admitted. 'The Poynders keep themselves to themselves most of the time. Even the neighbours' maids don't see much of Matilda. She doesn't have a beau or any friends they know of. Susie, the kitchen maid, was being courted by a fish frier but he scarpered when she started talking marriage. The cook lives out, but she doesn't know anything except what they will and won't eat.'

I buttered a thick slice of bread.

'What about Wormwood?' I asked and Gerrund whisked the mustard away. I had had enough of that, he had decided. Smothers the flavour he used to complain, unlike his hot spices, of course.

'I was coming to that.' He recorked the jar. 'He's a strange cove too. Goes to the Weasel once a week for pint of best bitter and stands at the bar drinking it, but never speaks to anyone, just downs it, pays and goes.'

'No young lady?' I asked and he shook his head.

'Not unless it's Matilda.'

'She would not be the first maid to fall for the valet.' I chewed a morsel of beef. 'This tastes even better cold.'

'So you didn't like it hot?' Gerrund pouted, but I was not falling for that one. Women invented the turning-a-compliment-into-an-insult-to-get-another-compliment game and we had yet to be bested at it.

'What about Dr Poynder?' I stabbed my fork at an onion, which shot off my plate and scuttled in panic off the table. Gerrund kicked it out of the way. Floors were Agnust's responsibility but I suspected that, if I did not retrieve the onion later, it would mulch the rug before she had dealt with it.

'They see him come,' he informed me, 'and they see him go, but they don't see him between times.'

'And Mrs Poynder?'

'The neighbours like her,' he said. 'She takes tea with the ladies either side and she's always nice to their maids. Has a chat with them. Gave them some scented soap last Christmas which was as good as anything they got from their mistresses.'

'Sounds like a nice lady,' I remarked, which confirmed what Martha had told me.

'She does,' he agreed. 'When Millie, their old kitchen maid, was taken bad through her own fault, Mrs Poynder tended to her herself, sat up with her all night until she got better but the ungrateful wretch still left her service.'

There was a bang and the windowpane juddered as a pigeon bounced off it, leaving the distinct image of an angel on the glass. It being a sacred sign, Agnust would never allow the mark to be washed off.

'Why was Millie's illness her own fault?' I asked.

'Drank half a bottle of carbolic,' Gerrund reported. 'She said it was an accident 'cause the label came off but how can you mistake carbolic? It doesn't exactly smell nor taste like lemonade.'

'It is just about possible if she had a severe cold,' I postulated. 'And taste is a slow worker. We've all swallowed something and then realised that it was bad.' I pincered another onion between my finger and thumb to spear it, despite its struggles, successfully this time. 'But I agree that it seems unlikely. Do your acquaintances have any theories as to why she might have tried to kill herself?'

'Maybe she thought it would kill a stomach bug,' Gerrund suggested flippantly.

'I have heard of people who have done more idiotic things than that.' I took a drink of my pale ale but not forgetting to sniff it first and roll it around my mouth before swallowing.

I had had cooler cups of coffee.

'Even if she hated her job,' he continued, 'she was leaving soon anyway to marry the fishmonger's son, and by all accounts they were happy, only she ran off to Bournemouth.'

'Bournemouth?' I checked in surprise for we had both heard of the unspeakable things that happen there.

Gerrund cracked his knuckles and I winced. I thought I had cured him of that habit, but he claimed that it alleviated the pain from when his hand had been broken. *If only hearts could be eased that readily*, I reflected.

'Anyway...' Gerrund massaged his fingers. 'Nobody has seen Mrs Poynder since she came back off her travels and they've been told, more or less, not to enquire.'

'Do they have any theories?'

'They all think she's ill and doesn't want anyone to know.'

'Do they see any doctors call?'

'Difficult to tell,' Gerrund said. 'Poynder has always had medical visitors.'

'Nothing at odd hours?' I tried and he snorted.

'Roughly how many servants do you think sit up all night to spy on the neighbours?'

That was a fair point. Most maids hardly had the energy to drag themselves to bed.

'Have you made any progress in your enquiries, milady?' he asked.

'I met a man in the gardens,' I began and Gerrund sucked through his teeth.

'Many a dead woman could say that,' he warned then, realising the incongruity of his claim, tacked on, 'in a séance.'

'And he...'

Agnust came in with an empty tray clutched protectively to her bosom.

'Int you finished yet?'

'We were talking,' I explained, wondering, as always, why I should.

'Wint get fat on talk,' she warned, clearly under the impression that every lady's ambition was to be as voluminous as she was.

'Lady Violet was speaking,' Gerrund informed her sternly.

'Tha's wha' I scold her for,' she counter-informed him, dumping the tray on the sideboard and folding her arms.

'It's not your place to scold,' he corrected her.

'Int yours either,' she corrected him.

'I didn't say it was.'

'Dint say you did.'

The Oxford Union had not raised the art of debating to such heights.

'And I didn't,' he began, but he could tell my maid what he did not do another time.

'How was your meeting?' I asked her, not that I cared.

'Finish crossin' out a whole page,' she announced, bosom quivering with pride. 'Sister Sabrittle do say destroy it. All the others cut theirs in bits with scissors but I eat mine up and spit it out.' Agnust smiled fondly at the memory. 'I do it my way.'

'I need to speak to Mrs Poynder,' I told Gerrund.

'Why?' Agnust demanded. Her chest had risen one side and slipped down on the other. 'She wint at the meetin'.'

To give my maid credit she listened attentively while I explained.

'I have an idea,' Gerrund declared but Agnust batted it away unheard.

'I do have a better one,' she said, doing something odd to rearrange her bosom so that it was lopsided the other way round, which was not an especial improvement.

34: STRANGERS AND THE STRING OF PEARLS

MARTHA'S FACE WAS not so much pale as blanched with a tinge of grey. Her complexion reminded me of Mr Evans the grocer after he had died of a heart attack while his customer helped herself to a tin of peaches and a bag of tea.

Hefty consulted his notes.

Oolong, he informed me.

'What on earth is the matter?' I asked in concern, guiding Martha as if she were blind into an armchair and fetching the ashtray for the cigarette she was already smoking.

'A boy,' she said, staring straight ahead.

The Henderson twins went by riding a tandem while balancing milk churns on their heads, but I doubted that she even saw them. They did it every day regardless of the weather but nobody knew why.

What boy? Hefty interrogated her. *Come along now Mrs Ryan and no dissembling.*

'What boy?' I enquired less aggressively, I hoped.

'Bethany my maid saw him while she was dusting the drawing room,' Martha said. 'He was hanging by a rope around his neck.' She swallowed. 'From my monkey puzzle tree.'

Examine her fingerplates, Hefty advised. *Look for hemp fibres. When I went to...*

Be quiet, Ruby snapped, for we had all heard his account of his role *Strangers in an Omnibus* so often that we could, and sometimes did, recite it along with him.

'Was he dead?' I asked, for it was not impossible that they had managed to cut him down in time.

'Of course he was dead,' Martha snapped, clutching at what would have been her head if it were twice the size.

Twice, Hefty repeated thoughtfully, jotting the word down.

Without asking if she wanted one I poured her a sherry.

'How awful,' I murmured, not troubling to justify my enquiry, for I knew that agitated people do not thank you for correcting them.

They do not thank you for their drinks either, I discovered, when she took the glass from me without a word.

The size, Hefty cogitated.

'Have you called the police?' I asked.

'Well I could hardly leave him there,' Martha retorted and I began to regret having forced her to visit me by sending telepathic messages, as it was clearly my fault that she was in my home being forced to consume my amontillado and relate her experience.

Martha gulped her drink and then gulped nothing.

'I am sorry,' she said, gazing at her lap.

She was all in lilac that afternoon.

Not too emotionally distressed to attend to her wardrobe, Hefty commented.

Have you actually met any women? Ruby challenged him. She had spent twenty minutes selecting the correct string of pearls to wear while wading through the sewers of Prague being chased by a pack of wild dogs.

I would remind you, he reminded her, *that I was once engaged to be married*.

To whom? she challenged.

You know full well, he blustered, for neither he nor I could bring the unfortunate young lady's name to mind.

'My nerves…' Martha was mumbling, hardly audible above Hefty's claim that his were made of steel.

Which means your brain must be metallic, Ruby reasoned. *Small wonder it doesn't work*.

'Anybody would be distressed,' I told Martha, sweeping aside the dozens of murderers and executioners who were emerging from the shadows, insisting that they would not have been. 'Do you know who he was?'

'Not yet,' she replied a little more calmly. 'The police cut him down and took him away.' She looked about wildly. 'I cannot understand what he was doing in my garden.'

Hanging himself, Ruby suggested.

Ask her where she was at a quarter past one this morning, Hefty urged.

'I will call into the police station later and see if they have any ideas,' I promised.

Policemen having ideas? Ruby mocked, but Hefty was too busy scrutinising Martha's fingertips with his magnifying glass to be wounded by her barbs.

Her hands are clean, he declared and clicked his tongue. *Too clean for my liking.*

'I shall wait to hear from you,' Martha said and I struggled to remember when I became her personal investigator.

Around the same time that you became her maid, Ruby told me as Martha held out her glass for a refill.

–

As events transpired I did not need to call upon Alfred Stanbury because he called upon me.

'Your acquaintance does not have much luck,' he commented, fanning himself with his bowler hat.

'I assume you mean that poor boy,' I responded, pouring him a glass of lemonade.

It was sharp and cloudy as it was meant to be but, more importantly, it was chilled. My block of ice, which once rivalled Marvellous Farthingale's concrete tomb in scale – though not, I hoped, content – was now the size of a valise and I only hoped the weather would change for what we would normally regard as the worse before Gerrund had fetched the last sliver.

Stanbury nodded.

'A strange case,' he said.

I have known stranger, Hefty volunteered, but none of us asked him to elucidate.

'Nobody expects a child to hang himself in their garden,' I agreed, and he sampled his drink gratefully.

'I am not sure that he did,' he declared and, in response to my quizzical expression, proceeded, 'for a start how did he get there?'

'I do not know how easily the back garden can be accessed,' I admitted, though a real investigator would have asked for that information.

Or even visited the scene, Ruby suggested, too late to be helpful but not too late to make me feel foolish.

'That is simple enough,' Stanbury told me. 'There is a side gate which was left unbolted. I am more concerned with how he got up the tree.' He paused for another drink. 'His hands were cut as one would expect, but the marks looked a bit too regular to me and there was not a scratch on his legs. How on earth could he have climbed up the trunk and along a branch without cutting them to ribbons?'

'I assume there was no ladder.' I pressed my tumbler to my temple.

What about me? my other temple whinged.

For some reason it often felt ignored.

'None,' Stanbury confirmed. 'And he was too far along the branch and the rope too short for him to have jumped off the wall.'

'What then?' I enquired and he looked down thoughtfully for a moment.

'The rope was more proficiently tied than you might expect from a stray child,' he said, 'a bowline around the branch and a fisherman's knot for the noose.'

'A sailor?' I suggested though Montford, being far from any port, was not overrun with able-bodied seamen.

More's the pity, Ruby commented, for she was rather partial to a naval man.

'Know what I think?' Stanbury asked and I shushed her before she could make any sarcastic remarks about police officers thinking. 'And I don't want this to get back to the station.' He rubbed the back of his neck ruefully. 'I got more than enough mockery after I nearly arrested the mayor and mayoress dressed as burglars on their way to a costume party. I was wondering,' he said tentatively, 'if it could be a professional killing.'

'By whom?' I asked, saving *But why?* for my next question.

'Well...' Stanbury crunched on a piece of ice and winced. I had been telling him to get that tooth attended to for years, but the man who had not hesitated to rescue an old gypsy woman and her dog from a blazing caravan was too terrified to enter a dentist's surgery. 'I think you know there is a war brewing...'

With the perfidious Spaniards, Hefty predicted. *They have never forgiven us for the Treaty of Utrecht.*

Utrecht ended the war in 1474, Professor Mason chanted from the cell in Reading Jail where he languished for altering the Magna Carta so that it awarded Hampshire to his family in perpetuity.

'Between Anton Gervey and the Braise Shotten gang,' I confirmed.

That's not a war, Ruby maintained contemptuously. *The Russian invasion of Lincolnshire would have been a war had I not averted it.*

'I suspect that the woman you saw shot in Seraphim Square was a random victim intended as a public display of power,' Stanbury theorised, 'and that this was the response.'

'But why that particular boy?' I asked and Stanbury massaged his cheek over his troublesome molar.

'Both gangs use children as messengers and look-outs,' he said.

'But why that garden?'

'I was mystified by that,' he admitted. 'Remember the murder of Mungo Peers? – I wonder if that was the work of one of those hoodlums and that this was done to make things awkward for Dr Poynder. He interrupted that killing and his garden adjoins the Ryans'.'

'Then why not use one of his trees?' I queried and Inspector Stanbury rubbed behind his ear.

'It's just a theory,' he said weakly and finished his drink.

–

Somewhat to my surprise Martha, though alarmed, accepted the idea the moment that I proposed it. I had simplified the hypothesis and presented it as my own, not to take the credit but so as not to embarrass Inspector Stanbury, should it turn out to be the nonsense he had half-suspected that it might be.

'I did wonder,' she admitted even more to my surprise. 'You see, I know we thought that poor woman was warning you that *the Master* would kill you but, on reflection, I had a feeling that she was looking over your shoulder at somebody else.'

'At whom?' I asked, somewhat taken aback for admittedly the woman's eyes had been flitting side to side, but I rather thought that they had settled upon me.

'Me,' Martha whispered, the word almost lost in the turmoil of her fear.

35: THE SILENT MENACE, DIXIE AND THE ROCKING HORSE

GERRUND STRAIGHTENED HIS peaked cap.

'How do I look, milady?'

Quite the Sullivan, Ruby said.

John L. Sullivan was an American boxer and she had met him in *Sunrise Over Mars Manor.*

I did not just meet him, she protested. *I rescued him, though he always denies it.*

Gerrund looked rather smart in his grey uniform, but I was not going to tell him that. He was vain enough about his appearance already.

'Like an emergency man,' I said, not sure if that was the term I was seeking, and he sniffed.

'Here goes,' he said as we ascended the steps.

'Five minutes,' I reminded him.

Gerrund marched straight on while I turned right along the side of the house to stand at the corner out of the line of vision, I hoped, but within earshot, though I could not hear the bell.

'Good day, miss,' Gerrund said. 'We have had a report of an electrical leak in the area and I need to check your basement.'

'We haven't had any problems with it,' a voice I recognised as Matilda's protested and I could hear Gerrund sucking through his teeth even from six yards away.

'You wouldn't,' he assured her, 'until it's too late.'

'How d'you mean?'

A black-and-white cat appeared around the side of the house.

'It builds up,' my man was explaining, 'until your whole house fills with electrical gas.'

'I haven't smelt anything.'

'You wouldn't,' he assured her again. 'It's not like coal gas. It just gathers. The silent menace we call it.'

What a cheek! I had written *The Silent Menace* and Ted Wilton had assured me that it was almost publishable.

'Then, when it gets concentrated enough,' my man continued, 'the slightest thing – just one flash of your beautiful eyes – and up it goes – BOOM!'

'Do you really think they are?' Matilda simpered, more interested in the compliment than the threat of an imminent explosion.

'The loveliest eyes that ever graced a room,' he assured her, which I thought was laying it a bit thick, especially as he had pinched the line from *My Gorgeous Galway Girl*, but women, myself included, and men, come to think of it, will believe almost anything as long as it is flattering.

'But what can be done?' she asked.

'I need to come in,' Gerrund rattled his metal toolbox, 'and test for it with my sensitive scientific equipment.'

The cat tiptoed towards me.

'Welllll…' She hesitated.

'Starting in the cellar,' he told her. 'It usually seeps up from the underground pipes.'

'Welll…'

'And I shall need you to come with me because I am unfamiliar with the layout of the property.'

'Well…'

'And also,' Gerrund continued, 'I am frightened of spiders so I may need you to hold my hand.'

'You're awful!' Matilda cried, as if being awful were by far the best thing that a man could be.

'Given half a chance,' he agreed.

I would have shut the door in the face of any man who tried that one with me – unless he were very good looking and she probably thought that he was. Gerrund had a rugged quality that appealed to most women though not, of course, to me.

I prefer Anthony Appleton, Ruby said.

He is all yours, I told her, regretting it instantly for any man with whom she fell in love had to die and there had been nine so far.

'You'd better come in,' Matilda decided, and I doubted that she would have let him leave by that stage.

The cat strolled by.

'Good morning, Chaos,' I whispered but, my not being edible, he curled his tail contemptuously. 'I have a title,' I informed him, omitting to mention that it was only a courtesy one, to make it quite clear how important I was, but nobody – not the Empress of India nor the man in Bury St Edmunds who makes the finest kid gloves in East Anglia – is as important as a cat. He ambled past me, his nose in the air.

Gerrund, when I peered over, was stepping into the house.

'You lead the way,' he said. 'I'll shut the door.'

And he did not, I trusted, without leaving it off the latch.

I checked my watch. Time passed but boredom overtook it, closely followed by an itchy right foot. I glanced at my watch again and wondered if it were broken and whether I had time to take off my boot, but decided that I did not.

I looked back towards the gardens. They were busy. A red-haired, spangle-suited man was strumming a banjo and assuring us in falsetto tones that he wished he was in Dixie.

So do I, I thought because his voice was almost as out of tune as his instrument. People were shying away but a lady in white tossed a coin into his hat. Perhaps she was hoping that, if she encouraged him to continue, she would get the gardens to herself.

The minute hand of my watch moved on reluctantly.

I went to the door and turned the handle. Gerrund, as usual, had not let me down. Matilda was giggling somewhere distant and, presumably, semi-subterranean. I poked my head through, and Chaos shot past me into the hall.

'Come back,' I whispered, but cats are not renowned for their dog-like obedience. He ran into the front sitting room and under a sofa and I did not have the time to coax him out.

I had not noticed how noisy my leather soles were until it was important that they were not. Cautiously I crepitated to the stairs and up them. At least the treads did not creak, I was relieved to find until, my having reminded them, they all started to do so. It was unlikely that I could be heard from the basement, I told myself, but it had been unlikely that I would discover a prehistoric flint mine at Thetbury Hall by falling down it until I did. Luckily

I was holding my father's hand at the time. Unluckily the jarring dislocated my shoulder.

All the doors of the first floor were closed, which was a shame because I enjoy a good nose around other people's homes. I like to see what they have in the rooms they do not open to visitors. That was how I discovered Rodney Pelham's plan to assassinate his wife with a mechanical doll. He had been so preoccupied in its construction that he was not aware that she had died three years previously.

The mantles were turned down but plenty of light came through the back window, frosted with an etched fern pattern. The wallpaper was nice with little blue butterflies flitting between little pink flowers.

Nice does not mean anything, Ruby criticised, adding editing to her already astonishing list of talents.

Well it does not mean nasty, I argued though I took her point.

The next flight, which could probably have squealed at full volume without alerting anybody, was silent. The wallpaper was nice on the second floor too, as was the majolica jardiniere that I brushed against, steadying the wobbling plant pot just in time to stop it toppling over.

All the doors were closed here as well, including the one at the bottom of the last flight but again there was a rear window, etched in thistles this time.

The final flight was uncarpeted and the walls were distempered white, though scuffed and grubby in places where they had been brushed against over the years and by me that morning. I flicked my scarlet dress but the paint, so ready to quit the wall, had formed a firm attachment to my clothing.

There were no gas mantles on the top floor and no lamps hung from the hooks on the ceiling. All five doors were plain pine and they were closed too, but a skylight gave sufficient moss-filtered light for me to see clearly through the galaxy of dust hovering in the air. Servants would neither have the time nor the energy to perform anything other than essential cleaning in their own quarters.

I tried the first door — an iron lever handle, rather than the white porcelain balls on the lower storeys — and found a boxroom, empty but for one wall which was lined with steamer trunks piled two or three high. Through the cobweb-draped window I could make out the top of a fire escape.

There was a rocking horse in the next room. I had one of those and named her Penelope after Mrs Odysseus. She was my greatest treasure until I rode her down the main stairs. Penelope took them at a canter, I was thrilled to find, though less delighted to discover that, no matter how hard I hauled on her reins, she would not come to a halt.

The third room was half-filled with tea chests and had a long rack of coats and dresses that, presumably, Mrs Poynder did not intend to wear nor wish to give away. There was a silk taffeta ivory gown I would not have minded if it could be shortened and taken in.

Resisting the urge to try it on, I was turning the handle of the next door when I heard a small voice calling.

'Is that you, Matilda?'

I put my ear to the woodwork but heard nothing other than the allegro beat of my heart. I opened the door. More boxes.

'Tilly?' A little louder and coming from the fifth door, I judged and made my way to it.

'It might be,' I said, which did not sound anything like as clever a response when I heard it aloud as I had imagined that it would, and Ruby piffed contemptuously to drive the point home.

'Come in,' the voice said and I turned the handle.

As I had half-expected this door did not open. I wiggled the handle because it is an essential element of being human to rattle uselessly at locked doors, that and shouting down telephones when you know you have lost the connection.

'I have not got the key,' I told her.

'It must be somewhere,' she said, like a tiresome adult when a tiresome child has lost a toy and added, even more tiresomely, 'where did you leave it?'

Good question, Ruby commented.

No it is not.

One day I shall explain sarcasm to you, she promised.

Let me think, I huffed and, huffily, she did.

Dr Poynder would not have taken the key with him, nor would Matilda I reasoned; if either of them were out and there were a fire, the occupant would be trapped. I doubted that he would entrust the key to the kitchen staff. If it were me I would not leave it downstairs in case I forgot it and had to traipse all the way down and back up again. I would keep it nearby.

There was no furniture that it could be put upon or into, and no hooks other than the ones on the ceiling and there were only cobwebs hanging from those. I stood on tiptoe, reached up and touched the top of the frame. My fingertips came away clean and I could not imagine anybody dusting up there unless the ledge was in use. I ran my fingers along and felt it.

'Ping!' I breathed.

What on earth is that supposed to mean?

It is an expression of satisfied surprise.

Do not put it into my mouth when I manage to escape.

Do not assume that you will.

I inserted the key and turned it.

'I am coming in,' I warned in case the owner of that voice was standing or crouching just behind the door, though her voice had sounded further away.

The room had been dark with the curtains drawn but I could see fairly well with the light going in from behind me. There was an iron-framed bed, ornamented with enamelled flowers, against the middle of the wall straight ahead of me and the figure of a woman lay upon it, propped up on two pillows.

'Good morning, Mrs Poynder,' I said and stepped inside.

36: DRAPES, BANDAGES AND BETRAYAL

THE SMELL HIT me the moment I set foot in that room. It reminded me of my lovely visit to Lower Montford.

Lovely? Friendless echoed incredulously. *Int nothin' lovely 'bout...*

What on earth are you doing here? I demanded, but did not wait for him to explain that he was wandering around my cerebrum questioning my use of adjectives. *Inspector*, I called. *Do your duty.*

Hefty appeared from behind the sulcus where he had crouched in readiness.

Right chum. He marched up to the cabby. *This is a private brain and if you are not off the premises in one minute flat...*

Friendless put up his hands – *All right... All right I'm goin'* – and slunk off, and I could not help but feel a little sorry for him. He had washed and combed his hair and even put on a smoking jacket for the occasion. Perhaps he had been hoping to shed his name.

Dolores Poynder raised her head. That and her right arm were all that was visible of her above the sheets and blankets, and then not clearly in the gloom.

'Who are you?' she asked huskily.

'I am a well-wisher.'

'Do I know you?'

'We have a mutual acquaintance,' I told her, taking the key out and slipping it away. Agnust had been revolted when she had found that I had a pocket in my dress. Pockets were for men. What next, she had demanded? Would I start growing a beard? *A goatee might be fetching*, I had taunted her, hoping that a genie had not heard. I still remembered the time that my wish had been mis-fulfilled by a mastiff called Prince jumping up and slobbering over me.

The room was sparsely furnished even for what must have been a maid's quarters. Apart from the unadorned bed there was a pine chest in front of the curtained window to my left. It had a plain wash bowl and jug resting upon it but no ornaments or pictures. Agnust had framed photographic prints on hers but I had only glimpsed them as I passed, not being allowed into her quarters, for servants had more privacy than their mistresses. A simple wooden chair stood near the head of the bed and a scrap of possibly Turkish but badly worn carpet on the floorboards. A bird cage stood empty on a stand in the far, right-hand corner and that was it. No bedside table and no evidence of any candles.

I shut the door behind me and stood a moment, waiting for my eyes to adjust to the darkness. I was not sure what they were waiting for but they were in no hurry to oblige.

'Who?' Dolores asked and I scrambled back through my musings.

Your acquaintance, Hefty reminded me. He had been paying attention to the conversation while Ruby had wandered off to have another look at the dresses.

'Martha Ryan,' I replied warily. If Mrs Poynder had rejected her one-time friend, she might have reason not to welcome that news.

She raised her head an inch or two more into the little daylight that squeezed in over the top of the drapes.

'T?'

I almost said that I would prefer a coffee until I remembered her letter to Martha.

'Yes.'

I went to the window, sliding my feet so as not to trip over anything in my unfamiliar surroundings but still managing to trip on the edge of the rug, just about staying on my feet.

Well done, Ruby applauded, having changed at lightning speed into the silk taffeta gown, though I did not think it suited her.

You could have warned me.

Am I my creator's keeper?

'T has sent you?'

'She is worried about you.'

'I knew that she would rescue me.'

And there I had been, thinking that it was me coming to her aid. There would be time to claim my rightful credit later though, I hoped, and took hold of the curtains.

'No!' Dolores cried hoarsely and I turned my head towards her. 'You must not,' she insisted. 'I shall be punished.'

I pulled them closed again but in that moment of illumination I had seen enough to alarm me.

Dolores looked awful. Her hair was a tangled mess and her face was pallid but, most shockingly of all, were Dolores Poynder's eyes – small and sunken, staring wildly from dark swollen rims. Was that a bruise on her right cheek?

It looked more like a burn to me, Ruby conjectured.

Not troubling to give my eyes a chance to redeem themselves, I hurried towards the bed, no more than a shadow in the shadows, and stumbled again, my comedic little run being brought to a halt by banging my knee on the iron frame.

Mind the rug, Ruby warned just late enough to sound like gloating.

'Ouch!'

'Have you hurt yourself?'

No, I just like saying that, I wanted to reply but settled for, 'I am all right.' And rubbed my knee, making it worse.

Dolores Poynder shifted uncomfortably.

'Why are you locked in?' I asked and she cleared her throat.

'Edward says I have to be,' she rasped, her throat obviously unaware that it had been cleared.

'But why?' I persisted and she shuffled her shoulders in a figure of eight.

'To punish me.' She turned her face to the ceiling.

'For what?'

Had she been unfaithful? Many a gay philanderer, I knew, could not tolerate the slightest hint of indiscretion from his spouse.

'I forget.' Dolores shuffled her shoulders again though not in any recognisable numerical pattern that time. 'I forget a lot of things these...'

Her voice trailed off.

Days, Ruby contributed for she hated unfinished... *Sentences*, she put in, proving my point.

'Have you broken your marriage vows?' I asked as tactfully as I could.

That was tactful? Ruby checked dubiously. *Why don't you ask if she and Wormwood...*

'Never!' Dolores protested so vehemently that I wondered if she were responding to Ruby's suggestion rather than mine.

'Or embarrassed him in front of other people?' I tried again.

Dolores traced over the pattern on her bedspread with an idle index finger.

'I do not think so,' she decided at last.

'Then why would your husband want to punish you?'

Do you think it might be because he is cruel? Ruby suggested.

'Because he is cruel,' Dolores confirmed.

Was it possible that Ruby was coaxing her?

It is but I am not, my Extraordinary Investigator asserted.

'If you are being mistreated I can get the police to rescue you,' I offered and she jolted.

I had seen dead frogs leap less when they were galvanised.

Coated with zinc? Ruby checked incredulously.

Shocked with electricity, I clarified.

What a peculiar hobby, she commented, *though considerably less tedious than accumulating used postage stamps.*

It has something to do with us all being made of volts, I told her uncertainly because I had daydreamed through the explanation.

'But you would have to leave me here in the meantime,' Dolores objected in alarm.

'Are you in any immediate danger?' I asked, for if she were, I would yell for Gerrund.

How feeble, Ruby jeered, *I have never needed a man to help me out of a jam.* She stopped, but I knew that she had not finished. *And do not dare to have one rescue me from this situation.*

'You have no idea what he is capable of,' Dolores told me and struggled to raise herself onto her elbows. 'My husband is a monster.'

I squashed the image of a giant leech conjured up by my febrile imagination, but it still oozed out at the sides. Thoughts, like men and naughty children – who are much the same thing – do not care for being ignored.

'Does he hurt you – physically, I mean?'

She pulled a sheet up to her neck.

'He kneels on my tummy,' she said.

He what? Ruby expressed my incredulity.

'When?' I asked.

I think I can answer that, Ruby interjected. *When they are alone.*

'Sometimes,' Dolores said, not quite answering my question.

He is hardly likely to do it in the middle of a dinner party, Ruby expanded upon her theme.

'I wake up sometimes in the middle of the night and I cannot breathe.' She flapped her right hand in agitation. Was she wearing a glove and, if so, why? And, if so, why just one? 'He is crushing me.'

'Does he do it often?' I asked doubtfully for this sounded like she could be having a night terror like that painting of an incubus by…

Fuseli, Ruby supplied the artist's name. *Ask her if a black stallion sticks its head out through her drapes.*

'Once,' Dolores admitted and, before I could query her original statement, added, 'but it feels like sometimes.'

Her eyes grew wild, flicking side to side and I inched backwards, just out of reach.

'Did he say anything?' I asked.

'He said…' Dolores swallowed noisily and with difficulty, though, as far as I could tell, she had nothing in her mouth other than what was supposed to be there. 'He was sick of…' She gulped as if choking on a piece of meat. 'Me.'

'Did…' I stopped abruptly and raised a warning hand. Had I heard movements downstairs?

Only you know the answer to that one, Ruby told me and she always claimed to be able to hear a pin dropping.

No I do not, she protested. *I can hear a pin landing.*

'And it is not just me that he hurts.' Dolores's voice rose alarmingly as she ignored my shushing signs. 'The things he did to Colin.' She shuddered and pulled the cover over her chin.

'Who is Colin?' I asked.

The boot boy, Ruby asserted, though I knew that she was guessing.

'My friend,' Dolores corrected her.

Maybe he was a bit too friendly, Ruby conjectured.

'What happened to him?' I asked and Dolores flopped down again.

'He is in the top drawer of that chest.'

The madwoman in the attic, Ruby diagnosed. *How very Edgar Allan…*

'See for yourself,' Dolores urged.

Poe, Ruby concluded.

'But…' I began to begin but where, exactly, could I begin?

Thank heavens you don't use words for a living, Ruby said ironically.

I was only going to point out that he must have been Tom Thumb, I told her.

This may surprise you, Ruby warned, *but Tom Thumb's Christian name was Tom not Colin.*

'Go on,' Dolores insisted.

Humour her, Ruby advised. *Remember Muriel McManus? She only weighed six stone but had the strength of two strong men when enraged.*

And you have just given away the denouement of The Morecambe Mystery, I scolded her.

Only to you, she pointed out annoyingly reasonably.

I went over to where the chest stood in front of the window and slid the drawer open, recoiling instantly at a stench that flooded out, overpowering both me and the already fetid air of the room.

Rotting flesh, Ruby and I realised simultaneously.

37: THE LAST BREATH

I TOOK TWO things – a step back and a handkerchief from my handbag to cover my mouth and nose.

'What is it?' I asked, slightly muffled and trying not to retch.

Light your pipe, I instructed Hefty and he did but even the foul Venezuelan Otter Dung tobacco he reserved for such occasions, could not camouflage the reek.

'Speak up,' Dolores commanded. 'I detest this modern habit of mumbling. Oh, I have worked out what you said now.' She huffed impatiently. 'It is Colin of course.'

She never listens, Ruby told the woman who was not listening to her.

Yes, but what part of him? I asked, not sure that I wanted to find out for there were no bits of putrefying Colin that would be anything other than disgusting.

Look closer, Ruby, having a much stronger stomach than I, urged.

Not wishing to lean over whatever the thing was, I went around the chest and took hold of the right-hand curtain.

'No!' Dolores cried. 'You must not!'

'Just a crack,' I promised and pulled it a quarter of an inch apart from its companion.

Did you really have to do that? my eyes, almost accustomed to the dark, demanded angrily.

Yes, I told them. *Stop blinking and do your blinking job.*

She is a hard taskmaster, Ruby sympathised, unwisely taking their side against mine. *You have no idea what she puts me through.* And, with a lot of grumbling they complied.

I went back to the drawer, steeling myself. I knew, of course, that Ruby had had to hunt human limbs all over Peru but as an Extraordinary Investigator, she had a certain devil-may-care swagger. As a lady novelist, I had a Violet-does-care squeamishness.

If you really want us to work you have to separate our lids, my eyes informed me. Was this the start of a trend? Would my stomach start nagging me about being too full or too empty? *I do those things already*, it said. *Shut up!* I snapped, vowing that, from now on, only I would be allowed to talk to me, though I could not guarantee that I would do so articulately.

Whatever the part of Colin was, it did not smell any better on reacquaintance.

I opened my eyes and saw it – pinned out like one of the dissections Romulus was always performing in his youth.

'A bird,' I said.

It had been split open straight down the middle, its guts splayed to either side and shimmering with slime. Was that the liver? I had no intention of poking it with my finger to find out.

I tried to close the drawer but it went sideways and jammed and I saw the surface of the putative hepatic organ move. It was crawling with maggots.

'Yick.'

It does not matter how often you say the word, Ruby informed me frostily, though this was only the second time. *It is not going to become a part of my vocabulary.*

'Colin,' Dolores told me again. 'My parrot.' She triple-inhaled in a rapid whimpering snigger. 'I taught him to say, *Silly Edward*,' she squawked, 'and Edward…' She quadruple-exhaled as if blowing out a great many birthday candles. 'Strangled him.'

The final exhalation broke into a sob.

Into how many pieces, approximately, can exhaling break? Ruby wondered.

'Oh how…' I began but, before I got to *awful* Dolores raised her already raised voice.

'It was awful,' she insisted as if I had shrugged it off with boys-will-be-boys tolerance.

'But why would he do it?'

Many men killed animals for sport and I knew of incidences where it had been done in a rage or revenge. I myself had savagely battered a wasp to death once after it had scaled the inside of my dress without being invited to do so and stung me repeatedly on the knee. I did not further mutilate its corpse nor put it on display though.

I would have asked a hundred more questions.

I can only think of ninety-eight, Ruby mused, but I had no time to call her bluff for, as Dolores spoke, there were heavy footsteps on the wooden stairs.

'Who was with you last?' I asked urgently.

'Why Tilly of course.' Dolores's voice was all at once so weak that I could hardly hear her.

'If anybody asks you, you are alone and Matilda must have taken the key.'

Dolores smiled oddly, reminding me of my godmother when she had taken twenty fluid ounces of vintage strum in the hope of curing her Bell's Palsy.

'Is this a game?'

'A very important game,' I assured her, dropping to my knees.

There was a chamber pot under the bed halfway down. I pushed it towards the wall at the head of the bed, praying that I did not slop it because, being a major contributor to the stench, I discovered, it had been well used. As often my prayers were answered.

Thank you, Cuthbert, I said silently. I had adopted Cuthbert as my guardian angel when I was a child. Originally he was only supposed to protect against chimpanzees who – Miss Kidd threatened – would burst into my room and attack me if I did not practise harder at my needlework. Having kept the creatures at bay, his duties had expanded and he had looked after me on numberless occasions since then.

You never give me any credit, Hefty complained, forgetting that it was I who had made him famous or – to be honest – raised him from anonymity to obscurity.

I shuffled across the bare floorboards and under the frame, my head towards the foot of the bed. The mattress sagged in the middle, forcing me to lie with the side of my face in the dust.

'Are you hiding?' Dolores asked with an unerring knack of being loudest when she ought to be quietest.

The steps grew worryingly close.

'Yes,' I hissed and the steps stopped.

Whoever it was would be feeling for the key that was not there.

'Not a word,' I whispered.

'Only one word,' she said loudly enough to be heard at the back of a rowdy lecture hall, 'and that word is mum.'

Dolores giggled at her own joke.

You have given me worse quips that that, Ruby informed me when I winced, but I let her comment pass as there was only just time to pull in the hem of my distressed dress before the door swung open.

I blinked. A man stood in the open doorway or, to be precise, his boots and trousers to just below the knee stood there, so it seemed a reasonable assumption that there was a man inside and above them.

Ever heard of Burlington Bertie? Ruby challenged, though it was me who had taken her to see Vesta Tilley performing the song.

'Why was the door not locked?' a deep voice demanded, confirming my rather obvious deductions.

Deductions may be obvious but they are never rather, Ruby spouted.

Leave the pontifications to Sidney Grice the Personal Detective, I told her touching on a very sore point indeed for, while the Gower Street Detective was flesh and blood, Ruby Gibson the Extraordinary Investigator, was not.

I bled enough when that cardinal shot me, she refuted my assertion aggrievedly.

Dolores cleared her throat and I only hoped that she had a good lie prepared.

'Because we have an intruder,' she declared simply.

38: BIRD-EATING SPIDERS AND GOUTS OF BLOOD

I CRINGED AND prepared to slide out – on the opposite side I decided so that he could not kick at me or stand on my fingers, like Shillidge the pigman had when he failed to see me making daisy chains on the lawn.

Never trust a woman, Ruby advised, *except for me and Agnust and Hettie Granger and yourself, sometimes. In fact…*

'Can you not see him?' Dolores interrupted.

Rudely, Ruby added.

'There is nobody here,' Wormwood replied.

'Oh but there is,' she insisted and her voice rose. 'He is standing beside you.'

The bed creaked and sagged some more, pinning me to the floor.

Hefty, still puffing on his briar, went down on his haunches. *The frame is broken*, he diagnosed, which explained why such an otherwise good piece of furniture was in the attic. Servants' beds did not usually have enamelled flowers on them.

You never mentioned those before, Ruby complained.

They did not seem important.

'You are imagining it, madam,' Wormwood assured his mistress gently but firmly while Hefty lectured me on the importance of recording every detail. 'There is nobody here.'

Enamelled, Hefty wrote in his notebook while, unbeknown to Dolores and her man, a fourth physical party had just joined us at the end of the bed – not quite a bird–eating spider but one probably capable of nibbling a sparrow's drumstick.

'Have a care, Wormwood! He has a dagger!' Dolores cried so convincingly that a few atoms of me believed her and huddled with their friends for protection.

My new companion skuttled up and stopped about two inches from my face. I have never especially been afraid of arachnids, but this one looked like it thought my nose might make a good home.

'And on its blade and dudgeon...' Dolores bawled so loudly that, had I had room to leap out of my skin, I would have left it half a yard behind but I was starting to feel as if Dr Poynder were re-enacting his incubus imitation upon me. It was becoming difficult to breathe in, though breathing out was no problem at all as Dolores proved with an impressively energetic bounce. 'Gouts of blood!' she completed the line.

The recently knighted Sir Henry Irving could not have declaimed Macbeth's speech more dramatically or so I imagined, only ever having seen him in Harrods trying on a pair of kid gloves and saying, 'They are a little short on the fingers.'

Fascinating though your anecdotes of celebrated thespians in metropolitan department stores might be but are not, Ruby said acidly, *I think we have more urgent concerns.*

'Madam has had a bad dream.' Wormwood was trying to soothe his mistress.

He had very large expressive hands, I told Ruby, because I had not completed my account, and she sighed.

That is the forty-ninth time you have told me that.

'If he is not here, who took the key?' Dolores demanded and I rather wished that she had not, but a man who has made a statement will go to almost any lengths to defend it, rather than admit to the possibility that he could be wrong – especially to a woman.

'Matilda must have,' he theorised.

'Silly Tilly,' Dolores said and laughed.

'Indeed, madam,' he agreed.

The spider reared up and I toyed with the idea of blowing it away but was not sure if it could spring between my parted lips before I got the chance.

'Silly-Tilly-silly-Tilly-silly-Tilly,' Dolores sing-songed.

'I shall fetch madam's medicine,' Wormwood decided as her voice clambered up the scale.

'Silly-silly-silly-Tilly.'

The bed rose mercifully before plunging unmercifully and winding me. At least it proved that my blowing idea was not a bad one because, assailed by the typhoon forced out of my lungs, the spider scooted off in search of shelter.

'Please try to calm yourself, madam,' Wormwood said.

'Silly-Billy-Willy-Tilly,' Dolores's refrain rose to a wail.

'I shall be back in a moment,' Wormwood promised, clearly disconcerted.

'Silllllly,' she howled after him as the door closed and we were left alone.

Oh good, I thought and I could almost hear Friendless asking what was good about the situation.

Jane Eyre had got off lightly compared to me, I thought uneasily, for she had not actually been trapped in the attic with her madwoman.

Dolores must have moved again because the underneath of the bed rose, just high and long enough for me to squirm out, twisting my head as much as I could in an effort to ensure that she was not the one with the gory dagger of which she had talked.

'I think that did the trick,' she giggled.

You certainly had me fooled, I admitted silently.

But not me, Ruby claimed, though she was the one who had been muttering about madhouses.

If I might make an observation, Hefty said.

That would make a change, Ruby said.

Far from you being trapped, Hefty continued, *you are at liberty to leave immediately. Wormwood had no key with which to lock the door.*

'How long will your man take?' I asked Dolores.

'Only a minute,' she said. 'The medicine is kept in a cabinet on the first floor and he will not want to leave me unguarded for long.'

Unguarded? Ruby and I queried but I said, 'Then I must hide.'

'Back under the bed?'

'In another room,' I told her. 'I will come back when he has gone.'

'Promise?'

'Word of honour.'

It occurred to me that, if Wormwood glanced down, he might easily realise somebody had been there. The dust had been swept by my clothes, but I had neither the time nor the broom nor the spare dust for scattering to do anything about that. Regardless of those concerns, I reassured myself, and despite the real and imaginary detectives one reads about, men are unobservant creatures. Any wife who has been coiffured will vouch for that and few husbands will notice a new hat until the milliner's bill arrives with the breakfast post.

Do not look at yourself in a mirror, Ruby advised. *You may never recover.*

A glance at my dress was enough to convince me that it was good advice.

I went back into the corridor, shutting the door behind me, placed the key on the floor a couple of feet from the frame and hurried into the only room that I had not looked into yet.

There were footsteps on the stairs again.

'Silly-silly-sillllllly,' Dolores recommenced her wail and I just had time to close the door behind me before Wormwood returned.

It was musty in that room but, compared to the one I had been in, no mountain or seaside resort had fresher air than that which I inhaled now. It could not completely erase the smell, though, which had impregnated my dress and clung to the inside of my nostrils, and the taste of it coated my tongue.

You cannot taste smells, Ruby sniffed, *oh buwah! My mistake.*

What kind of a word is *buwah*? I challenged her, squatting to peer through the keyhole.

An interjection, she bluffed. *You will find it in the addendum of the* Oxford English Di… *He is coming back.*

I saw Wormwood from behind, a big, black-haired man in dove grey trousers and a plain black swallowtail coat. He grunted something about falling off and bent to pick up the key before re-entering his mistress's room.

With a name like that I will wager the Kohinoor diamond that his face is pock-marked, Ruby speculated.

You really must put that back before anybody notices that the one in the queen's crown is made of quartz, I instructed and Ruby fell into a silent sulk. She had intended to have the gem mounted on a brooch. *Where are you now?* I asked, glancing over my shoulder.

I knew that I cried out, but I did not think it was aloud. A tangled-haired woman in ragged clothes was crouching behind me, her eyes burning from her filthy face, her lips curled in a hideous snarl and her body coiled ready to spring.

39: WATER BABIES AND CONTORTIONISTS

I TRIED TO catch my breath, but it was trying even harder to flee for its life without the slightest qualm about leaving its creator behind.

The figure shrank back.

No YOU shrank back, Ruby informed me patiently. *It is a looking glass.* And, of course, she was right.

I had not looked so wild, grubby and bedraggled since the day I had played at being a caveman in what I had thought was a disused drain at Thetbury Hall.

I did warn you, Ruby reminded me and I returned to my spyhole, absurdly wary about turning my back on my own reflection.

It is said that insanity is catching and, if Dolores were mad, and I was half convinced that she was, her affliction could be highly contagious.

Calm down, I told myself and tried, but what was there to be calm about? Dolores Poynder was being kept prisoner and I was not sure that she was stable enough not to wittingly or unwittingly betray my presence. Also my concerns about smudged dust applied to the corridor as well. There must be a clear trail leading to my hiding place.

I scanned my surroundings. There were some more tea chests here, but they were full of books and, even if they were not, small as I was, I was not a contortionist.

The door to Dolores's room must have been open wide as I could hear their voices fairly clearly.

'It was the best of times, it was the worst of times,' Wormwood was saying.

What on earth is that supposed to mean? Ruby scoffed.

'It was an age of wisdom, it was an age of foolishness.'

It is A Tale of Two Cities, I told her.

Oh good, she said. *I have not read that one.*

I have.

Do not tell me how it ends – assuming that it ever does.

I am hoping we will not be here for quite that long.

'It was an epoch of belief, it was an epoch of incredulity, it was the season of light…'

Let me guess, Ruby yawned, for she bored quickly. *Was it, perchance, the season of darkness?*

'It was the season of darkness,' Wormwood confirmed. 'It was the spring of hope…'

Is this a long story? Ruby sighed.

About four hundred pages, I told her. *But it gets better.*

It would have to.

Wormwood droned on. We were up to kings with large jaws now. He was not a dramatic narrator. I once saw Miss Emma Gregory, a splendid actress, reading selections from *Oliver Twist* and she was marvellous, bringing every character, male or female, vividly to life with her awe-inspiring range of voices and facial expressions. Wormwood anaesthetised every word with his soporific tones.

My knees were getting stiff.

A sign of approaching middle-age, Ruby told me.

We are the same age, I reminded her.

Yes, but Gibsons live to be at least a hundred.

They live exactly as long as I decide, I asserted.

Some might have found the power of life and death over so many people intoxicating, but I found it burdensome for my victims never ceased to haunt me.

I shifted position and nearly overbalanced, my shoulder striking the door.

Why do you not just burst out shouting 'Surprise-surprise'? Ruby asked.

Shush.

Listening intently I put my eye back to the keyhole.

'Sleep well, madam,' Wormwood was saying as he closed the door. His hand went to his midriff but he was facing away and I could not see what he was up to.

I held my breath, a ridiculous thing to do since he could not possibly have heard it and I was more likely to make a noise when I needed to release it again.

Was Wormwood listening? He seemed to be and then he glanced at the floor.

'What a mess,' he muttered and still with his back to me – rather impertinently, I thought – walked away without explaining whether he meant the floor or the situation.

Only after the footsteps had faded and the downstairs door closed did I stand again, go back into the corridor and creep to Dolores's room.

I felt along the top of the frame, carefully so as not to send the key clattering to the floor, but I could have swept my fingers like Franz Liszt performing a glissando at his most flamboyant for there was nothing there. When Wormwood's hand went to his middle he must have been slipping the key into a waistcoat pocket. Presumably he was not going to trust Matilda to lock up again.

I tapped gently on a panel and pressed my ear to it but heard nothing other than the sound of my blood rushing about, pretending to be busy. I tried again but there was no response. Kneeling, I peered through the keyhole, but it was too dark to see anything in there.

Qué sorpresa, Ruby mocked. She had learned some Spanish during her pursuit of Pedro Rodriguez, the Mexican bandit. *Quelle surprise*, she translated to make it easier for me, for I had learned a little French during my pursuit of M. Arquette, my Burgundian tutor, who came three times a week and pretended not to ogle me while I pretended not to ogle him back.

I put my ear to the keyhole and tapped once more, but there was nothing other than the sound of my hair rasping on the woodwork and some heavy breathing, which I realised was my own. I quietened it and heard some heavy breathing which I realised was Dolores's. She must be fast asleep and I wished I knew what draught she had been given. I never found anything that put me to sleep that quickly other than laudanum or chloroform, both of which gave me nightmares. Once I fancied that the queen had turned into a trout.

That was not a dream, Ruby quipped unkindly.

I got up again. All I had to do now was creep out, but I had no idea if Gerrund was still managing to distract the maid or if he had been discovered by Wormwood, who could be returning or waiting in the hallway for me.

In the event my escape was, disappointingly – for Ruby but not for me – easy. I walked down and through the front door without coming across anyone except Chaos, who must have been put out and shot back in again.

Gerrund stood at the entrance to the gardens.

'I spun it out as long as I could,' he told me, 'but I could hear Wormwood moving about and I didn't want to try the story on him. Men aren't so gullible as women.'

'I beg your pardon?' I challenged indignantly.

'Present company excepted,' he added hastily but too late. 'Anyhow you aren't a woman.' But, before my simmering indignation could boil into wrath, he added, 'You're a lady.'

What about me? Ruby seethed. *I don't have a title other than Miss.*

I shall make you a countess one day, I promised.

Not a princess?

Be careful that I do not make you a Mrs, I warned but we both knew that Ruby, like her creator, would never marry. I may only have been bitten once, but some wounds hurt too much and I could not believe that mine would ever heal.

'Goff!' He flapped his hand. 'What a pong. They must be digging up a sewer. You'd think...' But Gerrund came to an abrupt halt, realising from where and whom the aromas arose.

Important police work, Hefty mumbled as he shuffled off to hail a separate cab.

40: TORTOISES AND MOTHBALLS

ALFRED STANBURY LISTENED carefully.

'It's a tricky one,' he said. 'Many a husband chastises his spouse.' He raised his hands to stem the storm he must have known that statement would provoke. 'I'm not saying it's right. I'm just saying what happens.'

'Only if you allow it to,' I retorted as he sampled his tea.

Constables and sergeants had mugs. Senior officers, to Stanbury's chagrin, were expected to use cups and saucers. He got less to drink, he had complained more than once, plus it grew cold more quickly and spilled more easily.

'The law does not like to interfere between a man and his wife,' he told me, as he had before, and I was not sure if his wry face reflected his opinion on that or his beverage.

'And you think that is right?'

'It does not matter what I think.' He clinked the cup down. 'There's many a man I'd like to slutch senseless for what he's done to his missus, but I know who'd end up before the bench with his career ruined.'

A slutch was a good slap – or a bad one, depending on whether you were giving or receiving it.

'But she is being kept a prisoner against her will.'

'By her own admission she was...' the inspector flicked through his memory, 'a naughty girl.' He drummed his fingertips on the wooden desktop. 'He could argue that she had to be restrained for her own good.'

His nails were chewed back though I had never seen him bite them.

Perhaps his wife chews them for him, Ruby suggested and I shifted on my chair.

Wood is not the most cushioning of materials.

'I wonder how a magistrate would view a woman who imprisoned her husband.'

The inspector snorted.

'What man would admit to being bested by his other half?'

'A man with any sense,' I riposted and he smiled drily.

'Like to meet that old boy,' he assured me. 'Never have yet.' He pushed his tea aside, slopping some into the saucer. 'Poynder is a man of some importance in this town. Apart from being a doctor he's something of a local hero after the Mungo Peers case – chasing the killer and saving a wrongly accused man's neck and I'm not sure he isn't something in the Lodge.'

Stanbury spoke sourly, for I knew that he was convinced a local squire had been acquitted of indecent behaviour after making a secret sign to a justice of the peace.

The Lodge was not a branch of the freemasons whose nearest meeting place was in Bury St Edmunds but The Warreners, an East Anglian organisation regarded by some as little more than a gentleman's club, but by others as distinctly sinister. Some of them wore a miniature silver rabbit's foot on their watchchains, but most preferred to remain anonymous.

'There must be something you can do.'

'What?' he countered. 'I don't like these situations any more than you, Violet – and believe me I have come across things that no man should have to witness – but I can't go barging into a gentleman's home demanding to see his wife.'

I ran a hand through my hair in frustration and dislodged a tortoiseshell comb which, not satisfied with sliding sideways, fell to the toast-and-burnt-toast-coloured oilcloth floor covering. I bent sideways to retrieve it.

The oilcloth? Hefty checked.

The comb, I clarified.

'Could you not have a quiet word with him?' I suggested and, as I straightened up, a long tress dropped in front of my eyes. I lifted it up and back but, after a brief pause to reacquaint itself with its fellows, it swung down again.

Stanbury puffed dismissively, more – I assumed – at my proposal than my coiffurial problems.

'Quiet words lead to quieter ones,' he pronounced, not usually a man for riddles. 'If I speak to him, he whispers in the ear of the chief keeper, who has the chief constable round for dinner and I get a visit. If I'm lucky I'm given a friendly warning, if not Sergeant Stanbury will be shaking the mothballs off his uniform and making a brew for Inspector Webb.'

We both shuddered at that prospect. The power would go to Webb's colossal though not fully tenanted cranium and, as for Alfred Stanbury, he made an awful cup of tea.

'What about the bird?'

I fiddled with the comb and it fell out again, creating an unkempt horse's tail to dangle over my face.

'You could report him to the RSPCA,' he suggested as I parted the curtain, 'only their chief officer is a Warrener too, I think. Anyway,' he turned his hands palm up in a manner that most locals would have regarded as repulsively French, 'with all due respect to your problem, we have more important cases to worry about at the moment.'

'Of course,' I muttered, a little ashamed now to have been pestering him with my concerns. 'The woman who was shot and the man in the drain.'

'And,' he stretched his arms forward, reminding me of a conjurer demonstrating that there was nothing in his hands, 'there is another case in the Lowers. Workmen clearing a collapsed wall found the body of a girl. They thought she must have been crushed under the rubble but her throat had been cut.' Stanbury grimaced. 'Not quite ear to ear but not far off.'

'Do you know who she was?' I asked.

'Beryl Walker,' he told me. 'Her mother reported her missing fourteen months ago and she identified the body.'

'It was still recognisable?' I asked in surprise and he placed his hands on the desk, pressing down as if trying to stop it from floating away.

'She was in surprisingly good condition,' he confirmed. 'Her body had been mummified.'

'Do you have any suspects?'

Stanbury snorted.

'Half the men in Lower Montford.'

So many victims and not a single person to pulverise into confessing, Ruby commented cynically as I pushed my chair back.

'Then I had better leave you to your work,' I mumbled.

'You had,' he agreed, 'but please do something about that before you go.'

I did not need to ask what that meant nor what conclusions the men would draw if I went back into the lobby in a state of disarray.

'You need a looking glass,' I told him and he laughed.

'It is not me who needs one, Lady Violet,' Stanbury replied as a second comb fell, this time skittering under the inspector's desk.

'Come back,' I cried, but if such a creature as an obedient comb exists, we have yet to be introduced.

—

I was about to step outside when I was almost bowled over by a woman barging in, holding a man face down by the scruff of his scrawny neck. It was not difficult to recognise either of them for their suits glittered even in the gloom of the station foyer.

'Constable,' Daisy the Diamond Queen bellowed, elbowing me aside and almost sending Hefty sprawling. Ruby, however, was too quick for her and pirouetted out of reach.

It was more of an elegant cabriole, she corrected me. *I did not spin on the spot with my foot on my knee.*

You jumped out of your skin, Hefty corrected her, dusting himself down.

I cannot imagine why you ever got into yours, she retaliated while Webb, seething at his demotion, tapped the chevrons on his upper sleeve.

'Sergeant,' he insisted firmly.

'Arrest this man,' she insisted more firmly.

For what, Ruby, Hefty and I wondered because adultery with a foul-smelling stewed eel seller might show a lack of discernment, but it had yet to be proscribed in law.

'For what for?' Webb snapped, incensed at being reduced to the ranks and ordered about by a member of the public, bejewelled though she was.

'Murder,' she declared, 'of my husband.'

Apart from the fact that he is obviously alive, Ruby corrected her. *If he kills himself it is called 'suicide' and, quite frankly, who could blame him?*

'Danny,' Daisy specified, as if to distinguish him from a legion of husbands at her disposal, and wrenched her captive into a more upright stance. His face, I saw at once, bruised and bloodied though it was, did not belong to the Diamond King. This was an old man, with an asymmetrical chin and moustaches so wild and bristly that they looked like two tom cats locked in combat.

Obviously alive? Hefty crowed and clapped his hands in delight for he rarely got a trick up on Ruby.

I was going by what Thorn told me, she sulked.

The man licked his lips. They were scaly and cracked and a shade of orange that might have made an attractive scarf but did not make for alluring facial features.

'I dint kill nobodyone,' he whined. 'I find these clothes in a dustbin and think I do better beggin' in them not that I do no beggin',' he concluded hastily, remembering that vagrancy was an offence.

'As if my Danny do leave his sparkles in the rubbish,' Daisy retorted scornfully.

Looking at the suit, though, there might have been a grain of truth in the old man's claim, for the coat had dark stains down the front of it.

Ask her, Ruby urged.

This is none of my business.

And since when have you minded that?

I cleared my throat.

'Excuse me,' I called and she twisted towards me. 'But I remember seeing your husband… with you,' I added hastily before she assumed that I had spotted him since she thought he had run off. 'And he had a protruding tooth, did he not?'

'I dint steal it,' the man in her grasp said and I was not sure if he was referring to the suit again or the tooth that I was trying to discuss.

The woman smacked his head so hard that it almost made mine ring.

'Never counted 'em,' she said shortly. 'I int Dr Blimmid Hickman.'

I was not sure that Hickman, the tooth puller, merited his medical title but it was on a banner over his stall set up in Pender Court, close enough to the main thoroughfare for people to find him but far enough for most visitors not to witness his *painless* procedures.

'But he had a front one that stuck out from all the others,' I persisted, and she shook the man for no reason that I could discern.

'What of it?' she demanded. 'Int his fault.'

'Indeed not,' I agreed and hurried off to pester Inspector Stanbury again.

–

Stanbury ran a finger under his collar. He would have given anything to be able to loosen it in the heat.

'The body was buried straight after the inquest and I didn't have any pictures taken,' he told me. 'It was too decayed to be recognisable and, anyway, his front teeth were missing.'

'I know that,' I said, trying to hide my exasperation.

Obviously he thought your female memory was too feeble to retain the information, Ruby muttered, making no attempt to hide hers.

'What then?' Stanbury demanded, making no attempt to hide his impatience with my silliness.

'If the man used to have an extra tooth sticking out,' I proposed, 'there would have been an oddly positioned socket in the jawbone.'

'How on earth do you expect...' Stanbury demanded in exasperation but stopped in his tracks. 'Now that you come to mention it though...'

–

Hettie was occupied when I paid her a visit, cooking a pan of something on her paraffin stove.

'I hope you are not going to eat that,' I said for the stench was truly awful.

'I am not quite that desperate yet.' She laughed. 'It is powdered rabbit skin. I boil it up to make glue to paint on my new canvases.'

'But why?' I asked, wrinkling my nose.

'If I don't seal the fabric, the linseed oil of my paints soaks in and rots it,' she explained, giving her brew a stir with a wooden

215

stick. She sniffed the concoction as appreciatively as a connoisseur with a vintage wine. 'I think that should be ready.'

Hettie turned the stove off and perched on a window ledge while I sat on the one wooden chair that was not already claimed by her paintings.

Excuse me but I was here first, a roll of cartridge paper insisted as I lifted it aside.

And so were we, a portrait of a King Charles Spaniel and another of a woman holding a lily dueted.

Stop it, I commanded; if inanimate objects started talking, I would go mad.

You cannot go to where you are already, Ruby assured me over a pandemonium of protests from palates, jam jars and brushes.

'Do you remember Danny the Diamond King?' I asked when the noise had died down.

Hettie looked at me quizzically though she was accustomed to witnessing my daydreams.

'The ukulele player,' she nodded. 'Of course. Why?'

'The police think that he was probably the body from the drain.'

'Oh dear.' Hettie rubbed her brow. 'It seems more awful when you know the person and I rather liked Danny. He helped me look for Grizelda when she went missing and wouldn't take any money, which was just as well...' she half-smiled, 'because I didn't have any.'

Grizelda was a stray cat that Hettie had semi-adopted, but the creature was forever disappearing, eventually for good.

So we are to believe that the disappearance of the cat and the suspect's cooking of animal skin are unrelated events? Hefty ruminated. *Then how do you explain this blood-soaked cloth?*

He pointed accusingly at a paint-stained rag.

'Do they know how Danny got there?' Hettie asked.

'They think he was murdered,' I said, sparing her any gruesome details.

'Goodness!' Hettie said. 'Do they know why?'

'Not yet.'

I could suggest a motive if it had been the hurdy-gurdy man, Ruby said unkindly but understandably.

216

'Oh dear.' Hettie was clearly shaken and, for a moment, I thought she was going to cry but she blew her nose, smearing her cheek in cobalt blue and her lips in yellow ochre streaks, exhaled and said, 'Would you like a cup of tea?'

Every English man or woman's solution to every problem, Ruby commented.

Milk and three sugars, Hefty told her.

Hettie did not stock coffee.

'Not until these fumes clear,' I replied and he clicked his tongue in disappointment.

'How are things going with Martha Ryan and her friend?' Hettie asked.

'I managed to pay Mrs Poynder a visit.'

'Her husband let you in?' she checked in surprise. 'From what Martha told me, he will not allow any callers, not even on the telephone.'

'He did not and he does not,' I replied to her question and her statement. 'I sneaked in.'

Hettie gaped.

'Like when you went into the vicarage to retrieve my tennis ball?'

'A bit like that,' I conceded, 'except that I crept in through the front door rather than climb through a window.'

'Crikey!'

Mind your tongue, young lady. Miss Kidd brandished a blackboard pointer.

'Did nobody see you?' my friend asked, reaching over to stir her glue again.

'Gerrund created a diversion.'

'This is sounding like an episode in one of your books.'

Not one of mine, Ruby objected.

Nor mine, Hefty added.

'Was she all right?'

I shook my head.

'She is bedridden and locked in an attic room.'

'But why?'

'She said her husband is a monster.'

'Most of my lady sitters say that about their spouses,' Hettie pointed out, fetching a four-inch-wide brush and dipping it into her brew to spread it over a stretched canvas. 'It gives a more solid working surface,' she explained, though I felt that I knew quite enough about the subject already.

One can never know too much about art, Hefty lectured me. *Remember how I apprehended an assassin by applying my knowledge of medieval tapestry?*

No, I replied.

It must have been before we met, he said airily and I decided to contemplate the possibility of that another time.

'He killed her parrot,' I told Hettie, 'for saying that he was silly.'

'Blimey!' Hettie expletived, unaware that Miss Kidd had rapped her knuckles but looking shocked nonetheless. 'Have you been back to see Alfred Stanbury?'

'I have but the police are too busy investigating the murders,' I told her. 'And another body was discovered in the Lowers.'

'This is getting as bad as when the Montford Maniac was on the loose.'

'God forbid.'

The town had been panic-striken while he was on the rampage.

Hettie propped the canvas against a wall and picked up another.

'So what will you do now?' she asked, dripping mucilage over her boots.

'There must be some way I can help her,' I said, 'but the servants will not let me into the house and I cannot force an entry.'

'What if you use a Trojan horse?' Hettie suggested.

'And trick them into knocking a wall down?' I dismissed her idea, but she shook her head.

'I didn't quite mean that,' she replied. 'Remember how Cleopatra got in to see Julius Caesar?'

'I am not going to have myself delivered wrapped in a rug,' I objected, 'not even an Armenian one.'

'It was just an idea.' Hettie frowned peevishly.

'And as good as anything I have thought of,' I conceded to mollify her.

Better, Ruby declared. *But, never fear, Thorn, I have a better one yet.*

41: STRONGMEN AND THE GALLOWS

I VIEWED THE ottoman sceptically.

'It does not look very big,' I said.

'Tha's only 'cause it int,' Agnust explained, 'but you int neither.'

I have often wondered what language she speaks, Ruby deliberated. *It is certainly not English.*

'Or comfortable,' I added, brushing my heroine's interruption aside.

'It's English oak, milady,' Gerrund assured me as if the quality and patriotic provenance of the wood made it cosy.

'And the lid is padded.' Agnust stroked the paisley upholstery with a strange fondness.

'On the outside,' I agreed, 'but I shall be on the inside.'

Gerrund scratched his chin.

'There might be space for a small cushion,' he speculated doubtfully.

'Will I be able to breathe?'

You did not worry about that before you shut me in my coffin, Ruby pointed out justifiably, for I had put her in a great many disagreeable and dangerous situations over the few years that we had known each other.

'You do manage this far,' Agnust reasoned.

'Not from inside a blanket box.'

'I have drilled airholes in the sides,' Gerrund reminded me, and I poked at one but could not get the tip of my little finger into it.

'They are tiny.'

'They need to be unobtrusive,' he reasoned, 'and, if I might make a personal observation about milady...'

Tell him he may not, Ruby urged, but Gerrund did not wait for the permission that he had requested.

'Your nostrils are no bigger and, while you only have two of those the last time I counted…'

Is he being sarcastic?

Yes he is, Ruby confirmed. *Tell him he has no business appraising your anatomy and dock his wages.*

'There are twelve holes in the wood for you to breathe through.'

I had an inkling that there was a flaw in that reasoning but could not put my finger on it.

Even you cannot touch an inkling, Ruby informed me.

Romulus would know, but he had gone to help with a measles epidemic in Anglethorpe and there was not the time to exchange correspondence with him.

'This was all your idea,' I said to Agnust, 'but I note that you did not volunteer to do it.'

My maid folded her arms like strongmen do when they are posing for photographic portraits.

'Why bless you,' she laughed, 'I wint get in tha'. I do be much too…'

Fat, I almost filled the pause for her.

'Sensible,' she ended for it was well known that I had never been that. Why, I had even slithered out of the midwife's hands and onto my head on the floor a moment after being born, which at least, or so my mother told me years later, gave them all something to laugh about.

'You could still try my idea,' Gerrund suggested.

'Do I look like Father Christmas?' I demanded. 'And think carefully before you answer that.'

Gerrund scratched his chin.

What? I fumed. *He should not have to consider the question at all.*

'You don't,' he decided.

'Then I have no intention of scrambling down a chimney.'

'You scramble up the kitchen one,' Agnust remarked.

'When?' I asked, because she had made it sound as if I had done that morning and I was almost sure that it was not something I would have forgotten so quickly.

'When you do three-year-old,' she told me, 'and Peewick put you in to clear a bird's nest.'

Peewick was the butler and I remembered now, me but not him, being smacked for that episode.

'It is almost time, milady.'

'We had better get on with it, then,' I decided and Gerrund looked discreetly away while I stepped into the box, sat down, shuffled along, rearranged my dress, and laid back. 'This would have been much easier in trousers.'

Agnust looked nauseated.

'And how do I explain to your dear mamma that you goo and suffocate in men's clothes?'

'Lady Violet is not going to suffocate,' Gerrund insisted furiously. 'Unless she runs out of air,' he murmured, and I was so pleased that he could make light of the situation.

'Leave the gallows humour to those who are on the gallows,' I snapped.

Not a bad parting shot, I told myself, hoping that it was not going to be my final quip.

The doorbell rang and, while Agnust went to answer it, my man handed me the key to lock myself in when he had carefully lowered the lid.

Now light a fire under her, Ruby urged.

If I do not survive this, who will write you out of your predicament? I challenged but did not wait for a response, for I had just discovered an interesting fact.

Give me a coffee and a Beeman's and you will find a contented lady novelist, for I no longer envied Ruby her adventures to the slightest degree.

It was not long before I discovered one of the flaws in Gerrund's nostralistic logic. The holes would have been, as he had claimed, sufficient for respiration had the cotton of my flamingo pink dress not billowed up to block them. It was too late to bang on the lid as heavy boots were clomping about already, carefully avoiding any carpeted areas in order to deceive any casual listener into thinking that a Lancashire clog dance was underway.

'There it is,' Gerrund announced loudly to make me aware that we were not alone, just in case I had dozed off in my cosy nest.

'Thought you said it was a blanket,' the cabby shouted, presumably deciding that my man must be deaf.

'Blanket *box*,' Gerrund bawled.

I cannot breathe.

You have gone an unusual but not unattractive shade of blue, Ruby told me and, with the cool-headedness that only generations of breeding and a disciplined upbringing can imbue, I panicked.

I am suffocating! I gasped, surprised to find that I had not whimpered it aloud.

If your air holes are covered, try uncovering them, Ruby advised and I would have thanked her had she not added, *you twit.*

As quietly as I could, I clawed the cotton down and was relieved to see a pretty display of light beams streaming in. Slightly reassured I forced myself to breathe slowly, not sure why that might help, but it was something that I had read one should do in order to stay calm.

A hip flask would have done a better job, Ruby told me but I thought it more sensible to arrive at my destination sober.

'Careful,' Gerrund yelled as I rose.

He must have had one end and the cabby the other.

'Somethin' precious in there?' the driver shouted.

Very precious indeed, I knew my man would answer.

'Not really,' he yelled, 'but it's fragile.'

'Fragile is as fragile does,' the driver observed, managing to be loud, philosophical and talk drivel simultaneously.

Balderdash is what balderdash is, Ruby spouted.

She had become quite fond of obviousisms lately and I resolved to do something about it.

You have more urgent concerns than that, she told me and I agreed heartily, though we were both selfishly thinking of our own situations.

'Mind the paintwork,' Agnust warned too late.

'Need another lick anyways,' the driver shouted, and I wondered in what kind of palace he luxuriated because I would love to pay him a visit and assess the chandeliers.

My new lilliputian home swayed and tilted.

'Mind the steps,' Agnust warned as the person at the front stumbled.

'Now she tell me,' the driver complained.

'They were there when you came in,' Gerrund pointed out, both continuing their intercourse at never less than full volume.

'I dint coom in backward,' the driver retorted.

Blimmid pest, I fumed for the hurdy-gurdy man was starting to grind out an alleged tune. 'I Lost My Love in Leamington Spa' I diagnosed, though it sounded more like 'How Can I Forget Her When She's Tattooed on My Arm?' – *Arm* being the printable version of the song.

It could not be the latter though because that sounded more like the former. Was I making sense or suffering from a lack of oxygen?

You are just being you, Ruby told me unkindly.

'May be fragile but it weigh a blimmid ton,' the cabby moaned, though I have never known one yet not to complain about effort involved in lifting the lightest of luggage.

Do not dare to comment on my weight, I warned.

'It's precious,' Gerrund said and, if the temperature rose in my ottoman world, it was because I glowed, 'little more than junk,' he continued, chilling the atmosphere instantly, 'but you know what women are like.'

All men know what women are like, which is why they never misunderstand or misuse us.

What are women like? I umbraged.

There is no such word, Ruby corrected me, lady detective and adventuress all at once transmogrified into my governess, but suddenly the blanket box was a rowing boat caught in a force twelve gale.

'Watch it!' Gerrund warned. 'You nearly dropped her.'

'Her?'

'Her box.'

Quick thinking Gerrundino, Ruby complimented my man in an attempt to Mexicanise him. She had never really cared for Englishmen. They lacked the fire of most of her would-be inamoratos or should that have been inamorati? Stupidly I had forgotten to take my *Oxford English Dictionary*. It is always the same when you pack in a hurry.

There was a bump. From the outside it probably didn't look like much. From the inside it was like being in a derailed train.

Which one? Ruby enquired because hers had gone into a ravine in the Rocky Mountains, which made my experience with Gerrund seem tame indeed. Nobody had died in our accident whereas only Ruby and Two-eyed Jake had survived hers.

'Slide it across,' the cabby said, and there was a grating sound reminiscent of that made by our railway carriage careering on its side over an unmade lane.

They must have put me on the parcel platform at the rear.

How does it feel to be an item of baggage? Ruby asked, never having forgiven me for smuggling her out of Brazil in a steamer trunk, and while I considered her question, we dipped.

That must be the men climbing aboard, I realised.

Leave the detective work to me, Lady Violet, Hefty said stiffly for he had been rather left out of things since rescuing Joakim Kodak in *The Acrophobic Man* or *The Man With a Fear of Heights* as it was titled for American readers, who were only slightly more numerous than the words in the title.

I only wish that I could, I assured him, for I should be enjoying being told by Agnust that I did not need that sixth cup of coffee.

Off we set fairly smoothly over the tarred road, leaving it not with a bump but with numberless clatters. The driver's and passengers' seats of a growler are upholstered, but luggage does not merit such comfort and being over the wheel, despite the suspension, I could feel every cobble as if I were being dragged over it.

This is awful, I moaned.

No it is not, Ruby argued. *That...* I was flung up against the top of the box and dropped clumsily back again... *was awful*.

'Blimmid potholes,' the driver cursed as we stopped. 'Rattle my bone they do.'

Want to swap places? Ruby offered as we set off again.

The whine of the hurdy-gurdy may have faded but not that of the cabby.

'Blimmid traffic,' he complained. 'Dint ought be allowed on the road.'

We rumbled forward over a bump and stopped again.

'Ow!' I cried aloud as my face hit the lid.

'What do you say?' the cabby asked.

'How much further?' Gerrund asked.

Was my nose bleeding?

'You dint know where Gainsbru Square do be?' the driver asked.

I felt it gingerly.

'How much further would it be to Plymouth?' Gerrund asked. It was certainly sore.

'Why you do ask tha'?' the driver asked.

'Just wondering,' Gerrund blustered, 'for a wager.'

'How far you say it goo?'

Ouch! I managed to say just to myself that time.

'I haven't placed my wager yet.'

'Put your tin on three thousan' six hundred and forty-nine mile,' the cabby advised, and I decided against using him for anywhere out of town.

Off we set again, any conversation, loud as it was, being drowned out by the thunderstorm of the wheels.

'Here we are.'

Oh thank goodness, I breathed, relieved that I still could.

'Not a bad gaff,' the driver assessed, 'though I favour neo-Gothic myself.'

I would not be employing him as an architect either I decided as I endured the scrapes, knocks and sways of being dragged off and carried what I assumed was across the pavement and, from the way I tilted forty-five degrees – head down of course because feet down would not have been uncomfortable enough – up the steps.

'Ring the bell,' Gerrund instructed.

'It do be 'lectric,' the cabby informed him.

'Good.'

'Tint good. Two men die ev'ry day from touchin' 'lectric bell buttons.'

This, I suspected, was another of those friend-of-an-acquaintance stories, though I had not heard it before.

'Leave it to me,' Gerrund huffed and I was dumped onto the tiles.

'Best protecting is to stand in a bowl of water,' the driver advised.

'Didn't think to bring one with me,' my man said and, even from my hiding place, I heard the distant sound of a bell. 'Ah!' Gerrund yelled in shock and it sounded like he had fallen against the door.

'I do warn him,' the cabby declared to the world. 'Dead,' he added more quietly. 'Dead as a puffin.'

Dead? I echoed in horror.

The key was still in my left hand. In fact I had clutched it so hard throughout the journey that a burglar could have made a copy from the imprint in my palm. Loosening my grip, I took the key in my right hand and was just about to insert it in the lock when I heard Gerrund gloat, 'Fooled you.'

'A miracle!' the cabby proclaimed. 'You do die and rise again.'

'How could I have been dead when I was still standing up?'

'Like a puffin,' the driver reasserted and I began to look back fondly to the time that his voice had been inaudible. 'They do die standin'.'

'No they don't.'

'Ever seen a puffin lie itself down?'

'I've never seen a puffin.'

'Well I see one in The Museum of Curious Things,' the cabby said. 'Dead as a puffin he is and standin' up.'

But before this interesting and informative debate could continue I heard a voice I recognised as Susie's say, 'What do you want?' and I hoped that she had no ambitions to rise from the kitchen to the parlour, for she showed little promise in that direction.

'Delivery for Dr Poynder,' Gerrund announced.

'I wint 'spectin' nothin'.'

'Your master confides in you, does he?' my man enquired.

'No he dant,' she replied indignantly. 'I do be a good girl.'

'He does not tell you everything that is going on,' Gerrund explained. 'We had better bring it in.'

I had taught him that trick I remembered proudly as she said, 'You had better bring it in.'

Up I went and along and down with a clomp onto the floor.

'We are to take it to your mistress's room,' Gerrund informed her. 'Not her bedroom, the one she is in now.'

'I dint know nothin' 'bout tha'.'

I was getting cramp in my right calf.

'He won't be happy if he comes home and finds it in the hall,' my man warned.

'But I int allowen in there.'

I tried to stretch but there was no room to do anything other than shrink, which encouraged the cramp but not me.

'Then we had better leave it outside her door,' Gerrund declared.

'I dint know,' Susie mithered.

At least the cramp was bearable, I consoled myself, compared to the pain in my other leg.

'Suits me,' he told her. 'I don't want to drag it up all those stairs but Dr Poynder will be furious.'

And my neck was cricked.

'Stairs?' the cabby protested. 'You dint say nothin' 'bout stairs.'

Get on with it, Ruby and I chorused.

'Think my mistress will give you that guinea tip for leaving it in the hall?' Gerrund enquired.

'Oh I dint know 'bout tha'.'

Neither did I.

'Tha's a diff'rent kettle o' water,' the driver decided and we were on our journey again.

Head first, I begged as my feet rose and I slid head down yet again. *Have I really been such a bad employer?*

You never remember Gerrund's birthday, Ruby accused me.

Neither does he, I rejoined, *but I give him a present on every anniversary of his entering my service.*

'Mind the paint,' the cabby warned, so it must have been better than mine though I had had it done five months ago. 'And the wallpaper,' he added.

My left arm had gone to sleep and I realised something else that had been bothering me all along. It was almost insufferably hot in there.

We levelled out but, before I had a chance to be grateful for miniscule mercies, we were on the way up again.

'You can leave it there,' Susie told them.

'We are all going downstairs now,' Gerrund declared loudly but, if either of his companions thought that odd, they did not think it odd enough to comment upon.

I heard footsteps and waited until they faded, and all I could hear then were the clink of me dropping the key and a woman crying 'don't leave me!' and neither I nor Ruby had spoken those words.

42: INDUSTRIAL STRIFE IN THE THORN FACTORY

THE KEY WAS not difficult to find. After all there were not many places that I could search. Inserting it into the keyhole was a trickier business because I needed to turn towards that side and I could not, but I twisted and stretched and managed to wiggle it in. Luckily it was only a struggle to unlock the lid. I raised it cautiously and painfully. Even my eyes complained about that action, though you might have expected them to be glad to have more to do.

I listened hard. Why should my ears be the only parts of me that were not strained? There were no more voices though, only the faint whimper of a *young lady of old breedin'* struggling to unpack herself from a box.

Hauling myself into a sitting position, I found myself where I had hoped to be – on the second-floor landing. Sitting up was easy enough – I simply grasped the rim and hauled – and the action only hurt most of my muscles, but the rest was not so simple.

Seven years too late my legs had joined the matchgirls and gone on strike for better conditions.

I will never force you into an ottoman again, I promised and they returned warily to work. *Unless it is absolutely necessary*, I provisoed, hoping that they did not hear me.

My blood was a little less cooperative and still refusing to go back into circulation, but I did not have time to sort out its legitimate complaints.

With no audience I raised my skirt to a height that would have caused a riot at the Moulin Rouge.

I... Ruby began.

Later, I snapped. We could wallow in Ruby's memories of being a can-can girl another time, but this might be my only chance to save Dolores.

Making a stirrup with my hands under my knee, I heaved my right leg up to swing it over the side then – using that side to lean on and almost tipping the box over in the process – managed to get to my feet, who were grumbling like dockworkers presented with an extra load during one of their allegedly many breaks for tea.

My joints had gone rusty from inaction. If this was what arthritis felt like, I was sorry to hurt its feelings, but I did not believe that I should ever welcome it.

My blood was working now, rushing through my peripheral arteries like sink water through unblocked drains and my nerves, which had been taking an unauthorised holiday, returned to work angrily, flushing all the pins and needles that had accumulated during their inaction into my feet.

When I was twelve I peeked into Romulus's copy of *Franken-stein*. It was a badly printed version. The *o* of *monster* looked more like a *u*, so that I went for years under the misapprehension that the doctor had assembled an Irishman and that this was a terrible creature indeed. Today I found myself doing an excellent impression of the stiff-legged manner of that unfortunate creature's walking but after a lot of calf-rubbing, I managed to totter to the door.

That's more like an Irishman, Ruby quipped, her opinion of Hibernians being coloured by a confrontation with a mob of navvies on St Patrick's night.

My brain, seeing no reason why it should be any more industrious than the rest of me, weighed my options carelessly before calculating that there were not any to measure.

Perhaps, instead of manufacturing manufacturing metaphors, you might like to concentrate on the business in hand, Ruby suggested, mildly for her. *In other words, buck up your ideas, Thorn*, she cajoled, and this from the woman who had fallen asleep when she was supposed to be guarding Princess Fogianna.

My laudanum was drugged, she bristled.

With opium? I enquired. *Surely not?* And, for once, Ruby had no reply, though I could still hear her cracking her knuckles. It was an unattractive practice picked up from Gerrund that she engaged in sometimes when she was cranky, which was frequently of late.

The key was back where it belonged on the lintel and I took it down, slipping it into the lock. Behind me a floorboard creaked and I pirouetted – though not with the grace that Miss Kidd had failed to instil in me.

There was nobody there.

It was merely springing back into place, Ruby explained provokingly for she knew I had realised that.

I turned the key.

'It is only me,' I whispered.

How informative, Ruby, rarely missing a chance to undermine me, jeered.

'I knew you would come to save me,' Dolores Poynder declared, and I only hoped that her faith in me was not misplaced.

43: THE MYSTERIOUS COLIN AND THE SHIVERING OF TIMBERS

I CLOSED THE door, dismayed at the loud click the catch made. It had not done that last time.

Why not slam it? Ruby suggested, but I did not have time to remind her of how she had knocked over a harp while creeping through Schönbrunn Palace on Christmas Eve at midnight.

After locking the door I took out the key.

Dolores, I made out in the gloom, was still in bed. I had considered borrowing Gerrund's safety lantern but, as he pointed out, the smell of the paraffin would give me away. That seemed sensible, but Ruby believed it was more because he did not want to lend it to me after I had bent a prong of his carving fork while trying to pick a faulty lock in my writing box.

'I need to talk to you first,' I said.

'Why?' she asked.

'To decide what is the best course of action.'

Dolores wriggled under the covers.

'I thought you had come to rescue me.'

'That was going to be my first question,' I assured her. 'Do you need rescuing?'

'I most certainly do,' she said. 'What is your name?'

'Violet.'

'That is a pretty name,' she mused. 'It reminds me of a flower.'

Well shiver my timbers, Ruby sarcasmed. It was an expression she had picked up from the odious and odoriferous Captain Fisheye.

She raised her head to look about. 'Why does Martha not come?'

'She is not allowed to.'

'Oh,' Dolores greeted my statement in surprise. 'Edward said that she did not wish to see me.'

'She called many times, in person and on the telephone, and she wrote to you.'

'I was not told,' she said, 'but then I suppose that I would not be.'

'Why not?'

'Why indeed?' Dolores coughed. 'I wrote a letter to Martha and threw it out of the window in the hope that someone would post it for me.'

'Somebody did,' I confirmed, 'and Martha went to the Café Cordoba every day for a week.'

'Oh,' Dolores mused. 'She must have consumed a lot of coffee and I am not sure that it is good for her nerves.'

'Can you walk?' I asked.

'I have not tried recently.'

In other words no, Ruby contributed, *or at least not properly.*

'Not even around this room?'

'Where is there to walk to?' Dolores asked with interest as if there were a scenic route that she had yet to discover.

'To the window,' I suggested.

'Edward says he will have me chained to the frame if I do that again.'

'Why does he keep you here?'

'It is our home.'

'But why are you locked in?'

'So that I do not escape,' she explained as one might to an especially simple-minded simpleton.

I tried a different approach.

'You used to be allowed out and about.'

'I know,' she agreed dreamily, 'but I was naughty.'

'In what way?'

'Very.'

Give her a shake, Ruby urged and I had heard worse suggestions.

'What did you do that was naughty?'

Dolores mulled that over.

'It is difficult to know where to begin.'

'Try the beginning,' I suggested tetchily and hoped that I was not in for a long and tedious catalogue of faults in household management or social blunders, like the time that my mother

232

had seated a man next to his wife at dinner, forgetting that they were happily married.

Dolores stroked her chin.

'Might I see the key?' she cajoled. 'Pleeeese.'

'Why?' I asked, but she held out her hand and I saw that she was not wearing a glove, as I had thought when I first visited her, but was wrapped from her knuckles to her wrist in a grimy bandage.

'I need to know what kind it is.'

She is either an imbecile or mad, Ruby declared.

Puzzled, I handed it over and Dolores turned it side to side.

'I can only tell by tasting it,' she said, giving the handle a lick. 'I think it is…' and, before I could stop her, Dolores popped the key into her mouth like a child with a sweet, savoured it for a moment and swallowed.

'What on earth!' I cried and she opened her mouth like a patient proving that she has taken her medicine.

'All gone,' she declared.

An imbecile, Ruby decided, while I stood ready to pat Dolores on the back, but a key it transpired, unlike a wad of Beeman's, slips down comfortably for she smacked her lips appreciatively and said, 'Delicious.'

'But now we are both trapped,' I told her, aghast.

'Do not worry,' Dolores reassured me, though I most assuredly would. 'Sit on the bed beside me and I shall tell you exactly how naughty I have been.'

And demented, Ruby added ominously.

44: WICKED WOMEN AND THE POISONED CLAW

I SAT CAUTIOUSLY on the edge of the bed near Dolores's feet, fairly confident that I could jump off before she could spring at me, should the fancy take her.

'But first…' Dolores primped her hair but it did not look any less of a mess. Long strands flopped over her left eye or rose in coils in odd tangles, reminding me of the snakes writhing on Medusa's head. I had seen an illustration of the gorgon in Professor Wheatstone's *An Abbreviated History of Wicked Women*, a much bulkier volume than its companion, *The Complete History of Virtuous Women*.

'Shall I tell you what attracted me to Edward?' she enquired, pulling her hand away gingerly.

His money? Ruby suggested.

'His kindness,' she answered her own question without waiting for me to say whether I wanted her to or not. 'He is a very gentle gentleman.'

I doubt her rotting parrot would agree with that, Ruby argued.

'But what about Colin?' I said, and Dolores stretched her neck as if trying to see over the heads of a crowd.

'My husband did not want to harm him,' she sniffed, clearly peeved by my criticism, 'but, as everybody knows, you have to be cruel to be kind.'

I never quite understood that phrase. It is something that adults say to justify their nastinesses, if that is the word.

It is not, Ruby informed me. *And the quotation is from* Hamlet. She snorted. *So it must be true*, she added bitterly, having hated the bard ever since being obliged to play the part of Desdemona with a theatre company touring Tasmania.

'You should have seen how upset he was when that poor boy died.' Dolores patted her serpents to pacify them, but one of them reared even higher.

'Mungo Peers,' I contributed, keeping a wary eye on her coiffure as it bobbed alarmingly towards me.

I knew, of course, that those untrained tresses could not bite, but then I had known, of course, that a dead grass snake I came across in the henhouse could not bite me either until I realised that it had been – as my grandmother's gravestone proclaimed – *not dead but sleeping*.

'And Sheba.' Dolores sucked her lower lip. 'Edward doted on that dog though I always preferred Chaos. He may be a scallywag but he does not bark at night.' She clicked her tongue. 'Or any other time,' she mused in all seriousness.

I do not suppose that Sheba got stuck up monkey puzzle trees, Ruby rallied to the deceased canine's defence. She had not been fond of cats since *The Case of the Poisoned Claw*.

'You must have been very proud of him,' I commented and she smiled sadly.

Smiled sadly, Ruby echoed incredulously. *Did she also frown happily?*

'He was quite the hero,' Dolores concurred.

There was a time I was quite the hero, Inspector Hefty reminisced reproachfully.

Yes, I agreed, *but you never made me any money*.

The root of all evil, he preached with a newfound piety.

Ruby said nothing but her smirk spoke paragraphs.

'And he was so attentive when I fell ill,' Dolores told me.

Attentive in what way? Ruby asked and I hoped that she was not being prurient, but she only urged, *Ask her.*

'Was this after your trip abroad?' I checked and Dolores wriggled her shoulders.

'I was unwell before that,' she said. 'That was why I went with him, to consult a professor who had written a paper about my condition.'

'May I ask what that condition is?' I enquired tentatively.

'Headaches,' she replied simply, and part of me was not surprised with all those creatures emerging from her scalp. She winced. Surely one could not really have struck at her?

You are letting your imagination run away with you, Ruby scolded, ignoring the fact that my doing so was how she had come about.

'Terrible headaches,' Dolores said, putting her fingertips to her temples.

'How awful,' I sympathised for I could guess exactly how she felt.

Especially after a few absinthes, Ruby put in, never burdened by empathy.

'Do you know what was really awful?' Dolores challenged.

The way that Bolton Wanderers played in last year's cup final, Ruby suggested, though neither of us had any interest in football and I only knew about it because Gerrund had lost five shillings on the match and was grumpy about it for days afterwards. *Sutcliffe was half-asleep in the goal.*

'No,' I said to be met with a blank look. 'What?'

Dolores picked something off her bedspread and pinched it hard between her forefinger and the plate of her thumb as one might crush a flea. Now that I thought of it, I had an itch on my waist.

So do I. Ruby scratched herself vigorously, secure in the knowledge that only I could see her.

'A crumb,' Dolores explained, and I hoped that she was right because she popped that into her mouth as well. 'Of toast,' she diagnosed.

I am sure it jumped, Ruby asserted, then hesitated because there were other specks on the bedding, none of which was leaping about. *Almost sure*, she admitted.

'What was really awful?' I struggled to steer the conversation back on track.

It was bad enough dealing with Ruby's constant interruptions without Dolores getting distracted too.

'Edwina,' she said with viperous venom. 'It was all the fault of that vixxxxen.'

With that last word something hissed and I did not think – not for more than a moment at any rate – that it was Dolores's hair, and I knew that it was not me, which only left Dolores herself.

Ruby jumped back. And I had thought she was fearless.

I have cramp in my leg, she explained unconvincingly.

'What did Edwina do?' I asked while Dolores inspected another crumb.

'Edward dismissed her,' she replied and failed to reply simultaneously.

Ruby and I looked at each other.

When did you get changed? She was in rather a nice silk dress, cornflowers on cream stripes alternating with hellebores on beige.

Oh ages ago, she replied airily.

Come to think of it, I had seen that material in Auberge's of Bond Street but thought it rather expensive.

I put it on your account, she said.

'Why?' I asked.

Because I lost all my money at Bezique.

'He told me,' Dolores began for she, at least, realised that I had been asking her, 'that he had caught Edwina stealing my jewellery but, when we came home from our trip, I came across a letter from a private detective who my husband was employing to discover her whereabouts.' Dolores held the crumb towards the pale light as if assessing its clarity, cut, carat and colour. 'When I questioned Edward he told me that he believed that she still had a necklace of mine and was much reassured when I told him that nothing was missing.' She tossed the crumb aside as carelessly as one might a…

What is the word?

Crumb? Ruby suggested.

'However,' Dolores said, with that sudden loudness that governesses use when their charge is falling asleep during an especially exhilarating chapter of Professor Ottermouth's *Brief* – though not brief enough – *History of Harpsichord Making from Blanchet to Kirkman*. 'Three days later I overheard my husband saying on the telephone that it was imperative to find her.'

I would strongly recommend him not to embark on a criminal career, Ruby advised but Dolores was still talking.

'When I challenged him he finally told me the truth.'

I doubt that very much, Ruby said disdainfully. She had a low opinion of husbands generally after her vows to Mr Dorchester had been interrupted by his indignant and heavily armed wife in the antithesis of a shotgun wedding.

'Edwina had made improper advances to my husband,' Dolores explained, 'but, rather than distress my stretched nerves with details of her lasciviousness, he had told me that she was a thief.'

'Then why…' I began.

'A doctor's reputation is paramount,' she insisted, though Rommy might have argued that a medical man's skills were more important, 'and that filthy hussy was threatening to make false allegations about him.' She swept her hand over the bedspread, the specks springing into the air with an athleticism which any flea might envy, if it were of a competitive nature. 'He was going to offer to purchase her a passage to America with enough money for her to set up a new life.'

Who said crime doesn't pay? Hefty wondered though he had told many a villain as much himself.

He was selecting fibres from the curtains and sealing them in envelopes.

'But,' Dolores continued, 'I have read enough of those awful Inspector Hefty stories to know better than that.'

Ruby's laughter could not quite muffle the sound of grinding teeth – Hefty's, I thought, until a complaint from my molars made me realise that it was mine. To be fair to Dolores I had written his tales under the pseudonym of Bernard Quartermaster.

Do not feel yourself to be under any obligation to be fair, Hefty fumed.

'Blackmailers can never be silenced with money,' Dolores propounded, though she was unlikely to have had a wide range of experiences with them. 'They can only be silenced by death.'

45: THE MOUSE TRAP

I CHEWED OVER Dolores's last statement, but it did not become any more palatable.

'Death?' I checked.

I was confident that I had not misheard her, but I rather hoped that she was talking theoretically.

'Indeed,' she confirmed 'And that is why I decided to take matters into my own hands.'

'What did you do?' I asked.

Feebly, Ruby chipped in.

'Why I started to kill people of course,' Dolores chuckled.

'Of course,' I breathed.

Punily, Ruby supplied another adverb no more welcome than its predecessor.

'The first person I killed,' Dolores continued, as chattily as she might explain her choice of footwear, 'was what I believe is referred to as a *busker*.'

Get out of here, Ruby advised. *Now.*

The door is locked.

Try the window.

It is sealed.

You never told me that.

I have only just remembered seeing the screws.

While we bickered as to whether I was merely or utterly useless I looked about me. There was nothing that I could use to pick the lock and, even if there were, I would have no idea how to go about it.

Utterly, Ruby asserted and I found myself unable to refute her claim.

'The one in the drain behind the rope factory?' I checked, though I did not know of any other murdered street musicians in the town.

'The very same,' she agreed happily.

'But why?'

'I wanted his coat,' she replied, folding her arms one way then the other as if not quite sure how to go about the procedure.

'His coat?' I hoped that I did not sound quite as incredulous as I felt. She had a great many serviceable clothes hanging in the attic and no doubt her wardrobes were stuffed to the gunnels with others.

Wardrobes do not have gunnels, Ruby nit-picked and Dolores smiled in fond remembrance.

'His coat,' she confirmed. 'It was all sparkly and I thought it would make a good costume for Oberon in a production of *A Midsummer Night's Dream*, if ever I produced one.'

'If ever...' I echoed.

And I thought the parrot was dead, Ruby quipped but suddenly grew serious. *If you want my advice, Thorn, you will bludgeon her unconscious and cut her stomach open with the miniature folding penknife on your charm bracelet.*

Even by Ruby's standards that was a gruesome suggestion and I was not tempted to take it up. The idea of rummaging through Dolores's half-digested breakfast was not an appealing one. Apart from being messily brutal, it would have been difficult to explain why I tricked my way into the room of a virtual stranger and performed a pre-mortem dissection upon her. After all, I had swallowed the key to my father's safe when I was a child and on neither occasion did he threaten to disembowel me.

What then? Ruby challenged. *Wait for nature to take its course like he had to?*

Though a much less cruel idea, it did not appeal to me either.

'I asked very nicely,' Dolores continued, 'but he would not give it to me and I have always believed that one should not offer money to beggars because they only spend it on alcohol.'

Tut tut, Ruby tutted.

Strictly speaking, he was not a vagrant, Hefty quibbled.

He was crouching to inspect a mousetrap loaded with mouldy cheese.

'He even turned his back on me,' Dolores complained, folding her arms.

'So you strangled him,' I prompted.

Cheddar, Hefty printed in his notebook.

'I know I did,' she huffed, 'with a bit of rope that was lying about. It is a lot more difficult choking people than you might think. You would not credit the fuss he made, struggling and trying to pull my hands away – as if anyone would miss him. He kicked my shins so hard I had three bruises later,' she complained.

The bandage was coming undone and Dolores tucked a loose end in around her wrist but really it needed changing.

If only there were a doctor in the house, Ruby sarcasmed. *And, it does not matter how often you use it, that is still not a word.*

It will be, I forecast without much hope because the *Oxford English Dictionary* had politely rejected my suggestion of *aroundipity*, the happy faculty of being around somewhere at the right time.

'I know what you are thinking,' Dolores told me, and I earnestly hoped not as it was bad enough having all my characters roaming unconstrained around my head, disorganising my ideas and reading my private thoughts.

'You are thinking that I should have stabbed him,' she said, which should have at least given me the comfort that she had not penetrated my meninges yet but – perhaps not strangely – I felt less than reassured. 'But how could I?' She held out her hands to ridicule the suggestion that it had not even occurred to me to make. 'For...' Dolores treated me to a giggle, 'I did not have a knife besides which...'

She stared blankly at the ceiling.

Besides which what? Ruby prompted, impatient in less than a tick of my watch.

I looked at the birdcage, buckled and empty in the far corner. Ruby would have dismantled it and twisted a bar into a lockpick. Lady Violet Thorn did not because she could not.

You would have been much more resourceful if I had written you, Ruby informed me. She had changed again, into a smart Prussian blue ensemble and put her hair up a little higher, which rather suited her. *And*, she continued, *I would not have got you into all the debacles in which you embroil me.*

'It would have damaged the coat and got blood on it,' Dolores was saying, having lost interest in the uninteresting ceiling. 'Eventually he sagged and I could not hold him up any further, but I kept my rope pulled tight as I was not sure if he was feigning death. Those people are most untrustworthy. One of them stole my purse once.'

'What happened then?' I asked.

'Nothing.' She clapped her hands together then, remembering that it hurt, winced and inhaled sharply. 'I told the police but they did nothing of course.'

'You told...' I began incredulously.

She is talking about her purse, Ruby explained.

'What happened after you strangled the busker?' I asked, and Dolores shook her injured paw.

'Well I thought, since he was departed – God rest his soul...'

'Amen,' I put in automatically.

'I might as well have all his clothes. They were no use to him now.'

'And so you stripped him.'

'Goodness.' She blew on her fingertips as if they were embers and she was trying to relight a fire. 'But it was such a horrid job.' She curled her mouth like I did when given cold trotters bathed in congealed fat for breakfast once. 'But I did it,' she declared proudly before wrinkling her mouth again. 'I was going to leave his combinations but...' She half-suppressed a retch. 'He was not wearing any.'

I do not suppose he was expecting to be undressed, Ruby defended him, just as she had the pauper outside *Mars Mansions* who turned out to be the son of a maharaja.

A Maharaj Kumar, Ruby tutted at my ignorance of the ranks of Indian nobility.

'What did you do with his body?' I asked.

'Oh that.' Dolores twirled her right hand as if I had asked where she had lost a handkerchief. 'I took the cover off a drain – it was jolly heavy I can tell you – and dragged him over and dropped him in.' She crossed her hands on top of the covers. 'I supposed he would be washed out to sea but...' Her lips twitched in the way that people's do when they are going to make a joke. 'At least he would be washed.'

'Was he dirty then?' The Danny Dixon I had seen performing was always quite particular about his appearance.

'He had bled from his mouth down his coat and he…' Dolores failed to suppress a retch this time. 'He had…' She struggled to find the right words. 'Made a mess in his trousers.'

Strangled people do that, Hefty explained, though they never had in any of my books.

'It was horrible,' Dolores complained. 'I did not see quite how bad they were until I had gone out of the yard and along the street to under a lamppost.'

'What did you do with them?'

'Well,' she waved her unbandaged hand. 'I threw them in the bin so the stupid filthy man died in vain.' She touched the mark on her cheek, almost fondly, it seemed. 'But worse was yet to come.'

Worse than murder? Hefty chewed on his pencil dubiously.

'My dress had become horribly soiled in the process,' Dolores told me, pausing, probably for the sympathy that would never be forthcoming. 'I could not possibly go home in it like that and all the shops were closed.'

Please don't say you killed a woman for her clothes, I begged.

'So I had to get them cleaned,' she said, somewhat to my relief until I remembered.

'The laundress,' I said aloud and, with those words, Dolores scowled.

'The laundressss,' she and her hair hissed menacingly again and even Ruby took another step backwards. The last time I had seen a snarl like that I had awoken from a nightmare in two things – a production of Turgenev's *Lack of Money* – or *Lack of Excitement*, as Ruby had rechristened it – and a cold sweat.

Ladies do not sweat, Hefty declared piously. *They glow.*

Woke up in a cold glow, I corrected myself.

Satisfied with that, Inspector Havelock Hefty cleared his throat and applied himself to the business in hand. This was always his favourite part of the job.

Dolores Poynder, he declared in his best official manner, *I am arresting you on a charge of murder.*

Hefty braced himself in case his suspect attempted to flee, but Dolores Poynder was not even listening. It was as if she and he were in different worlds.

46: BROKEN NAILS AND NERO

AS IF SHE had shared my ruminations over the subject of dreams, Dolores closed her eyes. Had she nodded off? The medicines she took might make her do that, but I could not hear if her breathing was slumberous or not and I was not going to risk putting my ear close enough to check, especially since her teeth were still bared and not as clean as they might have been.

This might be an opportune moment to leave, Ruby suggested.

How? I demanded. *I cannot politely excuse myself.*

You are supposed to be the one who gets me out of life-threatening situations, she reminded me, *not vice versa.*

Life-threatening? I repeated in alarm and, while Ruby began to calculate how long it would take me to hack through the wall with the heels of my cranberry Wilber-Lowe shoes, I went to double-check the window. Needless to say it was still sealed tight. I poked a fingerplate into one of the screw slots and twisted. My nail broke and I broke into an *ouch* but the screw had not turned one minute of one degree.

Next time go anticlockwise, Ruby advised, but we both knew that it was a hopeless task.

I could try shouting and banging on the floor.

We are not supposed to be here, she reminded me, *besides which do you think, perchance, it might awaken her?* Ruby put her hands on her hips. *And you know how cranky you can be when you are woken up.*

I am never cranky, I objected crankily.

'She was difficult from the start,' Dolores announced without raising even one of her eyelids.

'The laundress?' I checked just in case she had overheard and meant me, and Dolores nodded lazily.

'I had to knock and knock before she would admit me.' She raised one lid a quarter way reminding me of Rodrigo, my kitten, trying to lure mice out of the wainscoting to play. 'Even then she made harebrained excuses like lazy servants always do. Saying it was late and that she was closed and that the fire had gone out and she had emptied the copper.' The lid lowered. 'She demanded a great deal of money to wash and dry and press my clothes – almost as much as they were worth – and she took an age to do it. I told her that I had soiled them rescuing an orphan who had fallen in the sewers, but she did not seem to believe me.' Dolores scowled. 'She even asked what I had been doing down there in the first place.'

What a sauce! Ruby exclaimed in mock sympathy.

'A lady does not care to have her word brought into question by a low, fat, common laundry woman and I had no intention of paying her all that money and so...'

Let me guess, Ruby sighed, though I had already formed my own suspicions.

Dolores unfolded her arms carefully as if checking the parts in case she wished to reassemble them.

'In the end,' she continued dreamily, 'the slattern gave me no choice. I told her that she had left a pocket handkerchief in the copper and...' She raised her head. 'While she fished about for it with her wooden tongs in the dirty water, I crouched, pretending to be tying a bootlace, grasped her stout ankles, heaved with all my might and...' The lids sprang open and Dolores stared at the recalled images. 'Tipped her in.' Her head dropped back and she snuggled a little deeper into her pillows. 'That was most annoying and disappointing.'

She closed her eyes again.

'Why?'

'Annoying because the splash soaked my dress and hair.' She stuck her thumb up like Nero feeling magnanimous at the Colosseum. 'Disappointing because I had prepared myself for a fight but she just went limp straight away.' She popped the thumb in her mouth and sucked. 'Why do you suppose that was?' she enquired indistinctly between slurps.

'She probably gasped in surprise and inhaled the water,' I suggested, and Dolores nodded amicably and extracted her thumb to examine it.

'Then what happened?' I asked and she flapped her bandaged hand as if my question were a persistent fly.

'I took a bundle of clothes and my money – it was no use to her now – blew out the lamp – I am always telling Tilly off for wasting oil and it is important to lead by example – annnn...' Dolores drew out that last syllable so much that even the word lost patience and cast aside its final *d*. 'Shut-the-door-and-went-home,' she finished in a rush.

I absorbed that information with less shock than I would have half an hour previously.

'But did the servants or your husband not wonder why you had come home late and wet?'

Dolores, eyes still closed, turned her face towards me. 'Edward was out healing the sick,' she said in slightly mocking tones. Was she envious of his professional standing? If so, she should not have been for she owed her own status to it. 'And my bedroom used to be at the back of the house. It is quieter there and there is a fire escape. I had told them I had a headache and was not to be disturbed and they never even knew that I had been out.' Dolores smiled. 'That was rather clever of me, don't you think?'

'Quite,' I granted her, though Ruby had done much cleverer things without boasting about them.

'I should have been a criminal,' Dolores mused.

You ARE a criminal, I told her in my head but kept a tactful silence. *You have just confessed to throttling a beggarman, stealing his clothes and drowning a laundress. How much more felonious can you get?*

There is not a jury in the country that would convict her. Ruby came unexpectedly to Dolores's defence. *The woman is quite clearly and, probably incurably, insane.*

'Was it you who attacked that waitress in the Monastery Gardens?' I asked as undisapprovingly as I could.

'Is that what she was?' Dolores shrugged. 'It was her own fault you know.'

'For wearing that hat,' I recalled and Dolores beamed.

'I knew you would understand,' she giggled and nudged the air between us as if we were confederates in her deeds.

You appear to have a great deal of knowledge about these crimes, Hefty observed suspiciously. *Perhaps you would care to explain how you knew about that cup of cocoa, Lady Violet.*

He licked the lead of his pencil.

That was a different case, Ruby told him with glee. *Ununiformed buffoon*, she added, not quite under her breath.

Ah... yes... um, Inspector Hefty blustered, leafing through his notebook. *Ah... so this is not Mars Manor then?*

Old Queeny, I pondered, might not be the only one ready to be put out to grass.

Dolores yawned, covering her mouth with her fingers rather theatrically, I thought.

'I was hunting for Edwina,' she continued.

Edwina? Ruby and Hefty chorused in surprise, but I shushed them both.

Oh, I realised.

Bravissimo, Ruby applauded though I did not feel that she meant it.

'Shall I show you what I used?' Dolores asked, rooting under her bedclothes.

'Only if you want to,' I said nervously for, even through her counterpane, I began to make out the unmistakeable shape of the barrel of a rifle.

47: WRATH AND THE BONNET

RUBY THREW HERSELF on the floor and I was about to follow suit when Hefty courageously stepped between us.

Save yourself, my dear-heart! he cried. *Oh... sorry, I got you muddled with...* Hefty's voice tailed off in embarrassment.

It was then that I glimpsed the end of Dolores's weapon and saw that she was pulling out a walking cane.

I tripped over the edge of the carpet, my Extraordinary Investigator lied, picking herself up and sliding her foot in pretence of straightening the rug.

If you really want to save face you need to wipe the dust from it, I told her, *and remove that cobweb from your hair.*

Her beautiful dress did not look quite so beautiful anymore.

You thought it was a gun too, Ruby muttered, brushing a dirty patch from her hellebores.

'I came across Edwina quite by chance in the Monastery Gardens,' Dolores told me.

'But surely,' I said in confusion, 'Edwina...'

'She had her back to me,' Dolores continued. 'But I recognised her by her bonnet. It was a brown one with yellow roses tucked into the ribbon. She bought it, I knew, from Edgar's Exclusive Millinery Shop, where every item is unique.'

Oh Lord, Ruby sighed, giving up on a smudge on her sleeve.

We both knew that Mr Edgar produced identical *exclusive* hats by the dozen.

'I did not expect to encounter her so soon,' Dolores related, 'but I had come prepared with this.' She waved the cane, grasped in both hands like a two-handed sword. 'It is Edward's,' she told me, 'and he has looked for it everywhere.'

If he had, he would have found it, Hefty quibbled.

There was something odd about the way that Dolores was holding that stick and, as if reading my thoughts, she explained.

'It is filled with lead. Edward takes it for protection when he is called out at night.' She allowed herself a little smile. 'It was very exciting. I crept up behind her, the cane raised high over my head.'

Dolores brandished the stick like Cardigan – the man not the knitted garment – leading the charge of the Light Brigade at Balaclava – the battle not the headgear.

Please do not explain Wellingtons, Ruby appealed, though I thought them unlikely to enter the conversation during that heatwave.

'And BASHED her over the head.' Dolores smashed the cane onto the counterpane, just missing her legs and my hand, crumbs jumping in a grey parasitical swarm.

That bedding really needs changing, Ruby tutted. *I had cleaner sheets in Baron Ravenwood's dungeon.*

'She fell face down into the shrubbery,' Dolores told me excitedly, 'so I bashed and bashed…' she thrashed her bed in time with her words, 'and bashed her again and then…' she caught her breath, 'the girl turned her face to the side. She had her hand over it, as if that could protect her from my connubial wrath. She had to be silenced and I had her in my power and then…' The cane came slowly to rest by her side. 'She raised her arm and I saw that it was not Edwina at all…'

'But surely…' I tried again but there was no stopping Dolores.

'It was just a silly girl.' She licked her dry lips. 'How was I to know that?' she demanded. 'I told her. I said *You should not have worn that bonnet*. And then, because I partly blamed myself, I threw her some money to pay for a new one.'

The florin in the flowerbed, Ruby and I remembered.

'I was almost apprehended,' Dolores told me. 'Some nosey hag came running towards us, as if it were any of her concern.'

'That was me,' I said, and she cocked her head.

'You?' She fiddled with her hair coyly. 'Oh, my dear Violet, what must you think of me? If I had realised I should never have dreamed of snubbing you.'

'You did not know me then,' I reminded her and she scratched her scalp so vigorously that I began to question whether those dots were all toast after all.

'And I suppose,' she mused, 'I did not know that I did not know you then.'

Watch out Aristotle, Ruby mocked, *you have a rival in philosophy.*

'I thought I saw a man,' I puzzled, and Dolores giggled in, what in different circumstances, might have been an infectious way.

'Why do you think I borrowed that bundle of clothes?' she enquired, hands outstretched with palms up as if comparing the weight of two parcels.

And what EXACTLY was in those parcels? Hefty demanded.

'For a disguise,' I realised to Ruby's slow clapping.

'A *clever* disguise,' Dolores corrected me. 'But when I heard somebody shout out, *You there!*'

Her voice rose shrilly. Was that supposed to be an imitation of me? If so, it was not a good one. Most people say I have quite a deep voice.

For a child, one of my characters called out from behind the others and I resolved to track him down later.

'It must have been you, dear Violet.' Dolores exhaled heavily. 'But I was not to know that, of course, and so I ran away to lick my wounds.'

'Your wounds?' I was under the impression that she had not been the injured party.

'My hands.' Dolores let go of the cane and held them up, the left one still bandaged. 'They were blistered by their exertions.'

'Bad enough to warrant binding?' I queried because I had played rounders, tennis and lacrosse all in a day once and had very sore hands, but they had not needed swaddling.

'Of course not,' she replied irritably. 'That was a completely different incident.' She elevated her chin proudly. 'It was when I dealt with Edwina once and for all.'

Dolores tipped her head a little to one side as if listening for applause but, if she heard any, it was in her dreams.

48: DEATH IN THE LIMELIGHT

WHILE DOLORES LOOKED at me in expectation of my approval, I chewed upon her words and, though I did not care for their flavour, digested them.

Dolores cleared her throat to remind me politely.

'Did you kill Edwina?' I asked.

I realised, of course, that she had all but confessed, but it was difficult to see how she could have done it.

'What choice did I have?' she demanded and I could think of one other option, to wit not killing her.

'But how?' It would have taken a very skilled marksman indeed to have killed the woman with a shot to the head from that distance and angle, especially with so many other people milling about.

'How do you think my hand was injured?' Dolores waved the grubby, partly unwrapped bandaging towards me.

'Climbing to the roof?' I hazarded.

'Climbing?'

To the roof, Ruby finished for her.

'Or down from it,' I suggested uncertainly and Dolores grasped her cane.

'What roof? Are you mad?' she demanded, though I would take my chances against her with any reputable psychiatrist.

Not Freud, Ruby cautioned and I remembered Rommy telling me about the Austrian doctor's paper on hysteria. *There is a serious danger that he might understand you.*

There is only one thing worse than being understood, Hefty opined, *and that is having halitosis.* And not for the first time I regretted having taken him to see *The Importance of Being Earnest*.

'But she was shot from the roof... was she not?' I checked uncertainly and Dolores laughed, lightly, like a hostess putting a guest at ease after a slight mix-up over names.

'Forgive me,' she smiled graciously, 'but you are labouring under a misapprehension,' she rubbed the fingers and thumbs of her right hand together as one might when sprinkling a little seasoning on one's food, 'that it was I who shot her.'

She wiggled her hand and, in different circumstances at this point, would have wandered off to mingle with other guests.

'So, when you said you killed Edwina you did not?' I checked and she put a hand to her temple.

Was I giving her a headache? If so, I was awfully sorry. I had not even thought to bring a bottle of Bromo-Seltzer with me.

'It is hard work murdering people,' Dolores complained. 'And messy and there is always a danger of being caught.'

Caught by the neck until you are dead, Hefty remarked.

'But then I had a stroke of luck,' Dolores related. 'A certain gentleman who is in charge of a certain band of brigands...'

'Anton Gervey,' I guessed, if only to make her stop trying to be mysterious when there were more than enough true mysteries already.

Dolores scowled.

'He came to see Edward,' she continued. 'Apparently he had cut his thumb while trying to do something to somebody's smile. He did not tell me exactly what. I knew that he owed my husband a favour, and so I told him that Edward could not say so himself but he wanted to get rid of Edwina and Mr Gervey, though not quite a gentleman, was perfectly happy to oblige.'

Dolores took a breath.

You do surprise me, Ruby said.

'I had a photograph of Edwina,' she continued. 'Edward had taken it but, unfortunately, her dress had come undone and slipped down her shoulders just as he opened the shutter-thing and so he put it away in his desk. I only came across the picture when I was hunting for poisons which I thought might come in handy for my quest. Unfortunately Mr Gervey's man still had trouble finding her. It was then that I had a stroke of luck.' Dolores scratched at an eyebrow. 'I was passing through on my way to Mrs Pilkington's, the floristry shop, when I spotted Edwina. She was in rags and much changed. I followed her and saw her standing in Seraphim Square. I could not do anything there and then but, after I saw her there the next day, I notified Mr Gervey. He said that, since she was altered, it might be best if I could point her out to his man. *Stand well back and use a parasol*, he suggested but, since I intended to wear my disguise again, I took an umbrella instead.'

Dolores inhaled deeply, probably exhausted by her recital.

'But...' A thought occurred to me.

And not before time, Ruby commented, her words almost lost beneath Dolores's heavy exhalation.

'At the appointed hour,' Dolores continued, 'I sneaked up to Edwina in my disguise.'

'But,' I returned to my rare but nonetheless welcome thought. 'You cannot have been the blind beggar. He wore a hat with a shallow crown. You could not possibly have tucked all your hair into...'

'It,' Dolores broke in, putting up her hand to lift her hair six inches from her head.

I knew it was false, Ruby asserted.

You might have told me.

You told me to stop maundering about wigs, she reminded me.

That was ages ago.

It was on Martha's second visit, as I recalled.

But you did not tell me I could start again.

Since when have you...

'Some of my own hair dropped out after I fell ill.' Dolores ran her fingers through the sparse strands with more equanimity than I could have mustered under the same circumstances. I did not need Ruby to remind me how much I had bleated over my singed eyelashes. 'And Edward very kindly bought me this.' She waved it about as if it were an especially shaggy badger in the jaws of a triumphant dachshund. 'But it is so hot to wear when it is so hot already.'

Dolores let her trophy fall limply on her lap.

'I still do not understand what happened to your hand.'

'Oh for goodness sake!' Dolores snapped. 'Who is telling this story?'

'You are,' I confirmed meekly and she stroked her wig affectionately.

'I pointed Edwina out, as arranged.' She patted the wig. 'But she must have sensed my presence and turned towards me. I think she was about to say something but I shall never know what, for at that very moment, Edward's umbrella was smashed.' Dolores flung out her arms. 'In my face.'

The first shot, Inspector Hefty deduced, looking up from the dead moth that he was examining with his magnifying glass.

I saw now that her right cheek was not bruised but wrinkled into an angry scar probably too wide to cover with a playing card.

Why would you want to? Ruby enquired.

It was then that I realised why Dolores had allowed her false hair to hang over her face. Even a woman alone does not like to sport her imperfections.

No we do not, Ruby confirmed sourly, never having forgiven me for giving her a birthmark similar to Alfred Stanbury's.

'And injured your hand,' I added and Dolores projected her lower lip.

'My poor sweet little hand.' She deserted the hairpiece to stroke her bandage.

Which also explains the broken umbrella we found in the square, Ruby jumped in to pilfer my thoughts, though I had not realised that she had helped in its discovery.

'And it nearly deafened me,' Dolores complained, putting her bandage to her ear.

'Which is why you waited for the motor car to go by,' I realised in begrudging admiration of her resourcefulness.

'Motor car?' she puzzled. 'I did not notice.'

'Oh.' I retrieved my admiration only slightly tarnished, but left her with full rights and possession of my begrudgement.

Begrudge-what? Miss Kidd interrogated me.

Ment, I said defiantly, for I was not very afraid of her now.

'But I heard the second shot almost immediately and Edwina's face splattered and she staggered away.'

You told me that the second bang was an echo, I complained and Ruby softly whistled a bar of the Bragislanian national anthem.

Did I? she enquired innocently.

'I scarpered,' Dolores recounted, which sounded more like the sort of thing a street child would do. 'Home.'

I took a breath and I must have got used to the air because it seemed less fetid than when it first assailed me.

I have laid down tools, my left nostril informed me, *in solidarity with my comrade.*

This was all a bit too redolent of the Paris Commune for my liking. What next? Would barricades be erected along the boulevard to my stomach, starving me into submission?

Let sleeping senses lie, Ruby advised. *Oh, and you can let your breath out now.*

'Did you kill that bird?' I enquired as casually as I could, though it was not the sort of question that I was used to posing when locked in an attic room with a homicidal maniac. The greatest risk I took as a rule was asking Agnust if she would mind dusting my study.

'Colin?'

Was avicide such a frequent occurrence in that household that she needed to check to which victim I was referring?

'Yes.'

Dolores crumpled her face in wounded outrage.

'Never!' she cried, her hand tightening so much that, if her wig were not a dead thing already, it would be presently. 'I would have died for my darling... darling...'

Her voice fractured.

I knew, of course, that the bible enjoins us not to judge others but to my mind Dolores's grief seemed a tad excessive, especially from somebody who held human life so cheaply. Fond as I had been of Rodrigo, I would not have sacrificed myself for him.

He knew that, Ruby told me, *which is why he went off on that cruise.*

My mother had told me that story, but I had another theory about what happened to my kitten and it involved...

Don't say it! Little Myrtle cried in horror from the depths of my parietal lobe.

I had quite forgotten that she ran a home for orphaned kittens.

'Edward did it,' Dolores insisted fiercely, 'to punish me for my misbehaviour.'

To my mind *misbehaviour* was talking with one's mouth full or tying the Minister of War's bootlaces together in revenge for him ruffling one's hair when he visited Thetbury Hall.

'I think,' Dolores sampled her thumb again, 'it was after I stabbed a little girl in the slums.'

'Beryl Walker.'

The mummified body in the Lowers, I remembered.

'Really?' Dolores looked at me with interest. 'I was unaware that she had a name.'

'Everyone…' I began but decided that the point was not worth pursuing. 'Why did you kill her?'

'Why not?' She smiled as if I had offered her a cucumber sandwich.

Yes please, Hefty said.

'But surely,' I returned to the reason for my earlier puzzlement, 'when you attacked that girl in the park, Edwina was already dead.'

We did try to tell you, Inspector Hefty remonstrated, *but you shushed us.*

I realised it too, I defended myself, *but she did not give me a chance to say anything.*

Dolores wiped her thumb on her nightdress.

'Dead?' she puzzled. 'Was she? Oh…' she laughed lightly, 'you must forgive me, my dear. It is all tooo bewildering.'

'But you cannot have forgotten,' I protested, reminding myself of Miss Kidd when I had not done my arithmetic preparation and shuddering because I had remembered that I was still afraid of her.

'I forget so many little things,' Dolores assured me.

'Hardly little,' I said, aghast at her choice of word.

Before I could pursue the matter, however, I heard a floorboard creak and Dolores must have heard it too for she lifted her head expectantly.

'Time for my snack,' she announced happily.

Oh Lord, here we go again, I sighed.

We? In this? I think not, Ruby sniffed.

I glanced over my shoulder and saw than she was in a flowing emerald ballgown, trimmed in ivory lace and richly embroidered in rambling roses.

You choose some odd moments to become skittish, I scolded, envious of a waist that I could not have achieved even with a corset and Agnust at her most brutal.

Besides which, Ruby reminded me, *he cannot get in without breaking the door down.*

'We must be quiet,' I whispered to Dolores and she wrinkled her brow.

'Are we playing that game again?'

'Yes.'

'But I do not want to,' she protested while I signalled urgently. 'How dare you attempt to extinguish me in my own house?' she demanded, her voice crescendoing from forte to fortississimo.

The footsteps quickened.

'Are you all right, madam?' the creator of those steps enquired.

'Help me!' Dolores shrieked. 'I am trapped with a madwoman who is threatening my life.'

I kept quiet, fairly confident that he would not try to force an entry. He must know from experience how his mistress imagined such things and that, at least, would give me a little time, though I had no idea how I intended to use it.

'I cannot find the key, madam,' he told her unsurprisingly – to me at any rate. 'But don't be afraid. There's a spare.'

His fetching it might give me a chance, at least, to sneak out, I was telling myself when I heard him add, 'In my pocket,' and slide it into the lock.

49: COLD SMILES AND HEADS ON SPIKES

WORMWOOD STOOD FRAMED in the frame and filling a great deal of it with his bulk, the light squeezing politely in around him.

Politely? Ruby echoed incredulously. *You need a new thesaurus, Thorn.*

It occurred to me that, of my needs, the one to escape was more urgent than the one to consult M. Roget.

Do something, Ruby urged and I blinked. *Do something else*, she urged adding, before I could ask, *Bluff*.

'What kept you?' If I had learned one thing from my upbringing in the minor nobility, it was when to talk to other people's servants as if they were one's own. 'I have been calling for half an hour.'

'What are you doing here?' he demanded, unput in his place by my peremptory tones.

'Waiting for you,' I replied, raising my chin, but it is difficult to look imperious when you are being towered over.

Shoot him, Ruby urged, knowing full well that I was not carrying a gun and that it would be murder if I had used one.

'How did you get in?'

He took a step towards me.

'Why was that door not locked?' I counter-challenged as he came closer. 'Dr Poynder will be very angry at your carelessness.'

'Violet has come to rescue me,' Dolores piped up helpfully.

'You are confused,' I told her.

'I most certainly am,' she said, 'not.'

'I am a servant,' Wormwood said, and I was clearing my throat to say it was about time he remembered that when he continued, 'not because I was born stupid but because I was born poor.'

How very careless of you, Ruby commented.

'I see,' I said carefully. He was starting to sound like a Marxist, and we all knew how they planned to overthrow us and substitute some outrageous scheme for allowing the workers to enjoy the fruits of their own labours.

'That box...' he said.

'It is an ottoman.' One should never miss an opportunity to educate one's underlings but, instead of thanking me for the information, Wormwood reached over and grabbed my arm.

I think he only meant to take my sleeve but this really hurt – though admittedly not as much as when I fell in a bonfire at Thetbury Hall – and I may have squeaked but my attention was taken elsewhere.

'You are pinching my skin.' I winced and he adjusted his grip, his long strong fingers closing completely around my short slender arm.

Kick him on the shin.

'How dare you?' I tossed my head, pretending that I had not cricked my neck in the process but, even as I said it, I knew it was one of those pointless questions that people ask when they know that they are disadvantaged. *What is the meaning of this?* being another useless favourite, but I reserved that for another occasion.

Rather impertinently, I thought, Wormwood did not even acknowledge my words, but began to haul me out of the room without even asking my leave to do so.

'Unhand me,' I commanded, cringing for sounding like Orphan Octavia in *Orphan Octavia*, a three-act melodrama that was three acts too long... 'At once,' I added firmly as we reached the doorway.

I could have clung to the frame, I supposed, but he could have wrenched me away easily, I supposed as well.

'Goodbye,' Dolores called merrily, 'and thank you for coming.'

'Otter-box,' he sniffed, parking me alongside the object of our discussion. 'Whatever it is, you came in it.'

'Stuff and nonsense,' I blustered. 'Nobody could possibly fit into that.'

Wormwood smiled. He might have had a nice smile for all I knew, but he was keeping it in reserve that morning or was it afternoon by then? This was a cold cynical smile almost worthy of Count Zugravescu.

'Oh, but I think they can,' he disagreed disagreeably, 'and I intend to prove it.'

A wild and ludicrous hope sprang to life in my breast.

'Are you going to get in?' I asked innocently.

'No, but you are,' he sneered and my wild and ludicrous hope died alone and unmourned.

'This is an outrage,' I fumed, dredging my repertoire of authority-asserting phrases but Wormwood's expression darkened.

'No, Lady Violet,' he told me. 'You breaking into this house is an outrage.'

'I did not break in,' I informed him frostily. 'Nothing was broken.'

That might have impressed an impressionable and sympathetic magistrate, preferably one who slaughtered pheasants on my father's estate, but it had no such effect on an angry and unsympathetic valet who had probably never shot anything in his life.

'Get in,' he ordered, jerking me towards it.

Ruby had loosened Ivan Kandinsky's stranglehold in *The Case of the Poisoned Claw* by bending his little finger back. I reached over for Wormwood's.

'Try it,' he challenged, raising his free hand. 'And I will slap your silly face.'

Silly? I seethed but reluctantly declined the invitation.

He is bluffing, Ruby assured me, but she did not sound very convinced and I was even less so.

I raised my skirt, colouring a little under his appreciative gaze.

Stop simpering, Thorn.

I am not, I lied and stepped over the side of the box.

'Sit.'

I was not a puppy but I obeyed as readily as one.

'You have no idea of the trouble you will be in,' I warned as I sat on the base.

'No, milady.' He made my title sound like it had been collected out of the gutter for tanning leather. 'You have no idea of the trouble you have caused.'

'Don't hurt her,' Dolores pleaded from her bed and I relaxed a little. At least I had one friend and her word must carry some weight in the house. 'I want to do that,' she concluded, a little less encouragingly.

50: TIBET AND THE SWAMP OF DESPAIR

HAVING HAD NOTHING to eat, I could not possibly have put on weight since setting off, but I was certain that the ottoman was a tighter fit when I squeezed back into it. Romulus had told me that he was corresponding with a Polish doctor who was extracting chemicals that he believed were excreted from kidney glands when animals are frightened. Perhaps these make one swell.

More likely you have gone rigid with fear, Ruby suggested. *Relax.*

And how am I supposed to that?

If only you had joined me in that Tibetan monastery, she said, but not everybody can take a year off learning how to levitate.

Meditate, she corrected me.

'Lie down,' Wormwood instructed me and I tried to consider my options but there were none, other than to do as I was told – not something about which Ruby and I were enthusiastic.

Ruby was doing some sort of prolonged monotonous *ummming.* I expect she had her reasons but I found it irritating.

There were the sounds of movement in the background – rustling and the padding of bare feet. It was obvious that Dolores, the madwoman, had been playing the part of an even madder woman to allay the valet's suspicions and was coming to prevent him from re-in-ottoman-ing me. She had better hurry though. He was ramming my head down as roughly as one packs an overfilled suitcase.

Ummmm, Ruby ummed and the shadow of Dolores crossed over me.

'Wait,' she commanded, restoring herself to her rightful position as mistress of the house.

'Go back to bed, madam,' Wormwood said calmly. 'I will deal with her.'

Amongst a dozen regrets that emerged from that yet-to-be-discovered part of the cerebrum known as the swamp of despair...

Puteum desperacionis, Hefty translated, having studied the classics at school.

…was the realisation that I had left the key in the inner side of the box but, if I could surreptitiously cover it with my elbow…

Wormwood reached down and pulled it out.

'One moment,' Dolores said imperiously and fiddled with her nightdress.

It was then that I realised she had something more than a trick up her sleeve. There was a glint of metal in the light and I saw that she was grasping a knife, a big one – not even just a carving knife but something a high priest might have used to slaughter an ox.

Wormwood did something that I would have done if there had been any room in which to do it. He jumped.

'Where did you get that from?'

'Where did you get that from, madam?' she corrected him and he added her title irritably.

From where did you get that, madam? Miss Kidd corrected them both.

'Why the kitchen of course,' Dolores replied. 'I knew you all intended to incarcerate me and so I wrapped it in a cloth and strapped it to my leg.'

Good for you, Dolly, I thought, preparing to rise.

'Take care, madam,' he appealed, foolishly stepping towards his mistress.

'I shall be very careful indeed,' she assured him with such a maniacal cackle that I resolved to offer her the part of the depraved twin sister should *The Mystery of Lamplight Road* ever be dramatised.

A little melodramatically, I thought – but a good director would curb her excesses – Dolores raised that wicked blade over her head.

'To make sure that I stick it in her throat.'

Should you not be threatening him? I wondered as she leaned over me and, jammed-in as I was, I could not even shrink back as the knife came swooping down.

It is said that your life flashes before your eyes when you are about to die. The only thing that flashed before mine was that long, steel blade, and I did not even have time to say more than 'No!' before I felt a sharp thump and my whole world went black.

51: *THE DAY OF DOOM AND DOOMSDAY*

DOLORES SCREAMED. I could have done that for her, but I was too busy rubbing my brow from the impact of the lid crashing on my head.

Good reactions, Wormy, I breathed mentally. In a twist that might go well in one of my Inspector Hefty stories, the villain was all at once the hero of the hour. *But oh my poor bonnet. Why did it have to die so young?*

There had been a second bang. Was that the knife striking the woodwork? That box had been in the Thorn family for almost a quarter of a generation.

I pulled the material of my dress away from the airholes and spotted a trouser leg. It was well-pressed. I had to grant him that much.

'Let me at her!' Dolores was shrieking.

'I am sorry, madam.'

The lock clicked shut from the outside and a twist of light showed that the key had been extracted.

'She murdered Colin.'

The killing of parrots is psittacide, Hefty informed me.

Sit aside? Ruby queried before realising what he had said.

'Colin flew away.' Wormwood was trying to pacify her.

'No! She killed my baby.'

'Your husband did that,' I yelled for I did not want to die, but I wanted to die even less with feathers on my hands.

'What did she say?'

'I believe she said *Your husband is fat*, madam.'

'How rude!' she complained, having behaved with the utmost decorum towards me.

'He killed her,' I tried again.

'Something about Ezekiel,' he interpreted. 'She is probably in one of those weird religious sects like Roman Catholicism.'

263

'She is raving,' the not-in-the-least-bit-mad woman in the attic diagnosed in disgust.

How could I hear them clearly when they could not make out what I was saying?

It could be something to do with the crook of your arm being forced over your mouth, Ruby suggested, correctly as usual, but I was wedged too tightly to do much about that.

'Perhaps madam would like me to take the knife now,' he suggested.

'Oh thank you,' Dolores said. 'She threatened to kill me with it.'

'I did not!' I objected, but even I could not hear that properly.

'Do you think she could be Jack the Ripper?'

'Quite possibly, madam, but you are safe now. She will not get out of there.'

What? Never? Horrible images swirled around my head. How long would it take to starve to death? Perhaps they would feed me pea soup – which I loathed – through the holes and I would live in my ottoman for decades, growing old stinking of legumes and shrivelling to end up like the Egyptian mummy I had seen in The Museum of Curious Things in Sackwater.

A terrible fluster swelled inside me. How could I wash?

'I do not have a toothbrush,' I called and, weirdly, they heard that.

'How disgusting,' Dolores pronounced. 'An alleged lady and she does not possess the simplest of hygienic devices.'

Alleged? I seethed for the Thorns had very nearly been mentioned in the Doomsday Book.

'I meant with me,' I explained, unheard again.

'Do not concern yourself with the wretch,' Wormwood soothed his mistress but not me. I had not been called a wretch since I had been accused unjustly of stealing my godmother's pearls, which I had accidentally fed to the goat. I shuddered at the memory for it had fallen upon me to retrieve them – one of the reasons I had not wanted to wait for the key. 'We must get you back to bed.'

'Can I have a story?' she said.

'Just a quick one, madam.'

The voices had faded, but I could still make out his droning.

'No, from the beginning,' Dolores cried, and he coughed.

'It was the best of times,' he began but, with all due respect to the late Mr Dickens, it felt like the worst of times to me.

52: MOCK TURTLE AND THE BLOWFLY

SOMETHING WAS CRAWLING over my face from the angle of my jaw across my cheek. It tickled, but not in the affectionate way that Uncle Postilius would tickle me when I was tiny nor in the even more affectionate way that he would tickle me when I was less tiny.

Was it a spider? I had heard of them laying eggs under people's skin and causing blisters that erupted into hundreds of baby spiders. It disappeared, buzzed and reappeared on my forehead – a bluebottle from the size and sound of it. I had heard of them laying eggs under people's skin and causing blisters that erupted into hundreds of flesh-eating maggots.

I tried to slide my arm up to brush it away with my elbow but, succeeding only in blocking my nostrils, I slid it down hastily. Even mock turtle soup, which I detested more than pea, might be preferable to suffocation by couture.

Wormwood had gone on to loaves and fishes.

The fly had reached my eyebrow and was carefully parting the hairs like a woman looking for a lost earring in the long grass.

You will not find anything of interest there, I warned, but blow-flies are not feted for their powers of telepathy – in fact I am not convinced that they have any at all – and it continued its painstaking if exceedingly irritating search.

At least, I consoled myself, I was not getting hot and bothered for I was both of those already.

Wormwood read out something about America. I had never been to the land of Beeman's and native peoples who, Romulus had told me, were not really Indians and were no redder than the average Englishman on Cromer beach. It did not look like I would be going there in the near future – unless the valet sent me in my ottoman by steamer in an attempt to dispose of my body.

It seemed an unwarranted expense and I bridled at the waste of his employer's money.

You could just as easily push me off a rowing boat into the North Sea, I suggested and hoped, that if I had said it out loud, nobody had heard.

The fly was on the bridge of my nose now, but there were no hairs there for it to explore because I had plucked them all.

'Christian pastures,' Wormwood narrated or was it Christian pastors? It was a long time since I had read the book.

If I die now I shall never get to know what happens to The Prisoner of Zenda, I pondered.

If you die now, the line dies with you, Ruby reminded me, but it did anyway for women are much too silly to be entrusted with titles that they can pass on, so the next of the Thorns would be my second cousin Romulus who, having an innate dignity, would take good care of his inheritance I felt sure. You would not find him squashed in a blanket box.

But I would not necessarily die with you, Ruby continued smugly. *Ted Wilton, your agent, might give* Dangerous Tuesday *to Grantham Hogarth to finish.*

'Never!' I cried as the fly reached my upper lip.

'What was that?' Dolores asked in alarm, though I could not help but feel that I had a great deal more than her to fret about in the immediate future. 'It sounded like a puppy.'

'Probably the yelp of a bitch,' Wormwood suggested, maliciously, I suspected.

That does it, I resolved indignantly. *I am definitely going to get out of here now.*

Now? Ruby checked.

The fly was investigating my nostril and no amount of blowing could dislodge it.

Soon.

How? Ruby challenged. *Have you got a spare key up your sleeve?*

Let me worry about that, I said as breezily as I could. All I had up my sleeve was an arm that managed to be numb and ache simultaneously.

Wormwood finished reading and, by the sounds that reached me, closed and locked the door.

'Try to rest, madam,' he said but not, I suspected, to me.

I bumped on the lid with my knee.

'Let me out,' I commanded as his footfalls faded.

You read about these things all the time – servants who pretend not to hear and will not do as they are bidden – but you never think that it will be a matter of life and...

Death, Ruby contributed portentously.

53: *LAZARUS AND THE ROOFTILES*

I SNEEZED SO violently that I banged my head on the wood-work, but at least it shifted the bluebottle from my nose.

Houses are never quiet. They creak and shift. Water pipes make water pipe noises and birds scrabble on rooftiles. Dogs bark, canaries twitter and cats miaow. Mice scamper over the floorboards and, if you are really lucky, rats scramble beneath them. Haglin House, however, was quiet as the...

Do not even think it, I scolded myself and lay still as there was not much else that I could do.

You could try lying still and thinking of a plan, Ruby suggested, *preferably one that involves escaping.*

I did as she suggested. If I pulled out my hat pin I might be able to bend it and at least try to pick the lock. It could not be that difficult.

It is, Ruby assured me, apart from which, I could not get a finger to my bonnet anyway.

What about your left hand doing something for a change, my right hand challenged, which was fair enough, I supposed, for – amongst other chores – it had to do all the writing and lifting of coffee cups, but my whole left arm had gone missing.

Only you could mislay a limb – and one of your own at that – in the confines of an ottoman, Ruby scoffed, sounding rather like Miss Kidd when I had lost a boot on my way to the chapel.

Here I am, it gasped from underneath me, which explained what that pain had been but, struggle as I might, I could not extract it.

Arch your back, somebody suggested but it was arched already and I was so busy squabbling with my character and my body parts that I did not hear any footfalls approach my prison or, if I had, I had not paid any attention. Nor – to my chagrin – had Ruby,

Hefty nor even Mrs Le Pram, the nosey old woman from *Death in the Parsonage*, warned me.

There was a metallic scraping sound that I had come to recognise as the key being inserted followed by the click of the lock being turned.

The roof rose and my world was flooded with light, only partly blocked by a figure and, after a lot of blinking, I made out that it was a man. A dark dot – the fly I assumed – flew off over his shoulder. I screwed up my eyes and saw that it was Dr Poynder and, because he did not look in the least bit pleased to see me, I did not feel in the least bit pleased to see him either.

'What in the name of the devil do you think you are up to?' he demanded.

'Your man locked me in here,' I explained, fully aware that that was not what he was asking.

This might be a good time to sit, Ruby suggested, though I was already twisting about and struggling to pull myself up. My left arm had expired, but I still harboured hopes that it might, like Lazarus, return to the land of the living.

'What are you doing in my house?' He rephrased the question, probably not sure if I was being awkward or stupid for both are proven feminine traits.

I could have told him that I was sitting in a box but that might well have overstretched his patience and – whilst I could match many a man in a game of croquet and quite a few at Beggar-my-neighbour but, even strictly adhering to the Marquis of Queensbury Rules, I did not fancy my chances against one in a fistfight.

You made me go against Killer Mulvane, Ruby pointed out, omitting to mention that she had a crowbar, which was yet another thing that I had neglected to bring with me.

Dismissing Ruby's suggestion that I claim to have been kidnapped and sent here against my will, honesty, I decided, might not always be the best policy but was the only option available to me.

'I wanted to see Dolly,' I told him, 'and your servants were obstructing me.'

'Why did you want to see her?'

'I was worried about her.'

He chewed my words more thoroughly than Agnust with her page of St Mark and spat his next words far more venomously.

'You were worried?' He bunched up furiously. 'YOU were worried?'

You can't accuse him of not listening, Ruby pointed out in his favour.

'Yes,' I mumbled nervously.

Anthony Appleton would not get away with the beautifully understated range of emotions that Poynder's face expressed, for nobody could have seen them from beyond the front row of the stalls, but they were all too clear to me and ranged from anger to loathing to resentment to indignation building up towards rage before the doctor inhaled profoundly and composed himself.

'Get up.' He exhaled so glacially that, overheated as I was, I found myself shivering as I struggled to oblige.

'My man is outside,' I warned, and he piffed.

'He would do well to get past mine.'

'He will call the police.'

'Then he will save me the trouble.' Poynder glared at me. 'Take my hand.'

He stuck it out and I poked mine up tentatively. He did not look like a man who would crush my fingers for a joke, but I had thought the same about Parson Gray, who had almost broken them to the hilarity of his cod-faced, halibut-breathed, bloater-shaped wife. She had not found him so amusing when he put chillies in her eye-drops.

Poynder grasped my hand firmly though not painfully and hauled me to my feet. My legs, taken off-guard, did what unprepared legs do best. They buckled.

'Oh!' I managed before I toppled over.

54: BEELZEBUB AND THE SCREAMING BRAIN

DR POYNDER CAUGHT me and Ruby rolled her eyes. Was I really such a milksop that I swooned into the embrace of a big strong man? I was about to deny it when, much to my chagrin, he scooped me up and held me for all the world the blushing bride except for two things. First I was dressed more like a vagabond – how on earth had my hem got so badly ripped? And second I was not blushing – whatever Ruby whispered in my auricle.

Though not especially big, Poynder must have been strong for down the stairs he went as easily as I used to carry Rodrigo, though, unlike my kitten, I felt no temptation to purr. The door at the bottom was open.

'Where are you taking me?' I asked nervously.

'Downstairs,' he said, which I had almost calculated for myself.

If he meant to strangle me, I speculated, he could have done it more conveniently in the attic.

He has a surgery on the ground floor, Ruby reminded me. *It must be well supplied with scalpels… and sawsssss.* She lingered gruesomely over her last word.

That would be much messier, I objected.

If you would care to inform me of the date upon which men commenced worrying about making a mess, she began, *I can arrange a soiree to celebrate the anniversary.*

Oh Lord, do not let me end my days like that parrot, I prayed and I could imagine Saint Peter making a note of my invocation. *Thou shalt never guess what I heardeth this day*, he would chuckle to entertain new arrivals.

Along the corridor we went and down the next flight of stairs. On the first floor I was reminded of when I had broken an ankle. Shillidge the pigman had carried me back to the house and I was almost sure that he had not meant to trip and drop me into that trough of swill. They probably had a good laugh about that too behind the pearly gates and I was not sure that I wanted to go there if they had such a peculiar sense of humour.

Dr Poynder, I discovered, used a slightly scented soap. This was a modern fad for men but I, for one, approved. Most members of the male sex were heavily scented with aromas of their own creation.

Was this the time to tell him that there was a cobweb dangling from the cornice? As we arrived safely in two pieces in the hall, I decided that it was not.

Into the front sitting room we went, where he deposited me gently to recline upon a chaise longue. The burgundy velvet might have complemented my attire quite nicely if my dress were in a state to match anything other than something the rag-gatherer might be content, though not thrilled, to come across.

Somewhat less than gracefully I hauled myself to sit somewhat less than elegantly upright.

Poynder stood at a mahogany cabinet with his back to me but it did not take any of Hefty's detection skills to deduce, from the clinks and plashings, what he was doing.

Mixing poisons, Ruby suggested, having narrowly escaped death at the hands of Docteur Charpentier in *The Tangled Sheet Murders*.

Does one usually add soda to strychnine? I had an idea that it was not traditional.

Poynder handed me a tumbler.

'Drink that.'

I sniffed it. Brandy. Not my tipple of choice but gamely I took a drink and found it rather welcome.

'Are you not having one?'

Ssstrongly sssussspicioussss, Ruby hissed.

'I have surgery in half an hour.'

But not on me! my brain screamed so piercingly that all my characters, except for Ruby – and Arturo who was deaf – fled and even she flinched.

The scream reverberated and faded, but there was still a commotion in the background. Somebody was hammering at something. Was Zugravescu's henchman Igor trying to break out

273

through my occiput? He had, after all, smashed through a wall to abduct Ruby.

Nobody could have taken me that easily, Hefty boasted.

Nobody would want to take you in any way, she retorted.

I was aware of heavy footfalls in the hall. The knocking stopped and the rattle of carriage wheels grew louder.

A servant is opening the door, Ruby explained, if only to prove that she could keep her head while all about were losing theirs.

'If you don't let me in this instant you'll be needing your master's attentions for a week,' I heard Gerrund threaten, for he could never wait and not be tired by waiting.

Actually that's quite poetic, Miss Kidd – rarely one to offer praise – commended me.

'Just try it and you'll be looking for an undertaker,' Wormwood challenged and Poynder managed a wry smile.

'It would appear that our men have introduced themselves,' he said before raising his voice. 'Show him in, Wormwood,' he called. 'I am sure Lady Violet will feel more comfortable with a chaperone.'

There was some muttering, the door closed and Gerrund marched into the room, Wormwood standing in the doorway in case we were thinking of making a dash for freedom or back upstairs or whatever he thought we had planned.

I was about to greet my man with something enthusiastic along the lines of *What in the name of Beelzebub kept you?* when he gasped as if he had been punched in the solar plexus.

'Oh my grandmother's bones, milady!' he croaked. 'What have they done to you?'

'Well…'

'You look dreadful.'

'Thank…'

'A complete mongrel's mess,' he assured me.

'I…'

'Like something fallen off the catmeat man's cart.'

'I am all right thank you,' I assured him coolly, not quite as pleased to see him as I had expected to be.

Poynder squirted a soda water into an empty tumbler. His fingers were even longer and thicker than I had remembered, not at all like the slender sensitive tendrils described by Penelope

Fitzbubble in *Dr Heaven's Hospital*. It takes a strong grip to saw a man's leg off, Romulus told me from experience, having had to do it when the field hospital had run out of ether.

Wormwood was still gawking at me.

'You don't look all right,' he insisted to clear any misapprehension I might have harboured that I was fit to be presented at court.

'Sit down.' Poynder indicated an upright chair against the wall.

Gerrund looked to me. I nodded and he crossed the room to sit ten feet away at two o'clock from me, arms folded but watching the doctor alertly.

'I could have you prosecuted,' Poynder warned, which I knew meant that he would not.

'For what?' I asked.

'Breaking into my house.'

'Nothing was broken,' I pointed out for the second time that day.

Except your bonnet, Ruby contributed, in case I had forgotten in the last three seconds how ghastly was my appearance.

'Trespass,' he tried again.

'Not a crime,' I told him. 'Though you are entitled to ask me to leave.'

Poynder brushed my remarks aside.

'I am sure my solicitor could build some kind of a case against you,' he said, rather lamely, I thought, 'but I am equally sure that none of us want to go through a trial.'

He sniffed his drink though it could not have had much of a bouquet.

'I am quite sure that *you* do not,' I told him firmly and he looked at me askance. 'Before I explain that statement, there is one thing I need to know.' I put a hand on my right knee to mask a tear in my dress, shushing Ruby's assertion that there were myriad things of which I was ignorant. 'Who killed Colin?'

Take a guess at Dolly, Ruby suggested, though I had not known they were on such casual terms.

I am not so sure, I reasoned. *She freely admitted all her other crimes, but she seemed genuinely distressed when I confronted her about that one.*

Poynder's expression was a study in puzzlement.

'My wife's parrot escaped when her maid failed to secure the cage and left the window open,' he protested.

'Escaped into her dressing table,' I said in disgust. 'Tell me, Dr Poynder, was the creature still alive when you dissected it?'

He put his drink down on the sideboard.

'You are quite mad,' he told me.

Only quite, Ruby queried.

'Shall I send my man to fetch it?' I asked, hoping that he would reject my offer for I had no wish to see the thing more clearly or to endure that stench again. It had reminded me of when I had discovered the family vault being ransacked at Thetbury Hall by thieves under the misapprehension that we were dull-witted and wealthy enough to entomb our loved ones in their finest jewellery. I had locked them in for twenty-nine hours before troubling to report the incident.

I don't remember that, Ruby said.

It was before your time, I told her for — flying in the face of arithmetic — Ruby, having been born four years ago, had always been twenty-five.

Gerrund half-rose uncertainly but the doctor raised his hand.

'I shall not have you invading my home any further. My man will go.'

'Don't try anything funny,' Wormwood warned, and I choked back a quip before it reached my larynx as he strode from the room.

Poynder took up his soda and went to stand with his back to the fireplace, a favourite position for Inspector Hefty while he explained to an aristocratic family how they were all suspects but the real murderer was…

'I do not know what you mean about the bird,' he said, 'but I am beginning to understand why you have been to such bizarre lengths.' He sipped his soda, and I resampled my drink. 'That damned woman put you up to this,' he asserted and, to save me the bother of not knowing who he meant, concluded, 'Martha Ryan.'

'Who?' I asked lamely, but he did not trouble to reply.

'I told her repeatedly to stay away.'

'She is Dolores's friend,' I protested, rather undermining my last question.

'Friend?' he spat. 'What species of friend pesters a dying woman?'

55: BROADMOOR AND
BERCHTESGADEN

I WAS STILL mulling over that enquiry when footfalls came quickly down the stairs and along the corridor and, unsurprisingly, Wormwood reappeared. He looked shocked.

'It is true, sir,' he announced. 'Colin is nailed out and cut open in madam's dressing table drawer. He must have been there a good while for he is crawling...' Wormwood did what I had struggled not to do at the time. He retched. 'With maggots,' he said.

His master put his tumbler down and I took a swig from mine.

'And how is the mistress?'

'She is sleeping, sir. I pulled out the drawer and put it in the boxroom for now.'

He spasmed again at the memory.

'Pour me a brandy,' Poynder said, 'and have one yourself.'

Gerrund perked up a little and cleared his throat but, if anyone other than me noticed, it did not have the result for which he was hoping and he perked down again, eyeing my half-full glass enviously.

'Thank you, sir.' Wormwood looked as if he needed one and poured two very generous measures, eschewing the syphon.

A coupe of champagne would not go amiss, Ruby suggested but none was forthcoming.

Gerrund looked at his boots despondently and I did not suppose that they appeared any different to the last time he had surveyed them.

'Let me get this over with,' Poynder declared, and I saw no reason not to oblige. 'About a year ago, my wife became unwell. There was nothing definite at first. Her spirits were low and she tired easily. I thought she might have anaemia because she had been troubled with that in the past, as many women are, and so

I prescribed Blaud's Pills. They are rich in iron and appeared to do her some good at first but the benefits were transitory. Her behaviour became erratic. She was always a gentle soul, but she would fly off into terrible rages.' He took a large drink. 'Dolores attacked her maid so badly that I had to pay the girl not to press criminal charges.' He clicked his tongue. 'I gave my wife sedatives which only worked in large doses and she could not live permanently anaesthetised. She attacked our dog.'

I saw the doctor's fingers blanch and hoped that his tumbler was sturdily made.

'And...' he swallowed and ran his fingers through his hair, 'that poor...' his voice broke.

'Mungo Peers,' I contributed, and he nodded miserably.

'I could not let the unfortunate salt man be punished for her acts.' He swirled his brandy. 'But neither could I let Dolores be taken to Broadmoor or even... condemned to death if the jury decided that she was simulating her insanity.'

Neither of which would do your practice much good, Ruby remarked rather nastily I thought for the man was clearly distraught.

'So what did you do?' I asked quietly.

'I consulted with Dr Cronshaw, who is a trusted colleague,' he replied. 'He specialises in the treatment of hysteria and there is no shortage of ladies suffering from that condition.'

Ruby's hackles rose, as did mine, but I shushed us both.

'Cronshaw recommended a clinic near the mountain town of Berchtesgaden,' Poynder continued. 'They have a robust approach there to the treatment of weak-minded women.'

By 'weak-minded' he means 'all' and by 'robust' he means 'cruel', Ruby chipped in. *They are a brutal race, those Prussians.*

Bavarians, I corrected her with mild though fleeting satisfaction, for it was not often that I was the better informed.

'Is that when you went away?' I checked and he nodded.

'I told people we were combining a lecture tour with a holiday. Friends knew that my wife was unwell and thought a change of scenery might do her some good.'

Poynder began to pace the room.

'It was obvious, however, that the journey only unsettled Dolores even more and her behaviour became so wild that she had to be restrained in a straitjacket on more than one occasion.'

He stopped to pour himself another brandy, watched balefully by Gerrund.

'After a month or so a nurse noticed nodules in Dolores's armpits and then elsewhere.' He took a good swig and I began to worry on his patients' behalves. 'She has cancer,' he announced flatly.

'Can anything be done?' I asked, with a sinking feeling that I knew the answer already, and he shook his head.

'We cannot operate because it has spread throughout her body and into her brain.' He took another drink. 'Which explains her behaviour. Her very mind is being eaten by this accursed disease.' Poynder's hand shook so badly that the brandy splashed over it and onto a rather fine blue Persian rug.

Note that he makes no attempt to mop it up, Ruby commented, and I had heard Gerrund sniff less loudly when he was taking his white powder. *Typical man.*

I stood. Sometimes I think better on my feet, but this was not one of those occasions for my mind was in as much of a turmoil as it had been while I was sedentary.

'I am truly sorry for what has happened to your wife,' I told Poynder, 'and I can appreciate your concern for her but Mungo Peers' parents are in purgatory. They do not know who killed their son.'

His jaw muscles bunched briefly.

'And what good would it do them?' he demanded. 'The details would have to come out. Damn it,' he cursed, his fingers tightening even more around his tumbler. 'My wife told me...' His face was a portrait of misery. 'She confessed...' He hesitated before plunging back into his statement. 'She told me that she tortured the child before she slaughtered him and she will tell the police that too.' He clutched his brow with his free hand. 'She boasted about it.' His head slumped and his shoulders shook. 'I am certain that his parents are – as you put it – in purgatory but...' He slammed the glass down onto the mantelpiece so violently that it shattered. 'Would you condemn them to hell?'

Edward Poynder glanced at his fingers and delved into his pocket for a white, though instantly stained handkerchief, to wrap carelessly around them before lowering himself back into his chair.

He has blood on his hands, Ruby observed grimly.

56: THE STAIN AND THE EVIL TWIN

I PACED TO the fireplace and stood with my back to it, only for Hefty to join me, his elbows resting casually on the mantlepiece that I could hardly see over unless I stood well back.

Before you announce the murderer's name, make sure he does not have a grenade, he advised, for that was how he lost three toes and the woman with whom he had fallen in love. *She had a name*, he reminded me indignantly but still – even more to his chagrin than mine – neither of us could recollect it.

I mustered my scattered thoughts and tried to drill them into some semblance of ranks but, as always, no sooner had I got those at the front into line, those at the back had wandered off.

'I have every sympathy with your desire to protect your wife,' I began carefully, 'but, in doing so, you allowed her to attack an innocent waitress and murder three more people.'

'I did not know,' Poynder protested, rewrapping his handker-chief around his first and second fingers. It was stained but not saturated.

He'll live, Hefty predicted.

Not if I have anything to do with it, Ruby vowed for she took great satisfaction in sending her villains to their deaths.

'You must have known,' I argued. 'Those murders were in all the papers.'

Poynder touched his brow with his uninjured left hand.

'I knew about the deaths of course,' he conceded, 'but I believed my wife to be restrained securely.' He fiddled with his watch chain. 'She slept at the back of the house because it was quieter there and she liked to wake in the morning sun. There is a fire escape.' He raised a hand to quell my incredulity at his lax security. 'But it is not directly accessible from her room. I was not to know that she had a spare key.'

'You must have suspected something,' I objected, and he shook his head.

Don't let him convince you that his wife has an evil twin sister, Hefty advised, having fallen prey to that ruse in *The Back Window*.

'The witnesses' reports implicated a man,' he protested reasonably enough and, to my surprise, his eyes filled with tears. 'I no longer care what happens to me,' he said, 'but the woman I know and love is kind, gentle and childlike.' He pinched the bridge of his nose. 'Quite literally she would not hurt a fly. She would go to great lengths to shoo one out rather than swat it. She has a matter of days to live. Would you have her spend her final hours being interrogated and imprisoned in a police cell? The disease committed those crimes, not my wife and most of the time she is still my sweet Dolores.'

I hesitated.

We let Quarry go free because of his work with the lepers, Hefty reminded me.

'Even if she had the means, she is too weak to escape now,' he argued. 'I shall have her manacled to the bed if you wish.'

Even you are not that cruel, Ruby breathed and, though I did not care for her use of the word *even*, I was forced to agree.

'Very well,' I said reluctantly. 'I see little to gain by making her suffer more.'

Poynder inhaled and exhaled slowly.

'God bless you, Lady Violet,' he said. The tears were flowing freely now. 'If Dolores can die in something approaching peace, I no longer care what happens to me. I have harboured a murderer and I shall pay the price.'

I took a breath and prayed that I should not come to rue my next words.

'You do good work in this town,' I said, 'and I see no reason to put a halt to it.'

How many other doctors, I reasoned, would respond to emergency calls in Lower Montford at night?

Poynder lowered his head.

'I shall do all that is within my power to ensure that you never have cause to regret that decision.'

I helped Poynder to bandage his wounds, a task that would have been difficult for him to perform one-handed.

'You could instruct some of the nurses at the infirmary,' he approved as I tied the ends.

'Romulus is a good teacher.'

'A good man altogether,' he concurred and accompanied me into the hall. 'Do you believe in the power of prayer?' A curious question, I thought, for an alleged atheist.

'I do,' I assured him, because at that moment I most assuredly did more than ever.

'Then pray for her.'

'I shall,' I promised and could not resist a glance up the stairs, all too aware of the monster lurking there.

A stooped gentleman was coming up the steps, leather bag in hand, as we stepped outside and stood on the path on either side to let him pass.

'Doctor Cronshaw,' Wormwood greeted him.

'How is the patient?' the gentleman enquired, a little out of breath from his ascent.

'Unsettled,' Poynder told him, 'despite this lady's kind ministrations.'

Cronshaw shot me a quizzical glance as he stepped inside, but the door was closed before he could say anything.

I hate it when men cry, Ruby snuffled, forgetting how she mocked Hefty's weeping by the grave of… oh what was her name?

He only knew her for two days, she pointed out.

The happiest of my life, he insisted. *I even paid for her gravestone and inscribed it to 'my one true love…'* He cleared his throat awkwardly. *It began with a P*, he mumbled, *I think.*

57: CONSUMPTION AND SEDUCTION

MARTHA LOOKED TIRED and tense when she arrived.

'You have some news?' she asked after she had kissed me.

'I have,' I agreed, ushering her into an armchair.

A salvation army band was heading towards the monastery gates. At least they played in tune and might deter the hurdy-gurdy man from setting up close by.

'You look grim,' Martha told me uneasily. 'What has happened?'

I crouched in front of her.

'It is not good news, I fear.' I took her hands. 'Dolores is ill.'

'Then I must go…'

'Very ill,' I broke in. 'Dr Poynder took her abroad for treatment but it did not work.'

'Consumption?' There were many clinics in Germany and Switzerland where it was hoped that the mountain air would help cleanse patients' lungs. 'I do not remember her coughing.' She stiffened. 'Did she tell you that?'

'Dr Poynder…'

Martha pulled her hands away.

'He is lying,' she insisted.

'I have seen her,' I said gently. 'Dolores is bedridden.'

'Did you speak to her?'

I nodded.

'She was very confused. Martha…' I looked up at her. 'Your friend has cancer.'

'No,' she corrected me. 'Dolores was healthy when she left.'

'It was probably in the early stages then. I am sorry.'

Martha stared at me.

'You cannot believe that. He has seduced you with his suave-ness.'

Poynder had not seemed especially urbane when I saw him last, but I could imagine him charming many women.

'She was being treated by Dr Cronshaw,' I continued. 'Did her behaviour not seem odd in any way before she went?'

Martha fiddled with the side of her hair.

'Perhaps a little distracted and forgetful,' she conceded, 'but that was because she did not want to leave me.'

'She had some trouble with a maid,' I reminded her.

'Who has not?' she demanded reasonably enough.

'And struck her,' I continued.

'Never!'

I did not even consider mentioning the killings of the dog or Mungo Peers. Martha would not have believed me for one moment and, even if she had, what good would the information do her?

I got to my feet.

'Why have I not been allowed to see her?' she demanded. 'I could bring her some comfort.'

'She is not herself,' I struggled.

'Dolly wants to see me – the letter.'

'Dolores is confused,' I said gently, but it was useless to hide the truth. 'I am afraid that the cancer has spread to her brain.'

'Then I must go to her.'

'You cannot,' I said. 'I am sorry.'

She jumped up.

'Did he pay you to tell me all this? How much? I shall double it for the truth.'

Throw her out, Ruby urged indignantly, but I knew that Martha was lashing out not at me but against what she had heard.

'Oh Martha,' I sighed. 'I have told you the truth.'

She looked about her, but there was no escape from what was happening.

'But I love her!' she cried and fell sobbing into my arms.

'I know you do,' I said uselessly, and even Ruby had no cutting remarks to make but hurried to look out of the window so that I could not see her face.

'It seems that I misjudged Edward,' Martha admitted when she had brought her tears under control, ignoring the large white handkerchief that Havelock Hefty was proffering.

'So did I,' I confessed shamefacedly as the door burst open.

'Misjudged?' Agnust repeated. 'Misjudged?' she echoed. 'Misjudged!' she parroted but, fortunately did not reiterate the word again, for I was running out of verbs to describe her action.

'Have you been listening to our conversation?' I demanded angrily and my maid gathered her arms under her bosom with some difficulty for they appeared to be struggling to conduct an orchestra.

'Course I have,' she replied defiantly. 'What are ears for but listening and what are conversations for but listening to? There's precious little object in havin' either without either.'

Moot points, Hefty conceded, refolding his handkerchief and tucking it away.

'It was private,' I scolded.

'It was until I hear it,' Agnust reasoned.

'It is not a servant's place to comment upon her mistress's intercourses,' I told her crushingly, but my maid was not so easily squashed.

'And it int a young lady of old breedin's place to goo scamperin' about town at all hours misjudgin' people,' she retorted haughtily.

Even by Agnust's standards this was going too far.

Dismiss her without a character, Ruby advised.

A character without a character, I mused before reminding myself that Agnust was not one of my creations and remembering my righteous wrath.

'And afore you remember your righteous wrath...' Agnust continued.

This was alarming. Had my maid been given access to my brain? I waited anxiously for her to deny it and thereby prove that she had, but she did not and thereby proved nothing.

'Get your things,' Agnust commanded, though I rather thought that should have been my line.

'What?' I asked, hoping I did not sound as confused as I was but knowing that I must have by the way that Ruby rolled her eyes.

'You're comin' with me,' Agnust said, though Inspector Hefty had rather thought that should have been his line.

'What? Where? Why?' I stumbled, more confused than it was possible to sound by then and Agnust's arms broke free.

'Do you want to know the truth 'bout Mrs Poynder,' she interrogated me, 'or do you not want to know the truth 'bout Mrs Poynder?'

'I do,' Martha chipped in, her hand shaking as she pushed a Little Queen into the mouth of the snake so clumsily that the paper wrapping split.

'You goo home,' Agnust told my guest, something else which I had thought was not a servant's place to do. 'Seek not the truth for fear it do seek you,' she advised sagely before turning a critical eye upon me. 'And you,' she pointed a sturdy finger, 'had best spruce yourself sharp. We have an appointment to keep.'

'Where are we going?'

'To sort this matter out once and for all,' Agnust said and I was still none the wiser.

Oh Lady Violet, Miss Kidd breathed despairingly, *despite your worst efforts you acquired some knowledge in all your years under my tutelage. Do not, however, delude yourself that you will ever be any the wiser.*

58: FORNICATION AND THE SIN OF SOBRIETY

I HAD EXPECTED Lower Montford to be less forbidding but it was not. While I had only imagined what lurked in the shadows, I could not avoid the sullen and menacing stares of the inhabitants in the daylight.

Luckily our destination was close to the outskirts of town and I had both my servants with me – Gerrund for protection and Agnust to affect an introduction. The three of us could not possibly have fitted in a hansom, even if I had sat on one of their knees – which I had no intention of doing – and so we took a growler. It rumbled, squeaked and jolted over every bump and divot, but I was a great deal more comfortable than when I had been packed on the luggage shelf.

'Waste of time,' Gerrund grumbled.

He had been looking forward to trying a new recipe for stuffed lambs' hearts, though I was less enthusiastic about ingesting them.

I had to eat their eyeballs in Morocco, Ruby reminded me.

They could not have been worse than the tripe sandwich I was given in Accrington, Hefty countered and, while they bickered about that, I tried to pay attention to Agnust.

'She need to speak to her herself,' she countered. 'There's things int decent for me to repeat.' And I only hoped that whatever was to be revealed would be worth the trouble.

The Convent of Saint Ethel of Ickworth was not an impressive building. Standing opposite the Stoat's Head public house, it had been a small factory for producing Salty Spud Slivers – thinly sliced fried potatoes in greaseproof paper bags sold as snacks. Unsurprisingly, the idea never caught on.

In response to Gerrund's hammering, the door was opened by an elderly nun, her tawny face shrunken inside her dark grey veil like a two-year-old windfall accidentally fitted with teeth.

'Marnin', Mother Mory,' my maid greeted her.

'Marnin' is as marnin' do,' the sister superior declaimed, her grey eyes searching the sky as if expecting their patron saint to drift over in a shining cloud.

Any kind of cloud would have been welcome that summer.

'Amen to tha',' Agnust endorsed the somewhat gnomic assertion. 'We come...'

'Come not to a place unless thou come from another place,' the nun advised wisely.

'We come from another place,' Agnust confirmed, 'seekin'...'

'Seek and thou shalt search,' Mother Mory declared, adding sagaciously, 'for he who searches shalt also seek.'

Poke a finger in her eye, Boson Briggs − who I had thought was lost at sea − advised, *any finger in either eye will do.*

Don't talk to me about eyes, Ruby protested, the memory fresher than the oculi had been.

'Amen.' Agnust glowed in the light of these revelations, but there was no stopping this marvellous old woman.

'Yea and I say unto you...'

'Millie Bull,' Gerrund barked, destroying my no-stopping theory before it had taken root and I sniffed peevishly for he had not entrusted me with the ex-kitchen maid's surname. 'We want to speak to her.'

'Then want shall be thy mistress and thy master,' that loveable old lady of the cloth continued, 'and he who...'

Shut up, Ruby snapped though, from the way they all looked at me, she had snapped aloud.

'Being shut up in a convent must give many wonderful opportunities for contemplation,' I bluffed, unconvincingly to me but not to the wizened anchorite.

'In contemplation do we ruminate,' she concurred, 'and in rumination do we ponder for...'

'Never mind any of that,' Gerrund interrupted rudely, but at least he had not said claptrap. 'Claptrap,' he ended and Mother Mory smiled beatifically.

'Do you wish to see your baubles hanging on a tree?' she enquired. 'Because, believe me, I can arrange it.' And, for reasons that were not at all clear, my man fell silent.

'May we come in please?' I asked.

'You may,' she said so simply that it took me a while to work out what she meant. 'But no man may enter this building.'

'That's a pity.' Gerrund puffed his cheeks in disappointment. 'Looks like I'll have to go for a pint instead.'

Think I'll join you, Ruby said.

'Good man,' the nun approved, 'for does not Saint Ethel teach us it is a sin to be sober?'

This was news to me and I began to develop a new respect for the Pre-Markians.

'But you do not drink alcohol,' I observed to Agnust.

'Before you condemn her, Agnust has a dispensation,' the nun told me, 'for she do have a wicked and troublesome mistress to attend to.'

'Is that so?' I asked sternly but my maid was unabashed.

'Since the day she's born,' she assured me, and we stepped inside.

The building was little more than a shell, with windows high enough in the flint walls for the workers to see but not see out of. All around the stone-slabbed floor were towers of Holy Bibles – hefty leather-bound volumes of family editions in one pile, smaller portable editions in another. Four even more elderly nuns were seated behind a bench, studiously turning to the offending pages to erase the next word on each. Two novices – to judge from their youth and simpler robes – trudged about, replacing each bible when the task had been completed.

'We do cross out *defiles* this marnin',' the young nun informed me.

'Congratulations,' I murmured.

'I already do mine,' Agnust announced proudly.

'You have not introduced me,' I reminded her but Mother Mory raised a hand.

'Those who have not foresworn the so-called gospel of the accursed Mark shall go anonymous in this wholly holy place,' she informed me.

'Can we speak to Millie?' I asked wearily.

'Sister Robinth has cast away her worldly name,' she told me and pointed to a solitary woman in black but no veil, sitting at a pine table in the corner, industriously chalking short lines in columns on a slate tile. 'She is practising the sacred task of striking out.'

'I do beseech the Lord every night that he summon me here to tha' work,' Agnust said fervently and I made a mental note to pray that her dream would come true.

'Can...' I began again, only to be interrupted by a piercing scream.

'Lord forgive me!' a young nun bawled, 'for I have blotted out fornication.'

I rather thought the Christian churches had been trying to do that for nigh on two thousand years, but from the general uproar it was clear that the premature erasure was almost as sinful as the deed itself.

Mother Mory rushed over to check, with Agnust close behind.

'Good day, Sister Robinth,' I said, squatting on a three-legged stool to face her.

'Millie,' she whispered. 'They do turn me as buffle-headed as themself with their muggled names.'

'You do not share their beliefs?' I checked quietly and she rolled her eyes.

'Int crackled yet,' she asserted – crackled being mad, I remembered. 'But they give me food and a bed. Bran my brain this do but it beat starvin' – just 'bout.'

'You used to work for Mrs Poynder,' I began.

'I know tha',' she told me.

'Why did you leave her employment?'

'Dint have no choice,' she said pushing the stick of chalk into her ear. 'Well I do but it int a choice I like.'

'What happened?'

I watched in concern as the chalk slid in. Surely her earhole could not be that deep?

'Poynder want his way and he do take it.' She tipped her head back, mouth agape like people do when trying to catch a grape.

'Is that why you drank carbolic?' I asked and she shuddered.

'My young man Habakkuk dint want spoiled goods,' she said bitterly. 'Like any good man he do want to spoil me hisself.'

'I believe that Mrs Poynder tended you.'

'She dint know what happen.'

'And then you left?' I checked.

'Dant no choice,' Millie told me. 'When I wint let the doctor spoil me more, he tell Mrs Poynder I do try frivollin' with him and she do dismiss me.' I had not heard of *frivolling* before but I could guess that it involved flirtation at the very least. She screwed the chalk further in. 'She dint want to but he say she must for it int the first time I do it and...' She puggled the stick about. 'He tell her dint goo and give me no character.'

To be sacked without a written character sounded the death knell to any servant's employment prospects for, in such a small town, it was a simple thing to contact her previous employer.

'Did she attack you?'

I might have asked if Dolores had performed a cartwheel in church for the incredulity that greeted my question.

'Wha' her?' Millie tugged at the chalk. 'If she hurt a spider she do 'pologise, put it to bed and call for the veterervin— animal doctor.'

'When did you leave?' I asked while she pulled harder.

'Year 'fore this after Christmas and 'fore the next,' she informed me not quite as unhelpfully as it sounded for it meant around the middle of last year and I was about to thank her when she said, 'maid 'fore me goo same way.'

'You mean...'

'I do.'

'Do you know her name?'

'I do,' she nodded vigorously, 'not.' There was a loud crack. 'Break off in my head,' she observed, eyeing the stump critically. 'Prob'ly melt,' she forecast with an optimism that I was unable to share.

Mother Mory rejoined us.

'Back to work, Sister Robinth,' she commanded, shooing me away.

I did not care for her, nor being shooed by anyone, but I had had enough of the Pre-Markians before I had even met them.

Agnust had her mouth full and was chewing vigorously.

'We are leaving,' I told her and she spat a wad of soggy paper at my feet.

'I 'member now,' Millie called after me, much to the mother superior's displeasure. 'Edwina Derisible.' She tapped her ear. 'Prob'ly best I push it right in.'

It probably would be, Ruby agreed mischievously as I opened the door.

The growler was parked by a shallow puddle of sewage, but that was small parsnips compared to the streams that I had waded through on my previous visit and so I tiptoed daintily into it and sank up to my knees.

59: FEAR AND THE COLLECTOR OF KIDNEYS

ONCE HOME I got out of my soggily stinking clothes and bathed. Millie's explanation had put rather a different complexion on my impressions of the good doctor, I contemplated as I struggled into a fresh, but slightly too tight, light rose dress and went to the sitting room.

'How are we provided for coffee?' I asked Agnust.

'I do get a bag yisdee,' she told me, clearly ruffled at my intrusion into one of her responsibilities.

'Bacon?' I checked.

'A good half pound of that,' Gerrund asserted, also discountenanced, for the kitchen was his realm and I had no visa to enter it.

'I am going for a walk,' I announced, 'possibly to purchase some cheese.'

'You do get delusionations with tha',' Agnust asserted.

'Only after a wheel of cheddar fell on my head from the top shelf,' I countered, 'and I thought that I was Miss Havisham, but that was just for a week or two. I sometimes have sick fancies, though, and today I have a craving for something savoury.'

'Miss Havisham?' Agnust ruminated, my exceedingly witty misquotation wasted upon her. 'Do she teach you the bagpipes?'

'She tried,' I agreed because I was already more than a third of the way through my allotted span.

–

Suffolk Crumble, I decided as I crossed the square and, at that moment, a much-welcome breeze sprang up.

Could it be that the Madonna of Woolpit was smiling upon me? She did not favour me for long though, because when I arrived at Peers and Sons Grocery store it had closed down.

It cost me tuppence to be misdirected by the mutton pie man and the same again to be correctly directed by a crippled seller of nutmeg graters.

Number sixteen Panford Road was not the sort of gaff to impress a cabby, but it was a pleasant little semi-detached house behind a neat garden. The white paint on the wooden picket fence was slightly worn and grubby, but the front door was washed and the single step freshly whitened. The iron knocker was shaped like a seahorse, an odd choice for an inland market town I supposed, but more pleasant than the grim reaper I had acquired with my front door and never got around to replacing.

A thin cheerless girl answered my tapping. Her uniform was crumpled with a greying apron, but a starched hat so white that she must have just clipped it on. It would appear that she was an up-and-downstairs maid otherwise known as a *general slavey*.

'Good afternoon.' I held out my card.

'We int buyin',' she warned, arm braced to shut me out.

'I am not selling,' I replied, a little put out that I had paid good money to look like a travelling representative.

'Tha's what I say.' She touched her hat.

'Is Mrs Peers at home?' I waited for the obligatory pretending-to-find-out routine.

'Yes,' she replied and stepped back to admit me.

The hall was short, wide and cheerless, the walls painted chocolate brown and the wainscoting cocoa brown for relief. The ceiling was white and I was deliberating whether the oilcloth floor covering was dark orange or very dark orange when the maid reappeared from a door to my left and said enticingly, 'Goo in.'

In contrast to the gloomy hall, the front parlour was painted a cheery shade of mud.

A unique blend of the soils of south-west Lancashire and central Dorset, Hefty diagnosed for he had caught the Kidderminster Kidney Collector by taking samples from the knees of his trousers.

Mrs Peers was standing by the window, scrutinising my card.

She was a tall woman and, sticking to her theme, dressed in burnt umber.

'Never have a lady in here before,' she told me, touching the top button of her dress as if to make certain that it was done up.

'Oh,' I said, at a loss for a response that did not sound condescending. 'I wonder if I might have a word with you?'

'Is it about Mungo?'

'I am afraid so.'

Mrs Peers nodded.

'It alway is,' she said. 'Are you from a newspaper?'

Uncertain if this was better or worse than being mistaken for a saleswoman, I replied simply, 'No.' Having thought long and hard about how to explain my interest in the death of her son and coming up with nothing satisfactory, I ploughed ahead. 'I wonder if you have any idea who might have killed him.'

'A catch-rogue, the devil rot his rotten heart,' she replied, clearly not a woman to beat about the bush.

'A policeman?' I checked in surprise for this was not a theory that I had heard proposed before.

'That's what I say,' she confirmed. 'Or a judge. Someone high up.' She touched the button again. 'Not the mayor for he's too chuffy.'

Chuffy means fat, I explained to a confused Inspector Hefty.

'What makes you think that?' I enquired.

'I dint think it, I know it,' she assured me, 'for I see him in his fine carriage, a regular jelly-boy.'

'No,' I clarified. 'I mean why do you believe it was someone of standing?'

She twiddled the button.

''Cause the catch-rogues never catch him,' she explained. 'He must be covered in my poor sweet Mungo's…' Mrs Peers' face showed little emotion, but her voice broke and she paused to take a deep breath. 'Blood,' she managed, twisting the button so hard that it came away in her fingers. 'And there he run through the square and the busy streets. Someone must have see him and yet the authority do nothin'.'

'Perhaps nobody reported it,' I said, confident that Alfred Stanbury would have told me if anybody had.

She looked at the button in surprise.

'Who goo and report a n'offical to a n'offical?' she reasoned with some justification. It was well known, that despite Alfred's best efforts, the police closed ranks to protect their fellow officers rather than bring them to justice.

'How did Mungo seem the day he…' I found myself unable to say the word to his mother. 'On his last day?' I ended as gently as I could.

Mrs Peers sucked in her cheeks.

'Worryin'.'

'Do you mean that he was worried or that he worried you?'

'Both,' she replied flatly.

'Do you know why?' I pressed and she blew out as if extinguishing a candle.

'Mungo come home one day,' she began, 'and tell me he goo to a house on his round with that old salt man.'

'Jacob Kaufman?'

'The same,' she concurred, starting on another button. 'Mungo see a maid up to no good with a man. She see my boy and look at him all afeared and he get all afeared and run off. I tell him forget it but it worry him and he decide he goo back the next week and tell her not to be feared for he wint say nothin', but he never get the chance for tha's the day he die.'

'Do you know which house it was?'

'A big one. He say he dint remember where exackerly it is, but he recognise it when he see it.'

Give me three guesses, Ruby said, *and I will save two of them for another occasion*.

I hesitated again.

Get on with it, she urged irritably for I was devoting far more time to the problems of other people than to saving her from the prospect of being roasted alive.

'Could it possibly have been Dr Poynder's house?' I suggested tentatively and Mrs Peers snorted disdainfully.

'Think I dint think on tha'?' she challenged me. 'Course I think on tha',' she answered her own question. 'But my old mother do have three survivable girls.'

'I am sorry,' I puzzled, 'I cannot see why…'

'For they help me,' she interrupted. 'Ethel call at the front door sayin' she look for work and Maude call round the back the next day askin' for a piece of bread what the kitchen maid kindly give her with a mug of tea. The over-stairs maid have corn colour hair the under-stairs do have red and say they only have two maids, but the one my Mungo see up to no good have hair the colour of a black cat, he do tell me.'

'Oh,' I breathed, taken aback as none of the information I was gathering was of the slightest use.

In my experience the information which is most useless is invariably the most useful, Hefty pronounced gravely, tipping his hat to a pretty young woman as we left Mrs Peers to sew on her button and stepped into the sunshine.

60: GREY WOLF AND THE GRIZZLIES

THE GREEN FAIRY was gathering herself in the bottom of my glass when the doorbell rang.

'Who on earth could that be at this hour?' I wondered aloud.

Shall I go and look? Hefty offered, though he could not possibly do so without my presence. He was being much more obliging since I had allowed him to speak again, though he had yet to apologise for naming me as his primary suspect in *The Woman on the Train Disappears.*

Stay with me, my absinthe whispered seductively.

Agnust had gone to bed early and Gerrund had retired twenty minutes ago. He would probably still be cleaning his teeth – a prolonged ritual for him since he had adopted a peculiar habit of working a silk thread between them, though heaven only knew what damage that would do to his gums.

I was rising from my chair as the last few drops fell through the corroded remnants of the sugar lump, when the door opened and Gerrund appeared in a rather gorgeous long silk dressing gown, gold with a black floral motif and blue velvet cuffs. Only a few inches of his blue silk pyjama trousers were visible below the hem.

His night attire is more expensive than yours, Ruby observed.

He plays a better game of brag, I told her.

'Would you like me to answer that, milady?' he asked while Ruby stifled a laugh.

She had just noticed the cream that he had applied under each eye to ward off wrinkles.

'Perhaps you could stand in the background,' I suggested, not wishing him and, by proxy, me to be subject to ridicule.

Gerrund followed me out into the hall.

Keep the chain on, Hefty advised for, if Marianne Crane had followed his advice, she might be on the earth rather than in it.

I had intended to take that precaution anyway, but a contrary part of me was inclined not to.

Fling the door wide open, Ruby egged me on.

When a sixteen stone, axe-wielding, grudge-bearing Albanian had burst into her mansion she had felled him with a secret blow shown her by her Red Indian guide for warding off grizzly bear attacks. Unfortunately Grey Wolf had not taught me that technique, so I kept the chain on while I peered out. There in the yellow glow of the gaslight, stood the tall, forbidding bulk of Wormwood.

'I am sorry to disturb you at such a late hour,' he began and, before Gerrund could tell him that he should be, I stepped back.

One glance at his face told me that he had not come to make trouble but to report it.

'You had better come in,' I said, half-closing the door to slip off the chain.

'And no funny...' Gerrund began before he too caught Wormwood's grim expression.

Wormwood removed his bowler and we went into the front sitting room where I flicked the light on. The brass toggle was supposed to be hot. Mr Poplar the electrician had told me so. Electrons are like tiny flames, he had explained, which is how they make the element in the bulb glow. If so, Rommy's switches were seriously faulty for they were always cool though his lights worked as well as mine.

'Take a seat,' I indicated but he remained standing, staring at the window though the curtains were closed.

'I shall not take up much of your time,' he promised as I went to stand facing him side on.

Not bad, Ruby assessed his profile. *I'll wager there is at least a drop of noble blood coursing through those veins.*

We both knew that many a maid had fallen for the lovesick son of her aristocratic master only to find that he had gone off the idea of marrying her when she was with child.

'I just wanted to say a few things,' Wormwood continued and ran a hand back through his hair. Could it really have become greyer since I saw him last?

It is the light, Ruby explained. *Electricity shows every one of one's flaws.*

She was very proud of her almost perfect skin, though not in the least part grateful for my giving it to her.

'My mistress, Mrs Poynder, passed away this evening,' Wormwood announced.

'I am sorry,' I said and Gerrund murmured something about God resting her soul.

'She is at peace now,' Wormwood said. 'It was a blessed release after all...' he swallowed, 'her sufferings.' He patted his pockets like men do when they are looking for their matches, but I suspected that he had no reason for performing the action other than it being something to do. 'I am just on my way back from Thackery's the undertakers.'

From the strong smell of spirits I judged that he had stopped for a stiffener on the way – the Splendid would still be open – and I could not blame him.

'They were closed of course and I had to go to Mr Thackery's house.' Wormwood slipped his hands into his trouser pockets but pulled them straight out again, it being far too casual a pose for a man of his station in the presence of a woman of my station. 'My master is anxious to have her made more presentable as soon as possible.'

'Of course,' I said. 'How is Dr Poynder holding up?' I asked and he tapped his pockets again.

'I think he feels guilty,' he said and I stiffened but he elaborated immediately, 'because he cannot truly mourn her death when it has released her from her sufferings.'

He pinched the bridge of his nose.

'That is understandable.' I nodded. 'Would you like a brandy?'

Wormwood raised a hand.

'No thank you, milady. I must get back to Haglin House. I wanted to apologise for what I did to you,' he said, his troubled eyes flicking to check my response.

'You were protecting your mistress,' I excused him.

And he saved your life by shutting the lid so quickly, Hefty pointed out.

It would not have been in danger had he not forced you back into the ottoman, Ruby argued.

Wormwood nodded gratefully.

'I wonder if I could trespass on your kindness,' he said.

You are doing so already, Ruby told him as he delved into a waistcoat pocket again, but this time produced a small oval gold locket scrolled in leaves and handed it to me.

I pressed the catch and it sprang open to reveal a dark lock of hair in the left-hand compartment and a miniature photographic portrait of Martha in the other.

'I do not think that my master would wish to keep this,' Wormwood said.

'I know he was angry with Mrs Ryan,' I agreed, 'but she was trying to help the friend that she loved.'

I imagined, with dread, how she would receive the news and resolved to call upon her first thing before she could see an announcement in the newspaper.

'I understand that,' he nodded, 'but my master felt frustrated in his attempts to protect his wife. He did not know...' Wormwood swallowed. 'Those things... a demon got inside her, but it left her in her last hours and she became my own sweet mistress again.' He looked at the ceiling and I glanced automatically up as well. Agnust always claimed to be busy but a spider had been busier. 'She had no recollection of what the monster had made her do and I shall be grateful to you all my life that you allowed her to leave this world in peace.'

I clicked the locket shut. Martha had been speaking the truth when she said it was nothing like as expensive as the one she had received, but it would still have cost a few guineas. On the back was engraved *To my dearest friend Dolly with love from T.*

'I shall give this back to Mrs Ryan,' I assured him.

'Thank you.' Wormwood said and peered more closely at my man.

'What's that white stuff on your face?' he sniffed suspiciously.

'Pearson's Cold Cream,' Gerrund replied unabashed. 'It stops me getting bags under my eyes.'

'Pearson's,' Wormwood sneered, for surely real men in his world never used cosmetic products. 'Try Haverstock's Night Lotion. It's a bit less greasy and much more refreshing.' Wormwood picked up his hat. 'I'll send you a pot,' he promised and shuffled his feet. 'Poor Dr Poynder. I don't suppose he imagined he would have to go through all this again,' he sighed and was gone into the night.

Gerrund went to bed shortly after that and I returned to my green fairy.

I am not a fairy, she claimed, *I am a nymph – Calypso, the seductress.* She sighed, yearning for the love that she had lost. *They say I drive men mad, but I say I help them find the madness that is in them all.*

That is nothing to be proud of, Hefty informed her primly, but Calypso laughed and lowered her eyes alluringly.

Lord you must be desperate, Ruby commented, but the green fairy made no response for she had disappeared and was coursing through my veins.

'Damn you,' I said aloud but to nobody in that room or even in my head, and slammed down the glass.

—

Martha took the news much better than I expected, her hands not even shaking as she loaded her cigarette holder.

The human brain copes with sudden shocks by sheathing itself in a cushion of denial, Doctor Heinrich Heimhock, the eminent psychiatrist – *i.e. quack*, Ruby opined – pronounced gravely as I poured Martha another sherry. He had no business at all in my brain for I had not fully imagined him yet. *The feminine brain is a confusion caused by its inability to override emotion with logic*, he continued, polishing his eyeglasses with an enormous white handkerchief and I resolved to unimagine him at the earliest opportunity.

Martha flipped open her locket and half-smiled at some remembrance.

'Why did Dolores call you T?' I asked, not that it mattered.

All facts matter, Hefty lectured me sternly. *Remember how I caught the Chessman of Chester by calculating that the king's pawn was one thousandth of an inch taller than its fellows because he had coated it with curare?*

Martha breathed smoke.

'It was just a silly joke,' she explained. 'Dolly called me Tich.'

'You are not especially small,' I remarked and she waved her Little Queen.

'I am compared to her,' she assured me. 'Why Dolly is… was nearly as tall as Edward.'

Was she by Jupiter? Hefty exclaimed.

You never told me that, Ruby complained.

I only ever saw her in bed, I protested.

And outside St Etheldreda's, Hefty reminded me.

Yes, but she was surrounded by a family of giants then and bent over. I thought she was looking for something but she was probably stooped by illness.

And when she tried to stab you, Ruby pointed out.

I was too preoccupied with not wanting to die to assess her stature, I objected.

One should always assess the stature of everyone and everything, Hefty preached, thumbs tucked smugly into his waistcoat pockets. *Remember how I caught the Chess...*

But, at that moment, a shot rang out. Well, I had to do something to distract them before their distractions drove me to distraction.

61: VIOLENT SPELLS AND DELUSIONS

IT WAS OVER an hour before Romulus rang me back. He had been helping at a difficult calving. Havinger, the horse quack, as he was known by the locals, was off work having been savaged by a pig.

'Must have recognised a rival bore,' Romulus had quipped, the vet being notorious for his rambling anecdotes.

'Is this about the Poynder woman again?' he asked. 'I did write to her husband asking if there was anything I could do, but he has yet to reply.'

'She is dead,' I told him and took a breath, 'and I think that she might have been murdered.'

There was a gasp.

'Stop listening to this conversation,' I snapped.

'A slightly odd request,' he observed a little stiffly, 'even for someone as eccentric as you.'

Eccentric?

'No not you, Rommy,' I hastened to assure him and raised my voice again. 'I was talking to the exchange operator.'

'But I wint listenin',' a woman protested indignantly, untruthfully and illogically. 'If there's a murder, thoughs, I best report it to a policeman.'

'He is a policeman,' I claimed and Romulus cleared his throat.

'No he int,' she protested. 'He's a human doctor. He see to my young Jessical when she do be taken sadly-badly.'

'Oh yes, it's Mrs Fox,' my cousin realised. 'How is your daughter now?'

'Nicely thank you,' the operator replied. 'Why yisday she walk all the way with young Jepsical to Stolham St Ernest.'

'I am very glad to hear it,' Romulus said. 'But you must excuse me while I talk to Lady Violet.'

'Lady Violet,' Mrs Fox exclaimed. 'Why I recollect you gettin' stuck in tha' witch hazel tree. Still up to all your capers, are you?'

'I am trying to make a private phone call,' I reminded her and, with some mumbling about me not being so high and mighty when she had helped to drag me out, Mrs Fox fell silent.

'Murdered by whom?' Romulus asked proving that he at least had not lost track of our conversation.

'Her husband of course,' I replied.

'Why of course?'

'Well,' I began, 'he is my only suspect.'

'Hardly compelling evidence,' my cousin pointed out, and I had to admit that my grounds for suspicion sounded rather feeble when I said them aloud. 'What makes you think Mrs Poynder was murdered?'

'I think she was poisoned,' I replied, my confidence probably in as much need of medical attention as young Jessical had been.

I do not feel well, my confidence admitted.

My cousin clicked his tongue.

'Why?' he asked simply.

'I do not know what his motives were,' I admitted and Romulus snorted.

'I meant what led you to suspect that?'

'He locked her in her room.'

'A wise precaution if she had violent spells.'

'It does not feel right,' I added weakly and readied myself to be patronised, but I should have trusted Romulus more.

'Describe her symptoms again,' he urged, though we had discussed this before.

'She was confused,' I said, 'and suffered from delusions.'

'Not inconsistent with a cerebral malignancy.'

'And she told me that she had bad headaches.'

'Ditto.'

'And she fell asleep easily.'

'Again ditto.'

'And, to judge by her chamber pot…' I recalled with a shudder.

'Loose bowels?'

'Yes.'

'How was her hair?' he asked quickly.

'She lost a great deal of it.'

'Did you touch her?'

'Only her hand. It was cold and clammy.'

'Arsenic,' he pronounced.

'Are you sure?'

'I would need to get some tests done, but the symptoms are highly suggestive.'

'Then we must apply to have an autopsy performed.'

'Easier said than done. Dr Poynder is a respected man, as is Dr Cronshaw. Both are in the Warreners, and Wilson, the coroner, is the chief keeper of the Montford Lodge.'

'Are you in the Lodge?' From that and previous conversations, he seemed to know a great deal about it.

'I would be snared and skinned if I told you that,' he replied, and I was not sure if he was joking as I would have thought that any secret society would be anathema to him. 'And my foot made into a lucky charm,' Romulus added, confirming my suspicions.

'What about the home secretary?'

'Asquith might have obliged,' Romulus mused, 'but Ridley has only just been appointed. Post-mortem examinations against the wishes of the next of kin tend to be highly unpopular, especially if they are inconclusive.' He puffed. 'Besides which, if it is poisoning, it must be chronic and arsenic is excreted into the hair.'

'How much would you need?'

'As much as possible.'

'And how would I get hold of that?'

'What would Miss Gibson do?'

I was wondering when somebody would ask for my opinion, Ruby said, *because I have already devised a daring plan.*

I did not care for the sound of that, especially as I would be the one who had to execute her scheme.

'She would think about it,' I told my cousin.

'Well don't think for too long,' he advised. 'If Dr Poynder did murder his wife he will hold the funeral as soon as possible.'

Does this plan involve hot air balloons? I asked warily.

It might, Ruby admitted.

I have a simpler and safer idea, Havelock Hefty announced.

Then that is what I shall do, I decided. *Probably*, I added because, when I thought about it, Hefty's plan may have been simpler but it did not seem especially safe either.

62: THE RACK, THE THUMBSCREW AND THE TERRIBLE GUILD

MR JANUS THACKERY was, as befitted his profession, a mournful man and one might have thought that Dolores had been his daughter from the tragic way that he spoke of her. His right shoulder was lower than his left and I wondered if that came from a lifetime of carrying lead-lined coffins, and if *Undertaker's Stoop* were a recognised medical condition. If not the journals might name it after me.

'Are you a relative?' he enquired tremulously, his bulbous whiskers quivering in lieu of the jowls he lacked.

'Her sister,' I said confidently.

'Oh,' he said, and it was then that I recalled Martha telling me her friend had been an only child.

I could say that I meant she was like a sister, I mused.

Highly convincing, Ruby sarcasmed.

'May I confide in you?' I asked and he leaned his lean face towards me.

'But of course,' he assured me, dipping his head so low as to give me a glimpse of a scalp stained in a vain – in vain – attempt to disguise his balding crinkled pate. 'For I have undertaken the Undertaker's Oath and neither the rack nor the thumbscrew would induce me to break a confidence.'

'Good,' I said, fairly well satisfied, but he had not finished.

'Why Countess Canelo herself entrusted me with the knowledge that her children were not sired by the count.'

'Oh,' I said, a little less well satisfied.

'And I will take the secret of Bishop Foster's gonorrhoea to my own magnificent tomb,' he vowed, which was good enough for me.

'Dr Poynder denies my existence,' I improvised, 'because…'

He is your lover, Ruby prompted.

'I discovered that he is an imposter,' I explained, highly gratified to observe the man's avid interest in my fiction. 'The weal Dr Poynder's body lies in five ditches awound Wutland,' I concluded with no idea as to why I had W'd my Rs.

'Rutland?' the undertaker checked in shock, for few worse fates could befall a corpse than to be disposed of in that county, and I found myself torn between relief at his gullibility and chagrin that he had not recognised the plot of *The Disappearance of David Divine*.

'Wutland,' I confirmed, having been committed to that pronunciation.

'Have you told the police?' he gasped, forgetting to be lugubrious.

'I cannot for they are all in The Guild.'

'The Guild?'

In for a penny, I told myself and glanced over my shoulder.

'A nefarious, secret and murderous organisation.'

'Oh my goodness!' he gasped again. 'They sound awful. Do you happen to know if they are looking for new members?'

'They are looking for new victims,' I told him and I saw him hesitate. Did he really want to associate with an enemy of that terrible Guild? 'To keep their brother undertakers in business,' I put in quickly and he smirked.

'I knew there was something wrong with the man,' he asserted. 'He was far too pleasant to be a doctor.'

Just get on with it, Ruby nagged.

I snuffled.

'I loved my sister,' I said and he reverted to his melancholy manner.

'Indeed.' He wrung his hands, much too Uriah Heepishly to be convincing but, as Romulus once told me, insincerity only works if you smother people in it.

'And, since I cannot attend her funeral...'

'The best that money can buy. In fact...' he broke in, appraising me in what I hoped was a professional manner. 'I could possibly let you have a little discount since your final home would require less material than usual.'

309

'Why is that?' I asked innocently and watched him flounder for a full three seconds before I quavered, 'My only wish is to bid my darling Dolores farewell.'

I tried but could not manage to make my lip tremble and Thackery touched his cheek. Did he think that I was blowing him a kiss? If so, it had failed to melt his sepulchral heart.

'I am not sure the putative husband of the deceased would approve.'

'And to make a substantial contribution towards a wreath.' I baited my hook.

'How substantial?' he sniffed at my lure.

'Would five guineas be sufficient?' I asked, calculating that I could buy the contents of Mrs Pilkington, the florist's, window for less than that.

'Ten would provide a truly magnificent tribute,' he wheedled.

'Ten it is,' I bargained.

Have you lost your mind? Ruby scolded me. *If he knows you are not attending the funeral, he will not provide so much as a daisy chain.*

There is method in my madness, I asserted.

There is madness in your madness, she counter-asserted.

'Come this way, madam,' Thackery ushered me, struggling to hide a smirk behind his mask of tragedy and almost skipping as he led me down a corridor lined by genuine plaster of Paris marble statues of mourning Greek women.

The coffin lay on a table which was draped with black crepe, as were the walls and the unlit chandelier, only the flicker of an equally genuine ancient Greek oil lamp in each corner illuminated the black curtained room.

'I would like a moment alone with her,' I said, hoping the catch in my voice was not too theatrical but in the land of hams, the hammiest ham is queen, I told myself, ignoring Ruby's tuts.

'But of course, madam,' Thackery murmured and withdrew backwards, hardly grunting as he caught his hip on a side table decorated with wax lilies.

The coffin was rather a splendid construction – oak carved with fat-cheeked, trumpet-blowing cherubs on the sides and – just in case anybody forgot its true purpose – a skull and crossbones on the lid.

Rather piratical, Ruby commented, though the word I would have chosen was gruesome. The body would decay soon enough without any pictorial encouragement. *But a tad more decorative than the steel box to which you have condemned me and I have yet to detect any progress in my escape plans.*

I have more immediate concerns, I told her impatiently, blocking my mental ears to her indignation.

'Botheration.' The lid of the casket had been firmly screwed down.

This was not a complete surprise, but it was a completely unwelcome one.

At least it is not padlocked, Ruby commented.

Gerrund had called on Snail's hardware store that very morning, having first visited the parlour, ostensibly to choose a suitable casket – for Agnust he had joked to her chagrin – but really to find what type of screws were most commonly used.

Many undertakers contented themselves with ornamental thumbscrews at every corner – not the instruments of torture to which nice Mr Thackery had alluded but ones with large, flanged heads for ease of use. Thackery, however, had used square, slotted brass screws in such profligate quantities that his charges might have difficulty being resurrected in time for judgement day.

It occurred to me that I had never actually handled a screw-driver before. Why would I? I was not a craftsman, and if I wanted something made or repaired I employed a man to do it for me. I took the tool out of my bag, mortified to see that it had torn the cotton lining, and set to work.

Was always this difficult or did the man who had fixed the lid down have the grip of Hercules? Either way I managed to extract the screw and put it carefully on the table behind me. Even I had worked out that it – the screw not the table – might roll away.

Only fifteen to go, Ruby encouraged me but failed to do so.

'Oh good,' I said aloud, glad that Friendless was not there to question me.

Two more screws and my wrist started complaining. It was not designed for that kind of work I was told and, if I forced it to continue with its labours, it would be obliged to commence aching. I did and it did. Perhaps I was getting the hang of it, but some of the other screws rose quite readily from the lid for removal.

Soft footsteps approached.

Howl, Ruby advised, but I had beaten her to it.

'Ohhhhhhh,' I wailed. 'Ohohoh oh oh.'

There was a rustling.

'Ohhhhhhh.'

The footsteps began again but faded. Undertakers must be used to dealing with weeping relatives. In fact most of them carry black silk handkerchiefs to offer the bereaved and add to their final account. The average man, however, would rather be confronted by a spear-waving savage who was unable to see the advantages of having his home stolen and his family enslaved, than a caterwauling female.

'Ohohoh-oh.'

You can stop now, Ruby said irritably, having little patience with even feigned weaknesses in her own sex.

I went back to work, my wrist having been distracted, forgetting to grouse at the action. There was not much to being a craftsman after all, I considered with great satisfaction as I put my screwdriver down though, possibly, there were other skills involved in the construction of funeral furniture. I had seen carpenters using saws but they seemed simple enough to operate.

Do not even think of it, my right shoulder cautioned.

I slid the lid, or at least I tried to, only to find that it would not move. There must be a lip on the rim so I would have to lift it. It was heavier than I had expected. I adjusted my grip and heaved. Even if it were lead-lined, surely it could not be that heavy.

I'll wager you wish you had given more attention to your arithmetic classes, Ruby jibed and it took a moment to realise what she meant. There were fifteen screws on the cloth and I had not dropped any. I had missed one at the corner and extracted it with the practised ease of an experienced screwdriverist.

'Right.' I pushed on the head of the lid, fully aware that shifting it would take a great deal of force. Fully unaware that shifting it would take a great deal of force the lid shot sideways. It lay askew at about sixty degrees, I calculated, despite my poor performance in geometry. This was ridiculous. I had not even pushed in that direction. I went around to the top overhang, hardly brushing against the bottom overhang, but the lid leapt as if I had prodded it with a white-hot poker.

'Stop!' I commanded but lids, like most men, never listen and it positively flew to the edge of the coffin, hovering tantalisingly.

'Come back!' I implored, but it fell before I had a chance to add, 'please.'

The floor was richly covered but even the thick pile could not muffle the sound of the impact. At least it had cushioned the fall, I consoled myself, hurrying round to the unconsoling sight of a crossbone lying detached from its fellow on the carpet.

Butterfingers, Ruby jeered as I heard a distant grunt of surprise and the approach of no-longer-soft footfalls.

63: STRONG SEA BREEZES AND THE COUP DE GRÂCE

DOLORES LOOKED DREADFUL. Her face was waxy yellow and her mouth gaped, no attempt having been made to strap her chin with a cloth. Her sparse hair was uncombed and she was dressed in a skimpy cotton shroud. Her hands had been put on her chest but not even crossed properly so that I could see three gashes in the left one, now that its bandage had been removed. Most shockingly her eyes were wide open, staring pallidly upwards.

I delved hurriedly into my handbag.

'Where are you?' I tossed my notebook and handkerchief onto the table. 'Where... Got you!'

Snatching my scissors by the handles, I was fumbling them clumsily as the door swung open.

'What the blazes are you doing?' Janus Thackery shrieked in an unattractively high register.

Answer a question with a question, Ruby advised.

'How dare you burst in on me like that?' I demanded, though I knew his wrath arose from a rather more solid foundation than mine.

'This is an outrage,' he raved, possibly the first time – I reflected – that he had exhibited a genuine emotion in all his professional career. 'What are you? A resurrectionist?'

Quite how he thought I might carry Dolores out under his undulating nose I could not imagine, but his accusation of bodysnatching was no more implausible than the explanation I was about offer.

'I wanted to see my fr...' I amputated the end of friend and inserted, 'sister one last time.'

'Then you could have asked me.'

'I did not want to trouble you and you might have refused. There could have been anyone or no one at all in the coffin for all I knew,' I rambled. 'I had to make certain that the imposter husband had not substituted my sister with an imposter wife.'

'And what about those scissors?'

'I only wanted a little keepsake.'

He stared at me and the carnage I had created.

'I am calling the police.'

He means that he intends to summon them rather than he is actually doing so at the moment, Ruby quibbled unhelpfully.

'Good.' I folded my arms. 'Then perhaps you could use the opportunity to confess to your fraud.'

Thackery's hackles did what hackles do best – in fact it may be their only skill – they rose, but I did not give him the opportunity to repeat my last word with mock-incredulity.

'I have no doubt that this coffin is supposed to be carved oak,' I continued, 'but it has been constructed from pine with cheap decorations glued on it.'

I prodded the fallen rib with the toe of my crimson shoe.

'It is what Dr Poynder requested,' he informed me frostily.

'I wonder what happened to the expensive dress in which Mrs Poynder almost certainly arrived,' I said with a wintry smile, determined not to be out-chilled. 'Did he really request that you take it and barely clothe her in this rag?'

'Yes,' Thackery asserted. 'As you yourself told me, the man is a cheap fraudster.'

'I said no such thing at all,' I lied furiously. 'Edward is a dear dear friend of mine.'

'You said he was your brother-in-law.'

I sniffed the air between us.

'You do not smell of whisky,' I conceded. 'Have you been habituating an opium den?'

And, if so, would you recommend it? Ruby chipped in.

'This is outrageous,' he bristled in a way that would be a credit to any homdehod – as locals termed spiny slug-eaters. 'She is only attired in that simple but elegant shroud while I have her clothes laundered and pressed.'

I hesitated. Even if he were lying…

Of course he is lying. You can tell it in his name.

Janus? I checked, referring to the two-faced Roman god.

Thackery, she corrected me. *Remember how Thackery Thibbon cheated his sister in* The Man with the Golden Revolver?

He could probably retrieve her dress and deny everything, I concluded my train of thought.

'Indeed, even if you are correct, which you most certainly are not,' he told me with a sneer, 'I can retrieve her dress and deny everything.'

You need to stop thinking aloud, Ruby advised.

'Whereas,' the undertaker delivered his coup de grâce, 'you cannot repair this damaged lid.' He leaned backwards like a promenader resisting a strong sea breeze. 'It will cost you a pretty penny, my little one,' he leered, 'unless…'

Oh Lord he is not going to suggest… I shuddered.

'Unless…' he drooled.

He is, I continued to shudder.

Pretend to oblige then club him with a statue of Osiris as I did in Death on the Amazon, Ruby urged but, while she revelled in past glories, something – or rather the lack of something – caught my eye.

'Where is Mrs Poynder's wedding ring?' I demanded and his grey complexion did the impossible. It greyed.

'She was not wearing one,' he blustered.

'I look forward to hearing Dr Poynder corroborate that claim.'

'It must have slipped off.' He fiddled about with the shroud. 'It must be here somewhere.'

I took a closer look.

'You have cut off her finger.'

'Her knuckle was enlarged,' he defended himself.

'Well that makes your action perfectly acceptable.'

'Indeed,' he nodded before his fallen expression fell some more. 'Oh. You are being sarcastic.'

'Graverobbing is an offence punishable by imprisonment,' I informed him, 'with hard labour.'

'But I have never done a proper day's work in my life,' he protested before he realised. 'She is not in her grave yet.'

'And mutilating a corpse is a capital one,' I bluffed, snuffing out his last ember of defiance.

'Surely not?' He ran a finger over his wrinkled stain.

'Ethan Grimes was hanged and flayed for cutting an ear off a zookeeper's body only sixteen years ago,' I lied.

'I do not remember that.'

'You cannot hold me to account for your ignorance being laced with amnesia.' I had had enough of this gruesome man and his gruesomeness. 'I am going to take a lock of my friend's hair. If you try to stop me I shall call upon Dr Poynder on my way to Montford police station.'

'And if I do not?' he enquired cagily.

'Then I shall not feel it necessary...' I paused just long enough to observe his relief, 'to stab you with my scissors,' I ended and watched that relief vaporise before setting to work.

'You will need a substantial locket,' Thackery commented sourly and I had to admit that he had a point. Some of Dolores's hair was longer than I had observed in the gloom and I was having trouble stuffing it into Uncle Hawley's old cigar case that I had brought for the purpose.

'Where are you going now?' Thackery asked uneasily.

'That is my concern,' I replied loftily, 'and I shall not ask you the same question for I know the answer already. You, Mr Janus Thackery, are on the path to hell.'

64: CATCH-THIEVES AND JUMPNIPS

THERE WERE TWO developments the next morning.

Romulus dropped me a line. There were possible traces of arsenic in the hair that I had sent him, but it was too small to make an accurate measurement. Could I get a larger sample and closer to the head for recent growth? Not without the aid of a gravedigger, I replied.

And Inspector Stanbury called. A Mrs Fortunate Flock had gone to the police station concerned about a missing person. He had had a photograph taken of the victim and, tactfully covering the wounded part of her face, shown it to the woman who immediately identified it as that of her sister, Edwina Derisible, an out-of-work kitchen maid. Could I guess in whose employ Edwina had been? I did not need to. A strange coincidence, we both agreed over a pot of coffee.

When one is faced with two tasks it is an invariable rule of mine to do them in reverse order, Inspector Hefty counselled sagely. *That way the second becomes the first and, when it is done, the first becomes the first thing to do again.*

In hindsight that was not especially useful advice, but it seemed so to me as I selected a parasol to match my cerise bonnet while Gerrund hailed a cab.

'I'm not happy about you going alone,' he grumbled.

It is not your vocation to make him happy, Ruby pointed out but I said, 'I appreciate your concern,' and set off alone anyway. Ruby had a very low opinion of any woman who cowered behind a man and I had no desire to be despised by one of my own creations.

–

Mrs Fortunate Flock lived in a good-sized Georgian house on the outskirts of Upper Montford. This had been a prosperous part of town until the philanthropic Dr Horbin Angel – a removed sort of cousin of mine – opened the asylum in Dewbury Hall. Nobody wants to live in or near a mental hospital. People began to sell their houses and move away until word spread and, unable to sell, they rented them out, dividing them into increasingly smaller apartments. Mrs Flock occupied a back room on the ground floor of one such house.

'You can't come in,' she whispered as she opened the door. 'My old boy do sleep and he slutch me 'bout somethin' fine he do if he do get woke.'

Mr F must have been awoken a great many times, I judged by his wife's misshapen face. 'He int a bad old boy,' she assured me, stepping out and carefully closing the door behind her. 'Just a nasty one.'

The corridor was papered in what was probably perfectly nice floral paper once but was damp and peeling now, with broken laths jutting in a bulge in the wall behind her. Some of the floorboards were missing, probably having been torn up for firewood in the winter.

'I wanted a word about your sister,' I told her.

'Edwina, Edina, Edwona, Edona, Edorna, Edarna or Clurance?' she rattled off.

'The first,' I replied, taking a step back for her breath did not smell like meat. It smelt like rotting meat. 'Edwina Derisible.'

Mrs Flock slipped a hand through a rip in her blue, brown and browner patchwork dress and scratched her belly vigorously.

'Dead,' she told me. 'The catch-thief show me a beauteous portrait of her.' She smiled fondly, though with more gaps than teeth. 'Dead as a clock. Have you observe,' she asked with interest, delving deeper and lower under her dress, 'how people alway die on a Tuesday?'

'I think they die on other days too,' I suggested, turning my face away from the miasma.

'I used to think tha' also as well,' she said so amicably that I let the matter drop.

'I believe Edwina used to work for Dr Poynder,' I continued. *Please do not go any further down.*

'Did but dint now,' she explained, moving further down.

'I believe that he dismissed her.' I continued watching with horrible fascination as she rooted around.

'I do believe you do believe wrong,' she told me.

'So what happened?'

'I have a scratch so I itch it,' she explained, pulling her hand out.

'Why did Edwina leave Haglin House?'

'She dint stay there,' she said, 'after wha' happen.'

'What did happen?'

'I dant know.' She screwed up her face. 'Hungry jumpnip,' she commented and her hand went in through a lower rip. A jumpnip was a flea though I doubted that it was a solitary creature. 'BUT,' she continued with sudden vigour, 'I do know she's afeared somethin' chronical.'

'Of what?'

'Of somethin' of course.' She hunted about. 'I do have a fish paste sandywich in here somewhere.'

'Do you know what that something was?'

'I ask her tha' very same questyon, but she dint say even when I make her. Goo find someone else to bite,' she told her friends, squirming almost as much as I was trying not to.

I took two steps back in case they were paying attention and, seemingly unaware of my repulsion, she followed.

'It's bad manners, steppin' backward,' she observed, seemingly aware of my repulsion and I resisted the temptation to riposte with any comments upon her etiquette.

'Do you know what date your sister left Dr Poynder's employment?'

'Course I do,' she insisted. 'It's a Tuesday.'

'What month?'

'An old one afore this one.'

'Before or after Christmas?' I pressed, for everybody remembers when that is.

'Every month is before next Christmas and after last Christmas,' she told me. 'You decide.'

With such impeccable logic she extracted her hand.

Thank goodness for that, I breathed until she sniffed her fingers.

'Goh,' she puffed. 'Wha' a stink.'

'Goodbye,' I said.

'Found it,' she called after me. 'Want a nipple?'

I assumed that Mrs Flock meant a nibble but, either way, I declined – a decision I was not to regret later.

The horse dung in the gutter was alive with maggots, but it was wholesome and fragrant compared to what I had just encountered. There was a horrible sourness in my mouth and nostrils which would require at least two sticks of Beeman's to overcome, and I was just about to unwrap the first one when a funeral coach approached drawn by two plumed black horses. I lowered my head and Hefty crossed himself, but Ruby was preoccupied with a stain on the hem of her dress.

Somewhat to my surprise the hearse pulled up a few yards down the road. I would not have thought that any of the local inhabitants would be able to afford such a luxurious conveyance for their dearly beloved. The driver climbed down from his lofty perch and strode towards me.

'The Master wants a word,' he announced, towering over me.

Everybody towers over you, Ruby yawned. *Even Mrs Poynder though you did not trouble to notice.*

He would tower over Gerrund too, I told her, for she had often told my man that he was too tall for his station.

Big for his boots, she corrected me.

And I would like a good few words with him, Hefty declared, primping his moustaches.

'If he wishes to make an appointment,' I told him, 'he may call at my house and leave his card.'

'You dint want to see his callin' card,' the man snorted, and I was fairly confident that I did not wish to find out what he meant by that remark either. 'In his coach.' He jerked a gloved thumb over his shoulder.

Run for it, Ruby advised, but she must have known as well as I that I had little chance of outrunning a man whose legs were a good eight inches longer than mine and clad in trousers rather than wrapped in a dress.

'Very well,' I said haughtily.

Shakily, Ruby amended.

But it doesn't show, Hefty reassured me with his habitual loyalty as the coachman opened the door, sweeping his left arm with exaggerated courtesy to usher me in.

I hesitated because, as everybody knows, the purpose of a funeral coach is to convey bodies and I did not wish mine to be amongst that number as I had not even completed my one score years and ten yet.

'Need a hand?' the coachman asked with an air of menace I had not seen since I refused to tip a crossing sweeper for not sweeping his crossing.

Need a gun? Ruby proffered her silver revolver, but I brushed it and him aside and stepped aboard alone.

I am with you, Hefty reminded me as the coachman shut the door.

And us, several dozen characters chorused, though I could not think what use Little Myrtle would be if I were attacked.

I could knit a pretty pink scarf that you could use to blindfold him as you make your escape. And, not for the first time, I wondered about the reason that Boson Briggs had not hurried home.

Anton Gervey sat in a high-backed black leather armchair, his legs only just reaching the Persian rug. He was dressed in black as he had been when I saw him in the cellar of the Green Munky, his clerical hat hanging on a peg beside him. The interior of the hearse had been converted into a miniature drawing room in deep mourning.

'Ah the rat woman,' Gervey greeted me, though this was not an epithet that I would have wished to have attached to me. 'Take a seat,' he said, his voice just as high as Gerrund's imitation of him had been on our excursion into Lower Montford.

I would have preferred to remain standing, but the carriage creaked and jolted off and I toppled heavily back into a similar chair to that of my host.

'What do you want, Mr Gervey?' I asked, trying to rearrange my attire without appearing to do so.

Gervey's spindly fingers rested upon the arms of his chair, and I saw that he had a gold ring on his left little finger inset with onyx carved in the shape of a skull.

'The truth,' he said simply. 'You tended the maid Edwina Derisible when she was dying.'

'It was outside my house so, of course I tried to help,' I agreed. 'What of it?'

'She spoke to you,' he told me.

'How do you know that?'

'One of my men was there.'

322

'And you want to know if she identified him,' I surmised but Gervey sniffed loudly.

'I want to know if she identified her killer,' he said as we turned sharply left and up a cobbled street.

'Is that not one and the same thing?'

Gervey raised his hands as if he were carrying a tea tray.

'Why would you think that?'

I piffed.

'Why should I tell you?' I asked as coolly as I could.

'I could hurt you.' Gervey put his hands together as if in prayer.

'And you could make me talk, but you would not know if I were telling you the truth,' I reasoned and leaned forward wishing that I could untwist my petticoat.

Though the carriage was only dimly lit by a safety lamp hanging from the ceiling, his pupils were very small, I noticed.

'I shall put my cards on the table,' he said.

I bet he's got a double bezique, Ruby said bitterly, having wagered everything on four jacks in a Mexican casino.

'Please do,' I said uneasily, for we had turned right and I feared that we were heading towards the Lowers.

'Seraphim Square is disputed territory,' Gervey told me.

'With the Braise gang,' I guessed, and he raised his skimpy eyebrows.

'You are well informed.'

'I am,' I agreed though I was not. 'There must be rich pickings in the square with the market traders and the tourists.'

Gervey looked impressed, though it did not take many observational powers to see large quantities of money changing hands there.

'So about a year ago we came to an agreement,' he continued. 'We would operate in the square on alternate weeks.'

'And when Edwina was killed it was Braise's turn.'

'Precisely,' Gervey nodded. 'My man was passing through. He was not supposed to be there and I have punished him accordingly.'

'A Suffolk Smile?' I shuddered.

'The very same,' he agreed as the carriage swung right again.

'So Braise thinks that you had Edwina killed on his territory.'

'Exactly,' Gervey said.

'Did you not?'

'No.'

'Oh,' I puzzled. 'I rather thought that you did.'

Gervey interlocked his fingers tightly.

'And why would you think that?' he asked icily.

'Because, before she died, Edwina told me that you would kill me too if I did not stop interfering.'

'She used my name?' He looked genuinely surprised.

'She called you *the Master*,' I said and his left cheek ticked.

'Damn it!' he cursed. 'Why the hell would she say that?'

Watch your frebbing language, Ruby scolded.

'Presumably she believed it,' I replied, and Gervey fell silent rotating the ring with his thumb in agitation.

We bumped over a pothole, the lamp swinging wildly, illuminating his face, then mine and Gervey grabbed the arms of his chair to steady himself.

'Interfering with what?' he demanded at last.

'I have no idea.'

'You must have been up to something.'

'I am a novelist,' I told him. 'I live a quiet life.'

I did not need Ruby to remind me how inaccurate that claim had been recently, but she did.

Murders, madwomen and mayhem, she scoffed. *I had a quieter life in* The Case of the Poisoned Claw.

Gervey tapped his pointed upper right canine tooth with a fingerplate.

'Did she say anything else?'

'Only that she was in pain.'

'And who have you told this to?'

'The police,' I replied and he tapped an incisor as if to check whether or not it was hollow.

'I hope you realise, Lady Violet, if you are lying or holding anything back and a war breaks out, you could be responsible for the deaths of many men.'

And who would miss them? Hefty enquired with some justification.

'I have told you everything,' I insisted, countering his cold, almost colourless stare with an open gaze.

'One last thing.' Gervey treated me to a gelid smile. 'Keep out of it, Lady Violet, and you might see Christmas yet.'

'It was you who dragged me into it,' I reminded him, 'and I shall be perfectly happy if I never come across you, your employees or your rivals ever again.'

Gervey sniffed, reached out and tugged a cord at his side and we came to a halt. I heard the driver's boots on the woodwork and a moment later the door swung open. Was this where I was to be left dead in a ditch?

No ditches here, Inspector Hefty reassured me as I stepped out into the daylight and found myself in Seraphim Square.

Do you know what I found most frightening about that man? Ruby asked as the hearse pulled away at a suitably stately pace. *The fact that he was not in the least part frightening.*

That makes no sense at all, Hefty argued but I knew exactly what she meant.

There was a terrible chill in Anton Gervey and I had a feeling that it came from the depths of his soul.

So, Hefty wondered, *if Gervey is to be believed — and I think, in this instance, he is — and neither he nor Braise killed Edwina, who did?*

He glanced about us as if expecting the murderer to reveal himself immediately, but only a scruffy tabby came towards us as I made my way to Break House, and the cat showed no inclination to confess.

–

'What can I do?' Stanbury asked, busily spreading a sheet of brown paper over his cleared desktop. 'It is all conjecture and hearsay.'

He delved into a cardboard box to produce a length of electrical cable.

'But Mrs Flock...' I faltered, knowing already what the inspector would say.

'More conjecture,' he pointed out, laying his find in a coil on the paper. 'What could she tell a court? Her sister was frightened but she doesn't know why? How do you think that story would impress a judge and jury? Come to think of it, how do you think the woman herself would impress the twelve good men and true?' He looked about. 'Now where did I put that string?'

I followed suit and spotted it cowering under his chair.

'What are you doing?' I asked as he retrieved the ball.

He is wrapping up a length of electrical cable, Hefty explained, even more anxious to be helpful since I had scribbled some notes on the subject of his demise and Ruby clapped derisively.

Stanbury folded the paper.

'They are starting a black museum in Ipswich,' he explained, leaving me not very much the wiser until he added, 'and this will be placed on display as the weapon in a murder.' He put the string around his parcel and I placed a finger over the knot without being asked. 'In their section of unsolved cases,' he admitted ruefully and unfolded his pocketknife. 'The body in the...' he began to clarify.

'Drain,' Ruby, Hefty and I chorused as Stanbury cut the string.

65: SALOME AND PANDORA

GERRUND PLACED MY plate in front of me – a mound of scrambled eggs, sausages, bacon, liver and fried potatoes.

'Delicious,' I crooned, uncertain that I would be able to eat a quarter of it.

There was an interesting article in *The Englishman's Weekly* warning mothers to stay indoors during the heatwave or their unborn babies' brains would be coddled and they – the children not their mothers – would have to be put into asylums. I made a note to ask my father to stop forwarding it to me.

'The condemned woman do eat a hearty breakfast,' Agnust announced as she entered bearing a coffee pot on a tray, in a manner reminiscent of Salome triumphantly parading the head of John the Baptist.

'They are unlikely to kill me,' I protested, wondering if I felt like eating at all.

'You say it's unlikely man goo to the moon,' she reasoned, 'but he never do goo yet.'

If there was a logic in that argument it eluded me, and Gerrund who rolled his eyes despairingly.

I took a golden triangle of toast from the silver rack and dipped my knife into the butter, liquified, despite having been stored in the cellar and brought up in a pottery cooler.

'Gerrund will be waiting outside,' I reminded her.

'Rather be inside with you,' he muttered.

'I do not think they will let us both in,' I reasoned, 'and I will not intimidate them.'

'They might need intimidating,' he pointed out.

'Then I shall blow on this.' I touched my silver whistle.

'If he hear it,' Agnust said. 'He never hear me asking for the rubbish to goo out.'

'Didn't know you wanted to go out,' he mumbled.

'Anyway,' I broke in before they came to blows. He would be no use to me with a broken jaw. 'I shall be quite safe.'

Agnust cleared her throat.

'Old Gerrund is all very well if you want that kind of thing,' she conceded, 'but what use is a man in a n'emergency?'

I was preparing a list of times men had been useful when he rounded on her.

'Saved your life when you were caught in that fire.'

'Yes, but who started it?'

'Placton the footman,' he said and Agnust crossed her arms, the sleeves of her black dress rising. Was that a tattoo on the back of her forearm? Surely not?

'There you goo,' she snorted triumphantly. 'A man.'

And you wonder why men think we are irrational creatures, Ruby chipped in. She was not in the best of moods that morning, regarding any outing as a distraction from her predicament. *What if I have secreted an electrical drill on my person?* she proposed.

Where would you insert the plug? I objected and she huffed.

'Well I must not keep you from your tasks,' I told Gerrund and Agnust and they left reluctantly, for they liked to watch me relishing his food and fattening myself.

I jumped up, hurried to the sideboard, opened it, scooped almost all my breakfast into a soup terrine, put the lid on and was at my place, opening my letters. This was a propitious start to the day indeed, for I had won a diamond tiara once the property of Marie Antoinette. All I had to do was send ten guineas and my prize would be securely delivered the very next day. Reassuringly they would only accept cash payment to a post office box in Whitechapel.

'That was quick,' Gerrund commented, materialising at my elbow.

'I was hungry.'

'Good,' he said as my eye fell upon a sausage that had rolled off my plate and onto the floor. 'There's plenty more.'

'There is no need.'

'It's no trouble, milady,' he assured me, 'just as soon as I get Agnust to clear that trail of food leading towards the sideboard.'

'Oh,' I said, never at a loss for the bon mot, as I followed his gaze to the bits of egg and the rasher of bacon now carpeting the carpet. 'Goodness.' I looked at the clock. 'Is that the time? I must get ready.'

You will never be ready, Ruby warned forebodingly and, as usual, she was right.

As always, she corrected me while Gerrund opened the sideboard door.

'I was saving it for later,' I protested.

'What?' he puzzled, taking out a clean plate.

–

Old Queeny trudged wearily. She had looked exhausted before we had left the square.

'She stay up late chin-waggin' with next door's cat,' Friendless fended off the criticism that he was certain would be levelled at her.

'If you ever feel that the job is too much for her,' I called up tactfully.

'Years and years in her yet,' he insisted, for he could not bear to think of his companion as cat food and glue. 'And weeks,' he added for good measure. 'And days.'

'I was reading about a charity,' I continued, 'for retired horses.'

'She dint want no charity,' he told me. 'She do got her pride.'

'It is only for deserving horses.'

'Of good character?'

'The best,' I assured him and he screwed up his lips.

'Do you being sarsastic again?'

'Certainly not,' I said, and he spat with impressive accuracy at a telegraph pole, though I had no idea how it had offended him.

'We do talk it over and she might may consider it,' he conceded and it was probably my imagination but it seemed to me that Old Queeny walked, if not with a spring in her stride, at least a little less listlessly.

Her owner must have taken a tentative step towards cheerfulness as well, for he cleared his throat – a long and loud process – before treating us to a revolutionary revision of the musical scale.

'My true love is sent to Bot'ny Bay,' he squawked, 'and she int been there more than a day when she fall in the water and drown-ded.'

'That's a cheery song,' Gerrund commented.

'It is,' Friendless agreed. 'Alway give me a laugh, 'specially when the shark do come.' He raised his voice again. 'To that fish human legs is bacon and human arms is eggs and human arms is EEGGGGGS.'

Gainsborough Gardens was busy as we entered the square. A small crowd had gathered around a man in the middle who was playing a penny whistle while jigging about on stilts.

'He int really that tall,' Friendless explained for our edification.

'I think milady knows that,' Gerrund told him.

'How?' our driver enquired. 'Do she seen him 'fore?'

'Feminine intuition,' I said.

'Fem'nin int wha'?'

'Int sitting in this cab all day,' Gerrund replied and Friendless unlocked the flaps.

'Clear off,' Friendless yelled, and for a moment I thought he meant me, but he was cracking his whip harmlessly in the direction of Chaos, who was ambling towards us. 'If they get into conversatin' I'll be stuck here for hours,' he explained, though we had already arranged that he would wait. 'Four hours and eight minutes prob'ly.'

'I hope not,' I said.

'So do I.' Gerrund climbed out. 'Got a certain for the three thirty at Newmarket to lay a bet on.'

'Which horse?' I asked, taking his hand to clamber out.

'Pandora.'

I had never heard of the nag but I said, 'Not a hope,' just to annoy him and, from his grimace, I succeeded.

66: FOWLER'S SOLUTION

I WAITED UNTIL Gerrund was safely out of sight before ringing the bell. Matilda answered, bracing herself, foot against the door the moment that she saw me.

'Dr Poynder has given instructions you are not to be admitted,' she informed me.

'Tell your master,' I emphasised the last word to remind her of her place, 'that I have important information regarding his wife.'

'Then you had better come in, Lady Violet,' Poynder said from somewhere close behind.

'But you said,' Matilda began.

'Do not argue with me, girl,' he snapped.

Where had I heard that *girl* before?

Matilda opened her mouth to object but shut it and stood back.

As was to be expected Poynder was in full mourning, only the white of his shirt visible behind the black frockcoat, waistcoat and neat bow tie. A black-banded silk hat stood on the side table beside a tray of calling cards.

'May I offer my condolences,' I began.

'Come through,' he told me with barely a nod but – concern-ingly – instead of taking me to the front right-hand sitting room where I had been on the previous two occasions, he led me towards the back of the house on the other side. Gerrund would never hear me from there.

I told you to bring a gun, Ruby reminded me. *Lovely wallpaper.*

You never say that about mine.

You may draw your own conclusions.

We entered a shady study, oak-panelled with a large oak desk and a glass-fronted oak bookcase filled with hefty medical tomes, a great many journals stacked on the top shelf. The maroon velvet

331

curtains had not been drawn. Poynder flicked a light on without appearing to burn his hand and I wondered if I should tell him how dangerous that was. If they could not escape through the switch, the electrical flames would build up in the walls, Mr Poplar had explained when I had called him back a third time.

'It is cooler in here,' Poynder observed and it was, despite the French windows overlooking a well-trimmed lawn, for the sun beat on the other side of Haglin House.

A door was open on the left side of the room and it led into a large cupboard also crammed with books and papers.

I sat in one of the two dark tan leather armchairs facing each other at forty-five degrees to the unlit fireplace.

'You claim to have information,' he began, sitting upright in the other chair and I took a breath.

'I had your wife's hair analysed,' I announced.

I had not expected him to break down and confess when confronted with that information, but he might have done me the courtesy of blinking.

'You had a sample of her hair?' he challenged, and I hesitated.

It would not go down well if I described how I had obtained it, and a pretence that I had clipped it from Dolores's head while she was ill would not have been received with much more equanimity.

'She gave a locket to a friend as a keepsake,' I stated, not entirely untruthfully, and he exhaled heavily.

'Martha Ryan,' he declared. 'That woman is a pestilence. I had to threaten her with the police before she would keep away.'

'She was concerned for her friend,' I protested. 'Perhaps if you had explained...'

'Had my wife no right to privacy?' he demanded. 'She did not want the world to know of her illness, and telling Mrs Ryan would be tantamount to announcing it in *The Times*.'

'The tests showed traces of arsenic,' I told him, and he blinked that time, but we all have to occasionally.

'I would have been surprised had they not,' he countered. 'Amongst other tonics, Dolores consumed large amounts of Fowler's solution, which has an arsenic base.'

I never knew that, Ruby admitted and neither did I.

Hefty opened his mouth but thought better of it. If he claimed to have known, he would have to explain why he had not informed me.

'The tests showed a much larger concentration than would be expected from any medication,' I lied.

'It can build up to a surprising degree.' Poynder brushed a speck of something invisible from his lapel.

That voice, I realised. *Come here, girl.*

'I saw you,' I said, though in truth I had only glimpsed a muffled figure. 'In Lower Montford.'

'I sometimes do charity work there.' He shrugged.

'Outside the Green Munky public house,' I continued. 'Soliciting the attentions of a young girl.'

'You are mistaken.'

'I have other witnesses.'

'They are mistaken too.'

'You have something of a reputation, Dr Poynder,' I told him. 'Servants who will testify to your lascivious behaviour.'

'Which servants?'

'Edwina spoke to a number of people.'

'What a pity she cannot do so now.'

'How did you know she was dead?'

'Word gets around,' he replied without pause.

That is a circular explanation of nothing, Ruby pointed out. *He might as well say that he knew because he knew.*

If he was going to lie, I decided, I would not be outdone.

'Edwina made a sworn statement,' I said, and he shifted slightly in his chair, the brown leather creaking with his movement, 'testifying that you made improper advances to her.'

'Servants often make these absurd claims to explain their lack of employment,' he told me smoothly. 'Edwina was a nice girl but dim and clumsy. She left a trail of breakages far too numerous to be docked from her wages and so my wife had to dismiss her.'

'Would you say that she was honest?' I probed, and he leaned back in his chair.

'Clearly not in the case of her allegations.' He shrugged with one shoulder. 'Truth and the lower orders are not always comfortable bedfellows.'

'And yet a number of people believed her story,' I said and he touched his fingertips together, his elbows on the arms of his chair.

'People will always give credence to gossip and scandal.'

'I am talking about a different story.'

That was not at all clear, Ruby said.

'About what?' Dr Poynder asked, a smidgen too casually, I thought.

If it involves Count Vorolski Zugravescu it is my story, Ruby objected, pacing the room.

Wormwood came into the room and his employer looked up. He had not touched the bell rope.

'Might I have a word, sir?'

'What?' Poynder snapped irritably.

'In private if you please, sir.'

'Oh very well.'

His employer got up and marched into the corridor, his valet closing the door so that all I could hear was a low buzz before Poynder reappeared.

'Thank you, Wormwood,' he said, a great deal more civil than he had been a few moments ago.

Poynder shut the door but it swung ajar again.

'Shoddy catch,' he muttered, fiddling with the door handle before returning to his desk.

'I am a busy man, Lady Violet,' he declared, hands flat on his blotter. 'Perhaps you would like to tell me what Edwina's *different story* concerned.'

'Mungo Peers,' I replied, my eyes fixed upon Dr Poynder.

67: THE STRANGLER AND THE SÉANCE

RUBY BANGED HER knee on the corner of a Canterbury magazine rack though, strangely, it did not move.

Blimmitation! That hurt.

Poynder interlocked his strong fingers.

The hands of a strangler, Ruby commented unhelpfully as she rubbed her knee.

'And what did Edwina have to say about that unfortunate child?' he enquired lazily.

He killed the boy, Ruby realised annoyingly because I wanted to reveal that theory to her.

'I think you can guess.' That was exactly what I was going to do, and I was playing for time to wind up the clockwork of my imagination.

'I fear I cannot,' he assured me smoothly.

Here goes, I thought and pulled a lever to set the cogs in motion.

'Edwina was not unreceptive to your advances,' I began and saw an eyebrow twitch.

Clearly that was not the impression that she had given him.

'Then the girl was a fantasist,' he told me, 'for there were no advances to which she could respond.'

Deciding against a were/were not argument, I ploughed on. 'Though she feigned reluctance.'

Poynder took an interest in his fingerplates and so I did. They were not as well manicured as they had been when I first met him, but were chewed so far back as to expose the flesh underneath. That, I conjectured, might make intricate tasks problematic. It would be difficult, for example, to pick up a needle.

Not that you have ever tried, Ruby mocked, for she knew that I was hopeless at that kind of thing. The tester I had begun as a kneeler cover when I was eight years old still lay in a drawer at

Thetbury Hall with its inspirational message *The Lod is my Shep* embroidered upon it.

'And what does any of this have to do with the Peers boy?'

'He saw you together,' I announced, and he blinked lazily.

'Where?'

I could only have one guess at that and so I kept my answer vague.

'In the basement.'

Poynder scrutinised his palms and I wondered if he had a long lifeline. I knew that I did not.

'And he told you that in a séance, I suppose,' he mocked.

'He told his mother and,' I added hastily in case he saw fit to silence Mrs Peers, 'his uncle and aunt and two cousins.'

And Uncle Tom Cobbly and all, Ruby ridiculed my claim.

'Quite an audience then,' Poynder snorted.

'Mungo was worried that you might both think he would cause a scandal,' I continued, 'and so he returned to reassure Edwina that he would be discreet, for he was a good-natured child.'

The doctor watched me coolly, fingertips touching again.

'His mother believed that he was killed before he got here, but he found you both together again,' I conjectured and was treated to a twisted smile.

'Did he tell you this through a medium or did he rap on a table?' he asked, quite reasonably, for we both knew that my claim was mere conjecture.

'Either you thought that he could not be trusted or misinterpreted his words to mean that he had come to blackmail you,' I postulated, 'and so you took a knife and stabbed him.'

'This is absurd.' Poynder managed a chuckle but not to make it convincing.

I ploughed on. 'Mungo, however, managed to run away. You followed, knife in hand, into the square and almost ran into Jacob Kaufman, the salt-block seller.' I paused.

Go on, Hefty urged.

'This presented you with something of a dilemma to put it mildly,' I went on. 'You could not kill him on the street while there were people in the gardens, but how could you explain being seen covered in blood, knife in hand, running after a dying boy?'

'How indeed?' he enquired. 'I would appear to have been caught literally red-handed.'

'I loathe you, Dr Poynder,' I told him and he looked affronted.

My accusations of philandering and murder might be water off a doctor's back, but to tell him that we were not going to be friends really hurt his feelings.

'But,' I continued, 'I have to admire your cool-headedness. Somebody else, you decided, must have committed the crime, but there was nobody else around and so you invented the tale of a maniac who had killed your dog...'

'Poor Sheba,' he sighed with patent regret at his creature's fate.

'To explain why you and your kitchen were covered in blood,' I postulated, my confidence building up steam. 'This elusive lunatic – you would have us believe – having stabbed Mungo on the street, went in search of more victims only to find himself confronted by your pet.'

'What an extraordinary tale,' Poynder scoffed.

'Almost as extraordinary as your claim that he threw away the knife he could have used to fend you off or even kill you when you went to investigate, thereby giving you the opportunity to pick it up and possibly use against him.'

Are you quite sure that sentence was long enough? Ruby asked as I replenished the air in my lungs.

'He probably dropped the knife in panic,' Poynder countered, an idea so preposterous that I did not trouble to refute it.

'I thought at first that you acted kindly in speaking up for Kaufman,' I said, 'but then I realised that, if you had had to go in the witness box, your account might have met with more scrutiny than it would bear.'

Time for another refill, my alveoli clamoured.

'Whereas your account bears no scrutiny whatsoever,' he pointed out with considerable justification, but I had set my course and must sail it because I had gone too far to merely apologise and make a polite exit.

'There is more,' I assured him.

Is there? Ruby asked in surprise, for I could always rely on her to set my mind at unease.

68: CAESAR'S WIFE AND THE PAPERKNIFE

I PEERED AROUND my brain for an idea to feed it, but the larder was not particularly well-stocked that morning.

Waffle, Ruby advised, *like you do in your books.*

This was good, if pejorative advice, I decided.

'I was puzzled as to why Edwina was murdered in such a public place,' I floundered, fumbling along the back of the bottom shelf of my cerebrum until the tips of my neurones felt something.

'Perhaps it was an unfortunate accident,' Poynder suggested, 'and the gun went off by mistake.'

'What gun?' Ruby and I asked simultaneously and, for the first time, he was discomforted.

'The one that shot her,' he replied uneasily.

'And how, exactly, did you know that?' I pounced, for *The Chronic* had said that Edwina fell onto a spike, but the good doctor regained his composure rapidly.

'I have contacts in the police force.'

Please say Inspector Stanbury, I urged, but he was not foolish enough to dig such an obvious trap for himself.

'Before she died, Edwina warned…' I struggled on.

'So not in another séance?' he mocked.

'Edwina warned Martha that you would kill her if she did not stop interfering,' I ploughed on.

Hold both your horses, Ruby objected. *I thought she was talking about Anton Gervey.*

So did I, I confessed, *but she meant her own master.*

'Strange,' Poynder commented, 'how all your fantasies are backed up by alleged hearsay and witnesses who are dead.'

'It is only strange because you killed them.'

'Are you rehearsing one of your ridiculous novels?'

Ridiculous? Ruby fumed. *You do not have to tolerate that. Stab him.*

With what?

His paperknife.

I glanced at the desk and saw his letter opener – six inches of steel projecting from a deer's foot. I had never understood why people described blades as *wicked looking*, but there was a distinctly evil glint in that cold metal point.

'I am rehearsing the truth,' I replied, not completely confident that that was what I meant to say. I had Dolores's version of events, but her widower could dismiss them as the creation of a diseased mind.

Pretend that you have worked it out yourself, Ruby advised. *It is about time you had some thoughts of your own.*

'For a long time I doubted that you, a well-known local figure, would take the risk of committing the crime yourself,' I waded on.

'Your doubts are well-founded,' Poynder assured me.

'And I believed that you employed the services of a professional assassin.'

'Your fantasies might sell books…'

Not very many, Ruby inserted.

'But they would not convince the most gullible of juries.'

'But then I realised that the very unlikeliness of you committing a murder in public in broad daylight was your protection.'

Poynder laughed.

'I have employed a great many servants who had only the most rudimentary education.' He twiddled with his watch chain. 'But even they never presented me with such convoluted illogicality.'

I half-suspected that this was true but, having alighted on the idea, I was not going to let it escape easily.

'Not in the least.' I struggled to hold it in my mental fingers.

Your mental what? Ruby glanced up from the fashion plates in her *English Ladies' Magazine*.

'The very idea is so incredible that no policeman would entertain it,' I concluded.

'The idea is incredible because it is pure fantasy.' Poynder batted my suggestion away with a flick of his left hand.

'You boasted to me that you have the protection of Anton Gervey,' I reminded him, 'and led me to believe that he might owe you more than that.'

'What of it?' He let go of his chain as if it were burning his fingers.

'But you are not the only one to be acquainted with him,' I said, 'and he did not arrange that killing.' I waited for Poynder to enquire how I had come to that conclusion, but he merely stifled a yawn. 'I know that,' I answered his unasked question, 'because he enlisted my help to identify the killer and avoid a conflict with the Braise Shotten gang, and now I have identified him.'

The umbrella! Ruby shouted so loudly that I put a hand to my ear.

'You left one crucial piece of evidence at the scene,' I said and Poynder shifted his feet. 'The umbrella,' Ruby and I dueted. 'You shot Edwina with it.'

'Come now, Lady Violet...' Poynder tried to look amused.

'Your wife thought that it had been hit by the assassin's bullet,' I continued, 'but I have seen that umbrella, Doctor, and it had not so much been shattered by a stray bullet as exploded and you dropped it, partly in surprise, but also because it was hot.'

For a moment I saw something resembling a flicker in those cool grey eyes but, instead of breaking down and confessing all as Hefty's suspects could be relied upon to do, Poynder murmured, 'And how do you work that out?'

'The first time we met your left palm was burnt,' I told Poynder.

You told us it was iodine, Ruby reminded Hefty.

Lady Violet put the idea in my head, Scotland Yard's premier detective defended himself perfidiously.

'I spilled some carbolic acid while I was sterilising my instruments.'

'You did not tell your wife about the umbrella for fear that it could be traced from where you purchased it to you.'

Poynder pulled out his hunter. 'I am a busy man, Lady Violet.' He flipped the lid up. 'I admitted you out of gratitude for allowing my wife to end her days peacefully and me to continue in my practice. As you are fully aware, Dolores confessed to the crimes of which you are accusing me so...'

So it is all right for him to rely on her evidence? Ruby threw up her hands, almost catching him on the chin.

'That is as may be,' I broke in. 'But there are too many inconsistencies in her accounts to hold water.'

If an account holds water, Hefty pontificated, scratching his ear, an annoying habit of which I thought I had cured him. *It is not an account. It is a bucket.*

Has Scotland Yard's premier detective really made an appearance just to tell me that? I checked but he had wandered off.

Poynder closed the lid, put his watch away and leaned back, arms folded, with an expression one usually reserves for tolerating irritating children.

'For example,' I said. 'Dolores talked of raining blows down on that waitress in the Monastery Gardens and the unfortunate woman did have wounds on her crown, but she was taller than your wife and so, until she fell to her knees, the blows would have been on the back of her head, where there were none.'

Excellent observation, Hefty complimented me, but I had not forgotten his attempt to blame me for his mistake.

Excellent bluffing, Ruby complimented me, for she knew that I had not examined the waitress's wounds and also that Poynder was probably no taller than the waitress but no man will admit to being short, unless he makes a living from it. *Especially as it doesn't make any sense.*

Poynder shrugged.

'Unfortunately my wife cannot give you an explanation of that.'

'Danny Dixon the Diamond King,' I announced and he shifted in his seat.

'As you are all too aware, my wife confessed to that crime and disposing of the body.' He brushed his shoulder down. 'She thought the thunderstorms that were forecast at the time would wash it away but we have had an arid summer.'

Got you! Ruby crowed, but I had already reached the same conclusion.

'How could you know when the body was put in the drain?' I pounced on his claim prepared to destroy it. 'The police do not.'

Far from being disconcerted by Ruby's and my brilliance, Poynder piffed.

'Dolores told me,' he said simply as his claim slithered away unharmed.

'She also said that she throttled Danny with a length of rope from the yard,' I recalled, 'whereas he was found with an electrical cord around his neck.'

Poynder put his hands together like a man in prayer, though his expression was far from devoted.

'As you are doubtless aware, she was confused.' He separated his palms as if releasing a butterfly, but they were all in my stomach. I was unused to confronting killers in their lairs – or anywhere else, on reflection.

'She was lucid enough to give me detailed accounts of the crimes,' I retorted.

'Detailed but, as you have pointed out yourself, contradictory,' Poynder reasoned smoothly.

'The person I saw running away in the gardens had the gait of a man,' I said. 'Dolores would have had to be a very clear-headed and accomplished actress indeed to give such a realistic performance while absconding from the scene of the crime.'

'As I have told you…' Poynder tapped his waistcoat pocket over the bulge of his hunter.

'I was misled into believing your wife's claims,' I stumbled onwards, 'because she knew so much about the murders.'

Poynder treated me to a raised eyebrow.

Not my idea of a treat, Ruby commented, flicking over a page of her magazine.

'But all of her information was second hand,' I continued.

Pause for dramatic effect, Ruby urged.

Suck thoughtfully on your long-stemmed cherry-wood pipe, Hefty advised, but I did not want to give my suspect the time to formulate a response.

'Courtesy,' I paused for dramatic effect after all but decided against nipping out to the tobacconist's, 'of you.'

I think I swung my arm up to point at the accused man, but I was too busy watching his reactions to worry about my own actions.

The eyebrows rose a fraction more. They were so tidy that I wondered if he trimmed them himself, for nobody would trust Dolores with a pair of scissors near their eyes.

Men never do their own, Ruby asserted. *Matilda does it for him.*

Speaking of Matilda, Hefty began, and I hoped that he was not going to launch into an account of Matilda Mattingly, who poisoned all her classmates to be sure of getting a front seat because she did not wish to wear eyeglasses. *If I might bring up a rather delicate matter.* Hefty blushed. *Where do you suppose she has a bedroom?*

That was a good point actually. As he had already calculated, Susie the kitchen maid probably slept in the basement. Wormwood would have his butler's room down there and Dolores had occupied the only bedroom in the attic.

Poynder lowered his eyebrows one at a time.

'Every theory you have proposed is half-baked nonsense,' he declared, but the hard edge in his voice convinced me that they were not, and it was only then that it occurred to me that he must have thought I knew something when he admitted me to Haglin House. 'You have done nothing but sling mud but, as we all know, it sticks and like Caesar's wife, a doctor must be above suspicion.'

'Why did you let me into your home?' I asked, before remembering that he had already told me that.

'Because you intrigue me.' Poynder leered, rejecting his own explanation. 'A woman who looks like a beautiful child.'

He licked his lips and I made no attempt to hide my shudder of revulsion. That was a dangerous admission, and I had a horrible suspicion that I knew which of us was more imperilled by it.

I marched to the door, but I did not need Hefty to explain – as he did – that when Poynder had been pretending to be dealing with a faulty catch, he had been locking it.

'Is that why you killed Dolores? She had found out about your predilections?'

'My wife had not the slightest idea. She regarded me as the epitome of propriety,' he said. 'But she was getting old...'

'She was thirty-six.'

'A man needs young flesh,' he said, 'and I have found such a girl who, conveniently, comes with a substantial dowry...'

'Adelaide Cotton,' I realised. 'The heiress to the traction engine company.'

'You have done your research.'

'I have a loud scream,' I warned and Ruby Gibson, Extraordinary Investigator, groaned. She would never have made such a craven threat.

'Which will not be heard below stairs from this end of the house,' he assured me.

I still had my charm bracelet and, by pretending to adjust my hat, got the whistle to my lips and blew as hard as I could. It sounded even louder and shriller than usual in the confines of the room and Poynder winced, but the moment I stopped he composed himself and smiled sardonically.

'If you imagine that will summon your man to the rescue,' he told me airily. 'I am happy to disabuse you.'

'Gerrund has excellent hearing,' I said almost as airily.

'That is as may be,' Poynder shrugged, 'but Wormwood has him locked in the boiler room.'

Got anything clever to say about that? I challenged Ruby.

The French windows, she suggested.

They would be locked as well, I assumed, but with few options left to me, it was worth a try. I had only taken two steps though, when Poynder was upon me. He was not a big man but, at that moment, he seemed it. One hand wrapped around my throat comfortably – for him but not for me.

I told you he had strangler's hands.

'Let go of me,' I protested.

That will do the trick, Ruby jeered. *Throw him to the floor.*

How?

Apply your jujitsu training.

I have not had any, I objected.

Use your opponent's weight against him, she told me, which might have been helpful advice had she explained what it meant.

Poynder's grip tightened and I remembered one piece of advice Ruby's Japanese trainer had given her. Everyone being throttled fights their attacker's hands, which are his least vulnerable part. I raised my right forefinger as one might to attract a waiter's attention, levelled it and prodded him in the eye. I had imagined it squelching into the jelly but eyeballs, like women, are tougher than they are given credit for and it felt no different to me to poking him on the cheek. It must have felt very different to Poynder though, for he yelped, let go, clutched his face and glared at me monocularly.

'Damn you, you damned little bitch!' he cursed and, leaving his eye to the ministrations of his left hand, strode towards the desk.

Realising what he was after, I developed an instant aversion to the idea of having it inserted into my heart and I leapt alongside of him, sprawling over the desktop, but his hand closed over the paperknife, even as I sent his brass letter rack flying off onto the floor. I grabbed the matching brass inkwell with my left hand, turned it, spilling black ink all down my once-cerise sleeve as I crashed it into his temple.

Poynder grunted, more in anger than pain I suspected, and lashed out with his left hand, catching me with the back of it on my mouth, my parted lips hardly cushioning the blow to my upper incisors. I twisted sideways to face him and raised the inkwell again, splashing ink down the front of my already ruined dress, but he was ready for me that time and pulled back so that I smashed it onto the desktop, barking my knuckles in the process.

'Ow!' I yelped. *Frebbit that hurt!*

It will hurt a great deal more later, Hefty assured me. He had hardly felt his grenade injuries at first but they plagued him still, especially in damp weather.

Arrest him, I demanded, but Hefty shook his mighty cranium.

I fear I have no jurisdiction in your world, Lady Violet, he told me regretfully, a fine time for him to discover that.

Poynder got to his feet. He was clutching his eye again but, more alarmingly, he was also clutching the knife. I snatched up the blotting pad to cushion the blow, but he wrenched it from my grasp, tossed it aside, took his hand from his eye to claw at my throat again, raised the knife, daggerlike over me and laughed. Count Zugravescu would have been proud of that cackle and Poynder obviously liked it too for he did it again but, instead of stabbing me, pressed the point of his knife to that hollow at the base of my neck – the supraclavicular notch, I recalled proudly.

'Well fought, little girl.' He grinned though his appearance left little for him to be cheerful about.

His left eye was bloodshot, his usually immaculate hair hung over half the right eye like old seaweed on a rock. His face was splattered with ink and he would never be able to wear that shirt again.

345

'Let's see what's inside that finery,' he suggested, though I already knew the answer to that. It was me and it was private and I preferred it to stay that way for the time being.

Poynder had tugged open my top button when he stopped and cocked his head to one side to listen. There were footsteps in the corridor growing louder. He put a finger to his lips.

'All right, miss, you can go now,' a man's voice said.

'But you were supposed to wait in the hall and I'm supposed to announce you,' another voice, Matilda's I decided, argued.

'That will be all thank you, miss,' the man said firmly. 'Now you go about your duties.'

Poynder looked as puzzled as I was.

'Very well, sir.'

The maid's footsteps had faded before the door handle turned. It rattled and there was a knocking.

'Not now,' Dr Poynder snapped at the impertinence of his caller, but the knocking continued.

'I am a police officer,' the man announced. 'Open the door, Dr Poynder.'

'What?' Poynder cried in disbelief. 'What do you want?'

'Let me in and I will explain, sir.'

'You will have to come back. It is not convenient,' Poynder blustered, but the knocking recommenced.

'One word and it will be your last,' Poynder hissed at me, looking about his study as if he hardly knew it. 'One moment,' he called, grabbed a fistful of my hair, sending my almost new hat flying into the wall to flop dented onto the floorboards, and dragged me across the room to the cupboard, tossing the hat after me. 'Get in.'

'Your luck has run out, Dr Poynder,' I told him. 'Let me go and it will be one less crime for which you will have to answer.'

Poynder snorted contemptuously and pushed me inside.

'I have nothing to lose,' he told me grimly, 'but you have everything and I will be sure to take you down to hell with me if I am arrested.'

The knocking became a pounding as he shut me in and slid the bolt home. It was dark in there, the only light coming through a knothole in a lower door panel and I crouched to peek through it.

'Open up in the name of the law.'

Poynder strode to the French windows, the knife no longer in his hand, but I could not see what he had done with it. Surely he was not going to try to abscond? He threw both the windows open and marched back to admit the policeman.

'Thank heavens you are here, officer,' he cried. 'They went that way.'

A constable stepped forward.

'And who might *they* be, sir?'

I could not make out what I hoped would be my saviour's face.

'The burglars,' Poynder said hoarsely. 'I disturbed them and they attacked me. They tried to make me send you away and, when that failed, they made off across the lawn. They can't have got far.'

The policeman stayed where he was.

'What's behind that door, sir?' he enquired, and for a moment I thought I recognised that voice.

It cannot be.

'What?' Poynder snapped. 'A cupboard. Books and stationery. What does that matter? There are two dangerous felons on the loose in my garden. You cannot let them escape.' He pointed the way. 'Quickly, man.'

'Open that door please, sir,' the officer said, turning towards it.

I still could not see his face clearly, but I had glimpsed enough to recognise him.

'Oh, you fool,' I whispered all too conscious of the danger that he was in.

Anthony Appleton looked every inch the part in his stage uniform and false moustaches. He stood erect with an air of authority that I had not suspected he had in him.

'One moment. I feel unwell,' Poynder breathed, stepping unsteadily sideways towards the fireplace and bending almost double as if in pain.

Anthony hurried to release me.

'Are you all right?' he asked anxiously, for I could not have looked anything of the sort, but it was then that I saw Dr Poynder taking a fire iron from its stand.

'Look out!' I yelled. 'Behind you!'

Anthony spun round, his hand going to his truncheon, just as Poynder brought the poker sweeping down and struck him on the side of his face. I burst back into the room in time to see my friend crumple at the knees.

'Oh, my dear!' I cried as he toppled forward, his helmet flying off, but Anthony was not finished yet.

Jabbing his truncheon up, he caught Poynder under the chin causing him to stagger backwards. Anthony sprang towards him, almost knocking him off balance, but Poynder recovered surprisingly quickly and, with a great grunt, flung him aside and almost onto the floor. Anthony was made of sturdier stuff, however, than I had given him credit for. He regained his footing and closed in on his opponent again. I grabbed the arm that wielded the poker, but Poynder brought his elbow back, catching me on the jaw and sending me reeling to collide with his desk. I wrenched open a drawer in the hope of finding something I could use as a weapon, but there was only a sheaf of papers, and I turned back to see Poynder lash out with the fire iron, catching Anthony with a vicious thwack on the left temple. Anthony toppled twisting around, his brow striking the edge of the mantlepiece with a horrible thump as he crumpled to the floor.

I hurled myself at Poynder, but he took me by the throat in one hand and, tossing his weapon away, slapped me hard in the face with the other. I choked and tried to kick out, but he had me at arm's length, grabbed a fistful of my hair again and produced his knife from a rolled copy of the *Englishman's Journal*, which he had been using as a sheath, tucked into the back of his trousers.

'Hold still damn you,' he swore and leaned over the recumbent form of my friend.

'Out cold,' he announced as he straightened up. 'Some policeman.' He laughed thinly and I saw that one of Anthony's moustaches was hanging loosely adrift.

'Dear God,' I said, though he did not feel very dear to me at that moment for allowing those things to happen.

Poynder drew back his foot and gave Anthony a sharp kick in the face. I heard a horrible crunch, but my friend did not even stir.

'You vile...' I began, lost for a strong enough epithet.

'Sit in that armchair,' he commanded, shoving me to stumble to the other side of the room.

Blood was pouring from Anthony's nose.

'If you try to escape I will slit his windpipe,' Poynder vowed and I knew that he meant it.

He put the knife piratically between his teeth and grasped Anthony's wrists to drag him with great difficulty into the cupboard, bolting the door and leaning heavily back on it, breathless from his exertions, the knife in his hand again.

'I'll deal with him later,' he panted, hurrying to secure the doors into the garden and corridor.

Shakily Poynder poured himself a very large brandy and gulped it down, his breathing almost back to normal. I surveyed the room. There were ornaments which I could use as weapons. That onyx pot on a pedestal would make a good club. I might be no match for a man with a knife, but I would not give up without a fight.

Where were my characters when I needed them? It was not difficult to calculate the answer. This was the real world and there was no escaping into that of my imagination.

Poynder came over and grabbed my hair again to haul me to my feet and force me back to the desk. 'Now then,' he said. 'Where were we before we were so rudely interrupted? Oh yes.' He put the knife to my neck again. 'I was about to enjoy you.'

I straightened my finger, but he would not fall for that move twice and I felt the tip of the blade press harder.

'Try it,' he snarled, 'and I will skewer you to my desk. Do not imagine that I am bluffing.'

'I know you will,' I assured him. 'Just as callously as you cut the throat of...' I clicked my mental fingers. This was where I needed Hefty with his notebook, until I reminded myself that I did not need him at all. 'Beryl Walker,' I remembered.

Poynder greeted the name so blankly that I wondered if my shot had gone wide of its mark.

'The little girl whose body was found in a derelict house in the Lowers,' I explained and saw the realisation dawn on his damaged face.

'I never knew her name,' he said.

'So you admit it?' I pressed and he tipped his head sideways.

'Why not?' He shrugged and he did not need to add that I would not be getting out of there alive, but nobody had told him that so he added, 'You will not be getting out of here alive.'

69: THE PITY AND THE PANE

I CONSIDERED DR Poynder's words before considering my options before realising that there were hardly any for me to consider.

Keep him in conversation, I advised myself. *No man will kill a woman while he has the opportunity to talk about himself.*

'Why did you kill Beryl Walker?' I asked.

'Because she was stupid,' he explained, which seemed a little harsh to me for, by the same yardstick, half the population of Suffolk and three quarters of the House of Lords deserved to be slaughtered.

'I only wanted her to give me some relief,' Poynder was explaining. 'Such acts are nothing to those guttersnipes, but she made a fuss and pulled my muffler down and recognised me.' He huffed in exasperation. 'If she had spoken out I would be ruined. What else could I do?'

'And so you put your professional standing before her life,' I pointed out in disgust and winced as the point dug in a little further.

'What was the life of one street slug to the lives that I have saved and shall save?' he demanded. 'I delivered twins by a caesarean on a dead woman last week. Those two lives more than expiate the taking of one.'

I had a feeling that there was more to morality than arithmetic, but I had a stronger feeling that this was not the time to debate utilitarianism.

'Dolores knew a great many details of the killings,' I recollected. 'Surely you were taking a risk in telling her?'

Poynder wiped a tear from his damaged eye.

'It was partly vanity,' he admitted. 'Since my wife met that Ryan woman, her respect for me declined noticeably. She even questioned some of my opinions.' He surveyed my face but, unable to detect my disapproval of such headstrong behaviour, continued, 'I wanted her to remember how clever and resourceful I am but, when she expressed her horror at my actions, I increased the doses of her medication.'

'Arsenic,' I said.

'Amongst other things. Some of the other drugs cause hallucinations and delusions. I told Dolores all about the slayings in detail, but in a way that suggested I was merely reminding her of what she had confessed to me. She was so muddled by then that she firmly believed she had committed the deeds. My wife was my insurance policy. Should the police trace any evidence to this house, I had a culprit ready to deliver into their hands.'

'Speaking of which, what happened to Dolores's hand?' It was obvious that the cuts I had seen when she lay in her coffin were not caused by an exploding umbrella.

'Oh that.' He flapped his own ungashed hand. 'She broke a window in a foolish and ungrateful bid to escape.'

'Ungrateful?' I queried and he nodded.

'She had everything that she needed here.'

'Except love,' I pointed out, though – amongst other things – I could have listed freedom, a bathtub and clean bedding.

'Women talk a great deal about love, but they do not understand how it is inexorably bound to lust,' Poynder told me. 'If it is not then it is merely affection and one can get that from a dog.'

I knew that he was trying to provoke me but I battled on, determined not to take the bait.

'And the burn on her face?'

'She had many more on different parts of her body,' Poynder told me. 'Dolores set fire to her mattress in an absurd attempt to burn her door down. I had to ban all candles and lamps after that.'

It was clear that he was getting restless, for he had plans other than making conversation, I suspected.

'What about Wally Hopkins, the boy you hanged?' I tried and the blade dug in. 'Ouch.'

I was almost certain that my skin was pierced.

Not fisherman's knots, I realised. *The bowline is used for tourniquets and the reef was probably, in fact, a surgeon's knot.*

'Sorry,' Poynder apologised, as if he had tangoed on my toe at a tea dance, and he eased the pressure a fraction. 'He saw me with his sister, followed me home and attempted to blackmail me. Need I say more?'

'*Forgive me, Lady Violet. Allow me to summon you a cab,*' *might be a good start*, went through my head.

'I see,' I floundered. 'I suppose you felt that you had to silence him.'

'Well of course I did,' Poynder concurred, my remark being obviously obvious, but he relaxed a little at hearing what he took to be my approval of his actions, for even ruthless multiple murderers do not care to have their actions depreciated.

'I was just wondering…' I struggled on, but there was such a jumble in my head. This was worse than when I had tried to write *Who Killed Rock Cobbin?* in which there were thirty-nine victims and forty-two murderers, some of whom went on to kill each other.

'Go on,' Poynder coaxed me, in much the same way that he might encourage a patient to describe her symptoms.

You really should get that eye seen to, I almost advised before remembering what had made it so angry.

'About Danny the Diamond King,' I dredged from the swamp of confusedness.

And, to my astonishment, the doctor blushed.

'Oh yes,' he laughed sheepishly. 'That was all a bit of a misunderstanding,' Poynder admitted and sucked his lips. 'Dixon consulted me at the clinic and foolishly said that he had seen me in the Lowers and was going to tell *The Chronical*. I told him that his problem required specialist equipment and to come to my house that evening. It was simplicity itself to strap him to a chair. You would be surprised how much people trust their doctors. As luck would have it I had recently acquired a new set of dental forceps, and so I extracted an upper incisor. What exactly had he seen and who had he told? I wondered. He screamed, of course, and claimed that he had only meant that he wanted everybody to know what good works I performed. I took out another tooth but he stuck to his story. He still stuck to it when all his incisors and dog teeth were gone and it was obvious that he was telling the truth, but I had some hawksbills and eagles that I was keen to put to the test.'

'And so you took out all his teeth,' I contributed and he clicked his fingers.

'I could hardly let him go after that, and I was just looking through my scalpel drawer when the asinine oaf rocked the chair over and smashed a brand-new electrical table lamp,' Poynder recalled furiously. 'I was so angry that I ripped the flex out and strangled him with it. Well,' he held out his hands like Tom Harley, the Sudbury Football Club defender feigning innocence after tripping up the referee, 'can you blame me?'

'Some people might,' I suggested tentatively. Much as I was loath to antagonise a man who had the means to impale me so conveniently to hand, I could not bring myself to condone his actions. 'Another thing puzzles me,' I remembered.

'What is it this time?' Poynder sighed like the pestered parent of a small child.

'Dolores thought that the woman who was attacked in the gardens was mistaken for Edwina,' I said, 'but your maid was already dead.'

'But was she?' Poynder countered. 'The Edwina I knew was young and beautiful but, at close range, I saw that the woman in the square was haggard and grey. I knew that Edwina had several sisters.'

'Five,' I confirmed, but he wafted the number away.

'I did not even know if one of them might have been a twin.' He rubbed the back of his neck. 'So I began to worry that I may have assassinated the wrong woman.'

'There was never a right one,' I said and realised that Martha must have seen her friend's maid at Haglin House but had not recognised her in the square, so changed Edwina must have been by poverty, grime and her disfigurement.

Poynder hardly paused in his narrative.

'I went in search of her and, when I saw what looked like Edwina in the Monastery Gardens, I decided not to take the risk of letting her live. Besides which,' he chuckled, 'I was rather enjoying exterminating those creatures by then.'

'Those *creatures*,' I responded in horror, 'were all human beings.'

'Hardly.' No matter how often Miss Kidd had told me that there was no such verb, Poynder piffed.

'I do not understand,' I admitted, 'how the bullet entered Edwina's head from above.'

'A simple stratagem.' He tugged lightly at his mutton-chops. 'I tossed a shilling at her feet to ensure that she looked away and did not see me approach. At the last minute she bobbed to pick it up. I spoke her name; she glanced up and I shot her in the face.' His cheek ticked. 'The gun was supposed to be silenced but, as you must have heard, it was not. It was also designed to fire two bullets in quick succession but the second jammed in the barrel.'

'You should ask for your money back,' I advised and he glowered.

'Enough of this.' He glanced at the garden.

Did that mean he was going to let me go? I wondered fleetingly while Poynder fiddled with his trousers.

Was he checking the buttons?

Unchecking them, I diagnosed.

'Women are lucky,' Poynder informed me, though I did not feel especially fortunate at that particular moment. 'They do not have desires.'

I would not have minded a good strong cup of coffee, but I did not think that one was likely to be offered.

'Men have such powerful needs,' he continued, 'that they must satisfy or be consumed by them.' He licked his lips. 'Luckily you are here to satiate my urges.'

'I most certainly am not,' I assured him, but Poynder's fingers slid under my collar and he wrenched, ripping my dress down to my shoulder, buttons flying off at the back.

'Come to Daddy, little girl,' he rasped, his spittle spraying into my face.

'Stop now before it is too late,' I said firmly but Poynder's hand had slipped under my dress.

'A pity you have breasts,' he commented, though he must have guessed that already and I could have named a few men who would have disagreed with him.

Kick him, I urged myself, but my lower legs were pinned against the side of the desk and, even if they had not been, I could not argue with six inches of sharpened steel at my neck.

He adjusted his grip on the material and I felt it rip further. Poynder was panting already.

'Give Daddy a kiss,' he urged and lowered his head.

I twisted my face away and yelped as I felt the point dig in.

354

'A kiss, little girl,' he insisted, and it was then I decided he could do all the skewering he liked but I was damned if I would cooperate.

I might die, I knew, but in my situation, Ruby would go down fighting and so would I. I would chew half of Poynder's disgusting lip off or go for his eye again.

'I must warn you, Dr Poynder...' I began, but was interrupted by a crash and the sounds of breaking glass.

Poynder's head shot up.

'What the...'

'If you dint let milady goo this instance,' a familiar and very welcome voice yelled, 'I do make a hole in your face what wint never take repair.'

Poynder stood up and back.

'This woman tricked her way into my home and threatened me with my paperknife,' he protested as I struggled to stand upright.

'And I do break my way in and threat you with a revolver,' Agnust told him, poking the barrel through a broken pane. 'Open the door.'

Poynder hesitated but reached into a waistcoat pocket and brought out a key to do as he was told.

'Stand you back against the wall,' Agnust instructed and, mindful of her unwavering aim, he obeyed, slowly edging away.

'Do he outrage you, Lady Violet?' she enquired without taking her eyes off him. 'For, if he do, I make certain sure he never do vi'late another silly girl.'

Silly girl? Much as I tried to tell myself that this was no time to take umbrage, it was.

'Luckily you arrived in time,' I assured her, making hopeless attempts to straighten my attire.

'Luck int nothin' to do on it,' she asserted scornfully. 'I tell you Gerrund is all very well,' she reminded me, 'but you need a good woman in a n'emergency.'

'And you are a very good woman indeed,' I assured her, and Agnust was still blushing when she pulled the trigger.

70: SECRETS AND SUSPICIONS

THE SHOT WAS not as loud as I had expected. It was louder. Big Ben was clanging wildly in my skull as I spun around.

Poynder was still standing, but there was a hole in the wall to his right as big as any workman could have made with a pickaxe.

'Drop it,' I made out Agnust yelling and the knife fell, bouncing on the floor only just audibly as the bell rang thirty-four o'clock.

Poynder chewed his lower lip, though not as hard as I had planned to do with his upper, and I felt quite sick now that I thought about it. It would have been like eating a raw hairy steak.

'Nnnnyah,' I mouthed in disgust and they both looked at me in puzzlement.

Nnnnyah? Ruby echoed in equal disgust. *You are not in the nursery, Thorn.*

I did not need her to tell me that as I held my ripped dress up around my neck.

'Want you me to decease him?' Agnust enquired as casually as, though less reluctantly than, she might proffer a second cup of coffee, and I remembered the first time she had offered to kill a man on my behalf.

'And how,' Poynder demanded, struggling to unfluster himself, 'do you intend to explain to the police that you broke into my home and murdered me?'

'Let me worry about that,' I assured him, for Agnust's offer was a tempting one but, apart from the fact that I could not answer his enquiry, I was not a murderess.

It would be an execution, Ruby argued.

I cannot be a witness to it, Hefty excused himself as he left the room.

Why was he able to do that when I was not?

Leave the executions to… I began but could not remember the hangman's name. 'Warbrick,' I said aloud and touched Agnust's hand. 'Not just yet,' I told her, hurrying to pull back the bolt on the cupboard door.

Anthony still lay crumpled with his eyes closed, but I was relieved to see his chest rise, fall and rise again.

There was an urgent knocking from the corridor.

'Are you all right, sir?' I heard a woman call.

'Put the key on the sideboard,' I told Poynder, 'and step aside.' I took it and opened the door.

'Your master is uninjured,' I assured Matilda, 'and you are quite safe.'

She edged warily into the room.

'They are all mad,' her master claimed and, catching sight of a revolver-toting Agnust, Matilda drew back nervously.

'And how do you explain my ripped dress?' I demanded.

'You ripped it yourself in order to lay false claims against me,' he claimed outrageously and turned back to his maid. 'This woman persecuted your mistress and now she fixed her attentions upon me.'

There were the sounds of running and Wormwood burst in.

'What the…'

I put a hand to my throat and saw a smear of blood on my fingertips. I was bruised and still half-stunned by what had happened, and I did not feel like explaining anything.

'Release my man and return with him immediately,' I commanded, 'or my maid will shoot your master.'

'I kill a man 'fore now,' she assured him.

Did she? Ruby checked but, if true, it was news to me.

'Do as she says,' Poynder instructed.

'If you harm him or Tilly…' Wormwood began to threaten but, catching his employer's eye – though not as hard as I had – he turned and strode back into the corridor.

Agnust examined me.

'You do need a doctor,' she decided.

'Oh Agnust,' I sighed. 'I have had quite enough of doctors for one day.'

357

'Did you really kill a man?' I asked on the way home, and I could not tell if my maid was nodding or it was just the motion of our cab.

'Best you ask him tha',' Agnust advised, 'but you wint get a n'answer.'

–

Inspector Stanbury called. I would have offered to go to the police station, but I did not want to go there in my dishevelled condition and he wanted to see me as I was – for evidence, he claimed, but also I suspected for his own diversion.

'You look like a street slug,' he assured me though I knew that much already.

Agnust had pinned my dress up for decency, but I was still far from presentable.

'You say Dr Poynder did that to you?' he checked.

'She say it for it's true,' Agnust insisted. 'I catch him sprawlin' all over her like somethin' a po-lice-man...'

'No officer of mine would ever behave in such a manner,' Stanbury protested indignantly.

'Like somethin' a po-lice-man do arrest him for,' she completed her statement and the inspector did not so much climb down from his high horse as fall off it.

'You had better tell me everything,' he said then, as if anticipating a quip from Ruby, added, 'about the attack.'

And so I told him almost everything but nothing, to her chagrin, about Ruby's part in the events. People tend to look at me oddly when I mention her.

You should hear what people say about you, Thorn, she retaliated.

Nobody should hear that, I told her, having hidden all the nasty reviews of *Blood in the Gaslight* away from her ever-inquisitive eyes.

–

When Stanbury returned that evening his face was grim.

Did he put up a fight? Ruby wondered. *Did he flee over the rooftops and fall into the Thames in the path of dredger?*

He would have had to run a long way for that, I argued.

Pheidippides ran twenty-five miles from Marathon.

He was not in a frock coat with the Central Suffolk Police Force on his tail.

'He denies everything,' he told me, which was not astonishing. Being given Pineapple my pony when it was not even my birthday was a bigger surprise than that. Being bitten by Pineapple on the shoulder was an even bigger one. 'He says that you broke in through the French window – I saw the smashed pane – and attacked him with Gerrund and Agnust, all three of you armed to the teeth.'

I laughed – not the sort of chuckle I might emit while reading *Three Men in a Boat* nor the devil-may-care guffaw of Pedro Rodriguez the Mexican bandit. It was more of a cynical pull-the-other-one that employers employ when the parlour maid claims that the Meissen shepherdess jumped suicidally off a shelf when nobody was in the room.

'I rang the front doorbell and was admitted, unarmed, by Matilda the maid,' I protested and the inspector clicked his tongue.

'The trouble is, Lady Violet, Matilda claims the first she saw of you was after she heard the sound of breaking glass.'

'He battered Anthony Appleton unconscious,' I said furiously, and Stanbury puffed out his cheeks.

'Mr Appleton tricked his way into the house pretending to be a police officer – a serious criminal offence in itself – and tried to arrest Dr Poynder,' he said. 'A man is entitled to protect himself from fraudulent intruders.'

'He was trying to protect me,' I objected. 'And Wormwood locked Gerrund up at gunpoint.'

'He says he found your man skulking in the shrubbery armed with a revolver.'

That much, I had to grant him, was true.

'Unfortunately, the only evidence we have is a broken window and the conflicting statements of three intruders against three residents.'

There had been four of us, but Anthony was in no state to make any kind of statement.

'He murdered his wife,' I insisted.

'And, if you have evidence of that, I would be very interested to investigate further.'

'Her hair contained traces of arsenic.'

'Traces?' he queried, but did not wait for a reply. 'And can you even prove that it came from Mrs Poynder?'

'Yes,' I insisted. 'If the coffin is opened up, you will find her hair has been cut. In fact,' I speculated, 'we can have her whole body examined. My father has contacts in the government. He can apply to the home secretary to have her exhumed.'

Stanbury rubbed the back of his neck.

'And he may have succeeded for all I know,' he said, 'but according to Dr Poynder his wife had a terror of being buried alive and was cremated at Woking Crematorium.'

'That was quick.'

'She did not wish to be embalmed either.'

'Her ashes will still have arsenic in them,' I floundered, having no idea whether or not the element would survive incineration.

'Scattered, at her request, into the sea at Sackwater.'

'Does none of that strike you as suspicious?'

'A great deal of it,' he admitted, 'but I have my suspicions about many people who are walking free and enjoying their coffee,' he added hopefully, and I poured him another cup.

'His first wife,' I recalled.

'Was part of some weird religious sect,' he told me, 'and was buried in a shroud with no coffin. After all these years there will be nothing left of her.'

'Dr Cronshaw,' I recalled, 'treated Dolores and...' I waved a hand to forestall any interruption, 'his wife died in similar circumstances.'

Stanbury screwed up his mouth and, for a moment, I thought that he was going to blow me a kiss, but he unscrewed it and said, 'I can't simply march into his house making allegations.'

'Probably not,' I agreed. 'But, with a little more preparation, I can.'

Stanbury half rose.

'You are not going to do anything reckless, Violet?' he worried, my title lost in his concern.

Please do, Ruby urged.

'Do not worry,' I reassured him, but did not make any promises.

71: *WHITE RIDLEY'S EAR*

A PLEASANT PORTLY porter admitted me to Marmaduke Maudsley Mansions.

'Mr Appleton dint have many of callers,' he chatted as he directed me to a flight of stairs. 'And never no shiny young ladies.'

Shiny meant well-presented rather than luminous.

Tell him it is not his place to remark upon our appearance, Ruby had simpered, though I was not convinced that he was including her in his remark.

He means nothing by it, I assured her.

Then why are you simpering, she challenged. Needless to say, I was not, but I did have to admit to an irrational glow of satisfaction upon learning that Anthony was not in the habit of entertaining female admirers.

'Number six,' the porter told me. 'The door int locked for he can't come to it.'

Ruby skipped ahead while Inspector Hefty trudged behind, but somehow he managed to be on the second-floor landing before us both. I knocked and entered a pleasant, though sparsely furnished, lounge overlooking the park with a telescope set up by a window. It looked like it was trained towards Haglin House but I had no desire to take a close look at that property again.

'Who is it?' Anthony called through an open doorway to my left.

'Violet Thorn,' I replied, not going straight through in case he needed time to arrange himself.

'Oh,' he said without enthusiasm, and I resisted a temptation to let myself out. 'I've already told you I can't pay the rent until I am on my feet again.'

'Violet Thorn,' I repeated more loudly.

'Oh,' he said again, 'I thought you said Mrs Brown. It's difficult to make things out above those church bells.'

I could not hear any.

'Can I come in?' I asked.

'Please do,' he said. 'Oh, thank goodness they've stopped.'

It was difficult to judge how Anthony looked. His whole head was bandaged rather as mine had been when, as children, Rommy and I used to take turns at being doctor and patient, and my cousin was getting his revenge for me having splinted both his arms. There were holes for Anthony's mouth and nostrils but only one of his eyes – the right – was visible and that was bloodshot.

'How are you feeling?' I asked.

'I have rarely felt better,' he replied indistinctly and untruthfully.

He lay propped up on a ramp of pillows.

'Are you in any pain?'

'Only when the effects of the laudanum wear off,' he told me, 'which they do after a couple of hours. My aunts have been looking after me very well, but they have an idea that too much opium is bad for one.'

'And I have an idea that they are right,' I told him. 'Where are they now?'

'One is having a lie-down at home, complaining that my complaining had given her a sick headache, and the other has gone to buy a handbag to cheer herself up.' He managed a chuckle. 'They will both be needing laudanum when they hear that I have been entertaining a lady in my bedroom without a chaperone.'

He has a peculiar notion of what constitutes entertaining, Ruby scoffed.

'I came to thank you,' I said, 'for trying to rescue me.'

'I wasn't much use, was I?' Anthony said modestly.

None whatsoever, Hefty concurred.

'It was a very brave thing that you did.'

He waved a bruised hand dismissively but said, 'Yes, I suppose it was.'

I smiled and he tried to, but drew a sharp breath in and touched his upper lip gingerly.

'Anyway,' he continued, 'it was not as brave as your actions, going into that house to confront a murderer and then fighting to save me.'

If I'd been there I'd have given that doctor a taste of his own medicine, Ruby declared pugnaciously.

'Did he break your nose?' I asked.

'Yes,' he replied, 'but the surgeon assures me he has straightened it out.' He sniffed. 'If not, I can always play the villain. I can be quite menacing you know.'

I found that difficult to imagine but I said, 'You make an excellent police constable.'

Might even make a sergeant out of you, Hefty said generously, for nobody else was worthy of being an inspector.

Grunting with the effort, Anthony raised his head an inch or two, cocking it to the left to survey me.

'Did you call out *Oh my dear* when he attacked me?'

'Certainly not.' I drew myself up, trying to look indignant. 'I said *Oh my. Dear me.*'

'I thought so.' Anthony managed a smile this time, but then it dropped. 'What time is it?' he asked.

'Ten minutes before midday,' I replied, consulting the brass carriage clock stationed between the masks of comedy and tragedy on his mantelpiece.

'Then, regretfully, I must evict you,' he said. 'My doctor is due at noon and is bound to report to my aunt if he finds us together.'

'Are you frightened of her?'

'Of course I am,' he admitted. 'She gives me an allowance.'

'Then I had better go,' I said. 'Besides which I am going to see a doctor myself.'

'Oh.' I thought he frowned, but it was difficult to judge as his bandage had risen. 'I trust there is nothing seriously amiss.'

'Not with me,' I reassured him, 'but I believe there is something very seriously wrong with him.'

–

Dr Cronshaw had a pleasant villa on the outskirts of town. It was just far enough out for Friendless to regale me with everything that I could possibly want to know – and a great many things that I most certainly could not – about a fare he had taken to Stolham St Ernest when Old Queeny was Young Queeny.

'Losted a shoe just past Lower Downhill Up,' he had told me mournfully.

'Oh dear,' I said.

'One on her favourite.'

'Oh dear,' I said again.

'Never do find it,' he concluded that part of his adventures to a third 'Oh dear' from me.

Fitterby House was tall and thin and set in extensive, treeless, flower-free lawns.

Like a miniature Pampas, Ruby observed wistfully, for she had fallen in love with an Argentinian prince found murdered by a gaucho's bolas on their wedding morning.

A bored maid took me through to Dr Cronshaw's consulting rooms, where I sat in a creaky leather armchair and he in another, his fingertips together in a very Poynderish manner. Was this something that doctors are trained to do in the same way that builders are taught to cluck and suck their teeth?

'I believe you have been suffering from nervous anxiety,' he began after a few pleasantries, including an accord we reached on the almost insufferable nature of the summer heat.

'Then you have been misinformed.' Before he could say – *But my maid* – I added, 'by me.'

'I see,' the doctor said, though clearly he did not, and leaned forward. 'Haven't I seen you somewhere before? No, don't tell me. I never forget a face.'

'It was as I was quitting the house of Dr Poynder,' I explained and, before he could point out that he had asked me not to say, jumped in with, 'while you were assisting him in the process of murdering his wife.'

I was not sure that *process* was exactly the word that I had intended to use, but it was a minor detail.

It was a minor detail that put a rope around Linocker Bloom's skinny neck, Hefty recalled with great satisfaction, for Bloom had set fire to the inspector's favourite oyster shop.

Cronshaw considered my claim and decided to gape.

'Just as you aided and abetted him in the murder of the first Mrs Poynder,' I continued. 'By colluding in the misdiagnosis of their illnesses and in providing death certificates for both of those unfortunate women.' I took a quick breath. 'And Edward Poynder reciprocated when you poisoned your own wife.'

Cronshaw shut his mouth and licked his lips.

'It is simple enough to prove,' I ploughed on, for I could not stomach being asked what on earth I was talking about and told how outrageous were my allegations. 'My father, the Earl of Thetbury, is a close friend of the home secretary. One word in Sir Mathew White Ridley's ear and we shall have your wife's remains exhumed for analysis.'

Dr Cronshaw put his head to one side, reminding me of a blackbird listening for a worm.

'Is that true?' he enquired as politely as a man might ask if I were sure that the capital of Australia is Constantinople.

'Yes,' I said simply, but he still looked a little sceptical and so I added, 'it is,' which appeared to satisfy him.

'I see,' he said quietly. 'In that case, Lady Violet, I regret to say that you leave me with no choice.'

He stood up and I braced myself. If Dr Cronshaw was going to attack me, I would put up a better fight than I had with his colleague, but he was walking past me and around his desk to open the middle drawer.

'I was in the Suffolk's,' he told me with justifiable pride, and I was about to tell him that my second cousin had been too when he added, 'and this...' he reached into the drawer, 'is my service revolver.'

72: *THE HAMMER AND THE INVISIBLE ONES*

I WEIGHED MY options. Dr Cronshaw was not a powerful man but he held a powerful weapon, and I could not hope to overpower him because there was half a room and all of a desk between us. The door was too far for me to reach in the time that it would take for his finger to bend, the hammer to fall and the bullet to fly towards and into me. I could beseech him to be merciful, but Thorns – though I am not sure why – do not beg.

Distract him, Ruby advised.

How?

Offer him favours.

'Certainly not.'

'Certainly not, what?' Cronshaw enquired.

'I was not talking to you.'

'There is nobody else here.'

'That is what you think,' I bluffed.

Really? Ruby piffed. *Is that the best you can do? Threaten him with invisible rescuers?*

'Yes it is,' he agreed, not even troubling to glance about.

'Is that gun loaded?'

'But of course.'

'Then it is foolish of you to leave it unsecured,' I scolded. 'Any burglar could break in and use it.'

Dr Cronshaw shrugged.

'In which case he would save me the trouble.'

'I meant he could use it on you.'

'So did I,' he concurred and, turning the gun, pressed it against his temple and I saw his finger blanch as he pulled the trigger.

Uselessly I shouted, 'No!'

The left-hand side of Dr Cronshaw's head erupted, his upper face a gaping crater, spewing blood thick with brain and flesh. It splattered over the wall beside him bestrewn with the splintered bones of his skull.

His hand, clutching the handle of his revolver, finger still gripping the trigger, fell onto the desktop, but Dr Cronshaw remained seated, though tilting to his right, the wound spurting bright crimson blood, splotting onto his blotting pad and over the maroon leather.

'Dear God in Heaven!' I cried, my voice muffled by the booming in my ears. 'I was bluffing.'

His right eye opened or had it not closed? Was it my imagination or was it following me as I staggered to the door?

His maid stood in the hall, clutching her apron in a ball at her waist.

'What have you done?' she gasped, eyes wide in horror, but I had been about to ask myself the same question.

73: THE NOTE

MARTHA GAZED AT me.

'There must be something.'

'Not without more evidence,' I told her.

'He cannot murder Dolores and God knows who else, walk free and prosper.'

'Perhaps Matilda's or Wormwood's consciences will trouble them, or they will fall out with their employer and decide to change their stories,' I said, 'but I do not know what else the police or I can do.'

Martha stood up grimly.

'Then I shall have to deal with Edward myself.'

I did not like the way she had said that and eyed her uneasily.

'You will not try to kill him?' She shook her head.

'I do not need to,' she said and held out her hand.

There was no hug or kiss this time.

'Goodbye, Lady Violet,' she said coolly, slipping her fingers away.

No thanks? Ruby demanded indignantly. *You risked your life for her.*

She is upset, I said, not mentioning that I was too.

From my sitting room window I watched Martha Ryan stride across the square. The crowd parted and closed behind her and I glimpsed her again as she went up the hill. She was walking fast and she never looked back.

–

Exactly one week later I received a note. It was on Dr Poynder's headed notepaper, but it had not been written by him. The handwriting was tidy in small block capitals and the spelling was inaccurate but logical.

369

Dear Lady Vilet.

   By the time you receeve this we do be far gone.

   Susy goo home allredy.

   We sort of believe what you tell us but we do not want to then Mrs Ryan come and explane.

   Most it is what you say but she know more about Mrs Poynder and she know us and we know we can trust her for she is always kind to us.

   We make our master confess by promises to stop hurting him and he tell us things Mrs Ryan and you do not know.

   Then we hurt him more.

   Mrs Poynder is a lovely mistress and hanging is too good for her murderer. He die squeeling like the pig he is.

   We leeve him in his consulting room.

   We are only sory we dint believe what you say or we may have save her.

   Thank you for trying.

   With best regard from myselve and Wormwood.

   Matilda.

PS The key is under the mat by the kichen door round the back.

—

'We need goo and tell the police,' Agnust declared firmly.

'And we will,' I promised, 'but I need to see for my own eyes, and they will not let me into the house.'

'I suppose it isn't some kind of joke,' Gerrund suggested without conviction.

'That is what I intend to find out.'

'Then I shall come with you,' he announced as Agnust marched out of the room.

'We shall see 'bout tha',' she muttered.

'What are you doing?' I asked.

Was she going to call the police?

'Gettin' my hat,' she replied, and neither Gerrund nor I attempted to talk her out of it. We all knew what had happened the last time we had tried to go there without her.

74: LOVE AND THE MAWKIN

THERE WERE DARK patches on the patio at the back of Haglin House. Could they be from the blood of Mungo Peers, the innocent child, ruthlessly slaughtered for his good intentions, or poor Sheba, Poynder's English Setter?

They are rust from that leaking drainpipe, Hefty diagnosed.

He had made a study of corrosive stains, following the wrongful conviction of his grandmother for amputating an engineer's toe.

The key, as Matilda had written, was under the mat from where Gerrund retrieved it to unlock the back door. We found ourselves in the kitchen.

I was not aware that you had lost yourselves, Ruby quipped, only for Hefty to explain patiently what I had meant.

It was almost as unnervingly quiet as it had been in the attic when I was re-en-ottomaned — another word I intended to send to the Oxford Dictionary. I had never thought of the place as noisy, but there were no footsteps, no voices, no clatter of pans as we made our way through. At least, though, I had the footfalls of my companions and the rustle of their apparel as we passed; it felt as if we were making a rumpus during an especially sacred part of a church service.

The kitchen was much like any other — quarry stone slabs — a large, scrubbed pine table, scarred by knife wounds and burns from pots. The twin Belfast sinks were marked by iron rubbing on the ceramic surfaces. Copper pans dangled from a rack and jelly moulds hung on the walls.

To our left was a closed door marked *Pantry* and, straight ahead, an open door to a corridor.

It all reminded me of the times I would sneak below stairs at Thetbury to cadge raw pastry, which my mother had warned gave one worms. Sometimes I would be allowed to scrape out the cake mix from a huge brown bowl. Cook took my small stature and skinniness as a personal insult.

You do be ganty-gutted as a mawkin – which meant *thin as a scarecrow* in the official language of her county – she was telling me as I toyed with a wooden spoon.

'This way, milady,' Gerrund was calling, and I put the spoon back with its companions in a large old marmalade jar.

The kitchen maid's room was first, plainly furnished, the bed unmade.

The door to the butler's pantry was unlocked and I stepped in to see a neatly made bed, a pine table with two brown account books upon it and a chair tucked underneath.

Agnust opened a wardrobe to find it empty and Gerrund peered into the silver cupboard. It had been cleaned out.

'Don't blame you,' he muttered as he closed it again.

There was a housekeeper's room though, to my knowledge, there had been nobody fulfilling that role in the short time that I was there. Increasingly, many an employer saved money by getting their other employees to share those tasks, it being well known by masters, but less well known by their underlings, that servants have little to occupy their time.

Up the wooden stairs we went, past the study, the window repaired and the desk set out tidily again with a fresh blotting pad. Agnust ran her fingers proudly over the bullet-crater in the wall and wandered off. Gerrund was looking into the room opposite when we heard a sharp breath.

'Lady Violet,' Agnust called urgently.

I heard footfalls and followed.

'Jesus!' Gerrund breathed, and I do not remember what I gasped.

Dr Edward Poynder was spreadeagled on his back in what must have been his consulting room on an operating table. It surprised me that he had had one, for I understood that he only carried out minor procedures there, but that was the least of my concerns. There were cords tight around his wrists and ankles running to each of the four wooden legs. He was naked, his torn clothes thrown in a pile in the corner. He had been cut open from ribs to groin and his intestines pulled out, hanging from his abdomen onto the floor in a coiled slimy mess. His limbs all bore multiple wounds from scratches to deep incisions. His face was mutilated with his nose cut off and his eyes gouged out, but less hacked than I might have suspected.

'They wanted us to recognise him,' Gerrund answered my unspoken question.

Agnust rattled a kidney dish and I saw that it had broken teeth in it, and I could only assume that they came from that gaping, clot-filled mouth.

'They weren't lying about hurting him,' Gerrund said grimly and pointed to Poynder's right hand. Every plate had been torn out of his fingers. I peered over and found the same had been done to the left and all his toes.

'Oh God,' I breathed.

'Satan more like,' Agnust corrected me and I could not argue with that.

I knew he had murdered two wives, Mungo Peers, Sheba his dog, his ex-maid Edwina, Beryl Walker, Danny the Diamond King, the laundress and Wally Hopkins, not to mention the waitress who he had attacked, but even so, I was shocked.

'How could they have been so cruel?' I whispered.

'They loved him,' Gerrund stated, walking slowly around the table.

'You mean her,' Agnust corrected him.

'No,' he stated flatly. 'They were fond of her but they loved him.'

Nothing kills like love, Ruby whispered as I gazed about in fascinated disgust.

I thought that I had witnessed terrible things in the Poynders' home with the imprisonment and slow murder of an innocent woman. I could not have known, the last time I left, that the true horror of Haglin House had yet to begin.

75: THE BOMB, THE SNAIL, THE MESSAGE, THE BETRAYAL AND THE GREAT ESCAPE

WE WERE HAVING a lazy morning. I was reading an account in the *Suffolk Whisperer* of a snail who was carried from a vegetable plot in Great Bardham to Sackwater in a lettuce but turned up back at home three months later. The head gardener recognised it from its markings and regretted having stamped on it now.

Ruby was practising her Italian in the hope that I would send her to Venice next.

Io ce l'ho, Ruby announced suddenly and loudly.

You have what? I asked, having learned a little of the language from a pastry chef in Thetbury, before finding out that he was Scottish, which explained why *Awa'* and *bile yer heid signor* earned me blank looks when a Sicilian count visited my father.

The solution. Ruby cleared her throat noisily to remind me that we were talking about whatever it was that she had got. *I had uncovered Count Vorolski Zugravescu's fiendish plan and placed a bomb under his furnace, which went off when he lit it. The steel coffin protected me from the blast, which maimed him and blew the lock off.*

I am not sure, I dithered, having decided to invent *Professor Schuman's Rapid Rusting Agent* to dissolve the hinges.

Never mind any of that, Hefty jabbed his churchwarden pipe towards her. *I have remembered my fiancée's name.* He waited in vain for our excited enquiries. *She was Pauline*, he announced through a cloud of smoke before a puzzled look came over him. *Or was it Penelope?* He clicked his fingers. *Persephone?*

It was certainly not the last of those. I would never have given him a fiancée whose name he had mispronounced to rhyme with *telephone*.

See what your agent thinks, Ruby suggested, for she had such a low opinion of his profession that she could not imagine him finding fault with her scheme.

-

Ted Wilton sipped his gin and tonic thoughtfully. He had not even offered me a glass of water.

'I have to say it's not very convincing,' he told me. 'Perhaps you should go away and think about it.'

'I have been thinking about it,' I protested.

'How about an acid?' he suggested.

'I have already used that,' I reminded him.

Twice, Hefty reminded me. *Once for me and once for that Gibson woman.*

Ted Wilton blinked slowly.

'I'm sure you'll come up with a better idea.'

He reached over to pat my hand but something, perhaps a warning snarl, made him pull away sharply.

He should not have had a mirror on the wall by the door for, even as I left his office, I saw my agent reaching for his telephone.

I stopped outside to retie my bootlace, and it was not my fault that my ear was so close to the keyhole.

'Grantham, old man,' I heard the cheery greeting. 'Remember how I suggested that Hydrangea Devine gets trapped in a steel coffin over a furnace? Well I've had a terrific idea how you could extract her from it.'

-

There were so few words and I knew them all by heart, of course, but something compelled me to read them again.

Forgive me for I am not worthy of you.

Burn it, Ruby urged as always and, as always, I demurred.

With all my heart, your ever-loving Jack, I read, bowing my head despondently.

It still smells of scallions, Inspector Hefty observed, though he was supposed to be on his way to Hong Kong.

I lifted the paper to my nose and sniffed.

So it does.

I told you the whole thing stinks, Ruby reminded me.

I thought that was a metaphor.

I met a four-legged dog this morning, Little Myrtle contributed in all seriousness.

'I wonder,' I said.

What? Ruby and Hefty chorused in exasperation, for all this was interrupting their argument about which of them had suspected Dr Poynder first.

It was a trick that Rommy taught me when we were children, I recalled.

Not the one where you pretend to pull off the end a child's nose? Ruby groaned, though I could not remember ever having done that.

Invisible ink, I said, walking to the middle of the room.

Not much use if you can't see it, Hefty grunted.

Onion juice, I explained and, getting up from my bureau, held the paper up to the electric light. The bulb was still reassuringly or worryingly hot, depending on whether or not one trusted Mr Poplar the electrician.

'It is working,' I whispered as faint shapes began to appear.

Was that an L? I moved the paper sideways, trying to ignore the burning of my fingers.

And that's an E before it, Ruby said.

And an I, Inspector Hefty contributed. *No, wait, it's a P.*

E. L. P. and then an M. Ruby spelt out.

And I was almost certain that I spotted another E at the end before the note curled at the edges, the paper toasted opaque brown.

'Oh Jack!' I cried aloud and all of my characters slunk away before I drowned them in my grief.

–

Free at last! Ruby cried, arms outstretched triumphantly to the rising sun.

But how? Hefty enquired disappointedly, for he had been urging me to let my Extraordinary Investigator roast and replace her with the future Mrs Hefty, preferably a princess called Lavinia.

Work it out for yourself, Ruby taunted him and the inspector looked askance at me.

It is too complicated to explain, I mumbled and returned to watching the green fairy gather drip by drip in the bottom of my glass.